TRAINED ROYAL

CLUB ROYAL, BOOK FIVE

ELOUISE EAST

CONTENTS

DEDICATION

To Brandi
For checking through these books with single-minded focus and helping me rectify any mistakes. You're amazing. Thank you.

SUTCLIFFE ROYAL FAMILY

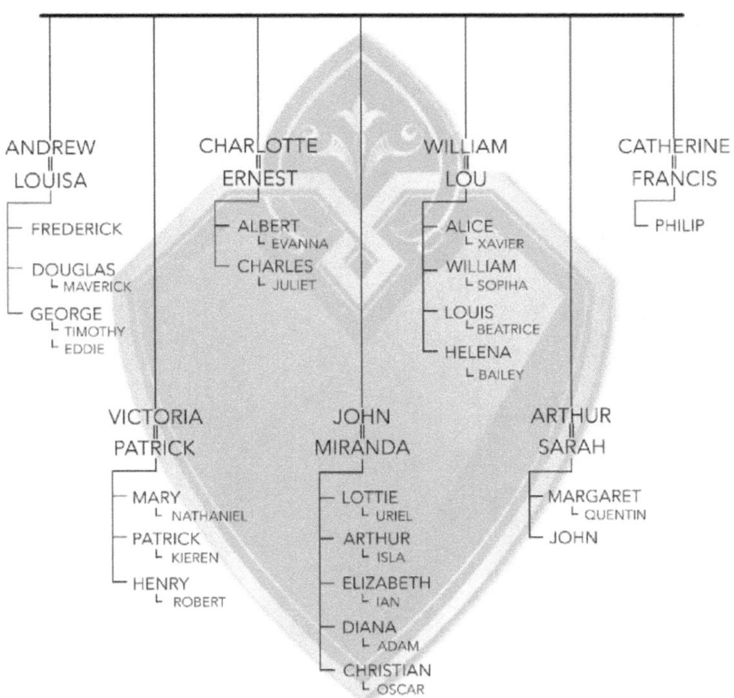

LIST OF CHARACTERS

(ALPHABETICAL ORDER)

Andrew, King of England, Patrick's uncle

Charles, cousin, Charlotte and Ernest's child

Charlotte, Patrick's aunt

Christian, Patrick's cousin, Oscar's boyfriend

Clarice, Club Royal's receptionist

Damon, Frederick's best friend

Douglas, Patrick's cousin, Mav's boyfriend

Eddie, barista, George and Timothy's boyfriend

Frederick, Patrick's cousin, heir to the throne

George, Patrick's cousin, Timothy and Eddie's
    boyfriend

Henry, Patrick's brother, Robert's boyfriend

John, Patrick's uncle

John, Patrick's cousin

Kean, Henry's best friend

Kendal, friend of family, submissive

Kieren, Patrick's bodyguard

Louisa, Queen Consort, Patrick's late aunt

Maverick, social media manager, Douglas's
    boyfriend

Oliver, Club Royal bartender
Oscar, owner of Book Drunk, Christian's boyfriend
Patrick, financial advisor
Quinn, friend of family, submissive
Randall, King Andrew's assistant
Robert, florist, Henry's boyfriend
Timothy, teacher/therapist, George and Eddie's
    boyfriend
Victoria, Patrick's mother
William, Patrick's uncle
Zane, Kieren's best friend

BODYGUARD LIST OF CHARACTERS

(Showing royal member they are assigned to. If blank, not yet assigned)

Aaron = Andrew
Brett = Christian
Colt = Andrew
Des = Henry
Dominic = Andrew
Eric = Douglas
Felix = Oscar
Ford
Gerald
Greg
Isaac = George
Jade = Patrick
Jared = Andrew
Landon
Locke = Frederick
Matt = Robert
Nick

Nina = Kieren
Owen = Frederick
Rae = Mav
Sam = Eddie
Selena = Andrew
Simon = Andrew
Tobias = Andrew
Van = Timothy
Viola = Andrew

AUTHOR NOTE

If you would like to see any potential triggers for this book and any other books I've written, please go to this link on my website: https://elouiseeast.com/triggers

TRAINED ROYAL

1

PATRICK

The music flowed through the air as Patrick Sutcliffe let his fingers do the talking. He didn't even look at the keys as he played, closing his eyes and letting the notes rise and fade into the spacious music room at his home in Bagshot Park. This was *his* room. His space to disappear into the sounds he could create. Be it his piano, violin, flute or clarinet. Any of them could take him away from the present and into a world of whatever he wanted: peace, fire, danger. He could make it all with the notes he chose.

That day, he needed to breathe. He needed to be at peace, and the music held a lilting quality, soft, melodic tones that calmed his soul and rested his mind.

Unfortunately, the moment his fingers stopped, the roar of reality intruded.

He held his hands over the keys, wanting nothing more than to continue, to stay in the bubble he'd created, but he had work to do. Work he'd initiated himself and couldn't bring himself to get out of. Work that made him feel weaker rather than stronger as it should. He pulled the lid down over the keys and stood, sliding the stool into place. He preferred things to be just right because it felt a lot like control. Something he didn't consider he had a lot of.

He shuffled towards the door, pausing with his hand on the handle, then opened it with a jerk, coming to a stop when he found his brother sitting on a bench opposite. The man who'd been keeping secrets from him for over eighteen years. Although he'd forgiven Henry, it was hard to not let the hurt of knowing he hadn't come to him when he'd needed help from intruding whenever they spoke.

"I loved that last one you played," Henry said. "What was it?"

Patrick leaned back against the closed door. "It doesn't have a name. I just played."

"It was beautiful."

Patrick gave a small smile and pushed off the door. "Thank you." He inhaled. "What brings you here? I thought you'd be with Robert?"

"He has a busy day and practically shoved me out of the flower shop, saying I was distracting him. I thought we could have breakfast together." Henry stood, the two inches height difference making them almost eye to eye.

"I'll have coffee."

Henry tilted his head, reminding Patrick of the puppy he sometimes was, and said, "Do you want to stay here or go somewhere else?"

"Let's stay here. I have somewhere to be in an hour."

Henry scrunched his nose as they started walking. "Anything interesting?"

"Not really. Why is Robert's day going to be busy?" Patrick diverted the subject because no one knew about his extracurricular activities yet.

Henry chuckled. "He has an entire list of bouquets and centrepieces to make for a wedding reception taking place this afternoon. Naomi and Finn are there to help, but Robert has had to call in help from his grandpa. I keep telling him he needs to get someone else trained up, but he keeps putting it off. Maybe this will be the reminder he needs."

They entered the dining room, and Henry had let the kitchen staff know they were there. Patrick made himself and his brother a drink and carried it over to the large table, settling into a seat opposite where Henry sat. He could feel Henry's gaze on him, but he ignored it. At least until he spoke.

"You seem forlorn, Paddy. What's going on?"

Patrick sipped his coffee, biding his time. How could he explain how useless he felt? How incompetent? Each of them—the Tantalising Twelve as his cousin George had coined them—had brought something to the table when it came to all the problems they were facing except him. His aunt Charlotte and her cohorts had been on a decade-long campaign to eradicate the LGBTQ+ community within the royal family, trying to force those "affected" to shed their true personality and regain her favour as heterosexual allies. In the last year, she had upped her game, ending the life of their beloved aunt and queen, Louisa. It was entirely possible the bomb that had taken her life was meant for her son George because he and his mother had swapped places at the last minute. Regardless, Charlotte's reign of terror continued, and Patrick felt helpless.

"Paddy?"

Patrick lifted his gaze to Henry. "How does it feel to be engaged?"

Henry narrowed his eyes, his gaze boring into Patrick, but after years of living with the man, it no longer worked. Henry sighed and smiled. "It's great."

"Even after only a week?" Patrick chuckled. "I didn't think it would make a difference."

"There's something about seeing my ring on Robert's finger that makes it all seem…more real, I suppose." He shrugged. "I don't know. Have you seen anyone you like the look of? We're all dropping like flies at the minute."

Another subject Patrick wanted away from, but he indulged his brother as he hadn't answered his previous enquiry. "No. I don't see many people. I doubt I'll meet anyone soon."

A household staff member entered the room, and they stopped talking while Henry's plate was set down.

"Thank you."

"You're welcome, Your Highnesses. Do you need anything else?"

"No, thank you."

When the server left, Henry continued, "We need to get you out and about. We have Christian's birthday party coming up, and aren't you attending the Halloween charity auction at the end of the month?"

Patrick nodded, watching Henry cut up his toast. "I am attending both, yes. Did you decide on a gift for Christian?"

"Robert had a great idea. We're making a photo album of him and Oscar in their Daddy and little roles. We have plenty of pictures we can use from the times we've been together. Robert said he's going to make it into a scrapbook—with Naomi's help —and make it special for him."

"I'm sure he'll love that. I still have no idea. I might have to ask Oscar to give me a clue." He sipped his drink.

"You'll never go wrong with something book-related."

Patrick grimaced. "But that's the easy option. I want some-thing different."

"Maybe some bookmarks or covers? I don't know. I was wracking my brain trying to think of something before Robert's idea."

Patrick waved his hand. "I'll find something."

They finished breakfast, thankfully without returning to the two subjects Patrick had avoided. As they wandered in the direc-tion of Henry's rooms, silence descended. He knew Henry, and the others, were worried about him, but he couldn't find it in him to explain to them. They were happy in their relationships, and Patrick felt like he was alone. Although Frederick was single, he had Damon, his best friend, by his side almost daily. Patrick had no one.

Suddenly, Henry stopped. "You can talk to me, you know? To any of us. I know you're struggling with something, and I wish I knew what I was, but I know you like your privacy. I won't push but talk to one of us. Please."

Patrick sighed and shoved his hands in his pockets. He was just as bad at keeping secrets as his brother was, but this wasn't something that would harm him. "I'm fine. Honestly."

"You're not, but I know you won't admit it." Henry wrapped his arms around him and hugged him. "You're my brother. I know you. But I also know you hate being pushed, so I won't. Just remember what I said, okay?"

"I will."

Henry stepped back, thumbing over his shoulder to his rooms. "I'll catch you later."

His brother disappeared, and Patrick understood without needing to see him that Henry was upset. Not with Patrick, but because he couldn't help. This was something Patrick didn't want help with. He needed to do it himself. Was that why Henry hadn't told him of what he'd witnessed when he was thirteen years old? Had he thought he could handle it himself?

Pivoting on his heels, he retraced his steps, diverting down another hallway towards the gym they had recently installed at Patrick's request. His excuse had been that he needed to work out his frustrations, which was true, but the real reason was something no one knew but him and one other person.

He entered the room they'd dedicated to changing and showering and changed into his workout clothes. He was early to their session, but he could warm up ready for when his companion joined him. Losing himself in the stretching of his muscles, he flinched and swiped his leg out behind him when someone grabbed his arm. The two of them fell to the floor in a heap, and Patrick rolled away and jumped into a crouch, facing his attacker.

He swore long and loud when he saw his bodyguard, Kieren, lying on the floor with a smirk on his face.

"Good reflexes," Kieren said, climbing to his feet. "I wondered how long it would take you to act before you thought. Seems like your body and brain are working together—at least when you're not focused on trying too hard."

Patrick stood, his chest heaving as his lungs strained for air, both from the fright and the adrenaline coursing through him. "Bloody hell, Kieren! You scared the shit out of me!"

Kieren grinned, unrepentant. "That was the plan. I wanted to see how you reacted to something you weren't expecting." He wandered over to where they kept the pads for sparring. "We're going to concentrate on your footwork today."

Patrick groaned, resting his hands on his hips and dropping his head back. "Bloody feet."

Kieren chuckled. "You did good just then, but we need to get your feet to cooperate with your brain."

"Good luck with that," he muttered.

"As you're all warmed up, let's get to it." Kieren paused. "Unless you've changed your mind?"

The hopeful note in his voice raised Patrick's hackles. "You know why I'm doing this," he grated.

"I do, but I also know you don't *want* to do this."

Patrick spun around, stalking to the other side of the room and back again. "It's a necessary evil."

Kieren sighed and pulled on the boxing pads, clapping them together. "Start with the punches."

They went through their usual routine: a variety of punches and kicks, then working through a specific routine meant to get Patrick's feet to obey his commands rather than do whatever the hell they wanted to in a fight. The session was more successful than the previous ones, and Kieren said as much.

"Thanks." Patrick pulled his T-shirt away from his chest, desperately needing a shower but not wanting to share the space with his bodyguard for reasons he tried to hide, even from himself.

"Let's shower, and I'll rub some ointment onto your lower back. I can see you've been stiffening up on certain stances." Kieren headed towards the bathroom area, and Patrick hesitated. "You won't be able to reach it yourself."

Patrick sighed, knowing he was right. It would be hell, but if he had to think about his brother or his cousins to stop himself from reacting to the sight of Kieren naked in the shower, he would do it. He followed in Kieren's wake, shedding his clothes and throwing them in the hamper before entering the shower area. Kieren already stood under the spray, the water cascading down his muscled back, flexing with every movement of his arms, to his tight ass.

Patrick jerked his gaze away, choosing the shower one away from him. He stood underneath, letting the water wash away the grime and sweat and hiding his face. If the shower was spraying him with water, he wouldn't be able to ogle his bodyguard. It was a cliché, after all—the lonely guardee falling for his guard. He could even pinpoint the moment it happened. A week after the problems Douglas had with the asshole Talon, who had assaulted several subs from their club, Kieren had been assigned to him permanently. A short while later, he'd heard Patrick playing the piano and had, uncharacteristically, started gushing about his talents. Patrick had been enamoured from that moment, that unguarded joy Kieren had shown.

"You'll look like a prune if you stay under there much longer," Kieren said, his words muffled by the water rushing over Patrick's ears.

Kieren disappeared into the changing area with a towel

around his waist, and an ache pressed on Patrick's chest. He'd ignored Henry's question about finding a partner because he knew who he wanted, and he knew he couldn't have him. He didn't want anyone else.

Sighing, he finished his shower and grabbed the other towel, drying off and securing it around his waist. Taking a deep breath, he entered the changing area, finding Kieren in shorts and nothing else.

Kieren glanced at him. "Lay on the bench. I'll rub the cream in."

Patrick peered at the bench, where two large towels lay to cushion him, and laid on his stomach, resting his arms beneath his head. Kieren came to stand beside him.

"Ready?"

No. "Yes." He closed his eyes, not wanting to see how close, yet how far, Kieren was.

Warm, firm hands pressed against the skin of his lower back, just above his ass. They spread the cream around, and then Kieren used his thumbs to push a little harder. It felt amazing, and Patrick lost himself to the rhythm, not realising until too late that he'd started making noises. Every time Kieren pushed against his back, his cock pressed into the bench, and a moan left his mouth.

Kieren's hand moved a little lower, sliding under the edge of the towel and working the top of his ass cheeks, and Patrick instinctively clenched, eliciting a chuckle from above.

"It's supposed to relax you, not make you clench."

Patrick let out a slow breath and relaxed. Kieren worked for a few minutes more, then his hands retreated.

"All done."

Patrick wanted to think Kieren's voice was hoarse because the act affected him as much as it did Patrick, but he was delusional. He knew he couldn't move at that moment, though. Not unless he wanted to show Kieren exactly how much the massage had affected him.

"I'm staying here for a few minutes," Patrick murmured, pretending to be completely boneless when, in fact, he was anything but.

When Kieren said nothing, Patrick opened his eyes and squinted at him. He stood, staring at Patrick's back as if he'd seen something confusing, and Patrick took stock of his body. There shouldn't be anything to make him look like that.

"Everything okay?" he asked.

Kieren flinched and stared at Patrick for a moment before nodding. "Yeah. Yes. Perfect. Okay. I'm going to wash…" He held up his hands before disappearing.

Patrick stayed where he was, frowning. What was that all about? Closing his eyes again, he thought about his brother, his parents, anything and everything that wasn't Kieren and, finally, he felt able to sit up without poking someone in the eye. He dropped his head into his hands, resting his elbows on his knees, and exhaled. What the hell was he doing? He needed to get this infatuation out of his system so he could concentrate. It was too early to visit the club, but he could play again.

He stood and dressed quickly, wanting to be done before Kieren came back, but when he still hadn't after he was ready to leave, he stuck his head around the corner. Kieren stood with his hands braced on the sink, his head lowered, and his eyes closed. That wasn't what caught Patrick's attention, though. It was the bulge in his shorts and the heaving of his chest.

Patrick licked his lips and opened his mouth to say something, but nothing came out. Instead, he retreated to the bench and called out, "Thanks! I'm heading out."

Kieren cleared his throat and said, "Okay."

Not waiting to hear any more, Patrick left, heading straight for his music room. He had a feeling peace and harmony were not what would be coming from his fingers this time.

And he was right. Devastation, mourning and despair were the topics of his song, and he felt every note arrow through his body as if they were physical strikes making him bleed. He tried to tame the music coming from the strings of his violin, but the ebb and flow of the tide was unresponsive, his body undulating with the haunting piece.

He had no idea how long he played, but when the last note rang out, he sank to the floor, tears streaming down his face. This was the version of himself he wouldn't allow anyone else to see. The weak, pain-filled man who only had the strength to pretend he was okay. To pretend everything was fine in his little corner of the world. To pretend he was of some help.

But he was none of those things. He wasn't okay, things weren't fine, and he was of no help. He was fooling himself with this need to train. Thinking he could become stronger, faster. That he could save them all from what was undoubtedly coming their way.

He couldn't.

He was useless.

2

KIEREN

Kieren Young stood with his hands braced on the sink in the gym changing room, his head lowered, and his eyes closed, breathing deeply until he felt he had control of his body. He hadn't expected to react to massaging Patrick's back. It had been a long time—a very long time—since he'd had any relief that wasn't his hand, but he also hadn't reacted to anyone either. Not until now. It wasn't like he hadn't been close to Patrick before. Why was this time different?

He glanced into the mirror, blanching when his reflection sent back the look of a man on the edge. On the edge of what, though?

Inhaling, he washed his hands again, not wanting to chance having the muscle cream get in his eyes if he'd missed any when he'd distractedly washed the first time. As he dried them, his phone rang, and he rushed back into the changing room to grab it.

It was Brett. "Hey, everything okay?"

Brett chuckled. "Everything's fine. Can't I call you just because I want to talk to you?"

Kieren exhaled, his body unclenching. "Of course. What's up?"

"We've been invited to a party?"

Kieren groaned and dropped his head back against the wall. "No."

"Yes."

"You know I hate parties."

"This one's different."

Kieren waited for more information, but when it didn't come, he sighed and bit the bullet. "Why is it different?"

"Because the princes are asking for our attendance," Brett said, and Kieren could hear the smile in his voice.

"Which princes?"

"All of them. Well, the ones we protect, anyway. Prince George called and requested our attendance."

"So, it's not a party. We're working."

"No. We're off duty. It's at Timothy's house, and I've been told there'll be alcohol, music, games and a barbecue. He also said we were allowed to get drunk." Brett laughed.

Kieren rubbed a hand over his face. "Do I have to?"

"Yes."

"Why?"

Brett sighed. "You need more time off than you're taking, Kieren. This way, I can see that you're taking it."

Kieren banged his head against the wall several times and blew out a breath. "Fine. When?"

"Saturday afternoon. It starts at three o'clock. I expect you to be there for as long as I am. Understood?"

"Yes, sir."

"Don't get cocky, asshole. Just because this is off duty doesn't mean I won't make your life a living hell as your superior if you mess me around." Brett sighed. "It will do you some good to get to know some of the other guys a bit more, too. You're not a loner, Kieren. We have your back."

"Okay. I'll be there."

"Anything I need to know before our meeting tomorrow morning?" Brett asked, slipping into work mode.

Kieren stood upright, flicking through his mental diary and notebook. "Not that I'm aware of. Patrick has work shortly, and I'm on standby tonight."

"Good. Call me if you need anything."

"Will do."

He ended the call and dropped his hands to his sides. A fucking party. What the hell was he supposed to do at one of those? The last "party" he remembered attending was his family's wake, if he could call it a party. Before that, it would've been something he'd attended with Norton, his ex, while they'd been attending university years ago.

Pushing aside the uncomfortable thoughts, he pulled a T-shirt on and headed for the room the household staff had allocated him. He hadn't needed to be a live-in guard, but when they'd asked him if he wanted to, to put them at ease, he'd agreed. It made no difference to him where he slept. He didn't own any properties, except for one house in the Lake District that had belonged to his parents, and he didn't have the heart to sell. It was a place they'd spent many of their childhood holidays and held many memories.

He rubbed a hand over his face and wandered through the hallways, a haunting melody reaching his ears. He knew where it came from, and he couldn't stop his feet from taking him in that direction. Stopping outside Patrick's music room, Kieren closed his eyes, resting a hand on the door as the pain vibrated through the air, sinking into his chest. He wanted nothing more than to go in there and wrap his arms around Patrick, shielding him from whatever ailed him, but it wasn't his place. He was a bodyguard, and the only thing he should shield him from were bullets and security concerns. Emotional pain was out of his jurisdiction.

When silence descended, Kieren pulled free of the hold it had on him, inhaled and continued the journey to his room. Patrick's musical ability was breathtaking, and Kieren had received many opportunities to see and listen to him perform. But his favourite performances were the ones from behind closed doors when Patrick let his emotions free—like he had done then—and played from his heart rather than sheet music. Music was an art form, just like drawing was, but Kieren didn't have an ounce of the talent Patrick did. It always surprised him Patrick didn't follow that career path instead of following in his father's financial footsteps.

He shook his head as he let himself into his room. Dropping his bag on the floor, he strode to the wardrobe and pulled a suit from it. A black jacket, white shirt, black tie, black trousers and steel-toe capped boots completed his working outfit.

Ever since the fire took out Floresco, the flower shop Prince Henry's boyfriend—no, fiance—owned, the royal family had increased their security. But when the bomb took the life of the queen, security had increased tenfold. Initially, they'd brought him on to guard Patrick only at the events he attended, but since the bomb, he'd been on full-time day duty with a standby duty overnight because he lived in their home. The weekends were his to do with as he pleased.

Kieren was lucky because Patrick was easygoing, and they got along well. He spent his days following Patrick around the office, attending meetings, and doing anything else Patrick had to do. Apart from filling out the paperwork, Kieren could've probably done Patrick's job from how much he heard and saw. Not that he'd want to.

He smoothed down his jacket and headed back out into the main house, aiming for the front door. He stepped outside, as always, waiting by the car and scanning the property for anything that might look out of place. The property was well secured, but he couldn't help his training.

The door behind him opened, and Patrick exited, wearing a sleek, dark grey suit with a black shirt.

"Ready?" Kieren asked.

"I'm good." Patrick nodded, and Kieren opened the passenger door of the car, letting Patrick climb in. Kieren shut the door, rounded the car and took a seat beside the driver, Kevin.

The journey into London took over an hour, and Patrick used the time to make phone calls and do paperwork—Kieren could see it through the soundproof glass. The entire journey, every day, Patrick did the same thing, rarely taking any time to just relax or watch out the window. Even when he was on a call, he'd be staring at the paper or writing something.

By the time they got to the high-rise building Patrick worked in, Kieren was antsy for no other reason than being locked in a car for any length of time. Fresh air while walking was better than any other mode of transport, as far as he was concerned. Being trapped within moving transport was at the very bottom of his list of favourite things to do, not that anyone knew that.

The day went as slowly as it usually did, but Kieren remained alert. When they had first requested that he stay by Patrick's side for the entire day, he hadn't realised it meant *every minute*. But on the first day he'd accompanied Patrick to work, he'd asked where he should wait, and Patrick Senior had given him a confused look and pointed at a chair near the window of Patrick Junior's office. From that moment forth, he and Patrick spent eight to ten hours a day with each other. It was tough to keep things from getting personal, but he did his best.

A similar routine happened on the car journey home, and Kieren found himself wishing for something to shake it up, then cursing himself for thinking such a thing.

After delivering Patrick safely home, Kieren headed for his room, changed into his workout clothes and strode for the gym. He rolled out a mat and sat cross-legged in the centre. His twice-daily yoga practice always helped get rid of the tension in his body. Working through his years-old routine, he ended on his back, in savasana pose, eyes closed, legs and arms spread.

He jerked to his feet, crouching with his arms in a fighting pose when the door slammed open.

"Oh, shit. Sorry. I didn't think anyone was here," Patrick said, freezing several steps into the room.

Kieren exhaled, dropping to his knees and lowering his head. "It's okay. I wasn't expecting you, that's all."

"I'll just go." Patrick stepped back towards the door.

Kieren held out his hand. "No, it's okay. I was done." He rolled his mat and tucked it under his arms, heading towards the door.

As he passed Patrick, the man said, "Are you joining us at the barbecue this weekend?"

Kieren glanced to the side, freezing at the look in Patrick's eyes. He was caught in those ocean blue orbs, the pupils dilating above flushed cheeks and a heaving chest. Licking his lips, he focused on Patrick's mouth as his tongue copied the motion. He leant to the side, wanting to taste them, to see if they were as soft as they looked.

Jerking himself out of the dream, he stepped back and cleared his throat. "Um, yes, I'll be there."

He gave a small smile and left the room, closing the door behind him and leaning against it. Exhaling softly, he whispered, "Damn it."

Saturday dawned bright and warm and stayed that way throughout the day. Patrick offered him a ride to the party, and as they both lived in the same house, he accepted. It would've seemed strange if he hadn't. After almost losing his head the other day, he had tried to take a step back from Patrick. It wasn't easy, especially as he trained him every day.

It hadn't been *his* idea to train Patrick. In fact, Patrick had cornered him the day after the bomb and implored him to help him learn to fight. The man had tears threatening to fall at the slightest provocation, and Kieren had been helpless to decline. The prince shouldn't have to learn how to fight. It was Kieren's job to protect him, but he understood the need to feel something, anything, other than fear and grief. It was what had turned Kieren towards security detail in the first place. A need to protect. That same need coursed through Patrick.

They hadn't spoken about the whys of it. All Kieren had done was take stock of where Patrick initially stood in relation to training and started from there. For him to have taken Kieren down to the floor the other day meant the training was becoming part of him, instinctual, which was what Kieren had been hoping for.

"Are you looking forward to relaxing with your friends?" Patrick asked after several long minutes of silence. He didn't look at Kieren, his eyes completely focused on the road ahead of him as he traversed the roads towards Windsor.

Kieren resettled himself and tapped his fingertips on his thumb, a nervous gesture he had never curbed himself of. "Yes. It'll be nice."

He didn't know how relaxed he could be with at least six princes, five partners and several other royally related people, and that's without including his colleagues.

"Can you say that with more feeling?" Patrick glanced across at him and back to the road, his mouth quirked at the corner.

Kieren huffed a laugh. "It *will* be nice. I'm just not a very social person—as you might have gathered."

"Well, I know you like yoga," Patrick cleared his throat at the probably inadvertent reminder of the other day, "but what else do you do when you're not bored out of your brain looking after me?"

Kieren stared out of the window, not seeing the passing scenery. "I don't know, really. I watch TV a little, read a little. That kind of thing." He wasn't discussing what he really did. That was no one's business but his own.

"Hmm. I don't see you as the type of person to sit around doing nothing."

"You'd be surprised."

"What do you read?"

"Mainly sci-fi. I'm not a fast reader, by any means, but I read a couple of chapters a night."

Patrick chuckled. "It's more than I do."

Their easy conversation continued for the entire journey. When Kieren climbed out of the car, he automatically studied their surroundings but snapped his head around when Patrick laughed.

"You're not on duty. Chill."

Kieren pursed his lips. "'Chill?' What year did you come from?"

"I'll have you know there's nothing wrong with the word 'chill.'"

"Maybe from a teenager." Kieren bit his cheek.

Patrick's mouth twitched, and then they both laughed. "Come on. I need a drink."

Patrick led the way to the door, which opened before they could even get close.

"Come in, come in!" George said, waving them through. "The Tantalising Twelve Plus are out the back. Have you got your sun cream on? It's going to be a hot one!"

Patrick embraced his cousin. "Plus?"

"Well, there are too many to include in one name, so I just called all the guards 'plus.'" George shrugged. "It's not the best choice of words, but I asked their permission first. Brett said it was okay." He glanced at Kieren. "Is it all right with you, Kieren?"

Kieren shrugged. "Not a problem for me."

George fist-bumped the air. "Great. Let's get some drinks."

They wandered through the large house, down the hallway, through a kitchen and conservatory and out into the enormous back garden. It was something Kieren loved about this house—the privacy. It wasn't completely blocked off, but it was better than some were. Journalists were still able to get the occasional photo through the trees, but the security team had added cameras to those areas to identify those and warn them against doing it again. So far, it had worked beautifully, and Prince George and his partners were able to live in relative peace.

"Kieren! I didn't think you'd show," Brett said, grabbing him in a back-slapping hug.

Patrick elbowed his side. "I could see he was wavering, and I offered him a lift." He winked at him and wandered off.

"That true?" Brett raised his eyebrows.

"Not that I was wavering, but yes, to the lift."

Brett gripped Kieren's nape and guided him to where the group sat. He'd expected the security team to be separate from the royals, but he was pleasantly surprised to see them inter-mingled. Doing a quick tally in his head, there were roughly thirty people in attendance because each of the royals and their partners had individual security guards. There were a couple of people Kieren didn't recognise, but he didn't know *all* the royals, just the ones he interacted with regularly.

"What're you drinking?"

Wasn't that the question of the evening? He blew out a breath. "Beer?"

Brett laughed at his questioning tone and grabbed him an ice-cold bottle. "Sounds like you need it."

"If all I'm going to get is your sass, boss, I'm going home," he grumbled, lifting the bottle to his mouth. The bitter taste coated his tongue, and he grimaced, remembering why he didn't often drink alcohol.

Brett laughed and held up his hands. "I'm off duty. No 'boss' here tonight." He picked up a bottle of his own and gulped it down. "Ahh. That's the stuff."

"Are you not worried about what the royals think of us?" Kieren murmured.

Brett shook his head. "Other royals, maybe, but not this lot. We're human. They're human. We see them at their lowest and highest points, day in, day out." He tilted his head. "These men are the cream of the crop. The men pointing us towards a decent future. If we can't be ourselves around them, who can we?"

Brett clapped him on the shoulder and sank into a chair, crossing his ankle over his knee. Kieren didn't miss the way his eyes darted around the space, though. He wasn't the only one feeling like he needed to be working when that many royals got together.

Kieren settled into a chair beside Brett, getting comfortable. Everyone knew he wasn't much of a conversationalist, but he'd bring himself out of his comfort zone for a short time. He needed a little more liquid courage first, though.

3

PATRICK

*P*atrick could see Kieren relaxing the longer he stayed at the barbecue, and it made him smile. Kieren might be a self-proclaimed social pariah, but when he allowed himself to join in, it wasn't as visible as it might've otherwise been.

"What's got you smiling, Paddy?" Douglas asked, dropping into the vacant seat beside him and tipping his bottle to his mouth. "Anything interesting?"

Patrick chuckled. "No, just remembering the last time we tried for a barbecue. The birthday party after-party wasn't the success we hoped it'd be, was it?" It wasn't the truth, but the memory had been close to the front of his mind several times since he'd arrived.

Douglas threw back his head and laughed loudly, garnering several gazes in their direction. "True. So true. How we made such a cock up of that, I'll never know."

"It might have had something to do with how drunk we all were." Patrick finished his shandy and put the cup aside. He hated the taste of alcohol, but the lemonade mitigated the taste a little. It was only on rare occasions that he allowed himself to drink despite the taste, and his joint birthday party with George and Freddie had been one of those occasions.

"I can't remember much of the following day, either. There was nothing in the media when I checked, and I'm taking that as a win for all of us," Mav said, coming to stand behind his partner in crime and sliding his arms around his neck and down his chest until he rested his chin on Douglas's shoulder.

"I can just imagine the headlines now," Patrick said, holding his hands up and spreading them wide as he continued, "'Royal heirs three sheets to the wind.' Can you imagine the picture they'd get to go with it?"

They laughed, and a cup appeared in front of him. He jerked his head up to meet Kieren's gaze.

"I saw you were empty." He shrugged.

Patrick took the cup and smiled. "Thanks."

"I have evidence of that night. I can use it as blackmail should I need to." Kieren winked and strode off, leaving Douglas and Mav laughing hysterically while Patrick's mouth gaped.

"Cheeky bugger," he muttered, his mouth twitching to keep a smile from blooming on his face. It wasn't often he saw the playful bodyguard appear instead of the serious one, but he relished it when he did.

"I dread to think how we all looked. Even Freddie was gone, and you know how little that happens," Douglas said when he got his breath back.

Patrick's stomach growled, and he pressed a hand against it. "Any idea when the food will be ready? I've not eaten yet."

"Damon said it would be about half an hour, and that was…" Mav checked his watch, "about half an hour ago." He stood upright, groaning. "I shouldn't lean like that. It kills my back." He sighed. "I'll go check with him."

Mav wandered off, leaving Douglas and Patrick alone again.

"Any news?" he asked.

Douglas glanced at him with a small smile. "We're supposed to be relaxing today, remember?"

Patrick stared at him. "And I bet it has been *far* from your mind all this time, hasn't it?"

Douglas snorted, then sobered. "It's never far from my mind, Paddy. We just don't know any more than we did before. Neil, Daniel and Gia are going through the information as much as Christian still is, but they're hitting roadblocks in every direction. There's more information there, but no one can seem to figure it out."

"We still have dates and locations, don't we? It'll make things easier."

"Let's hope. The next one on the list isn't until near Christmas. If they stay true to that, we have a bit of leeway to relax."

Patrick scoffed, "None of us will relax until this is over." Douglas nodded slowly, a frown on his face as he fiddled with his cup. "What are you thinking?"

Douglas sighed and rubbed a hand across his face. "I don't think that list is any good now," he whispered.

Patrick blanched. "What! Why?"

"Shh." Douglas held out a hand. "Keep your voice down. I haven't told anyone about this yet, only Mav." Patrick's heart pounded as his cousin kept talking. "If they knew Miranda had turned her back on them, what's to stop them thinking she gave Christian information?"

"There's not."

Patrick jumped at Christian's voice, having not heard him step up behind them. He faced his cousin. "Where does that leave us?" His body felt like jelly, trembling as if he was a slant away from sliding off into a mess on the ground.

"It leaves us where we are. Working our asses off to figure everything out before anything happens. We assume the dates and locations haven't changed. And if they have..." Christian met his gaze. "If they have, we adapt."

Patrick dropped his head into his hands, scraping his fingers through his hair and linking them at his neck. Why did nothing go their way? Why couldn't they cut a break? Having the information Christian's mother provided had proved invaluable, but to know it was potentially useless made Patrick feel even more powerless than usual. Douglas and Christian tried talking to him, but he was too wrapped up in his head to do anything. They rested their hands on his back and left him, knowing him too well to stay while he was like that.

Someone else took the seat beside him, and he closed his eyes, not wanting to invite conversation when he wasn't sure he could form a sentence. Having to adapt to things wasn't his forte. He much preferred a well-thought-out and detailed plan of action, but it was why he'd been training, wasn't it? In case he needed to step up to the plate.

A hand rested on his lower back, the heat soothing him despite it being hot outside. Instinctively, he knew it was Kieren, but he lifted his eyes to check. The man's eyes broadcast a wealth of emotion as his thumb smoothed across the fabric of his T-shirt. For a moment, he wished he wasn't wearing one, wanting to feel it against his bare skin. Their gazes locked, the moment extending far longer than it should. If Patrick had more confidence—and fewer witnesses—he would've closed the distance between them and kissed him. But he didn't, leaving him to wallow in the "what-ifs" of his life.

What if Aunt Charlotte had never started down this path? What if he had the confidence to kiss his bodyguard? What if he had the strength to fight back? What if he...?

"Stop," Kieren murmured, leaning a little closer.

Patrick's eyes widened. "Huh?" It was all he could manage.

"Your brain is going too fast. Slow it down. You'll never work yourself out of the maze you've got yourself into unless you slow down. Now, breathe. In," he paused, inhaling, "and out."

He exhaled, and Patrick found himself following the action automatically.

He kept his eyes on Kieren, not wanting to be set free on the water slide just yet. With his concentration on his breathing, the tumultuous thoughts were able to settle.

"I wish they hadn't left you alone like that," Kieren said.

"Who?"

"Your cousins. They do it every time you get like this, and I've never understood it. All they need to do is help you calm your thoughts, and you'll be back with them. Whereas if you're left alone, it takes you longer." He pursed his lips and broke the staring match, looking at the ground instead.

How did he know that?

"I'm observant," Kieren answered.

Patrick stared at him, overwhelming feelings bottling up inside him. No one else had seen that. Not even Patrick had realised. How had Kieren? He sat upright, swallowing hard, and dislodged Kieren's hand unintentionally. He missed the warmth the moment it left him.

"He's right," Freddie said, approaching from Patrick's left.

Patrick peered at him. "About what?"

"Us leaving you alone. I can collectively say that we thought it was what you needed, but I can see we were wrong. We'll do better." Freddie nodded at Kieren and crouched beside Patrick. "Are you okay, Paddy?"

Patrick tried for a smile, though he wasn't sure he succeeded. "I'm... I'll be fine," he amended. "Let's forget about it for now, except for me to say we need to have a discussion soon about everything. I feel out of the loop."

Freddie nodded and squeezed Patrick's knee. "I'll arrange it."

Patrick chuckled when his stomach growled again. "I need food." He grinned, feeling calmer. "Preferably a cheeseburger so I can watch Henry's face when I eat it."

Freddie laughed, rising to a stand. "That never gets old."

Kieren's forehead creased, and Patrick explained, "He hates them with a passion. I don't know how you missed that." His mouth twitched when Kieren pursed his lips.

"My focus is you, not your family," he stated, sending tingles of heat through Patrick as his mind conjured up being his sole focus in other ways.

Patrick cleared his throat and stood. "Food," he said, his voice cracking.

He strode across the grass, not stopping to talk to anyone until he reached Damon. "Are there any cheeseburgers?"

Damon grinned. "I might've made a special batch of them just before Henry came to pick up his jacket potato." He winked. "I don't think he likes me anymore."

Patrick chuckled. "He probably does, but you'll have lost a few points on his scale."

Damon passed him a burger and pointed to the table. "Everything you need is there. Including everything you don't need." He rolled his eyes. "Douglas insisted on every condiment and ingredient he could think of."

"Sounds like him." Patrick paused. "Actually, that sounds more like Mav."

"I agree."

"Don't forget to eat yours, too," Patrick reminded him.

"Not gonna happen."

Patrick chuckled and added fried onions and salad to his burger before christening the top with ketchup. The best way to eat a cheeseburger. He grabbed a jacket potato for good measure and headed back to his seat, glad to see no one waiting for him; he needed a few minutes' peace.

He savoured the food, made to perfection, while his brain simmered, not running rampant as it had earlier, but trundling along. He couldn't hide from the glaring fact that he wanted Kieren and had for a while. The fact he didn't have the confidence to try for what he wanted was also blatantly clear, which put him in a conundrum. If he thought it would make any difference and wouldn't affect Kieren or his job, he would've requested a new guard, but he couldn't imagine his life without the man in it, and he trusted nobody else to protect him. Plus, he'd badgered the man enough to get him to train him; he could hardly go back on that now.

Should he cancel their training sessions? It would give him less time with him, which might help with his crush. He doubted it would help because he'd still feel the same way, and it would mean he wouldn't be as well trained as he hoped he would be. He still needed to feel he was helping in some way, and he had nothing else to offer other than his body.

He switched to lemonade for the rest of the evening, knowing he wanted to drive home instead of crashing in one of the many bedrooms in the house. He also didn't want to leave Kieren stranded after giving him a lift. More than one person was worse for wear by the time Patrick and Kieren left. Luckily, they had already decided on designated drivers before the evening had started.

Silence filled the car on the journey home, but Patrick had something he needed to say.

"Thank you for your help back there."

"My pleasure."

He would never tire of hearing Kieren talk. The soft but deep tones seemed to vibrate through the air and surround him before soaking into him. Patrick shook his head minutely. Such whimsical vocabulary for saying he loved the way he spoke.

"My cousins and brother mean well. I'm not just saying that, either. I didn't know what I needed until you sat there and helped."

"It's not easy to figure out what helps when pain and frustration get the better of you. Sometimes, you need someone on the outside looking in to see what you're blind to."

Patrick tapped his thumb on the steering wheel. "Sounds like you have experience." He didn't want to pry if Kieren didn't want to tell him, but he wouldn't deny that he wanted to know more about the man who played everything close to his chest. Had the alcohol he'd drank loosened his tongue?

Kieren stared out of the window, the same as he had done on the drive earlier that day. "I do."

That was all he said, and Patrick could understand him wanting to keep his personal life to himself. "Understood."

"It's not that I don't want to tell you, Patrick." Kieren faced him. "I've vocalised what happened precisely three times in the years since it happened, and none eased the pain of it."

"It's okay. You don't have to—"

"Seventeen years ago, my family was killed in a plane crash."

Patrick's heart broke. He'd not expected that. How could anyone live with being the sole survivor of something like that? "How did you survive?"

Kieren scoffed. "I wasn't on the plane, though I should've been."

"I'm sorry for your loss."

"Thank you."

They drove in silence until Patrick stopped the car outside home. He put his hand on the handle, pausing when Kieren said, "I know you have a lot going on in your head. Although talking to a therapist didn't help me, it might help you."

Patrick stared at the steering wheel. How could he explain how he felt to someone else when he didn't know himself? He nodded to show he'd heard and climbed out of the car. He was sure a therapist would have a field day with him.

"Keep your arms up," Kieren called, stepping to the side as Patrick took a swipe at him. "You're leaving your head undefended."

Sweat dripped off Patrick's forehead and into his eyes, momentarily blinding him, but he ignored it, focusing instead on where Kieren's voice advertised he was. He punched with his left hand, grazing Kieren's shoulder and, gaining the knowledge of his position, he swiped his right hand out, aiming for his jaw, but Kieren caught it in his hand and spun him until his back rested against Kieren's heaving chest. His wrists were secured in Kieren's grasp, his left arm between their bodies, his right arm across his stomach.

"Good. Using your other senses to figure out where I am."

Patrick wanted to lean back into him and close his eyes, but he kept himself rigid, not knowing what his next move would be.

"Escape," Kieren demanded.

Patrick quickly ran through his options and let his knees go weak, dropping to the floor and twisting to bring his hands to the front. As he fell, he yanked on his arms, bringing Kieren tumbling with him. When Kieren landed on top of him, unable to break his fall because he still had hold of Patrick's wrists, the air shoved out of Patrick's lungs, winding him.

"Fuck! I'm sorry. Are you okay?"

Patrick stared at how close Kieren was, and Kieren scrambled to rise, but Patrick gripped his shirt. As if he watched from afar, his hand cupped the back of Kieren's head and pulled him closer as he lifted his own head to close the distance between them.

The moment their lips connected, Patrick moaned and opened his mouth, wanting to taste Kieren, but Kieren pulled back.

"Wait…"

Patrick opened his eyes, not realising he'd closed them, and stared at him. Cold seeped into his body, and he trembled, pushing against Kieren so he could get up. Kieren's body came to fully rest on his, his forearms bracing by his head. Kieren came close enough that Patrick could see different coloured flecks of blue in his irises.

"Wait," he murmured.

Patrick's breathing increased, not wanting to hear a story of how it was Kieren and not him. "Let me up," he whispered, closing his eyes.

"Patrick, look at me."

Patrick shook his head, reacting like a teenager who didn't want to accept his crush knew how he felt about him.

"Patrick."

He squeezed his eyes tighter as heat flooded his cheeks. How could he have been so stupid?

A brush against his lips had his eyes flicking open, and Kieren stared down at him, the lines around his eyes tightening. They stayed staring for several long seconds or minutes, he had no idea, but the answering heat in Kieren's eyes—and the bulge in his shorts—gave him the courage he needed. He slid his arms around Kieren's waist, following the waistband, and let his fingers drift up and down his spine.

Kieren's eyelids fluttered, but he kept his gaze on Patrick. "No going back," he whispered.

Patrick smiled. "No going back."

Kieren's pupils flared, and he slammed his mouth onto Patrick's, stealing his air. Patrick tightened his hold, letting Kieren take whatever he wanted from him. His brain was firing his nerve endings, sending sparks of fire along his body and into his groin. It had been a long time since he'd done anything with anyone, but he would keep himself from exploding within the first few seconds if it was the last thing he did. He didn't want this to end sooner than it had to because the moment reality intruded, it would be over. He knew it.

Kieren straddled him, making it impossible for him to wrap his legs around him like he wanted to, but he circled his hips, brushing their groins together. He could feel Kieren's cock against his own, and it was glorious. He slid a hand into Kieren's waistband as Kieren grasped Patrick's head in his hands. While Patrick's hands wandered onto his tight ass, which flexed when Patrick squeezed it, Kieren's mouth devoured him.

Patrick couldn't remember a time when a kiss had felt life-changing, yet right at the same time. He never wanted it to end, but he needed more. He turned his face to the side to grab some air and whisper, "More."

Kieren took his mouth again, but this time, his hand moved down his body, tugging at Patrick's shorts at the same time. Patrick got the message and pulled at Kieren's shorts, too, taking them below his ass and freeing his cock and balls. Patrick wriggled to get his shorts down, and when his dick met Kieren's, he groaned into his mouth.

Kieren wrapped a hand around both their shafts and pumped. Electricity sparked through Patrick's groin, and he knew he wouldn't last long.

"Fuck! You feel too good," Kieren gasped, resting their foreheads together.

Patrick stared down at their dicks, squeezed in Kieren's fist, their tips leaking fluid and making a mess of Patrick's stomach. It was a sight he'd remember as long as he lived.

"Patrick..." Kieren's eyes bored into his, and Patrick knew they were in the same boat.

"Come for me, Kieren," he whispered against his lips.

Kieren tensed, biting down on Patrick's lower lip as he came. Patrick wanted to watch his cock, but the expression on Kieren's face transfixed him. His own body seized, and his nails embedded themselves in Kieren's back and ass when his orgasm hit him. The way they stared into each other's eyes as their releases claimed them should've been strange, but it was more real than anything Patrick had ever experienced.

4

KIEREN

ieren stared at the man beneath him as his mind cursed him from heaven to hell for what he'd done. As their joint releases cooled between them, he realised he still held their cocks in his hand. He gently let go and braced himself on two arms again, sighing. Finally breaking eye contact, he closed his eyes and shook his head.

"Don't," Patrick said, his voice breaking.

Kieren opened his eyes again, and he flinched at the pain filling Patrick's eyes, the pain that had vanished while they were...together. "I'm—"

"If you say sorry, I'm going to kick your ass."

Kieren couldn't help the quirk of his mouth at the words. "Really?"

Patrick glared at him and lifted his chin. "I got you down to the floor, didn't I?" His cheeks flushed an adorable red as he unintentionally referenced their current predicament.

Nodding, Kieren said, "You did. Well done." It had impressed him that Patrick had got himself free, even though it ended with them both being winded. If they hadn't been distracted by...other things, Patrick could've easily pushed Kieren off and escaped.

He sighed, and his dick nudged Patrick, causing a ripple of awareness to flow through him again. Swallowing hard, he lifted and set his shorts to rights, wanting to do the same for Patrick but not knowing if he had permission to. He glanced at him, finding his gaze already on him, and made a split-second decision. Tearing his gaze from Patrick's, he pulled the waistband of Patrick's shorts up over his spent cock and smoothed the T-shirt back into place, covering the evidence of their releases.

"Sorry about that." He waved a hand to Patrick's stomach without looking up at him.

"Don't be. Please, god, don't be sorry."

Kieren peered down at him, seeing a sheen of tears. "I'm sorry for the mess, not...anything else." He wasn't sure if that was true or not, but Patrick needed to hear the words.

Kieren stood, holding out his clean hand to help Patrick up. They stood facing one another in silence until Patrick whispered, "Shower with me?"

"It's not a good idea." Kieren couldn't in all good conscience let what they did become anything more than it was already. Patrick was a prince, someone completely out of Kieren's reach, especially as he was supposed to protect him. If they became more, he couldn't do his job. Plus, if anyone ever found out, they would probably reassign him. There was a reason people in relationships didn't work together.

Patrick nodded with a lowered head and turned to leave.

"Thank you," Kieren said.

Patrick paused and faced him, his expression one Kieren didn't remember seeing previously. Before he knew what had happened, he was on the floor on his back, the wind knocked out of him again, and Patrick was walking away. When his brain came back online, Patrick was gone, and Kieren was glad because he couldn't contain his laughter. The prince had taken him down with a well-timed foot behind Kieren's ankle and shove. If that didn't prove how much strength—not physical, but emotional—the guy had, nothing would. Kieren had shot him down and thanked him for the experience, making Patrick undoubtedly feel like shit, and he'd shown Kieren exactly how he felt.

He lay there for a long minute, debating what to do. He had been an ass, not thinking about how his words would sound. But he hadn't meant them like that. He truly had been thankful that Patrick had even given Kieren the time of day, let alone allowed him to share something so personal with him.

Standing, he collected his belongings and showered in his bathroom rather than using the ones next to the gym. With it being Sunday, neither of them had plans, and Kieren wanted to catch up on the project he was working on.

When he finally settled on the sofa with a cup of coffee and his tools, with a random film playing in the background, he took a breath and opened his drawing pad. If anyone saw what he drew, they'd think he was certifiable or a stalker. Page after page of hand-drawn pictures of Patrick lay before him, with a few of the view from the window of his room thrown into the mix. No one knew he could draw because it was something he had pushed aside when his family had died. He'd left university without the degree he'd been aiming for and thrown himself straight into security.

He'd only taken up drawing again when he'd taken the job with Patrick. He hadn't been able to resist capturing the expressive features. And once he'd started, he couldn't stop. It was like a fire had been lit within him as it had all those years ago when he drew anything and everything he saw, when he had visions of selling his artwork in galleries across the country or even the world.

He snorted at his immature dreams, but at the same time, he wished for the peace he'd had back then. Nothing to worry about, nobody to force him to do anything, nothing in his way. How life changed in the blink of an eye.

Picking up his pencil, he focused on the drawing he'd been trying to perfect. Patrick had been playing the piano for his parents a few nights ago. Kieren had been passing by the open doors and stopped, mesmerised. The serenity on Patrick's face had hit Kieren hard. He catalogued every nuance of his features while hiding in the shadows of the door, then immediately went back to his room and began drawing. His retinas retained the image, but something eluded him as he tried to capture the essence of the performance.

His phone startled him, and he checked the display before answering.

"Zane! Where the hell have you been?" Kieren chuckled.

His friend's voice came across the speaker in droll tones. "I've been on holiday, remember?"

Zane Turner and Kieren met at university. Zane was slightly older than Kieren, but they found their interests and humour aligned extremely well. They had hardly been apart during those first few years, even sharing a room, but when Kieren's family died, and he dropped out, they'd lost touch for a while. Only Zane finding him and badgering him had kept them from losing touch altogether.

"Ah, yes. Where was it again? Austria? Australia?" He knew exactly where Zane had gone, but he loved teasing him.

"Aruba, you ass."

"I remember now." He chuckled. "How's Viv?"

"Good, thanks. Even better now we're married."

Kieren froze, then shot upright, holding the phone closer to his ear. "What the fuck!"

Zane's laughter flowed down the line. "I planned to just propose, but when we saw the place we'd booked, we decided to go all in and make it a honeymoon, too."

"You actually got married over there?"

"Yep. I'm no longer an unmarried man. The ball, chain and anchor are firmly—and happily—in place."

He shook his head. "Oh, my god! Congratulations! I'll kick your ass when I see you, though, because I wanted to see you get hitched. But wow. I'm happy for you."

"Thanks. We're planning on arranging a reception here soon, but we're not sure when yet. As soon as I have the info, I'll let you know."

"I'll be there." He huffed a laugh. "You are never one to have patience, are you?"

"Why waste time when this is the only life we have?"

The words hit harder than Zane probably meant them to, and Kieren slumped back, his hand barely keeping the phone to his ear. His parents and sister had their lives cut short. Shouldn't he be living his life to the fullest in memory of them?

"Kieren? You still there?"

He blinked repeatedly and cleared his throat. "Yeah."

"Sorry, man. I didn't think."

"No, it's fine. You're right. So, so right."

Zane said nothing for a moment, and Kieren lost himself in the memory of doing something for himself for the first time in a long time—being with Patrick.

"I take it you have something to share," Zane said finally.

"Huh?"

Zane chuckled. "You made it sound like there was something on your mind. Or *someone*. Who is it?"

"Nah. It's just..." He sighed. If he couldn't talk to his friend, who could he talk to? "Fuck it. This goes no further, Zane."

"Fuck you."

Kieren chuckled. "Glad you agree. It's the person I'm protecting."

"Holy shitballs. Seriously?"

"I really like him, Zane, but I don't want to lose him. I can't lose him like I did them, and with everything going on around here…" He bit his tongue, knowing he couldn't divulge any more than he already had.

"Bloody hell. You don't do things by halves, do you? A bloody prince, Kieren!"

"It doesn't matter who he is. There's nothing I can do about it." Except screw it up more than he already had.

"Does he feel the same way?" Kieren sighed. "He does, doesn't he? What are you waiting for? You might not find this again, Kieren. Don't borrow trouble. Take what you're given with both hands."

Kieren rested his head against the back of the sofa and closed his eyes. "I don't think I can."

"They wouldn't want you living like this."

Kieren stayed silent, knowing Zane was right but unable to change anything. His parents had always believed he would find the person he was meant to be with when the time was right, just like they had. He couldn't bring himself to forget the promises he'd made when he stood at their gravesides. Promises he knew they wouldn't want him to keep, but that he made anyway. Promises to protect those who needed it. With his own life, if necessary.

Zane sighed. "I know I won't change your mind. Just think on it, okay? Don't make any final decisions before you think long and hard about this."

"Okay." It was the best he could do. He cleared his throat. "Tell me about your wedding."

Changing the topic, he spent the following hour listening to Zane rave about their holiday, making Kieren wish he could join them one day. Unfortunately, that would never happen. As it was, he could barely sit in a car for any length of time. Going on a train, a boat or flying would never happen.

"Check in, please," Brett's voice came over Kieren's earpiece.

"Felix, main hall, garden exit door," Felix said.

"Isaac, main hall, front entrance door."

"Matt, entrance hall."

"Locke, main hall, side door."

"Kieren, main hall, emergency exit door."

The rest of the security team checked in with their names and locations, ensuring everyone was where they should be. Christian's birthday party was bigger than Christian was expecting, according to Patrick. He believed it was just immediate family, but Christian's boyfriend, Oscar, had gone all out for him. After what they'd been through, Kieren could understand trying to stamp out the terrible memories, but it made for a security nightmare. At least, as far as he was concerned.

Although the entire security team had to be alert for any dangers at all, they were also focused on specific individuals. In Kieren's case, if Patrick moved out of the room, Kieren would go with him, and another guard would take his place. Despite it being a nightmare, they were a well-oiled machine and had done it many times before.

Prince Douglas entered the room, calling, "The birthday boy has arrived!" and a cheer sounded as Prince Christian followed him. Christian greeted several people before racing across the room to Oscar and spinning him in a circle, ending with a kiss. Kieren's mouth curled, and he found himself searching for Patrick. He locked gazes with the man because Patrick had already been looking at him. Even across the distance, the look felt like a physical caress across his skin, and he repeatedly blinked before diverting his gaze. He tapped his fingertips on his thumb in order and surveyed the room, ignoring the fluttering in his chest and stomach.

It had been precisely one hour and nineteen minutes when the DJ announced, "Good evening! Please, could you give a cheer for the birthday boy, Christian?" A cheer answered him.

"We will need your attention on the stage at the front of the room for the next few minutes as we have a wonderful lineup of comedians—oh, I mean, men who'd like to dish the dirt—um, talk about how amazing Christian is. Over to the stage." Laughter filled the room.

The king, Andrew, took to the stage first, welcoming everyone and claiming Christian as his son, not his nephew. Kieren could see the prince was in tears because his parents and siblings had disowned him, but not this part of the family. These members were truly who you'd want by your side, as their stories and banter proved when they each took a turn to talk about Christian and what he meant to them.

When Oscar stood on the stage with the microphone, someone sidled up beside Kieren. He didn't need to look to know who it was. As Oscar began speaking, Patrick leaned into his side, not his full weight, but enough to show he was there. It took all the discipline Kieren had not to wrap his arm around his shoulders and hold him close.

"Everything okay?" he asked instead, his gaze scanning the room, though every atom of his body was attuned to the man beside him.

"Yes." It was all he said before he wandered back through the crowd to his family.

Prince Douglas and his boyfriend, Mav, carried a box up onto the stage. If it hadn't already been cleared with security, they would've been racing to that platform right then.

"Can you come up here, please?" Oscar asked Christian, who climbed up beside him. "I love you. I want to experience everything with you, and I thought we could start with this."

After some prodding, Christian opened the box and lifted out a beautiful chocolate brown Labrador puppy. There were some hushed words that were not picked up by the microphone before Christian passed the puppy to Patrick. The smile lit up Patrick's face as the puppy licked at his chin. Maybe a dog would help lift Patrick's spirits? It was something Kieren could manage.

His gaze snagged on the stage again when Christian dropped to one knee. Into the microphone, he said, "I truly thought you were going to steal my thunder when you brought me up here, but I'm glad I still get to do this." He held out his hand without moving his gaze from Oscar, and Prince Frederick handed him a box. "You mean everything to me. Everything. I refuse to live my life without you in it, and I want to ask you a very important question. Oscar Hall, will you do me the honour of marrying me in front of the entire world?"

Oscar said something and nodded, and Christian slid the ring onto his hand to an audience of ear-splitting cheering and whistling. Once more, Kieren scanned the room for Patrick, finding him at a table with the puppy on his lap, his cheek buried in its fur. Yes, a puppy might be a suitable gift. He'd have to check with his employer first, though. The last thing he wanted to do was bring a dog into a place where someone was allergic. That was a quick way to get fired.

"Check in, please," Brett said.

"Felix, main hall, garden exit door," Felix said.

"Isaac, main hall, garden exit door."

"Matt, main hall, side door."

"Locke, hallway to the right of the ballroom." Kieren glanced around, noticing Frederick was not present, hence why Locke and Matt had changed positions.

"Kieren, main hall, emergency exit door."

And so it continued. They didn't have to move around extensively because they had asked the royal family to keep within the ballroom wherever possible, meaning the security team could guard the party easier. The team was at least thirty strong at events like these, usually more when the king was in attendance, but they had vetted the people they'd invited extensively before being allowed to attend.

Incidents had been happening throughout the past year, and the security team was on full alert that anyone could be against the crown, even those who appeared to stand with them. The team's job was to keep the royal family protected at all costs. There were other people involved who were investigating who and how these incidents kept happening. From what Kieren had heard, Christian had been a vital part of that process.

Kieren hated the uncertainty that the family faced. With everything Patrick had entrusted to him, on top of what he'd been told by Brett, he couldn't imagine what they were going through. Losing Kieren's family was a devastating loss, but to apparently have Patrick's family gunning for them was cruel.

"Are you okay?"

Kieren snapped his head to the side, focusing on Patrick and grimacing to realise he'd moved without Kieren knowing. He brushed aside all other thoughts and refocused on his job. He couldn't afford to lose concentration like that. He could be all that stood between Patrick and someone trying to kill him.

"I'm good. Are you enjoying yourself?"

Patrick sighed. "Not really." He smiled as a guest wandered past. "But they're my family."

"Are you going to play for them?"

Patrick shook his head slowly. "Not today."

Kieren glanced out of the corner of his eye as Patrick leaned his shoulder against the wall, a glass held against his chest. He appeared worn out, and Kieren wanted to get him home. Unfortunately, it was not his choice.

"Do you want to visit the club with me?" Patrick asked.

Kieren raised his eyebrows. "What?"

5

____

PATRICK

*P*atrick had no idea why the invitation came out, but once it had, the better the idea sounded.

"Do you want to come to the club? I know you've never been inside before. You have a membership, so I can show you around if you like?"

He held his breath, wishing Kieren would take him up on the offer but knowing he wouldn't.

"I don't know if that's a good idea."

Patrick snorted. "I think it's a great idea. Once we're done here, we'll go. I'll show you how things work."

"We shouldn't—"

"I don't care," he said more forcefully than he intended if Kieren's expression was any indication. He inhaled. "Sorry. If you don't want to go, that's fine, but I'm going. I need..." He wasn't sure what he needed, but he needed something.

Kieren nodded. Whether that was in agreement to join him or just that he understood what Patrick was saying, he didn't know. Maybe it was the release of endorphins that impact play gave him that he needed. He was willing to try anything because playing his musical instruments wasn't cutting it.

Patrick wandered off to say goodbye to everyone. It was earlier than he'd planned to leave, but not early enough to be rude. Besides, his family knew him well.

He found Christian first. "Hey, I need to head off. Happy birthday and congratulations." He pulled him into a hug.

"Thanks for being here." Christian held his shoulders and stared at him. "Are you okay?"

Patrick smiled. "I'm good. Just a little tired."

Christian placed his forefinger under Patrick's chin and lifted slightly, raising his eyebrow. "You know where we are, all right?"

"Yes. Wherever there's trouble." He laughed with Christian. "Will you say goodbye to Oscar for me? I'm going to find the others before I go."

"Will do."

Patrick made his goodbyes to each of his cousins, but his brother wouldn't let him leave without an inquisition.

"Where are you going?" Henry asked.

Patrick sighed. He had never been able to outright lie to his family. Divert the topic and smudge some details, yes. Lie, no. "I'm going to the club."

"I'll come with you."

"No. You stay here. Enjoy the party. I'll be fine on my own."

"I'll be with him, Your Highness. You don't need to worry," Kieren said from behind him. Patrick's heart missed a beat, and his stomach started with butterflies.

Henry wanted to argue, but he nodded. "As long as you call me when you get home. I want to make sure you're okay."

Patrick shook his head. "I won't call you, but I will send you a message. I'm not purposefully waking you to tell you to go back to sleep again."

"Fine, but don't forget, or I'll be waking you."

"Deal." He hugged him and turned to leave.

"Kieren," Henry said. Patrick glanced over his shoulder as

Henry murmured, but not quietly enough, "Keep an eye on him, please."

Kieren gave a nod and followed Patrick through the remaining guests until they reached the entrance, which Kieren held open to allow Patrick to exit. The night had a slight breeze, which brought a chill to the air, but it was refreshing after being cooped up inside for so long. Patrick inhaled and exhaled as he wandered towards his car.

"Kieren, leaving the premises," Kieren said into his earpiece, then paused. "Understood." He pulled the earpiece out and slipped it into his pocket.

He glanced at him. "Are you okay to leave?"

Kieren nodded. "Yes. I spoke with Brett before I came to find you."

Patrick unlocked the car and climbed into the driver's seat, starting the engine while Kieren made himself comfortable. They said nothing for the first part of the journey, though Kieren's fingers were never still. He tapped each fingertip on his thumb, over and over again, while looking out of the window.

"Are you sure about this?" Patrick asked finally.

"I'll join you, but I won't take part in anything."

"Watching is just as good as taking part sometimes."

Silence descended again, and thoughts of what he planned to do when they got to the club distracted Patrick. When he pulled into the underground car park, he stopped the car and glanced at Kieren.

"Ready?"

"As I'll ever be."

Patrick led the way to the lift, putting his thumbprint on the sensor, then stepping aside so Kieren could do the same. The doors opened immediately, and they entered. The ride, as always, was smooth and quick, barely taking more than a few seconds to rise to the reception area. Patrick didn't have time to explain anything to Kieren before the doors opened into the club foyer.

"Clarice! How are you today?"

"Good evening, Prince Patrick. I'm very well, thank you." Her gaze flicked to Kieren. "Mr Young, nice to meet you."

Patrick chuckled at Kieren's raised eyebrows. "Clarice knows everything and everyone. Just because you haven't been here before doesn't mean she doesn't know everything there is to know about you. She's our gem and one we hope never to lose." He paused. "Although we would love for her to lose the titles when she speaks to us."

Clarice smiled and ducked her head. "Now, now, Your Highness. Don't make me blush." Patrick laughed. "Let's get Mr Young set up for the club, shall we?"

It was a rhetorical question, and while she did her magic on the computer, Patrick glanced at Kieren, who was looking around but whose posture screamed, "Get me out of here!"

Patrick studied their surroundings, trying to see it as if he'd never been there before. The dark wooden floors and furniture and emerald-green walls with various shades of cream accents gave the area an earthy feel, along with appearing smaller than if the decoration was lighter. The sconces on the walls helped, as did the spotlights in the ceiling, but why the designer went for such dark colours, Patrick would never know.

"Okay, Mr Young. If I could get you to read through this NDA agreement and sign at the bottom if you agree, then we can finish setting up your access." She handed Kieren a form on a clipboard and a pen.

As Kieren went through it, Patrick asked, "Clarice, who's around tonight?"

"The Monitors tonight are Princesses Lottie and Elizabeth, Princex Alice and Princes Albert and John."

"John?"

"Yes, Your Highness. Prince John is in Monitor training, but because of the external event tonight, he has taken a shift in the main area."

John was his younger cousin, barely twenty-one, but he seemed a nice enough guy, although he would reserve judgement with whom his parents were close to—Christian's parents. The ones who were working alongside Aunt Charlotte and her nefarious plans.

He stared at Clarice, who gave a slight nod. "He's being observed," she added softly.

"Anyone else around I should know about?"

Clarice inhaled. "Princes Charles and Arthur are inside."

Patrick sighed. "Wonderful." He smiled at Clarice. "Thanks for letting me know."

Kieren held out the clipboard. "I think I'm done."

"Any questions, Mr Young?"

"No, I'm good."

"Okay, then." Clarice clicked a few things on the computer. "Can you put your thumb on the sensor, please?" She pointed to the black square next to the screen, and Kieren followed her instructions until he was all done. "There we go. You should have access to the changing rooms and the main club doors."

"Can you add him to the Monitors' changing room and my locker, please?"

Clarice raised her eyebrows, hesitating. "I...can."

Her pause was brief but understandable. The only people who had access to the Monitors' changing rooms were the Monitors themselves and their partners. Kieren didn't come under any of those, but Patrick wanted him close, away from prying eyes, and this was the best way to do it.

"Done, Your Highness. Is there anything else I can help you with?"

"No, that's great. Thanks, Clarice. I'll see you later."

"Have a good evening, gentlemen."

Patrick led Kieren over to the changing room door. "Try your thumbprint to make sure it works."

The green light confirmed everything worked, and Kieren held the door for him to enter first. He turned right as soon as he entered, coming to stand before another door. "Check this one, too, please. This is the Monitors' room." Kieren pressed his thumb to the sensor, and the green light appeared again. "Good."

When the door closed behind them, Kieren asked, "Why do I need access to this room?"

Patrick wandered over to his locker before answering. "You don't, but I feel better with you having access here when I have no one else around."

"What do you mean?"

Patrick opened his locker, pulled out a shirt and faced Kieren. "Usually, when I come here, I have either my brother or my cousins or both with me, meaning there is always backup when some of the more unfavourable family members are around."

"Like Prince Charles."

Patrick nodded. "We know what he's capable of when he finds one of us alone. After getting into Christian's room at the barracks and holding a gun on him, I'm not taking chances."

"I agree. I didn't realise he had access here."

Patrick sighed. "He shouldn't, but they gave him access a while back, and no one is willing to rescind it in case it antagonises him. Even Uncle Andrew is cautious."

"I can imagine." Kieren glanced around and then down at his clothes. "Am I okay wearing what I have because I didn't know to bring a change of clothes?"

"You're fine, although I would remove the shirt and jacket. I have this you can try, but it might be too small." He held out the shirt he'd taken from his locker.

As much as Patrick wanted to watch as Kieren changed, he didn't. He turned back to his locker and chose another shirt for himself. He stripped to the waist and pulled the black PVC shirt on. Then, he removed his trousers and slipped into some leather versions, keeping his briefs on underneath to avoid any potential chafing. He tucked his shirt into the waistband and fastened the zip and button. Delaying turning around as long as he could, when he faced Kieren, he almost swallowed his tongue. The shirt fit him—just. It stretched beautifully across his muscles without giving away too many glimpses of what was beneath.

"I'll have to keep an eye on you in there. You'll be a new favourite in no time," he murmured. He cleared his throat. "You need to lock your phone in here, then we can check out the club."

Kieren handed him his belongings. "How did this place come about, anyway? It's not exactly hidden away from prying eyes."

Patrick chuckled. "Yes, my ancestors were not the most original for thinking of names. Club Royal has certainly had its fair share of the limelight. I don't know how long ago the club began, but one king had a kink he hid from most people, using a small windowless room for his own pleasures. Supposedly, his son grew out of control, and he introduced his son to the kinks, hoping to curb his wayward ways. From there, it expanded, involving more and more descendants until it became mandatory for all royals. I think it's mainly to keep them all in line. If everyone knows the secret, then it's less likely to be exposed because those who don't want it known will also be exposed." Patrick frowned. "Does that even make sense?"

Kieren chuckled. "Yeah, I get what you're saying."

"Come on, then. Let's go check out this place."

Patrick clapped Kieren on the shoulder as he passed, trying to keep things light, but all he really wanted to do was sink into his arms and never leave. They exited the changing rooms and strode to a door behind Clarice's desk. Patrick unlocked the door and held it for Kieren. This first area was what Douglas had coined the "conversation area" because it was a lot quieter than the rest of the club, and they were able to hold a conversation without having to shout or talk right next to their ear.

"Oliver! Two bottles of water, please. How's Griffin?"

Oliver was the bartender at the club for most of the nights they were open. His tanned skin and muscular physique always made Patrick's mouth water, especially in his uniform of a white waistcoat with nothing underneath, black trousers and white cuffs around his wrists. His black studded collar confirmed his "taken" status, although Patrick knew both he and his husband, Griffin, were open to anything. Some nights, one or the other were given free rein to play with others.

"Griffin is well, thank you, sir. Unfortunately, working tonight, though." Oliver placed two bottles on the bar. "Have a wonderful evening. Let me know if there's anything I can get you." He glanced at Kieren, looking him up and down.

Patrick felt a spindle of something poking at him, but he ignored it and faced Kieren, handing him a bottle. "Shall we explore?" He purposefully used words that had a double meaning, hoping to spark something in Kieren, and if he wasn't mistaken, his eyes narrowed. Only slightly, but enough to make Patrick believe his words hadn't missed their mark.

He led the way to the heavy wooden door, pausing to say, "The sounds are what seem to overwhelm people when they first visit. There's low-playing music and some conversation, but the sounds of sex and play are audible. Very audible."

Kieren nodded. "Okay."

Patrick unlocked the door, and the noises he'd just explained hit them. He didn't look back at Kieren, waiting until they were both through the door. Again, trying to see it from Kieren's perspective helped him to realise it looked just like an orgy. He peered at Kieren, the man's eyes darting around the area as Patrick had seen him do when he was assessing the security risk. He was probably doing the same thing there.

"Initial thoughts?" he asked, swigging from his bottle.

"A security nightmare." Score one for Patrick. "Overwhelming."

"There is a lot going on, but there's no rush for anything. Do you want to wander around for a bit? See what we can see?"

"Sure."

Patrick weaved slowly through the crowds around the perimeter of the room, greeting Quinn, a submissive who was friends with their group, as he passed until he came to a stage with the St Andrew's Cross on it. A man had strapped another man to it and was in the process of whipping him, the red streaks across the bound man's back easily visible against his skin. The Dom, he assumed by taking into account the outfit, pulled his arm back and flicked the whip through the air, sending the bound man arching into the cross.

"I don't understand," Kieren said.

"Understand what?"

"Doesn't that hurt?"

Patrick nodded. "It's supposed to. It's what he wants. It might be something he needs. Not everyone is the same. Have you any experience with BDSM at all?"

"Only what I've watched and read about."

Patrick chuckled. "It's both the same and different from either of those. If it's something you've never experienced and you look at it and go, 'No way in hell,' that's a hard limit. If you think, 'Hmm, maybe,' that's a soft limit. At least in my book. The things you go, 'Hell, yeah,' are good to experience straight away." He took another drink. "But even soft and hard limits can change, but only by yourself. No one can change your mind for you."

"Well, I think I would deem this a hard limit if I use that as my guide."

"Good to know. Let's continue." He wanted to find something Kieren might like the look of. It seemed extreme pain was a no-go.

They arrived at the next stage, which had a swing. A woman was strapped into it with her legs in the air, and a man was using the momentum of the swing to pound into her. He glanced at Kieren. His eyebrows were raised, but no disgust or negative emotions showed on his face.

"It would be interesting to see if that's as easy as it looks," Kieren said with a chuckle. "I have a feeling it isn't."

"It's not. If you get the momentum wrong, it's annoying as hell when you have an orgasm barrelling down on you, and then it disappears because the swing knocks you out of rhythm."

Kieren met his gaze, and something sparked between them. "Hell, yeah," Kieren said.

Heat bloomed in Patrick's gut, flowing outwards and upwards. He swallowed hard, then jumped when someone touched his shoulder.

"Sir, are you free for a session tonight?"

"Good evening, Cecily. I'm not sure if I'm going to—"

Kieren interrupted him. "You can. I don't mind."

Patrick weighed his options. It might be good for Kieren to see him in action. He'd be able to watch Kieren's responses as much as the submissives and gauge his reactions to them.

"Are you sure?" Kieren nodded, and Patrick faced the sub. "Okay, Cecily. Is the spanking bench free?"

"Yes, sir."

"Wait on the stage for me. I'll be with you shortly."

"Yes, sir."

He focused back on Kieren. "Would you like to watch or wander around?"

"I'll watch if you don't mind?"

"Not at all."

Patrick drifted towards the final stage in the room, nodding at John as they passed. Before he climbed onto the stage, he asked Kieren to stay on the floor. "This is where everyone watches."

He stepped up to where Cecily waited with her head lowered and her hands clasped in front of her. He'd played with her before and knew exactly how she liked things. "Remove your clothes and lay on your stomach on the bench."

"Yes, sir."

While she did as he'd asked, he went to a set of shelves to the side of the stage and chose a cane. He turned back around, glancing at Kieren as he tapped the cane on his opposite hand. Then he wandered over to Cecily and focused solely on the submissive who had asked for his help.

6

KIEREN

The change that came over Patrick as he stepped into his role as a Dom was breathtaking. Kieren had not expected the change to be visceral, but Patrick seemed to grow —not physically, but in confidence. It was sexy as hell. What Kieren didn't like, though, was Patrick's attention on someone else. That was something he hadn't anticipated. He wanted to push the woman aside and take her place, even though he had no idea if this was something he'd enjoy.

He shoved his hands into his pockets, trying to himself stop from going up there, especially when Patrick focused his attention solely on her. He'd been the recipient of his focus when they'd spent those stolen moments in the gym, and he wanted it again.

Pushing aside those thoughts, he refocused on the equipment Patrick was using. The bench that the woman was on reminded him of short stilts, which was an antithesis if ever there was one. It had a narrow padded cushion on which she rested her stomach and chest; a U-shaped padded headrest that appeared to rest against her forehead and cheeks, enabling her to breathe freely; and leg and arm platforms at adjustable heights. The frame of the bench itself appeared to be some sort of steel but didn't look like it would hold much weight.

Patrick placed the cane beside the bench and bent down to speak to the sub while fastening the straps to her arms. He continued to talk while he restrained her, though Kieren couldn't hear what he said. Then, Patrick picked up the cane and ran a hand over Cecily's back and ass.

"Ready?" Patrick said, louder than before.

"Yes, sir."

"What is your safe word?"

"Pineapple."

"I will be asking for your colours throughout the session, okay?"

"Yes, sir."

Patrick rested the cane on the top of Cecily's ass, then slid it to about halfway down, probably the fleshiest part, and paused. He pulled his arm back and shot it forward, the resounding smack loud despite the noise already in the room. Cecily flinched and made an almost bitten-off sound. Kieren couldn't see her face, but her hands clenched into fists.

"Colour?"

"Green, sir," she gasped.

Kieren could see the redness blooming on her ass cheeks already, and he winced. He wasn't sure how that could convert into pleasure, but maybe it was one of those things he'd have to try to find out for himself. He wouldn't do it for anyone, but if Patrick did it... His mouth curved. *Hmm, maybe.*

Another thwack sounded as Patrick caned Cecily again, this time against the tops of her thighs, just beneath her cheeks. Kieren winced again. That couldn't be comfortable. That area was really sensitive.

"Colour?"

"Green, sir."

Apparently, it was acceptable. As the caning continued, he

noted the places Patrick hit, the patterns blooming on Cecily's skin and how often he asked for her colours. He hadn't realised how long they'd been on the stage until Patrick put the cane down and unfastened the woman.

"Lay there for a moment, Cecily."

"Yes, sir." She sounded sleepy or drunk.

Patrick became a whirlwind of motion, grabbing several items from the shelves and a small fridge Kieren hadn't noticed before. He placed them all on a small table beside the sofa at the back of the stage before returning to Cecily and helping her climb from the bench. He guided her over to the sofa, helped her lay on her stomach and covered her with a blanket.

Kieren couldn't hear what was being said, but he watched their every movement, a warmth flowing through him at seeing the care Patrick took for her. He held a straw for her to drink some pink liquid and brushed his fingers through her hair as she drank. When she nodded, Patrick put the drink back on the table and grabbed a tube. He spoke to her, then lifted the blanket from her legs and ass, pulling another one from the back of the sofa and covering her legs, leaving just her ass exposed. He rubbed cream into the welts that were still visible, and Cecily barely flinched, a small smile staying on her face as she closed her eyes.

Once Patrick finished, he replaced the blanket over her and slid onto the sofa, lying beside her and obstructing Kieren's view. They stayed that way for a while, and Kieren glanced around, wondering whether he should stay or leave them to their privacy. He was about to leave when a hand clamped on his shoulder, and it took all his training to stop himself from throwing the person to the floor and subduing him.

Eyes narrowed, he turned his head, relaxing when Prince Frederick grimaced. "Shit, I'm sorry. I wasn't thinking," Frederick said.

Kieren inhaled and smiled. "No, it's fine. I was...distracted."

"I can imagine."

"I didn't realise you were visiting tonight," Kieren said, for conversation more than anything. He preferred having someone to talk with to stop him from looking out of place on his own.

"I hadn't planned to, but Henry mentioned Patrick was coming here. I thought some moral support would be good." Frederick slipped a hand into his pockets and stared at Patrick's back. "Has he explained about aftercare?"

Kieren waved his hand back and forth. "A little. I understand what he's doing, but not really the why and for how long."

Frederick nodded. "Every person who goes through a scene has the potential for a 'drop.' A drop is when the adrenaline and endorphins leave the body, causing an imbalance. There are many ways this can show in a person. It could be feeling lethargic or cold, nausea, headaches, and so on. A conversation about aftercare is an important part of a scene and always happens before the scene begins."

Kieren frowned. "Patrick didn't discuss much with her before doing this. Not that I heard anyway."

Frederick smiled. "Patrick and Cecily have played many times together. He probably spoke to her briefly as he was setting up the scene to check nothing had changed from the last time they played."

That made sense, although that tendril of unease at Patrick being with someone else wouldn't quit.

"What Patrick probably didn't tell you was that those drops don't happen *just* to the subs."

Kieren stared at Frederick, letting the words run around his head to make sure he understood what he was saying. "How do I help him?"

The knowledge in Frederick's eyes should've worried Kieren, but all he cared about was the potential drop Patrick would feel when he finally stopped caring for Cecily. He needed to do something.

"I booked room four for you when I saw Patrick on the stage. He never thinks to do it himself, but usually, one of us is there with him, and we help." Frederick pointed to a hallway at the back of the room. "Go through there and turn right. The doors are numbered, and your fingerprint will get you into the room. Settle him on the sofa or bed and get him to drink something from the fridge in there. Try to get him to eat if you can. If you're feeling up to it, a massage on his back or arms will help the ache in his muscles. There are some oils and creams on the shelves which you can pick from." Frederick sighed. "Just be there for him. He tends to withdraw into himself more than anything, becoming quiet and easily distracted. Oh, he might fall asleep, too. It's fine if he does."

"Okay. I can do that." He wasn't sure he'd be any good at it, but he'd do his best.

"One more thing." Kieren glanced at him. "He might fight you on it, to begin with. He's never been one to admit he goes through it. We're used to it and don't bring attention to it any longer."

Kieren nodded, his mind already planning how to get him to the room without causing a scene. He could tell Patrick he needed to talk through what happened on the stage and that he wanted somewhere quiet to do it.

"Why me?" he asked suddenly.

Frederick glanced around the room, seemingly collecting his thoughts. When Frederick squinted at him, Kieren felt exposed. "It's none of my business, Kieren, but I've seen how you both look at each other when you think no one's looking. Most of the time, no one is, but I look out for my family, and I see a lot of things other people don't. I have no problem with your relationship—if you decide to have one—because I think you're both perfect for each other. I can't see your journey being easy, but it will certainly be worth it."

Kieren's heart pounded, and his mouth dried up. "I don't know what to say to that."

"You don't need to say anything. Just know I have your back, and if you ever need anything, come to me. No matter what it is."

Kieren focused on Patrick's back, blinking away the stinging in his eyes. Frederick's hand rested on his nape and squeezed, helping to centre him. "Thank you," he rasped.

"You're welcome. Now, I'm going to disappear before Patrick sees me and gets angry at me for being here. I'll be around for a few hours. If you need anything, use the phone in the room to call Clarice, and she'll get a message to me."

Kieren nodded, inhaling and exhaling when Frederick let go of him. "Have a good evening, Your Highness."

Frederick chuckled. "Please call me Freddie. I'm tempted to abolish the titles if I ever become king."

Kieren snorted. "Good luck with that."

Freddie clapped him on the shoulder and pivoted away, disappearing into the crowd. Kieren crossed his arms over his chest and waited, watching over Patrick and Cecily until Patrick finally moved. His actions were slow but methodical, and he helped Cecily to sit upright, holding onto her until she nodded at him a few minutes later. He grabbed her clothes and dressed her, then pulled her to standing. He held onto her again, then wrapped his arms around her. When he let her go, he pressed his lips to her forehead, smiled and helped her from the stage.

Cecily gave Kieren a small smile as she disappeared, but Kieren focused on Patrick. His face appeared drawn, lines etched onto his features that hadn't been visible beforehand.

"Patrick?" He waited until Patrick faced him, a glassy look in his eyes. "Come with me." He held out his hand, and Patrick stared at it for several seconds before slipping his hand into it. Kieren said nothing, just tugged Patrick towards the room Freddie had pointed out.

His thumbprint opened the door, and he pulled Patrick inside, closing the door behind them. The room wasn't huge, but it had a two-seater sofa and a double bed, plus some other furniture items. At that quick glance, Kieren chose the bed and guided Patrick towards it.

"What are you doing?" Patrick asked.

"I'm taking care of you."

Patrick shook his head. "You don't need to do anything. I'm fine."

"I want to." Plain, simple words.

Patrick lifted his gaze to Kieren's, staring at him for an eternity before nodding once. Starting at the top of Patrick's shirt, he unbuttoned the shirt, pulled it free of the waistband, and pushed it off his shoulders. He grabbed his hips and settled him onto the edge of the bed, kneeling in front of him and removing his shoes.

"Scoot up to the headboard."

"I'm—" Patrick stopped when Kieren glared at him, earning a small smile. "Okay."

Patrick sat against the headboard and stared at his hands in his lap. Kieren would've been concerned about his "spaciness" if Freddie hadn't explained it to him. He rose and gathered a bottle of water that said it had electrolytes in it, a tub of cut-up fruit that had been left in the fridge and a small bottle of coconut oil.

He put the items on the bedside table and sat beside Patrick, opening the bottle of water and putting a straw in it. He held it to Patrick's mouth and raised an eyebrow. Patrick's mouth quirked, but he took the straw between his lips and drank, their eyes locked the entire time. When Patrick had his fill, Kieren put the bottle on the table and picked up the fruit. He used the fork to spear a piece and held it to Patrick's mouth again.

"I can feed myself," Patrick said.

"I know." Kieren wanted to do this. He hadn't realised how

much he wanted to look after Patrick. He knew the man was a Dom and probably didn't want this level of care on a normal day, but while he would let him, Kieren would revel in it.

As Patrick chewed the strawberry Kieren had placed in his mouth, he tilted his head. When he swallowed, he said, "Do you have any questions about the scene?"

Kieren lifted another piece of fruit while he organised his thoughts. "Did she orgasm?"

Patrick raised his eyebrows, then shook his head. "It wasn't about a sexual release for her. It's about a release of the tension in her body. Her job is very stressful, and this was what she found works best for her to let go of all that. She's happily married, and her husband can't do this for her because he hates seeing her hurt. As a compromise, she comes to me when she needs the release, but that's all it's about. She would never cheat on him, and she goes right back home to him after."

Kieren thought that through as he fed Patrick piece after piece of fruit until he finished it, then he offered the drink again. "Lie down on your stomach," he said when Patrick drank some more.

"Why?"

"I'm going to massage your sore arms and back."

"But they're not—" Patrick sighed and nodded. He manoeuvred himself further down and rolled to his stomach.

Kieren had never given a massage before. He'd only ever rubbed a warming muscle cream into his skin or Patrick's. That was different to a massage. He poured some coconut oil into his hands and rubbed them together, positioning himself on his knees beside Patrick's hips. He inhaled before resting his hands on his back and rubbing in small circles around his lower back. He started gently, increasing the pressure depending on the noises Patrick made. His hands moved to his upper back after replenishing the oil, but it wasn't an easy position, twinging his own back with his movements.

"Straddle my hips, Kieren. I don't mind."

"How did you—"

"Your movements aren't as smooth as they were before. I don't want you hurting yourself."

Kieren smiled. There was no giving the Dom a break. He grabbed the oil so he could reach it when he moved and lifted his leg over Patrick's thighs. It was an excellent position for many things, the least of which was the massage. He hoped he could get through it without popping a boner, but he doubted it.

Focusing on Patrick's upper back, he dug into the muscles there, earning several deep groans which vibrated through his back and into Kieren's hands. He rubbed his thumbs into the base of Patrick's neck and all along his shoulders. Grabbing some more oil, he moved to Patrick's arms, giving one side and then the other the same treatment the rest of his body had received.

When he couldn't find any more knots or tension in Patrick's body, he softened his hands for a few minutes, then paused. Soft inhales and exhales sounded, and Kieren smiled. It seemed Patrick had fallen asleep. Kieren had done something right. He glared down at his cock, hard and aching behind the zip of his trousers. Nothing would come from this, and it needed to fuck off.

Climbing off Patrick's body carefully, he grabbed another bottle of water and settled onto the bed beside him, his back to the headboard. He watched the rise and fall of Patrick's back as he drank. What the hell was he going to do? He wouldn't lie to himself and say he didn't want Patrick because he did. He wanted to see what they could make of their lives together, but could he let his heart out of its locked box and take the chance that Patrick would stay with him for the rest of their lives? Could he take the chance that the evil at work within the royal family wouldn't take Patrick from him before they were both old and grey and died peacefully in their sleep side by side?

He wanted to, but being scared did something to a person. It stopped their heart from making a choice. Logic won out more times than their emotions did. Was he ready for his heart and head to fight the big fight? He didn't know.

For then, he was where he wanted to be, with the person he wanted to be with. After that, he'd have to see which fights he won and which he lost. Having Freddie's approval helped, as did knowing Patrick felt something for him, but he had his own nightmares to fight against, as well as guessing what their future held.

He put the bottle on the table and lay down beside the man he wanted more than he'd wanted anyone else before. He didn't touch him, but he stared at him, mapping every laughter line, every hill and valley, every scar and hair on his face.

Did he have the strength to give Patrick everything he said he wanted?

7

PATRICK

*P*atrick woke surrounded by warmth, and for a moment, it disconcerted him. He studied his surroundings without moving his head, finding he was still in the room at the club, but the arm around his waist and the breath heating his neck was something he wasn't used to. Gently, he twisted his head to the side, and Kieren came into view. Patrick let go of the worry and smiled. This would probably be the only time he would get to hold and be held by him, and he wasn't going to do anything to mess it up. He wished he could roll over to watch Kieren as he slept, but he didn't want to take the chance he would wake and move away from him.

Instead, he lay there, relishing the hold Kieren had on him, the deep inhales of slumber, the heat of him pressed against his back. Having no idea what time it was because there were no clocks in the room, he let himself drift, half-dreaming, half-daydreaming about a life where he and Kieren could be together. Patrick didn't see a problem with them being together, but something was holding Kieren back, and he wished he could help him with it.

The body behind him froze, and Patrick realised Kieren was awake.

"It's okay," he whispered, tightening his hand over Kieren's, which was resting against Patrick's stomach.

A shaky exhale rushed over his neck, and he waited to see if Kieren would say something. When the silence continued, Patrick rolled until he faced Kieren, putting the man's hands back around his waist when he pulled them away. He placed his hands on Kieren's chest, rubbing his thumbs back and forth.

"How did you know what to do?" he asked. Kieren's forehead creased, and Patrick added, "The food, the drink, the massage?"

Kieren's lips pursed, and if Patrick hadn't known it was one of his tells that showed his embarrassment, he would've kissed him. "I had a conversation with someone while you were doing the aftercare with Cecily."

Inwardly, he rolled his eyes. "Let me guess, Doug...no, Freddie."

Kieren's eyes widening would've given it away even if he hadn't nodded. "How did you know?"

"I know him. He wouldn't have been happy with how we left things at the party. He would've come to check on me no matter where I was. I should've warned you."

"It's fine. I'm glad he was there. It let me help you."

Patrick moved his head a millimetre closer. "Thank you." He rolled his shoulders as much as he could without dislodging Kieren's arms. "My arms hardly ache, which is a first."

Kieren smiled. "I'm glad I could help."

Patrick dropped his gaze to Kieren's lips and licked his own before closing the distance. He brushed his mouth against Kieren's, then pressed harder, not trying to get him to open his mouth, but just so he could feel it against his. He pulled back after a moment, snuggling down until his head fit beneath

Kieren's chin and wrapping one arm around his waist and one leg over his thighs.

A chuckle vibrated through Kieren's chest. "Are you quite comfortable?"

"Yes." Patrick closed his eyes and breathed—just took a moment to soak in everything about the situation. He doubted they would have much time before someone knocked on the door to say the club was closing, depending on how long they'd been asleep, but he was determined to wrangle as much snuggle time as he could from Kieren before they went back to their real lives.

The knock sounded quicker than he'd hoped, and reluctantly, he pulled away.

"Who's that?" Kieren asked, sitting upright.

"It's what the staff does when the club is starting to close," Patrick said as he headed for the door. He opened it a crack and nodded his thanks to his cousin, Elizabeth, who just stared at him before turning and walking away. Closing the door again, he sighed. "And sometimes, it's the Monitors who do it." He shook his head.

"Who was it?"

"Elizabeth."

Kieren paused, then nodded. "Christian's sister."

Patrick snorted. "If you could call her that." He grabbed the bottle and oil from the bedside table, threw the bottle in the bin and replaced the oil on the shelf. Sliding his shirt on, he buttoned it while watching Kieren move closer. "See something you like?"

Kieren's heated gaze pierced him, reaching across the space between them to freeze him in place. "Definitely."

Patrick inhaled at the tone, knowing what was coming. "But?"

"I can't."

Patrick stared at his hands as they finished buttoning his shirt, then he fetched his shoes and put them on. "Time to go."

He refused to fight with Kieren about it. If the man didn't want him, he wasn't going to push him. The last thing he ever wanted to do was make someone do something they didn't want to do.

"Patrick."

"It's fine. We know where we stand."

He opened the door and led the way through the club, not checking to see if Kieren was following or not. He hoped he was when he saw Charles standing at the doors as if he was waiting for him.

"Patrick," Charles said in a condescending tone. "I haven't seen you with our cousins for a while. Had a nasty breakup?" He mockingly pouted.

"We're doing well. Thanks for asking. How are Juliet and the kids?" He tried to sidestep around Charles to get to the door, but Charles stepped in front of him.

"They're all doing well. Juliet is pregnant again."

Patrick bit back his retort about bringing another child into such a shit family. Instead, smiling and congratulating him. "When's the lucky day?"

"10 March." Charles smirked, and Patrick's hands trembled.

"I'm sure the kids are looking forward to having a brother or sister as much as you'll be happy for another child."

Charles crossed his arms over his chest. "Mother and Father are over the moon."

Patrick wasn't surprised. More brains to corrupt. "I'm sure they are." He nodded to the door. "It's time for me to go. Have a good evening, Charles."

Charles stared at him, unmoving, then he flicked his gaze to Patrick's right and sneered before stepping aside. "You, too."

Patrick opened the door and strode into the conversation area, not stopping until he was through reception and in the

Monitor's changing room. Then he sat on the bench and dropped his head between his knees. How could such an evil person act like he cared about his family? It wasn't that long ago that Charles held a locked and cocked gun at Christian's head and threatened to end his life. Patrick couldn't understand how the two sides could work together.

Kieren settled beside him, his legs bracketing Patrick, and pulled him sideways against his chest. The arms were just what he needed when his hold was fraying, but he needed to get out of the club before that hold disintegrated completely. He pulled free from Kieren and opened his locker, yanking his shirt over his head and his trousers down his legs. He quickly dressed in the clothes he had worn to arrive and grabbed his belongings. Kieren reached past him to get his things, then they were out of there.

They signed out at reception, Clarice giving them a small smile, and headed for the car.

"Give me the keys," Kieren said, and Patrick handed them over without complaint. He wasn't in any state to drive.

He stared out of the window on the journey home, his chin resting on his hand. Something was going on with Charles, and it had nothing to do with the new baby. Patrick's instincts were flaring, but he couldn't figure out what was prickling at him. He ran through his conversation with Charles again, but nothing stood out.

"What's wrong?" Kieren asked as they pulled into Bagshot Park.

"I don't know," Patrick said, distracted.

When Kieren parked the car, Patrick climbed out and headed straight indoors. He needed his music.

"Patrick." He continued on his way. "Patrick!"

Patrick whirled around. "What?" He glared at Kieren, unable to temper his expression right then.

"Make sure you rest," Kieren said, pivoting away and striding down the hallway.

Kieren turned the corner, then Patrick closed his eyes and shook his head. How he had ever been given such a nice guy as a bodyguard, he'd never know. He didn't deserve it with how he treated the man sometimes.

His music room calmed him the moment he shut himself inside it. He paused with his back against the door, looking at his instruments, deciding which would be the best for him to expel the feelings inside him. He hadn't played his flute or clarinet lately, but they weren't what he needed. Neither was his violin. He aimed for his piano, sitting on the stool and lifting the lid.

He rested his fingers against the keys, closed his eyes and inhaled. As he exhaled, his fingers began moving, but what came out wasn't the riot of noise Patrick had been expecting. Instead, tears sprung to his eyes as a melody with peaks and troughs filled the room. The peaks flew higher than the tallest tree, full of lightness and freedom, and the troughs filled with weights and darkness. With each peak, his mood improved, but with each trough, it fell. A never-ending cycle that seemingly wouldn't end.

But end, it did. As the last note drifted away, Patrick lowered the lid and left the room, eyes locked on the floor. By the time he reached his rooms, his body was a ball of tension, all the work Kieren had done to loosen his muscles after his scene at the club gone to waste.

He showered off the sweat, pretending the tears were just water droplets trickling down his face, then dried off and climbed into bed. As he stared at the ornately decorated ceiling, he did the only other thing he could think of to distract himself from what was trying to escape his control—he wrapped his hand around his cock. His eyelids fluttered closed as he stroked, his mind taking him back to the room at the club when he was enveloped in Kieren's arms.

Instead of them leaving the club, he deepened the kiss, licking into Kieren's mouth as their hands explored. He removed Kieren's shirt, exposing the tanned, defined abs and chest, and moved his mouth over them. Despite the hardness of the muscles beneath, the skin was soft, with minimal hair, unlike his own. When he reached Kieren's waistband, he glanced up at the man's burning gaze, smiling and unfastening the button and lowering the zip on his trousers. Kieren shifted his hips, allowing Patrick to pull the trousers down over his hips and freeing his cock.

Patrick licked his lips and grabbed the shaft, bringing it to his mouth. He laved the head, moaning at the taste of him. He sucked, wanting to swallow more of the liquid, then lowered his head, taking Kieren deep into his mouth. Bobbing his head, he used his hand at the base, adding to the sensation. He peered at Kieren, his eyes widening at Kieren's hands gripping the headboard. The man wasn't bound, but it gave the idea of it, and Patrick's arousal rose. He increased his speed, swallowing every time Kieren hit his throat, and within minutes, Kieren's body locked as his release spurted into Patrick's mouth at the same time Patrick's orgasm hit him.

Patrick opened his eyes, chest heaving, the ornate ceiling having not changed to the smooth one of the club. The release had calmed him, but wishing for something he couldn't have never helped. He cleaned himself up and climbed back into bed, rolling to his side with his hand under his pillow.

Seconds later, he shot up again. "Shit!" He scrambled for his phone and dialled. "Sorry, Freddie," he said when his cousin answered. "I spoke to Charles today, and something was bugging me. I finally figured out what it was."

"What?"

"Juliet's pregnant, and apparently, she's due on 10 March."

Freddie stayed silent, and Patrick hoped he'd figure out the connection without him having to explain. "The anniversary of the bomb."

Not the anniversary of his mother's death. "Yes." Patrick sighed. "I don't know if it's true because it's just scary if it is, but can we check if there's anything on Christian's list for that date? With it being the…anniversary, there would likely be some events happening."

"It's likely something is planned. It's only five months away, and usually, events are planned well in advance, as you know." Freddie cleared his throat. "The list is in my office. I'll check and let you know."

"Thanks, and sorry if I woke you."

He chuckled. "You didn't. I was still awake."

Patrick shifted up the bed and leaned back against the headboard. "Anything I can help with? After all, you helped me earlier."

"You needed it, whether or not you admit it. Anyway, we're not keeping a tally."

"I know, but a worry shared is a worry halved and all that."

Freddie was quiet for a while, and Patrick knew him well enough to know he was gathering his thoughts and deciding if sharing was the best course of action. "I'm worried about Damon."

Patrick raised his eyebrows. "How come?"

Freddie's sigh was audible. "He's been away more than usual. I thought his covert shit had stopped, but I'm not sure now."

He must be worried because Freddie rarely swore. "Did you ask him?"

"Yes. He told me he was doing some jobs for Father, but they were nothing to do with what we're doing."

"You don't believe him."

"I want to." He sighed again. "We seem to have grown apart lately. I feel like I hardly see him."

"Could you offer to go on the job with him?"

"I could, but I have many responsibilities here. It's not easy to just up and leave."

"When is he due back?"

"Monday."

Patrick mentally skimmed his diary. He had nothing planned for the next couple of weeks before the charity auction at the end of the month. "When's he next due to leave and come back?"

"Wednesday to Friday."

It didn't surprise him that Freddie knew Damon's calendar as well as his own. They were childhood friends who had been—until recently, apparently—joined at the hip ever since preschool.

"Okay, what do you have booked for those three days?"

"Paddy, I know what you're thinking, but it won't work."

"Humour me."

Freddie huffed a laugh. "I have three meetings on Wednesday, a ceremony on Thursday and an evening event on Friday. You can't do all of those."

"But you can?" He paused. "I'll be over in the morning, and we can go through each of them, and you can tell me what I need to know. I'll take over, and you can go with Damon. It sounds like you need to reconnect with him. It's putting the universe out of alignment with you not being together."

Patrick's mind brought up what Oscar had mentioned a few months back. When Christian had first begun a relationship with him, Oscar had wrongly assumed Freddie and Damon were a couple, but Patrick had been thinking about it, on and off, since then, and it made perfect sense. Except for the fact that Freddie was straight. If he pushed that aside, though, they were the perfect couple.

"I'm not used to it, either," Freddie admitted. "I didn't realise how much better my schedule was when I had Damon by my side."

Patrick smiled. Was Freddie as straight as they all thought? He wasn't sure now. "He'll be back before you know it. Then you can get to the bottom of what's going on. Uncle Andrew knows how you feel about Damon going off on his own. I doubt he'd send him to do something dangerous like he did before."

"I hope so, but there are many things going on at the minute. I'm wondering if it's a case of all hands on deck. We have a limited number of people who we trust implicitly not to turn against us."

"True. Maybe we can ask Uncle Andrew tomorrow."

Freddie was quiet again. "Do you know what? Let's get everyone together on Monday evening, including Damon, and go through everything. I know you said you were feeling out of the loop, but we'll go through everything. I'll get Father to come as well if he can. Maybe we can get to the bottom of it without making you take over where you don't want to." He chuckled.

"I don't mind at all. You know that."

"Not minding doing it and not wanting to do it are two different things."

"Are they?" Patrick feigned ignorance. "I'll let you get back to your work."

"I'm not working. I'm reading."

"Reading about something regarding work?" Freddie stayed silent, and Patrick laughed. "It's still work, no matter how you couch it." He closed his eyes and tilted his head back. "You need to rest, Freddie."

"I try. There's just so much…" He didn't finish, and he didn't need to. With everything that was going on with their family at the moment, it was a surprise any of them slept anymore.

"I know."

When they finally ended the call, both were tired, which

Patrick took as a good sign, at least for Freddie. As for himself, he wanted to lose himself in the land of his dreams, but the problem with that was that it hurt all the more when he woke the following morning. In his dreams, he could have everything he wanted. In reality, life was throwing more hurdles his way than someone taking part in the Olympics.

All he wanted was to protect his family, but that seemed less likely than ever. Despite his training, he would never be at the stage where his ability was of any use. Especially if he cancelled their training sessions because he couldn't stand not being able to be in the same room as the man he wanted in his bed and not have him.

Life wasn't fair.

8

KIEREN

When Charles started talking to Patrick at the club and stopped him from leaving, it took everything in Kieren not to intervene. Not only as his bodyguard but as his…whatever Kieren was pretending wasn't happening. He had seen Patrick trembling under the pressure of the conversation, but Kieren wouldn't do anything to make Patrick look weaker than he was, even if that meant keeping quiet. But he hated every minute.

He'd wanted to talk in the car because he'd looked worried, but Patrick hadn't given much response. Leaving him in the hallway when Patrick had snapped at him had been the last thing he wanted to do, but Patrick would've beaten himself up if his temper had got the better of him and he'd hurled words he hadn't wanted to, and Kieren refused to let him do that. It was the only reason he'd walked away.

He hadn't gone far, and as soon as Patrick had shut himself in the music room, Kieren crept back and listened at the door. The haunting song had him holding back tears, and he wished he could go to him. Lifting his head, he stared at the handle. Freddie had given them permission of sorts, and after what they'd been through at the club, could Kieren allow himself to give in to how he felt? He wasn't sure he was brave enough.

Resting his forehead against the door for a moment, he closed his eyes and wished for courage. Just not for tonight. He pivoted away and headed for his rooms.

"Kieren."

He whirled around at his name and paused. "Yes, Your Highness?"

Princess Victoria, Patrick's mother and Kieren's employer, closed the distance between them, stopping outside the music room and staring at it with pain in her blue eyes—the same blue as Patrick's. "He's hurting." Kieren didn't reply, not knowing what to say. "I've tried everything I can think of to help him, but nothing works. He just locks himself away and 'plays' his pain." She transferred her gaze to Kieren. "What can I do?"

Kieren's heart broke for more than one reason. She was hurting because her son was in pain, and Kieren wished he had someone who cared that much for him. It was selfish, but he'd missed out on much by losing his family. He cleared his throat.

"I don't know, Your Highness. I know it's not my job, but I'm trying to figure that out, too."

She sighed as the notes changed and rose, eliciting a sense of happiness in the air, but Kieren knew it wouldn't last. "We all feel helpless, but he seems to be taking it harder than I expected. Do you know why?" Kieren had an idea, but he wasn't sure it was his place to say. "Please. If there's anything I can do to help him…"

Kieren stared at the music room door. "He feels weak like he can't be of any help in this fight. It's why we…" He stopped. Patrick hadn't told his parents about his training.

"It's why you're training him." Victoria gave a small smile. "I have my sources."

He blew out a breath. "I apologise if I shouldn't have agreed, but I didn't know what else to do."

She waved her hand. "You're not in trouble. If my son needs to train to feel better about the situation, then let him. God knows I haven't been of much help." She sighed again. "I usually have more instincts to go on with these things, but this time…I feel as lost as everyone else." She shook her head. "I'm sorry to have kept you. Thank you for what you're doing. Whatever he needs, if it's within your power and will help, give it to him. And pass that on to your colleagues, too. Times are fraught with uncertainty, and we need to keep those on our side as close as we can. I believe it's only together we can fight my sister."

Kieren made sure he kept his expression neutral at her words. As the music grew sombre, Victoria placed a hand on her stomach, nodded and retraced her earlier steps. He watched her go, wishing he could do more. He needed to speak with Brett. There had to be something. He wouldn't interrupt him tonight, and tomorrow was Sunday, so he'd wait until their Monday morning meeting.

He slept like shit and felt even worse when he woke to find Patrick had left the house without him. It didn't matter that he was only visiting Windsor. He was still supposed to have a guard with him. When he'd spoken to Brett briefly, explaining what had happened, his boss had assured him it was okay—Patrick was with Freddie, who had guards on him constantly. It didn't alleviate his worry and, if he was being honest with himself, his anger. If Patrick didn't want him around, that was fine, but to risk his own life just because they were on an out wasn't good. They would be having words later.

He spent several hours in the gym, working his body to exhaustion, hoping to get rid of all the tension before he saw Patrick again.

But Patrick didn't return. He stayed at Windsor all day and overnight. Kieren had next to no sleep again, but as he dressed for his journey to Windsor, he knew there was no chance of him falling asleep during the day. His body was strung tight, and he was on edge. All because he hadn't seen Patrick for over twenty-four hours. Because he didn't know where Patrick's head was at. Because they hadn't talked through what had happened the other night. It was ridiculous.

He put a set of workout clothes in a bag to take with him. Depending on what Patrick's plans were that day, he might get the opportunity to train Patrick or just get a workout himself. Checking he had everything he needed, he strode through Bagshot Park and to the car he'd been given as part of his job. He didn't know if Patrick planned on going into the office that day, and until he knew for certain, he'd take his own car, and they could call for a driver if and when he decided.

The car was a sleek, black machine that probably cost twice as much as his annual salary, but it was a nice drive. He showed his ID at the gate to Windsor and parked in a vacant spot. He left his bag in the car for the time being and headed for Randall's office.

Randall was the king's personal assistant and the head of the household staff. He kept everything running smoothly and often appeared to know what he needed before he asked for it.

Kieren knocked on his door and entered when asked. "Morning, Randall. I just wanted to drop in to let you know I was on the premises, and if Prince Patrick needs to go anywhere, I will be with Brett for the morning meeting."

"That's great. Thanks for letting me know. I've already arranged for a suit for him if he goes straight to work from here, and a car is on call ready for if you need it."

"On top of things as always, I see." Kieren grinned.

"I hope so. Too many balls in the air to drop any." Randall chuckled. "If you need to see Patrick, he's with Douglas."

"Thank you, but I think I'll leave them to it unless he needs me."

"Understood. I'll let the guards know to call if Patrick tries to leave without you." Randall smirked.

Kieren felt his cheeks heat. "That would be much appreciated. Have a good day, Randall."

"You, too, sir."

Kieren trailed down the corridors and hallways until he reached the wing of the castle that held the security team's base of operations. It was just as grand as the rest of the property, but it was easier to ignore due to the sheer number of computers and gadgets the room held. Not to mention the number of people.

"Kieren! You made it," Brett said, coming over and clapping him on the shoulder.

"Morning. How is everything?"

"All running smoothly, though we'll go over that in the meeting. What's on your mind?" Kieren raised his eyebrows, and Brett chuckled. "I know you. I can tell when something's bothering you."

He sighed. "We have to do something, Brett. We can't keep living in the stasis of not knowing. Something's got to give."

Brett sighed. "I know. Even though we're just the bodyguards, we've been working with everyone involved and trying to help how we can. It's crazy how organised it all seems to be. So many leads heading to dead ends."

Kieren frowned. "Almost like busy work."

Brett's forehead creased as he stared at him, then his eyes widened. "As if they're trying to keep us busy..."

"So we don't see whatever's coming next. Fuck."

Brett shook his head. "I've never seen anything like this, Kieren. And you know how long I've been in security."

"I need that list."

Brett stared at him. "You don't have clearance."

Kieren rubbed his hands over his face. "Can you get me it?"

Brett's jaw clenched. "I don't know. I'll try."

Kieren nodded. "Okay.

"Brett!" He lifted his head when Felix called. "Christian called. They're ready to go as soon as we're finished here."

Brett nodded and clapped his hands. "Let's get to it, gentlemen. I have places to be."

Brett and Felix guarded Christian and Oscar when they were out and about and, sometimes, at Windsor if there was a particularly high threat like there had been a few months ago.

"Okay, this will be brief because there isn't much to tell you," Brett started. "We have a new set of earpieces that we're trialling. They have a greater range than our current ones, but we're not sure about what interferes with the reception. I want Eric, Rae, Isaac, Van and Sam to trial them over the next couple of days and report back your findings. We'll rotate them around until we've all had a try before we collate the information and decide where to go from there.

"Second, at the next event, which I believe is the Halloween charity auction, we need more volunteers to work it. Obviously, this will only be if your charge is not due to be elsewhere at the same time. It is a Saturday night, and most of you won't be working, but I would prefer volunteers rather than choosing."

That was one thing Kieren liked about Brett. He didn't push his weight around and make people do what he wanted when they hated something. He always asked for volunteers and preferences before deciding and only ever put his foot down if they weren't cooperating.

"Kieren, I know Patrick is the guest of honour, and you'll be there that night. I'll have you switch out a day that week to get your second day off."

"Don't worry about it. It's fine." Kieren didn't care about days off. It gave him too much time to think.

Brett glared at him. "Not up for debate. Finally, we have four additional guards starting with us this week. They will arrive on Wednesday, and I'll assign them to shadow all of you at some point. Their names are Jade, Nina, Greg and Ford."

"Yeah! Two more to add to our small contingent," Locke called and high-fived Rae.

They were two of only four female guards on royal duty. The other two, Selena and Viola, were the king's personal guards, along with six males. When Kieren had first joined the team, he'd expected to see some of the male guards causing problems for the females—it was what he'd experienced in previous positions more often than not—but when everyone was treated the same, it filled Kieren with a sense of contentment. He knew he'd picked the right job and would do everything in his power to stay in it.

"Yes, Locke. No ganging up on us now." Brett winked.

"Wouldn't dream of it, boss."

"Anyway, that's all the updates from me. Does anyone have questions? If so, make it quick." No one said a word, and Kieren glanced around, seeing shaking heads. "Good. Well, Felix and I are off on duty. You all know what you need to do. Get to it."

Brett and Felix left the room quickly, and Kieren followed at a more sedate pace. He hadn't been called to take Patrick to work, and he assumed he wasn't attending that day. He had his phone, and the team would contact him should Patrick need him; therefore, he grabbed his bag from the car and headed for the gym.

When he'd first arrived at Windsor, he'd been surprised by the location of the security team. From what Brett had told him, security used to hold up elsewhere and only attend Windsor when needed. But when King Andrew took over, he insisted the security team become part of Windsor, keeping them close at hand at all times. Kieren could see the reasons behind it, but the luxury was more than he could stand sometimes.

By the time he'd changed into his workout kit, he was ready to get rid of some of the tension that had seeped back into his body. He still hadn't seen Patrick, and he was uneasy. Not because he thought something was wrong, but because they were issues between them that needed settling. He should've fetched Patrick for his training session, but the man needed his family more than learning how to fight. At least, in Kieren's opinion.

He warmed up by going through the karate katas from white belt to black belt. As he finished the brown belt one, he felt eyes on him, but he didn't stop. If anyone attacked him, he could go into defending mode in a split second, but he didn't think they were there for that. As he ended the final stage, he closed his eyes and bowed his head.

"Can you teach me that?"

Patrick's voice sank into him and released the tension he'd not been able to get rid of. He glanced over his shoulder. "I can."

"It seems…peaceful."

"If peace is what you're looking for, tai chi might be a better choice."

Patrick stepped onto the mat, already wearing his workout clothes. "Do you know that?" Kieren nodded. "Show me?"

Kieren swallowed and stepped back. He knew several martial arts, and although karate was his favourite, tai chi was the best for relaxation and peace, although yoga was even better, in his opinion. He worked through some slow movements, focusing on his breathing and the position of his arms, legs and feet. Coming to a stop after several minutes of silence, he faced Patrick.

"Which would you prefer? Or would you like yoga?"

Patrick scrunched his nose. "I don't think folding myself into a pretzel is the best choice for me. I like the sound of tai chi."

"Okay. Stand beside me. Follow my moves, but don't worry if you get them wrong. You can learn the order of the moves with every repetition you do. It's not essential."

The more Kieren thought about it, the more he liked the idea of teaching Patrick tai chi or karate. It would help with his footwork, and tai chi would hopefully help to release him from the tension he carried.

"Can we talk while we're doing it, or does it need to be silent?"

"We can talk." It might make it easier for them. "Just focus on my movements and copy what I do."

He went through the first few moves, allowing Patrick to get used to the speed, before asking, "What did you want to talk about?"

"I wanted to apologise for leaving without you yesterday. I know I should've woken you, and I'm sorry."

Kieren bit his lip before he answered, taking a breath through his nose. "You should've, yes. Not only because it wasn't safe for you to drive alone, but because you took a chance with my job. If Brett hadn't been as understanding as he is, I could've been fired."

Patrick's moves stuttered, but he recovered. "I never thought about that. I'm doubly sorry, then."

"Apology accepted only if you promise not to do it again. No matter how at odds we are, I need you safe." That was more than he'd planned to give him and more telling than he'd wanted.

"Promise." A few seconds later, he asked, "We didn't have time to talk it through much, but what did you think of the club?"

"It was both what I was and wasn't expecting. I don't understand the need for pain, but then I've not been on the receiving end, so I can't form a full opinion. It doesn't seem like something I'd enjoy."

"Would you want to be on the receiving end to experience it?"

Kieren hesitated. While he didn't think he'd enjoy the pain, he'd seen other things that could lessen the sting. Was that something he would want to try? "Yes, but with some amendments."

"What kind of amendments?"

He pursed his lips. "The cane appeared painful, but I know there are other implements that wouldn't hurt as much."

"There are lots of different items, providing a wide range of pain levels or even no pain. Would you like me to show you?"

Wasn't that the question of the day? Of course, Kieren knew his answer, but was it the right answer? Would this bring them closer than they should be, or would it bring them to *where* they should be? He only had one answer he could give.

"Yes, please."

9

PATRICK

When Patrick had asked the question, he'd expected a resounding negative answer, but Kieren had surprised him. He didn't take his gaze off Kieren's movements, though, following with his hands and feet in a surprisingly easy set of actions.

"Okay, great. We can start with something small and see how it goes." Patrick already had ideas of what to use for the first time. "When would you like to try?"

Kieren stayed silent for a few moves and said, "How about Friday evening? You don't have to be up early for work the next day."

If Patrick had his way, he wouldn't be working there for long. He needed to have a sit down with his father and explain that finance just wasn't for him. He'd given it a good try, but after fifteen years, he couldn't do it anymore, though he didn't know what he would do instead.

"Friday is great. We can go to the club again and book a room, then take it from there."

Kieren hummed what Patrick took as his agreement and

changed the subject. "Did you ever figure out what was wrong the other day?"

Patrick frowned. "The other day?"

"In the car on the way back from the club, you were uneasy about something. Did you figure it out?"

"Yes. You remember Charles saying that Juliet was due on 10 March? Well, that was the date Aunt Louisa died. I don't know if it was a lie and he wanted to see how I'd react or if he was telling the truth and it's a cruel twist of fate." Patrick had paused when Kieren had, and when he didn't continue, Patrick glanced at him. "What?"

Kieren was frozen with his right leg in front of his left and his hands outstretched, but his gaze was on the floor. Patrick could almost see his mind working on something, but he didn't know what. He didn't want to ruin his flow; therefore, he kept quiet and still.

After several minutes, Kieren's hands dropped to his sides. "I need that list," he muttered.

"What list?"

Kieren blinked at him as if just remembering he was there and cleared his throat. "The list of dates and locations. I wanted to go through it and see if there were any links I could see." He shrugged. "I know plenty of people have already done it, but..." He shrugged again. "I don't know."

"Have you not asked for it?"

Kieren nodded. "I don't have the clearance for it, I'm told."

"That's stupid." Patrick headed over to the bag he'd brought in with him and left just inside the door. He grabbed his phone and dialled. "Hey, Christian."

"Hi, are you okay?"

"Yeah, good, thanks. Listen, can Kieren have a copy of the list of locations?"

"I don't see why not. I'll need to clear it with Neil, but as he's integral to our security, I can't see it being a problem. Why?"

Patrick stared at Kieren. "Just another pair of eyes, really. And a hunch."

"I'm happy for any and all hunches. Let me contact Neil, and I'll call you right back."

"All right." Christian hung up, and Patrick wandered over to Kieren, still holding the phone. "He's going to call back in a minute."

Kieren shook his head, a small smile playing on his lips. "As easy as that?"

"It all depends on your background check." Patrick winked.

"We're in trouble, then," Kieren joked. "I knew I shouldn't have stolen that creme egg when I was twelve." He swallowed some water from his bottle, and Patrick watched his Adam's apple bob before his phone distracted him. He put it to his ear.

"Hey."

"Okay, Neil says it's fine. I've let Brett know to include Kieren in the need-to-know information now. It shouldn't be a problem in the future. I've already sent it to the email address Brett has for him. He will need the password that I've sent to his phone. Ask him to only open the document on a computer, not his phone."

"Will do. Thanks, Christian."

"Anytime. I have to go because we've just arrived at the hospital."

"Okay. Enjoy yourselves, and say hello to the rascals from me." Patrick grinned, remembering the boys and girls at the Children's Hospital when he visited last time.

Christian chuckled. "I will. Bye."

Patrick locked his phone. "Christian says he's emailed the document to you, but you must open it on a computer, not your phone, and you'll need the password, which he's sent to you."

Kieren stared at him for a moment. "I can't believe that's all it took."

Patrick stepped closer. "They trust you. *I* trust you. Why shouldn't it be that easy?"

He didn't answer, and Patrick moved another step closer. And another. Until they were toe-to-toe, his gaze never wavering. "I trust you," Patrick whispered. "Do you trust me?"

"With my life," Kieren replied.

"With your body?" Kieren nodded. "With your mind?" Kieren nodded. Patrick lowered his voice. "With your heart?"

Kieren froze. Patrick had pushed too hard. He stepped back and smiled. "We can work on that." He changed the subject. "Are we training today?"

Latching onto the new topic, Kieren put Patrick through the motions, then sent him on his way with a reminder that if he wanted to leave to let him know. Patrick wouldn't make that mistake again. He refused to jeopardise Kieren's job.

He strode for the room he had at Windsor whenever he stayed for a visit and showered and changed. Then he picked up his phone and called his father.

"Patrick! How are you?"

He settled into a chair by the window, staring out into the bright October day and watching as the tourists wandered around the gardens.

"Good morning, Father. I'm well. How are you?"

A creak sounded over the line, and he imagined his father leaning back, resting his elbow on the arm of the chair as he held the phone to his ear. It was an image that he'd seen many times as a child and had stayed with him over the years.

"I'm great. Things are going well today. I can't ask for more." Patrick Senior chuckled. "Anyway, what can I do for you? Is everyone okay over there?"

He'd called his father earlier that day, saying he was going to take the day off to visit with his cousins, but he'd also needed a breather before he broke the news.

"Yes, everyone is fine." He cleared his throat. "I wanted to talk to you."

"Sounds ominous. What's wrong, Patrick?"

He searched for the right way to say it, but nothing came to mind, and he blurted it out. "I don't want to work in finance."

Patrick Senior snorted. "I never thought you did."

Patrick Junior was startled. "What?"

"Your mother and I had high hopes of you focusing on your music, but when you insisted on becoming part of my business —and no amount of dissuading from us helped—there wasn't much we could do but adhere to your wishes. Don't get me wrong, Patrick. You do an amazing job, and the company will miss you, but I'm glad you finally realise this isn't you."

"I can't remember you trying to change my mind," he murmured.

"We didn't make a fuss of it. We just kept asking if music was something you'd considered and what you'd like to do when you finished college. I'm surprised you've lasted fifteen years."

Patrick rubbed a hand over his face. "Me, too."

"What are your plans from here?"

He stared at the trees in the distance. "I'm honestly not sure. I won't stop working for you until I've figured something else out. Don't worry."

"Patrick, dear boy. I'm not concerned at all. If you want to stop working here as of now, that's fine. I have people who can cover your workload. And I know you will have money squirrelled away that will keep you afloat for some time. Take some time to decide what you want. I think it would be good for you."

Patrick chuckled. "You agree I should have no job security while I decide? Where's the financial advisor gone?"

"I left the financial advisor aside the moment I answered

your call." His father sighed. "I love you, Patrick, but I'm going to be tough with you now."

"All right. What?"

"You're fired." Patrick opened his mouth several times, blinking rapidly, but couldn't get anything to come out. "Now, go see your cousins and, no doubt, your brother, too, and let them help you figure out what the hell you want to be when you grow up."

That startled a laugh from him, and a tear trickled down his cheek. Only one, though. "Thank you, Father. And if you have any questions about any of the cases I handled, let me know."

"I won't, but I will."

Out of context, that wouldn't have made sense, but he knew what his father meant. He hung up, feeling lighter than he had in a long time. There were other things he needed to sort through, but the job had weighed him down the most, and now he felt freer. How could one conversation—and losing his job— make such a difference to him?

He slid his phone into his pocket and jogged through the corridors until he reached Douglas's rooms. He knocked and, when he didn't hear anything, popped his head through the door and called his cousin's name. Unable to hear anyone, he closed the door and headed for Freddie's rooms. He could've called one of them to find out where they were, but he wasn't in a rush. It wasn't like he had anywhere to be.

Freddie's rooms were empty, too. Patrick switched directions and knocked on a door.

"Come in!"

He smiled at Randall. "Morning."

Randall stood and bowed his head. "Good morning, Your Highness. What can I do for you?"

"Do you happen to know where my cousins are?"

Randall nodded once. "Christian is at the Children's Hospital with Oscar. Douglas is meeting with the Secretary of State with

Maverick, and Frederick is on his way back from collecting Damon from the airport as we speak. As for George, I believe he's in his suite working as Timothy and Eddie are at work, too. As for your brother, he's the only one I don't know."

Patrick chuckled. "He's probably bugging Robert at the shop. I'll give him a call and see if I can entice him to leave the man alone."

Randall smiled. "Is there anything I can do to help?"

Patrick paused. "No, I think I'm good, thank you."

He headed for George's rooms while he called Henry. "Are you bothering your man again, Henry?" he said when his brother answered.

"I wouldn't call it 'bothering,' but potentially, yes."

"Well, get your ass to Windsor. I'm in need of assistance." He hung up, leaving Henry sputtering. Knocking on George's door received a call for him to enter, and he grinned when he found the man lying on the sofa with a pile of sweet wrappers on the table beside him. "Have you had enough of those yet?" he asked, sitting on the sofa opposite.

"I can never have enough," George said, throwing another wrapper onto the pile and pressing a few buttons on the laptop resting on his lap before swinging his legs off the sofa and sitting upright. "What brings you to my humble abode?"

"I'm impatient for the meeting tonight because I also have some news to share. Do you fancy helping me waste the afternoon? Henry's on his way."

George grinned. "Sure! Any plans?"

"No."

The three of them ended up spending five hours playing board games, card games and watching films until the rest of the group turned up.

Freddie grinned at them, though there seemed to be extra lines on his face. "Shall we have dinner first, then we can get to the nitty-gritty stuff?"

The Tantalising Twelve headed for the dining room and ate their fill before relocating to Freddie's rooms.

"George tells me you have news to share, Paddy. Do you want to do that first?" Freddie said, settling beside Damon on the slightly more uncomfortable sofas than what George had.

"I got fired." He grinned at their shocked faces.

"What?"

"Why?"

"Your father fired you?"

He nodded and repeated his conversation with his father. "It means I need to find a job. Preferably, one I like this time."

"As you like music so much, why not something to do with that?" Damon said, pointing out the obvious choice.

"Do you want a job you can just walk into, or are you willing to work towards it?" Timothy asked from his perch between his two men.

Patrick sat forward, resting his elbows on his knees. "I'm willing to work for it. I just don't know what I want to do."

Timothy scratched his jaw. "Going the music route, you have plenty of options, depending on what you enjoy doing. A musician, fairly self-explanatory. A composer, a music director, a teacher. Even a conductor."

"A conductor?" Patrick said.

Timothy nodded. "You'll oversee different areas of whichever musical ensemble you choose to direct."

"How do you know this much about it?" Eddie asked, poking the man in the side.

Timothy twisted away with a chuckle. "One of my students asked about it a few weeks back. We've been looking into it."

"But you deal with psychology," Henry said.

Timothy nodded. "I do, but sometimes, students feel comfortable with one specific teacher, and when that happens, you do whatever you need to."

George pressed a kiss to his cheek, smiling. "You always go the extra mile."

The conversation continued, but Patrick got lost in his thoughts as an idea grew. It would be a few years in the making, but it might work.

"Patrick?" He blinked at Kean and found Henry's best friend staring at him in concern. "Everything okay?"

Patrick smiled and nodded. "A conductor slash teacher. But for kids who don't have the opportunity to learn instruments at home or school. I want to provide instruments and lessons for them, then we can put on a show at the end of the year. The money can be given to a charity of the children's choice or somewhere else. There are many children without these opportunities."

Freddie leaned forward. "I like it." He faced Timothy. "Do you know what qualifications he needs to do this?"

"Not exactly, but it won't be hard to find out. I'll start looking into it."

"Thanks," Patrick said. The idea that he could do something he loved and help children at the same time was perfect for him.

"We can get together to discuss charities and how to get this rolled out to the kids. Mav, would you help?"

Mav nodded, tapping away on his tablet. "Already on it."

Freddie chuckled. "Now, onto the other part of the meeting." He sighed. "In all honesty, we don't have much to go on. The next date on the list is 18 December, which is Uncle William's Annual Christmas Dinner. We have less than two months to figure out what the hell is going on."

"But do we?" Patrick said, gripping his thumbs in his fingers alternately.

"What do you mean?" Christian asked, scooting forward in his seat while Oscar slid an arm around his shoulders. "That's what's on the list."

Patrick inhaled. "You've probably already thought of this, but what if that list is no longer viable?"

Freddie nodded slowly. "We have thought about it, but what other option do we have? We have no one who can corroborate anything. Albert gave us what he could, but he's staying away from it all now. He's scared his mother will retaliate, and he's not willing to risk Evanna."

"Understandable," Douglas said. "We're going through every event we have booked, both the public knowledge ones and the private ones, to see if anything jumps out at us. So far, nothing does. But they're good. We probably wouldn't know anything until it was too late."

Silence descended when the reminder of how wrong it had gone before hit them. The bomb was nothing short of shocking, but wasn't that the reaction they wanted? It wouldn't be difficult to do it again, even though they were more aware of things now. Security measures were crazy for even small trips, and large events were a nightmare.

"Do we know anything?" Patrick asked.

Freddie sighed, and Damon rested a hand on his back. "No. We really don't." He dropped his head.

Damon continued, "We're checking all the locations continually in the run-up to events. We're checking cars, buildings, people, and we've reduced the number of tourists to Windsor, too."

Patrick shook his head. "Someone has to know *something*."

"Someone does, but they're just not sharing."

"Can we do this meeting again and include security, too?" Patrick asked. "Maybe with more security-orientated minds, we might be able to come up with something."

"I can ask," Christian said. He was the man most closely involved in the case. "Have you heard anything from Kieren?"

"No. I called him earlier, but he said he was still going through it."

"Did he explain his hunch?"

"No."

Christian chuckled. "These men who won't spill their secrets."

Patrick smiled, but his mind was on his bodyguard, who had told him more than he probably wanted him to know. After a lengthy discussion on Friday, they would experience a scene together, and Patrick couldn't wait. He hoped Kieren would enjoy their play, regardless of what it turned out to be because there was much he could show him. And maybe, just maybe, he might let Patrick in to steal his heart without him knowing about it.

10

GEORGE

At the reminder of what happened to his mother, George fell silent. Timothy slipped his hand into his and squeezed. George would never get over what happened, but with the help of his boyfriends and his family, he found the strength to carry on.

The idea that that could happen again left a sour taste in his mouth and made his heart pounded. How would they ever find out the truth before it was too late? Who knew what the final plan was? They had an idea but no solid proof that Aunt Charlotte wanted to take the throne for herself. For all they knew, she could pass it straight onto her son, which would be as bad as having it herself.

George listened to the conversation going on around him, but he didn't join in. Instead, he watched his brothers and cousins and their partners. Despite the heavy burdens on their shoulders, they seemed lighter. Even Patrick. George wasn't blind. Kieren would be a fine addition to their group if they ever decided to make a go of it—once Kieren let go of his job hangovers when they were all together in private. Patrick needed someone to see *him*, other than them, and George believed Kieren did.

Eddie sat beside him, having moved from the other side of Timothy, and placed a kiss on his cheek, whispering, "Are you okay?"

George smiled and nodded, turning his head to kiss him on the lips. "I'm good. I'd love to tease the crap out of Patrick about Kieren, but he's not ready for that just yet."

Eddie chuckled and rested his head on George's shoulder. "Yeah, maybe leave off that for the moment. He has a new career to distract him for now."

"I don't think that's what's distracting him. If I were to guess—"

Timothy squeezed his hand. "Shh."

George refocused on the conversation and realised Patrick stared at him with a creased brow. "What's wrong?" Patrick mouthed.

George smiled. "Nothing," he mouthed back.

He could tell Patrick didn't believe him, but he refrained from grinning like a loon. For now, anyway.

George pressed his lips to Eddie's forehead, then rested his own head on Timothy's shoulder. He wanted them to be snuggled up in bed where he could wind himself around them and forget about the world outside, but that wasn't possible. Real life intruded more than he wanted it to, but it was his father's legacy they were trying to keep alive as well as all the people who were supposed to follow after him. George included.

In the dark of the night, where no one could hear him, he told Timothy and Eddie of his wish that they could take things into their own hands and get rid of Aunt Charlotte and Charles, to name two of the people who were causing them harm. He knew it wasn't "royal" of him to think that way—or even decent of him—but when there was no proof pointing to those they *knew* were responsible, and that was the only way the law would penalise them, it wasn't the easiest pill to swallow.

They got to try and kill several members of their family and ruin other people's lives, but because there was nothing to show they were the people who did it, the police could do nothing to help them.

It sucked, to put it politely, and George was sick of it. It burned that they hadn't brought his mother's killers to justice and had to let them walk the streets as normal until they could prove it. And if he didn't have Timothy and Eddie to help him get through those dark nights, he wasn't sure how he could cope with the knowledge.

But then he remembered the amazing part of his family. Those surrounding him now and those not here, who were working tirelessly to help them in any way they could. If it was at all possible, they would find a way to send that...evil to hell. And George would watch with a grin as it happened.

1 1

KIEREN

In the past four days, Kieren had noticed a significant change in Patrick's demeanour. He walked with his head held high, he had a smile ready for those he passed, and he laughed more. But what was most noticeable was the music. It was lighter, happier. If he hadn't seen the change for himself, he wouldn't have thought being fired from his father's firm had been a good thing, but for Patrick, it might have been the best idea anyone had ever had.

Not to mention it had made Kieren's days less boring. Sitting in an office watching someone else work had never been on his bucket list, but he went where the job took him. Now, Patrick spent more time with his family and his music and was locked away in his room doing something Kieren knew nothing about. Patrick wasn't forthcoming about it either. When he'd asked, Patrick had just said he was working but had not explained what.

As for Kieren, work had been a bust. At least, the list had been. He'd been through it with a fine-toothed comb, but he couldn't find whatever had been bugging him. He thought if he saw the numbers in person, it would make something jump out at him, but nothing had. He wouldn't stop, though. He planned to keep at it because he didn't want the bad guys to win. They'd already taken too much from the royal family as it was.

Tonight was Friday, and his induction into impact play Patrick had told him. He hadn't realised that was the collective name for it, but he was learning a lot of new things lately. He'd chosen something simple to wear—black trousers and a black T-shirt—because he wasn't sure how long they were staying on. The thought of being naked in front of Patrick had him trembling, in a good *and* bad way.

Patrick had insisted on driving them, and it hadn't helped calm Kieren's nerves. The prince kept up a one-sided conversation all the way to the club and into the foyer, where they signed in with Clarice. When they'd locked everything away and wandered to the conversation room, Kieren was having second thoughts. What if he didn't like it?

Patrick grabbed two bottles of water from the bartender and led the way to a two-seater sofa on the opposite side of the room. Kieren frowned when Patrick sat and gestured for him to sit next to him.

"Everything okay?" Kieren asked, accepting the water.

"Yes. We need to chat before we go through those doors."

Kieren swallowed hard. "About what?"

"Our wants, needs, expectations, rules…everything. We need to be crystal clear about our plans before we get into it. If we don't, emotions and adrenaline can make you choose incorrectly in the heat of the moment."

"Similar to when you're protecting someone. You rely on instincts."

"Yes, but for Doms, we need clear-cut instructions. We need to know exactly what you do and do not want before the scene starts. Once it starts, we can use our instincts to guide us, but we'll never step over the lines you draw in the sand."

Kieren nodded. "Sounds fair." He lifted his knee to rest on

the seat to face Patrick. "What do you need to know?" He tapped his fingertips against the bottle.

"First, do you know the traffic light system that's used in BDSM?"

"Yes. Red for stop, yellow for slow down and green for keep going?"

Patrick smiled. "Perfect. That's what we'll use. If we find this is something you enjoy, we can always choose something else later if the traffic lights don't work for you." He drank some water and replaced the cap. "You mentioned you didn't like the idea of pain but weren't sure. What I usually suggest for newcomers is spanking, to begin with. It might sound rudimentary, but it does work to find out if pain is something you enjoy or not. And if it's not, that's fine. It's not for everyone."

Kieren nodded and inhaled. Talking about this in the cold light of day—or the dim lights of the club—had his cheeks heating, but if he couldn't talk about it, then how could he let Patrick do anything to him? "I liked what I saw last weekend. I might not have understood why Cecily needed to feel the pain, but I can see the beauty of it."

"I think of it as playing instruments. Finding the right note, the right tempo, the right combination of elements that make a melody work is a similar process as it is for learning how a submissive wants me to play with them."

A question had been niggling in the back of his mind since the previous visit, and he braved voicing it. "What do you get from it? Because from what I saw, you received no release from the scene."

Patrick tapped his thumbs against the bottle, staring down at it, and Kieren opened his mouth to take his question back when Patrick answered, "For me, it's not sexual. My enjoyment of the scene comes from the people I play with getting what they want from it. I don't need a sexual release." He cleared his throat. "Whether it changes tonight, I don't know," he murmured.

Kieren tilted his head. "What do you mean?"

Patrick huffed a laugh. "You would've thought with the number of times I've had this discussion with people, I'd be used to explaining things, but with you..." He inhaled. "I'm attracted to you. You and I both know that. If this turns out to be something you enjoy, I honestly don't know if I will stay true to form or if I will get aroused by it. I apologise in advance."

Kieren stared at him. "You don't need to apologise. I think I'd like it if you were right there with me," he whispered.

Their gazes met and held, the same frisson of awareness tingling through him as it did every time. More so when they'd come together in the gym that time. How would it feel to have Patrick's hands on him with the intent to give him pleasure and pain?

"Do you have any questions?" Patrick asked, breaking the silence.

"I don't think so."

"Are you ready, then?"

"Yes." He paused. "Sir," he added, remembering hearing other people say that.

Patrick licked his lips and exhaled. "Come on." He stood and held out his hand. Kieren hesitated before taking it. Patrick led the way through the doors to the main area of the club, keeping a tight hold of his hand. It kept Kieren grounded but also sent a wave of awareness through him about what they were about to do. As they hustled through the crowds, he took in the sounds and sights of their surroundings. His breathing increased, and he pursed his lips, wondering if he'd made the right decision.

Patrick paused at a door, unlocked it with his fingerprint and led him inside. When the door was closed, he faced Kieren.

"We can stop at any time. This is not supposed to embarrass or humiliate you." Patrick smirked. "At least, this time." He grinned, then became serious again. "It's to educate you like you said. Unless you know what they experience, it's difficult to understand the why of it. Do you still want to do this?"

"Yes. Sir."

Patrick smiled. "Sir works well in this scenario." He took Kieren's bottle from him and wandered over to the bedside table, placing both bottles down, and faced him again. "If it was anyone else, I would be taking over now and telling you what to do, but with you, I'm unsure. Not how a Dom is supposed to be."

Kieren inhaled and exhaled. "Treat me as you would anyone else. I need to understand, don't I?"

Patrick studied him for a long time before he nodded. "Colour?"

"Green, sir."

"Come here." Kieren stepped closer. "Undress."

Kieren swallowed but lifted his hands to the hem of his T-shirt. He'd kept on the clothes he'd arrived in, whereas Patrick had changed into a black shirt and some leather trousers. Kieren pulled the T-shirt over his head, folded it in half and placed it on the chair to his left. He swallowed hard again, then unfastened his trousers. As he did, Patrick unbuttoned and removed his shirt, and it temporarily distracted him. At least until Patrick cleared his throat and raised an eyebrow at him. Kieren pulled the trousers from his legs, leaving him in his boxers.

"Do I...?" He pointed at his underwear.

"Remove those as well."

Kieren's heart thudded, but he did as asked while Patrick climbed onto the bed and rested his back against the headboard with his legs stretched out.

Patrick patted his lap. "Lie over me, on your stomach."

Face heating, Kieren crawled over until his stomach was resting on Kieren's thighs.

"Shift up a little further."

He did, moving further until Patrick was happy, and Kieren's cock was far too close to Patrick for Kieren's comfort. How would he hide his reactions if he liked it? What if he came all over Patrick? The leather against his skin felt amazing, and he tensed to ensure he didn't do something embarrassing like rubbing against him.

"Colour?"

Kieren checked in with himself. "Green, sir."

"I'm going to rub my hands on you to get you used to the feel of me touching you."

It wasn't a question, and Kieren didn't reply, but he jumped a little when Patrick's warm hands touched his upper back. The soft skin traced over his shoulder blades, spine, sides and lower until he paused at Kieren's lower back.

"Colour?"

"Green, sir." Kieren wet his lips after hearing the hoarseness of his voice.

Patrick's hands smoothed over his ass cheeks and quickly to his upper thighs. With every move, Patrick's leather-clad thighs rubbed against his cock, and Kieren closed his eyes as he felt himself responding. The hands rose to his ass again, this time kneading his cheeks, pressing them together and digging his thumbs into his skin. He rested his forehead on his arms and breathed into the space between.

"Colour?"

"Green, sir."

"You're doing great. Are you ready to go a little further?"

"Yes, sir."

He tensed in preparation for the sting, but a hand moved to caress his back while the other stayed on his ass. Nothing happened, and Kieren felt himself relaxing again. Before he could react, the hand on his ass lifted and came down with a loud smack. An immediate sting spread from the point of contact on the fleshy part of his ass out across his skin. It didn't last long, instead turning into a warmth, and when

Patrick rubbed a hand over it, it soothed the leftover prickle effect.

"Colour?"

"Green, sir."

The hand came down again, and a similar experience happened on his other ass cheek. A sting, a warmth, then a soothing of it, along with a caress along his back or neck. It continued, and each time Patrick asked for his colour. He forgot to be bothered by his nakedness. He forgot about everything outside of what he was experiencing.

"You're doing well, Kieren. I'm proud of you."

The next smack sent a tendril of heat to his groin, and he jerked his hips automatically, biting his lip to withhold his groan when his cock rubbed against the leather.

"Don't hide from me. It's okay. Whatever happens is okay. Let yourself go. Let me hear you."

Another smack and Kieren lifted his head to move his hands to grip the covers beneath him. Another smack and he groaned, louder that time, his hips rocking into Patrick's legs. Another smack, the sting and warmth intensifying, and he hissed.

"Colour?"

"Green, sir," he panted.

Fingers threaded into his hair, scratching at his scalp as another smack landed. Kieren exhaled, twisting his hands in the fabric. He could feel an orgasm teasing his body, not quite ready to go but climbing slowly. His hips had a mind of their own, and every time Patrick landed another smack, he bucked, and with every soothing caress of his hand, he arched into it.

"Do you want to come like this, Kieren?" Patrick whispered.

"Please, sir. Please."

Several more, and Kieren's climax barrelled down on him. He curled in on himself as his cock erupted against Patrick's legs, pressing his forehead into the covers while his hands gripped tightly. He was aware of Patrick's hands on him but not what he was doing or saying. The release lasted longer than he could remember them lasting before, though his mind was fuzzy.

When the orgasm finally released him from its clutches, he sank into Patrick, breath sawing in and out and sweat coating him. He became aware of hands running over his back and murmurings he couldn't understand. He stayed where he was until Patrick lifted him and deposited him to his side, the cool air making his wet abdomen more evident, but not for long because a warm cloth washed it away. Kieren had no energy to open his eyes and figure out what Patrick was doing.

Something poked at his lips, and he opened one eye, seeing Patrick holding a cup with a straw. He sucked the sweet-tasting drink, his mind finally understanding what Patrick was doing. *Aftercare.* What he'd done for Patrick. What he *needed* to do for Patrick, too. He drank some more, then lifted a hand to Patrick, pulling on his shoulder until he lay beside him with a chuckle.

"Drink," Kieren rasped. Patrick held the straw to his mouth, but Kieren shook his head. "You drink." Patrick lowered his eyes until Kieren put a finger beneath his chin and lifted it. "Drink for me. Please, sir."

Patrick's eyes flared, and he put the straw to his mouth and drank, never once removing his gaze. When they were done, Patrick rose.

"I need to put some cream on you. It'll help."

"Okay, but before you do, can you get the oil so I can massage you afterwards?"

Patrick smiled. "This is supposed to be your aftercare."

"It is, but why can't it be both of ours? You look after me; I look after you."

Sleep pulled at him, but he refused to succumb to it until he'd seen to his...Dom? Partner? He mentally shrugged. It didn't matter what they called themselves, but he needed to do his part to help Patrick. As far as he was concerned, it wouldn't work unless they both did their bit because who would ease Patrick if he didn't?

Patrick stared for a moment, then nodded and climbed off the bed. He picked up an oil bottle from the shelf and returned, placing it on the bedside table.

"Roll to your stomach."

He did, resting his head on a pillow and closing his eyes. He could easily fall asleep, but he wouldn't. The cold cream touched his ass, and he inhaled. Patrick apologised and rubbed it in carefully. When it was done, it felt better, but every time he moved, it smarted. He assumed it would for some time.

He rose to his knees, ignoring the sudden reminder of his nakedness, and gestured for Patrick to lie down. Patrick rolled his eyes but did. Kieren reached for the oil and rubbed it into his hands. Straddling Patrick as he had done the previous time, he massaged the oil into his skin, starting at his lower back and rising to his shoulders and along his arms. Patrick groaned into the covers, and Kieren smiled. There was something about caring for another when they needed it.

When he was done, he climbed off and lay beside Patrick, who opened his eyes and stared at him sleepily.

"Sleep with me?" Patrick murmured. His eyes widened, and he rolled to his side. "I mean to sleep. I'm not trying to push—"

Kieren silenced him with a kiss. "I know. But to sleep, you need to get out of those trousers. You'll be more comfortable."

Patrick hesitated, and Kieren took matters into his own hands. He unfastened the buttons, pausing when he saw the result of Patrick's release. He glanced at him, Patrick's pink cheeks and lowered eyes evidence of his embarrassment. Kieren smiled, glad he'd been able to find his own pleasure in the scene. He dragged the trousers awkwardly down Patrick's legs. He'd gone commando, and all it took was a bit of pulling and yanking, and he was free. Kieren threw them to the side, uncaring where they landed, and pulled the covers back. They both climbed in and rested the cover under the armpits. As they faced each other, a few inches between them, Kieren understood what he got from the spanking.

"I understand. It's a release, like you said. The freedom to let things go, to not care about anything but what is happening here and now."

Patrick smiled. "Exactly. It's slightly different for everyone, but for something that is solely for pleasure, that's the consensus." He rested his hand over Kieren's between them, rubbing his thumb over the back of it. "How are you feeling?"

Kieren sighed, closing his eyes briefly. "Relaxed."

"Good."

Patrick rolled to his back and opened his arm, and Kieren snuggled into his side, not hesitating the slightest. As his heartbeat lulled Kieren towards the edges of sleep, he murmured. "How are you?"

The rumble of Patrick's laughter made Kieren smile. "Better than I have been for a long time."

Kieren slid his arm over Patrick's chest, resting his palm over his heart. As much as he'd baulked at trusting Patrick with his heart, he knew he could. He also knew he shouldn't. There was far too much going on for him to let himself get sucked into what he knew could be an amazing relationship. Because that relationship could be short-lived, he didn't want to take the chance that he was cursed and something would happen to Patrick. The man didn't deserve that.

As he lay there wrapped in Patrick's arms, he tried to remind himself of all the reasons they shouldn't happen. And as he drifted off to sleep, he found it harder and harder to remember.

1 2

PATRICK

*A*s Patrick held Kieren, the man's body relaxed into sleep. He could feel himself wanting to follow, but he enjoyed the sensation of holding him. He could imagine Kieren not allowing it often. When the man had willingly snuggled into his embrace, Patrick's heart raced and swelled. Patrick already knew he was in deep with Kieren, but how could he convince him to explain what was holding him back? Several options ran through his mind during the hour Kieren slept, and even though Patrick was tired, he refused to miss a minute of it.

When Kieren stirred, Patrick held his breath, wondering what his reaction would be, but when Kieren blinked and smiled up at him, Patrick exhaled in a rush.

Amusement shone in his companion's eyes, and Patrick leaned down to press a brief kiss to his lips. "Sleep well?"

"Yes, thanks. Did you?"

"Hmm." He smiled, refusing to acknowledge his creeper-watching habit had not let him sleep. "How do you feel?"

Kieren wriggled and grimaced. "It smarts, but it's not uncomfortable. More like a bruise you can't stop yourself from pressing."

"Good." He ran his hand up and down Kieren's back. "What did you think of it?"

"It's something I'd like to explore more."

Patrick kept his focus on the ceiling but couldn't contain his smile. "I'm glad."

"The question is, are you willing to teach me?"

Patrick lowered his head, meeting Kieren's gaze. "I'd love to," he whispered. "But only if that's truly what you want. I can find you someone else if you'd prefer."

Kieren's nostrils flared, and his fingers tapped a rhythm against Patrick's chest. "I wouldn't prefer. I don't know if I could trust anyone else enough to let them do this with me."

Inwardly, Patrick preened. It's what he wanted, but he couldn't refuse Kieren the opportunity to find someone else. "I'm glad you can trust me."

They lay in silence for a short time, and then Kieren made a move to get up. "I think I need some food."

It was probably a ruse to get him back home and away from Patrick, but he'd let him go. Everyone needed the chance to recalibrate what happened, even Patrick, and he wouldn't stop Kieren. They dressed, but the lack of conversation wasn't uncomfortable. Patrick stole glances at him and caught Kieren doing the same. He had no idea where they were going with whatever they were doing, but he was there for the entire ride.

Before they left the room, Patrick touched Kieren's arm. "Whenever you want—or need—to do this again, just say the word."

Kieren stared at him, and Patrick's cheeks heated under his scrutiny. "Friday?" he asked finally.

Patrick nodded, his mouth dry. He grabbed on to the future "date" and held it close to his heart. Opening the door, he led the way out, smiling when Kieren slipped his hand into Patrick's. Patrick threaded their fingers together and headed for the exit. It was time he took them home.

Patrick dodged the punch, spinning away from Kieren, and kicked his leg high, aiming for Kieren's thigh. He didn't make contact because Kieren grabbed his ankle and pulled, taking Patrick to the floor. He put his hands out as he hit the floor, but he misjudged it, and agony tore through his wrist.

"Ahh!"

He cradled his left wrist against his chest, panting with the pain.

"Shit! Patrick! Fuck! What's wrong?" Kieren slammed to his knees beside him. His hands hovered over him but didn't touch. "Where do you hurt?"

Patrick gritted his teeth and breathed through a wave of nausea. "My wrist."

"Can I see?" He removed his good hand, leaving his painful one resting on his chest. "It's swelling already. We need to get you seen by a doctor. Let me help you up." Kieren stood and moved to Patrick's head. He slid his hands under Patrick's armpits and lifted.

Pain tore through him again, but Patrick bit it back, not wanting to make Kieren feel bad. When he stood upright, he swayed as his head spun and arms came around his waist. Despite the dizziness, Patrick's skin tingled at the contact. It had happened few and far between in the six days since the club.

"I'm good now," he said a few minutes later.

"Let's get you to the doctor."

Patrick shook his head. "Just get me to my room, and I'll speak to the doctor over the phone. I don't fancy driving anywhere."

"But they might need to see you," Kieren argued.

"Then they can come here and see me." Kieren opened his

mouth, but Patrick stared at him, and he snapped his mouth shut again.

"Please, just help me to my room."

Kieren nodded and opened the door of the gym, resting a hand on Patrick's lower back and guiding him through the corridors to his room. Once he was sitting on the sofa in his living area, he cursed.

"What?"

"I left my phone in the changing rooms."

"I'll get it."

Before Patrick could decline, Kieren was out of the room. Patrick couldn't find the energy to chuckle. Instead, he leaned against the back of the sofa and stared at the ceiling. A throbbing sensation filled his wrist to the beat of his heart, and Patrick breathed through the agony. He'd had injuries before, and this one was just as unexpected as those had been.

Voices reached his ears, and his door opened.

"Patrick! What happened?" his mother asked, sweeping into the room with a pinched expression.

"I fell wrong, Mother. I'll be fine."

"Let me get some ice. Kieren, be a dear and call Dr Montgomery. His number should be in Patrick's phone." She disappeared through the door again, and Patrick closed his eyes.

"Do you want to call the doctor?" Kieren asked.

Patrick opened his eyes again. Kieren held the phone out to him. Instead of answering that question, he just gave Kieren the code to unlock his phone. He never used facial or fingerprint recognition for that. It would be too easy for someone to get hold of those things, or so he'd been told.

"Hi. Um, sorry. This is Kieren Young, Patrick's bodyguard. There's been an incident, and I think he may have sprained his wrist."

There's been an incident. If Patrick was a betting man, he would've placed money on Kieren blaming himself for this *inci-*

dent. Not an accident like it was, but an incident. It took everything in him not to yell at the man, but he sent a glare across the distance that Kieren either ignored or didn't see.

"Uh-huh. Yes, ice is on the way. Uh-huh. Okay. Does he not need to be seen by someone to make sure it's nothing more serious? Do you want to speak to him? Are you sure? Uh-huh." Kieren sighed. "Thank you." He ended the call and exhaled again.

"What's the verdict, doctor?" Patrick was concerned with Kieren's colouring.

"Um, he said to ice it for twenty minutes every two to three hours and wrap it in a bandage or brace to stop it from moving too much, to begin with. Paracetamol or ibuprofen for the pain."

Kieren twisted the phone between his fingers, and Patrick frowned. Were his hands trembling? Patrick couldn't tell.

"Come sit with me." Kieren shook his head. "Come—"

His words were interrupted by his mother's return. "I have ice, a bandage and a sling for you to get comfortable with." She held up her wares with a smile, faltering when she saw Kieren. She glanced at Patrick with a raised eyebrow, but he shook his head once, unable to give her an answer to the unasked question. "Kieren, could you help me, please?"

Kieren flinched but put the phone down and followed Victoria's instructions. He settled beside Patrick, bringing a cushion to rest on Patrick's lap. With his mother guiding him, Kieren methodically wrapped the bandage around Patrick's wrist, rested it on the cushion and applied the ice. When Patrick sighed and sank back into the sofa as the pain eased a minute amount, Kieren rose and stepped away.

"Do you need anything else?" he said in a hoarse voice.

"Would you stay with him and keep an eye on him?" Victoria asked. "I would do it myself, but we have dinner with the French ambassador, and I don't think it would be wise to cancel at such short notice."

"I'll be fine, Mother. Don't worry."

He'd finally realised what the problem with Kieren was. The trembling, the sweat beading on his forehead, the blood-drained face. Kieren was remembering his family, and Patrick didn't want to be the cause of such emotional pain.

Kieren closed his eyes, then straightened. "Of course. If you need me to." His reluctance was missing from his tone but not his demeanour.

"Thank you, dear. It would make me feel easier knowing someone was with him."

"Kieren, go and rest. I'll call one of my cousins. You don't need to babysit me."

Victoria raised her eyebrows. "That's kind of his job description." She snickered.

Patrick chuckled and groaned. "Yes, for when I'm outside, not here. It's not in his job description to work when I'm home."

"It's fine. I don't mind." He glanced at Victoria. "Would I have time to get changed?"

Victoria smiled. "Of course! I have another hour before I must leave. That's plenty of time."

Kieren nodded his head and left the room, closing the door quietly behind him.

"Mother, what are you doing?"

Victoria turned her innocent expression on him. "Nothing. You need some help, and Kieren is here."

Patrick inhaled. Did his mother know what had happened to his family? "I don't think he's in the right frame of mind to look after me right now."

"I think this is the best place for him to be." Victoria wandered over to the side table and grabbed a bottle of water from the fridge beneath it, bringing it back. She cracked it open and held it out.

"Thanks." He drank, then asked, "Why?"

Victoria sighed and sat down again, smoothing the front of her skirt. "He's worried about you, and if he's left to wallow in that by himself, he'll drive himself crazy. If he's here with you, he'll see you're fine."

Patrick stared at her. The pain in her eyes was visible. "You know about his family."

She nodded. "Poor boy has had much taken from him, but he takes too much weight on his shoulders. He needs to realise not everything is his fault."

"I agree. I'm working on it."

She glanced at him out of the corner of her eye. "Are you now?" Her mouth curled.

Patrick snorted. "If anyone knew you behind closed doors, they'd know you weren't the prim and proper princess they all think you are."

"Ah, but they don't, do they?" She smiled and lifted her chin. "A woman has to keep some parts of her life a mystery."

He chuckled and winced, removing the ice. "God, it hurts."

"Have you had any paracetamol?"

"Not yet. We didn't get that far."

She stood and bustled over to the bathroom, coming back with two boxes. "Keep this handy because you're going to need it." She helped him take two tablets. "What happened anyway?"

"We were sparring, and I fell wrong." It was only after he'd said the words that he realised she hadn't known about his training sessions. Although, peering at her showed no surprise at this supposedly new knowledge. He decided to come clean. "I've been training with him for months. I want to be able to…" He paused, swallowing hard as images of his aunt came to him. "I want to help however I can."

His mother rested a hand on his leg. "You do help. You don't need to fight to help anyone."

"What else can I do? Hypnotise them with my music?" He scoffed and looked away.

Victoria shifted closer. "My boy. Do you not realise what you do with your music?" Patrick didn't look at her. "You bring peace, contentment, happiness, joy, rage, anger, grief. For every single emotion there is a word for, you capture and bring it to life. When people want to be cheered up, you play for them. When someone needs a tribute to them, you play for them. When someone has something to celebrate, *you play for them.* That's not something small. That's an exquisite gift that few people have. The gift of being able to alter the mood of a room, of bringing memories to the forefront of people's minds, of giving yourself over to those who listen to you." During her words, Patrick had faced her, seeing the honesty in her expression. "Because that's what you do. Every time you play for someone, you give them a piece of yourself. You show them who you are, how you can help them."

Tears overflowed, and Patrick swallowed against the lump in his throat. No one had ever said something like that before. Sure, they'd told him he played well or that they loved what he'd played, but nothing so eloquent. But then, his mother had always had a way with words, just like George.

He sniffed. "Thank you." He cleared his throat. "It doesn't change that I can't do anything to help in our fight."

"Sometimes, we need distractions in the fight. Time to recuperate. Time to rest. You give us that."

Patrick wasn't sure he agreed, but he didn't argue. "I won't be doing that for a while." He glared at his arm.

"You could play the piano one-handed," his mother said before laughing.

"I suppose I could. The violin, clarinet and flute are out of the question, though."

A knock sounded, and she stood. "Not for long, sweetheart. You'll be back to normal in no time." She opened the door to Kieren and Grace, a member of the household staff. "Thank you, Grace. Could you please put it over by the window? Thank you."

Grace did, and Kieren hovered by the door, not meeting Patrick's gaze.

"Thank you, Grace."

"You're welcome, Your Highness. Have a wonderful evening." Grace nodded her head as she left, closing the door behind her.

Victoria bustled over to the trolley Grace had brought in. "I ordered some food for you both. I thought you might be hungry after your training."

Kieren glanced at him at that, and Patrick smiled and shook his head. "I'm not as sneaky as I thought I was."

Kieren's mouth curled for a moment, and Patrick was glad of the reprieve.

"Well, don't just stand there. Come on. Tuck in. After that, Patrick, you'll need a shower. As much as I love you, son, you stink."

Patrick gaped at her. "I can't believe you just said that!" he spluttered.

She patted his cheek. "I'm your mother. That's why I can get away with saying stuff like that. Have a good evening, boys. I'll check in on you when I get home, Patrick."

"Enjoy your evening, Your Highness," Kieren said.

"I will now. I know I have you looking after my boy." She patted Kieren on the arm as she passed. "Now, get some food in you."

"Yes, Mother."

When the door closed behind her, Patrick rose, trying not to move his arm too much. He wasn't very successful, but he made it to the table. Cutting up his food was a problem he hadn't thought of, but Kieren took matters into his own hands and cut it into pieces before handing the cutlery back and focusing on his plate.

They ate in silence until Patrick couldn't take it any longer. "It's not your fault, Kieren."

"You wouldn't have fallen if I hadn't been training you."

"I didn't give you a choice."

"I could've said no."

Patrick didn't argue. He could see he wasn't getting through to him. He wasn't sure how else to show it. Then he had an idea. He grabbed his phone, unlocked it and opened a message to George.

PATRICK: *Gather as many of us together as you can and meet at my rooms as soon as possible. We're in need of an intervention.*

Within seconds, George had replied.

GEORGE: *Understood. Anything in particular we need to bring?*

PATRICK: *Just yourselves.*

GEORGE: *Okay. Will be there in an hour, tops.*

Patrick didn't reply. He just put his phone away and continued eating.

"Everything okay?" Kieren asked.

Patrick peered at him. "Perfectly fine. I was thinking of watching a film. What do you like to watch?"

"I don't really pay attention to films much. It's usually just background noise."

"Let's go for a comedy, then. I think we could do with cheering up."

It took Patrick longer than expected to finish his dinner, but then he had the task of showering, which was something he realised he couldn't do without pain coursing through him.

"Do you need anything?" Kieren called through the closed bathroom door.

"A new wrist?" he called back.

"Funny," Kieren said. "I can't do that, I'm afraid."

"Well, in that case, clothes that I can easily put on and take off with one arm?"

Kieren was quiet for a moment. "Would you like some help?"

He could manage, but he wasn't going to turn down an offer like that. "Yes, please."

Kieren opened the door and slipped through. They stood facing each other, both breathing heavier than they needed to. Kieren closed the distance between them and grabbed the hem of Patrick's T-shirt.

"Take your good arm out first, then let me manoeuvre the fabric over your bad one."

Within seconds, he was naked from the waist up. "How did you know how to do that?"

"I've had to deal with many injuries in my profession."

Patrick's heart pounded as he thought of what Kieren often had to do as part of his job. "How many of them were your own?"

13

─────

KIEREN

*oo many.

But Kieren didn't say that. He'd looked after celebrities of all calibres, and several of them had been shot at, driven off roads and all sorts of other random acts of craziness.

"A few." He folded the T-shirt and put it on the cabinet. "Do you need help with your trousers?"

"I think I can manage them." Patrick's voice had lowered, and Kieren tried to breathe through his answering arousal. "Can you take the bandage off for me, though? I don't want it to get wet."

Kieren unwrapped the bandage, rolled it back into a ball and put it aside. "Be careful. I'll wait right outside the door. If you need any help, shout."

Patrick nodded, and Kieren retreated before he offered more than he should. He rested his head back against the door and closed his eyes. The shower turned on, and he imagined Patrick with water gliding down his muscles. Kieren clenched his hands into fists, tensing his body to stop him from taking what he desperately wanted. He glared at his cock, tenting the joggers he'd put on.

A hiss from the bathroom dulled his heated thoughts, and he tilted his ear to the door.

"Um, Kieren! I need some help."

Kieren inhaled and entered the bathroom again. The frosted glass of the shower cubicle did nothing to hide Patrick's body from his gaze. "What's wrong?" He cleared his throat when his voice came out raspy.

"I can't squeeze the shampoo from the bottle."

He stepped closer. "Okay, hand it to me."

Patrick opened the door with his good hand, then reached for the shampoo. "I need to get a pump-action bottle or something. I know I could do that one-handed," he grumbled.

Kieren withheld a smile and opened the shampoo, squirting some onto Patrick's palm.

"Thanks."

Patrick couldn't close the shower door because he had shampoo in his hand, so Kieren did, but not until after he saw Patrick's glare of annoyance. The man would find plenty more things to be annoyed about before he had full control of his hand again.

He stayed in the bathroom but turned his back to the shower to give Patrick some privacy. He knew he'd have to help with the shower gel and possibly even a towel at the end, but he'd let Patrick guide him on what he wanted help with.

"You know, you've been very quiet about what happened last week. Do you have questions about anything we did?" Patrick said, his voice slightly distorted by the sound of the water.

Kieren leaned his hip against the cabinet, taking his time to answer. "The only question I really have is what you're going to use next time. Which, by the way, will not be tomorrow."

"Yes, it bloody well will be," Patrick shouted. "It might not be the play I had planned for you, but we will be at the club, and we will be engaged in play of some kind. I just need to think it through."

"We can postpone."

"No!"

Kieren sighed. Patrick was as stubborn as they came sometimes. "You're in no state—" he tried again.

"I can do plenty with what I have."

Kieren didn't doubt it, but he also didn't want Patrick hurting himself further. But he could see he wouldn't be dissuaded.

"Can you help again, please?"

Kieren turned back to the shower and squeezed the shower gel into Patrick's palm, then closed the door and faced away again.

"As for what I'd use, I was thinking of trying a flogger, but I want to show you the different types first. We can still do that tomorrow, and I can explain what each of them can do. We can also have a look at the different restraint options." He paused. "If that's something that might interest you."

"I'm happy to look at it if nothing else."

They lapsed into silence, the quiet even louder when Patrick switched off the shower. The cubicle door opened, and Kieren held out the towel, averting his gaze.

"You can look, you know." The humour in Patrick's voice had Kieren doing just that, but the towel covered him, both sides gripped in one hand. "I think we're beyond the privacy stage now." He held out his bad arm and sighed. "This is going to get tiresome, but could you help again, please?"

Kieren carefully dried his arm, noting the swelling still evident, and wrapped a bandage around it. "You maybe shouldn't have had such a warm shower. I doubt that helped your arm at all."

"Too late now. Besides, if my mother said I was stinky, then I needed one."

Kieren chuckled. "When we get out there, you'll have to ice it again."

"Shit."

"What?" Kieren frowned.

"I forgot to bring any clothes in."

"These are your rooms. Why does it matter?"

Patrick winced. "Because we have company."

"I didn't hear anyone come in." Kieren straightened and glanced at the closed door as if it could reveal what waited for them.

"My family. I bet they're out there being all sneaky and shit."

"And why would they need to be sneaky?"

Patrick headed for the door. "Because they're nosey fuckers." He opened the door to a gasp.

"How dare you swear so heartily about us!" George said, his hands pressed to his chest.

Patrick ignored him and brushed past, heading for his bedroom. "Kieren, can you help, please?"

Kieren ignored the burning stares and his heated cheeks and followed Patrick, helping him into another T-shirt, some briefs and some more joggers. He kept his wits about him when he pulled the briefs up his legs and over the man's cock, though his mouth watered at the sight.

"Later," Patrick whispered.

Kieren shook his head. "No."

Patrick cupped his jaw. "Yes."

Kieren swallowed but said nothing.

"Come on. Let's see what damage the Tantalising Twelve have done in our absence."

"Are they all here?" Kieren asked as Patrick led the way to the living area.

"I don't know. I wasn't paying attention."

As it turned out, Freddie, Damon and Christian weren't present because they were working at the club, but everyone else was. Oscar had come with George and his partners instead of being left at home while Christian worked.

"I'll leave you in capable hands," Kieren said when Patrick settled onto the sofa.

"Nuh-uh," Patrick said. He tapped the seat next to him with his good hand. "I promised you a comedy, and you'll get a comedy. Sit your ass down, Kieren."

Henry grinned at him. "Better do as he says. Even with a bad arm—which, by the way, what the hell!—he could give you grief."

Kieren exhaled and sat beside him, feeling mightily uneasy around that many royals and partners when he was the only bodyguard present. The others' guards would be around somewhere but not in the room with them all.

"I really should—"

"No." Patrick's tone brooked no argument, and Kieren settled in, breathing deeply through his nose.

"Paddy, what happened?" Henry asked, nodding at his arm.

Patrick sighed. "I guess I have something to explain." He told them about the training sessions he'd started earlier that year and how he'd pushed Kieren into a corner to make him do it, then about the accident. "It was an accident. I fell wrong, that's all. But it means I'm down an arm for a bit."

"Well, if you need anything, you only need to call," Timothy said, sliding his arm around Eddie's shoulders.

"Thanks."

Henry's face was troubled, many questions running around in his head—his face was very readable, which Kieren found curious in a royal who usually wanted everything to stay hidden.

"Why do you need to learn to fight, Paddy?" Henry asked.

Patrick was quiet for a while, staring down at his hands. "I thought if I could learn something like that, I might be of use in an emergency. It might save someone who might otherwise have died," he murmured.

Silence descended, and Robert wrapped his arm around Henry's shoulders. Timothy and Eddie did the same for George, and Mav followed suit with Douglas and held Oscar's hand. The grief was palpable, and it took every bit of training for Kieren to sit still and not run from their pain.

"Life is poop sometimes." The words were spoken in a harsh tone but with such a small voice that it took Kieren a minute to realise it had come from Oscar.

"True, Ozzie," Robert said, reaching across to him. "So true."

Ozzie was Oscar's name when he was close to being little. Christian was his Daddy, but occasionally, Oscar regressed almost by accident. Robert had the most experience of being what Oscar needed when Christian wasn't there, with Henry being his pup, but Douglas and George—and he supposed Patrick, as well—all had training. No matter where Oscar, or Ozzie, was, someone could take care of him. Patrick had told him it had recently started happening, but they couldn't understand why. It wasn't a problem, but it was strange.

"You don't need to physically fight, Paddy," Douglas said. "We all do our bit behind the scenes. We don't need to be on the front line."

"But aren't we?" Patrick said. "We're the enemy they're attacking. We're the ones they're aiming for. We shouldn't put other people in front of us to save ourselves from it."

"That's our job," Kieren said.

Patrick stared at him, his jaw working. "It's not fair."

"It's what we're paid for."

Patrick averted his gaze. "Choose a comedy, George. We need to lighten the mood."

"*American Pie?*" George said with raised eyebrows.

Patrick frowned. "I said a comedy, not teen humour."

George huffed. "Fine. *Deadpool* it is."

Kieren had to admit he had a good time. When the film finally finished, he bid goodnight to everyone after making sure Patrick had everything he needed. As he walked down the hall, he paused and turned back at his name.

Patrick strode towards him, and Kieren tilted his head in question. Patrick didn't stop, though. He came right up to him, slid his good hand behind Kieren's head and slammed their mouths together. Careful of Patrick's wrist, Kieren slipped his arms around his waist and clung on, devouring every inch of Patrick's mouth. They had hardly touched since last Friday, and Kieren had missed it. Now, all the tension left his body, and he gave everything he was to the man before him. There was no hiding what he wanted. No pretending this wasn't going to happen. It was, but for how long was the issue. Kieren couldn't risk breaking Patrick's heart—or even worse, cursing him to death, but he could take these stolen moments for as long as he could stand it, then he would step back and let someone else take over the job of protecting him. As it was, Kieren was too close, and it scared him he couldn't do the job properly.

He licked inside Patrick's mouth, sucked on his tongue and pulled back, breathing heavily. He rested their foreheads together and closed his eyes. "You need to get back to your family."

Patrick lifted his gaze. "I need you."

"Tomorrow."

"Promise you won't back out?"

Kieren smiled. "I promise." That was one promise he could keep.

"All right." Patrick stepped back, and the cool air made Kieren wish he'd kept hold of him. The warmth of Patrick's body against his chased away the coldness in his soul, even for a moment.

"Get some sleep. Take more paracetamol, too."

"I will."

Patrick smiled and walked away, Kieren watching every move he made until Patrick waved before shutting the door. Swallowing hard, he drifted through the building to his room, sank onto the bed without bothering to change, and spent far too many hours staring at the ceiling, wishing tomorrow night would arrive.

The moment the time came, though, he wished it was over and done with. This time, they had company at the club. It wasn't just him and Patrick. The rest of the group had come, too. Not that they would be in the same room as Patrick and Kieren, but still. It felt weird that his employers knew what he was there for.

They had given Patrick a plastic brace to strap around his wrist to hopefully keep it from being hurt worse amongst the crowds of the club. Kieren wasn't sure what to expect when the entire Tantalising Twelve joined them, but they were no different than normal, which shouldn't have shocked Kieren, knowing them as he did, but it had. They'd also been joined by Quinn and his master for a few minutes.

He blushed furiously when Patrick had taken him by the hand, said goodbye to those who were with them and led him to one of the rooms. Nothing like advertising what they were going to do. Although not even Kieren knew what Patrick had planned. All he understood was that Patrick wouldn't be striking him that day because Patrick's wrist was still too sore.

As the door closed behind them, Patrick faced him. "As I said yesterday, today is about learning what other implements you might be interested in." He squeezed his hand and let go, wandering over to a cupboard.

Kieren followed behind, eyes widening when he saw the sheer number of items hidden behind the doors.

Patrick chuckled. "Don't be scared. Sit on the sofa, and I'll bring some stuff out."

"Let me help."

"No. Sit."

Kieren sank into the leather cushions, rubbing his hands over his face. What the hell had he agreed to?

Patrick brought several floggers—yes, he knew they were

floggers—to the table and then sat beside him. "I'm going to go through the different types of floggers, the materials and the type of pain or non-pain it could give." He picked up one that had a black leather handle with a rounded end on either side of it. Coming out of one end were several fur strips. "This is a rabbit flogger. It is one that would give little to no pain because it's made completely of fur. They're usually used more for sensation play. Feel it." He held it out for Kieren.

It was as soft as it looked, but he wasn't sure he believed it could give no pain. If that hit his ass, he was sure it would still hurt.

Patrick picked up another one. "This one is made from deer leather. It provides a light thud on your skin and is good for those who don't want severe pain, but we can also use it as a warm-up or cool down with other floggers."

This one looked more like the floggers he'd seen when he'd researched. A leather handle, as they all seemed to have, with individual leather strips of varying colours.

"This is a suede flogger. It gives a mix of a thud and a sting. And this is an oiled leather flogger. This gives a more severe sting."

"What's the difference between a thud and a sting in this case?"

Patrick tilted his head. "Have you ever high-fived someone and caught it slightly wrong and had that stinging against your palm?" Kieren nodded. "Think of the result of that as being the sharp, stinging sensation that fades fairly quickly. And when you fall to the floor unexpectedly in sparring? It's a deeper, duller sensation over a wider area, which lasts longer and often bruises."

"If you want to feel it for a while, go for the thud, and if you just want something short, go for the sting."

"Yes."

"What's best for beginners?"

Patrick scrunched up his face. "There's no best. It's whatever you think you might enjoy, then we try them out. Experiment. Nothing extremely painful, of course." He lifted his knee to the sofa and faced him. "Only if you want."

"I do. It's just a little overwhelming."

"I know." Patrick stared at the floggers. "How about this? Let's try the deer leather next time we do this and go from there."

"Okay." Kieren became distracted by Patrick's mouth because when he was that close, he could see the excitement in his expression, the quirk of his lips as he explained. He couldn't resist lifting a hand to his jaw, the stubble scratching his palm. Patrick froze, eyes locking with his, and Kieren closed the distance between them. Whatever was happening between them was a force he couldn't resist.

As their lips touched, Patrick groaned and pressed closer. Kieren deepened the kiss, and Patrick wrapped his arms around his neck but hissed. Kieren moved back.

"I can see I'm going to have to be careful with you," he murmured. He stood, pulling on Patrick's good hand to help him stand. He dipped and swept his arms under Patrick's back and legs and carried him to the bed. "I think it's time I looked after you."

Patrick grinned. "I like the sound of that."

Kieren paused. "Are you only a top, or do you bottom sometimes?" He hadn't thought to ask before.

"I'm vers."

Kieren's smile grew. "Me, too. How about that?" He winked, feeling more confident now that he was in charge.

"Hmm. Fate." Patrick lowered his hand to the button of his trousers, flicking it open until his cock sprang free. "But if you think you're in charge, you're wrong."

"Am I now? We'll see about that."

Kieren grabbed the waistband of Patrick's trousers and

tugged them off. He needed them both naked because he wanted to be inside him. They had yet to have intercourse, and Kieren was out of patience.

Let him just hope he could keep his libido in check and give Patrick an experience to remember.

14

PATRICK

As he watched Kieren get naked, Patrick's mouth dried up. The man was a god. Muscles that went on for miles, tanned skin from time out in the sun or just his genes, Patrick wasn't sure. He wanted nothing more than to spend hours worshipping every inch of him, but until his wrist was better, he wouldn't be able to do everything he needed to. Allowing Kieren to have his way with him—or at least thinking he was in charge of the situation—was a suitable compromise.

"You're a work of art," Kieren whispered, skimming his fingers up Patrick's legs and stomach.

"Look who's talking." They were both naked, and Patrick needed to feel Kieren on top of him. "Lay on me. I want to feel you," he said.

Kieren carefully lowered his hips, then chest, bracing his forearms on either side of Patrick's body. The feeling was exquisite. The warmth of him bled into Patrick, sending a sense of contentment through him. No matter how much Kieren protested, Patrick needed to get him to see what he saw for their future. Because he did see a future for them, and one he was reluctant to let go of.

Lifting his good arm, he slid it around Kieren's neck, pulling him down for a blistering kiss. The longer the kiss continued, the more they rubbed against each other. Patrick could feel their precome leaking enough to wet his skin.

"More," Patrick panted. "Wrap your hand around us."

Kieren smirked. "Topping from the bottom?"

"Of course."

Kieren ignored him and kissed his way down his neck and chest, lapping against his nipples. Patrick arched towards him and hissed as his bad hand tried to copy his good hand and grip the covers. Kieren peered up at him, then across to his hand. Sliding his own hand across, he stretched out Patrick's arm.

"Keep it there, or I'll find some way to restrain you, so you don't hurt yourself further. If you do, we stop," Kieren growled.

Patrick's breathing increased. "Yes...sir."

It was the first time he'd submitted to someone else, other than in his initial training, and he never realised how much of a relief it was to let go and give control to another person because, although he'd done it, he had never felt comfortable with it. He doubted he could've done it with someone other than Kieren, but his body and mind were in total agreement with the plan.

Kieren's eyes widened, and he inhaled through his nose, his nostrils flaring with the move. He lowered his head back to Patrick's chest, licking and nipping at his nipples and sending shocks of electricity down to Patrick's groin. His cock hardened further, and he thrust his hips up, pressing against Kieren.

Kieren pushed his hips back down with his hands but lowered his head to lap at the fluid collecting on Patrick's stomach. The groan that met his ears was full of desire, and Patrick wished he could taste it. As if Kieren had heard his thoughts, the man swiped a couple of fingers through it and lifted them to Patrick's mouth. He happily sucked them in, closing his eyes at the decadent taste. His eyes flew open when Kieren's mouth descended on his cock. His eyes rolled back as he lowered to the root, swallowing Patrick into the back of his throat.

Patrick slammed his head back into the pillow and moaned. It had been a long time since he'd had someone throat-fuck him. Kieren pulled off, breathing heavily, and lowered again, returning to his position. He kept Patrick in his throat for far longer than Patrick thought he'd be able to—when he could think clearly enough—and lifted clear again. He licked and laved the length of him, paying special attention to his frenulum—the nerves beneath the head of his cock. They were extremely sensitive and sent shooting arcs through his body every time they were touched.

"Fuck!" Patrick couldn't stop the curse from escaping, not just from the sensations but because he'd moved his bad arm again. Luckily, the pain wasn't enough to stop the pleasure from mounting, and before long, he called Kieren's name. "I'm going to come if you keep that up. I want you inside me first."

Kieren lapped at his nerves, making Patrick jerk and thrash, though their gazes remained locked. "Okay."

Kieren rose to his knees and stretched for the table. He retrieved condoms and lube. Patrick licked his lips, wondering if he should ask what he wanted to. He'd never been unsure, but he knew he wanted to feel Kieren as much as possible. And would he get the chance again?

"Kieren?" Kieren paused, staring at him. "I'm clear. We get tested every month." What Patrick didn't say was that he hadn't slept with anyone for too many years to count. He always chose partners who didn't want intercourse.

Kieren hesitated, and Patrick wished he'd kept the words back. "I got tested six months ago, but…I haven't slept with anyone in fifteen years," Kieren whispered in response.

Patrick's heart both broke and lifted with the words. He pushed himself to a sitting position and wrapped his good arm around Kieren's neck, sealing their mouths together again.

When they came up for air, Patrick said, "Thank you for telling me. It has been roughly the same amount of time for me. I don't do well with trusting those here at the club, and I definitely wouldn't trust anyone outside of it. Except for you."

"Let me take care of us both," Kieren murmured against Patrick's lips.

Patrick lay back down and smiled. "Go right ahead, sir."

Kieren threw the condom towards the bedside table and picked up the lube. Patrick widened his legs, bringing his knees to the side. Kieren slicked his fingers and lowered to his stomach. "Let's see how crazy I can make you with just my fingers—and maybe my mouth."

Patrick's shaft kicked at the idea, and he swallowed hard. He'd given similar treatment to other people, sending them higher and higher until they couldn't contain themselves, but had never had it reciprocated. He'd edged himself, however, and he was looking forward to what Kieren would try.

Kieren placed a lubed finger at Patrick's pucker, and Patrick bore down, knowing the first finger was always the worst, especially with how long it had been for him. A little resistance, but then Kieren was through, and Patrick groaned at the feel of his finger sliding into his channel. Kieren sucked on the head of his cock, his finger continuing to move back and forth. Then he added a second finger, and Patrick eagerly took it even with the slight burn. The burn for him was a precursor of what was to come, and he didn't mind the uncomfortableness of it.

"You should see yourself," Kieren whispered. "Your ass is sucking my fingers in."

The imagery was sexy as hell, and Patrick clenched around the intrusion. "More."

Kieren withdrew and slicked his fingers more before returning with three fingers. The sting increased, but Patrick breathed through it, not wanting Kieren to stop because it pinched. When the three fingers were in as far as they seemed able to go, Patrick released a breath and met Kieren's gaze.

"More," he growled, narrowing his gaze at the man currently holding his body hostage.

The corner of Kieren's mouth kicked up. He withdrew, thrust forward and paused again. Patrick groaned and circled his hips, trying to get some relief.

"Stop," Kieren said. "Otherwise, I'll drag this out longer."

Patrick pressed his head back into the pillow and stared at the ceiling, stilling his body.

"Good."

Kieren set a steady pace with his fingers now Patrick had accustomed to it, and the drag against his insides sent fireworks firing through his spine and groin. Then he curved his fingers, and Patrick's body bowed as they grazed his prostate. He tensed, trying not to move because he didn't want Kieren to stop, but he did anyway.

"Please!" Patrick said through gritted teeth.

Kieren sat up and grabbed the lube, slicking his cock generously. "Ready?"

"Yes!"

Kieren scooted closer and gripped Patrick's hip with one hand and his own cock with the other, positioning it at Patrick's hole. Their gazes met once more, and Kieren pressed forward. He didn't pause at all while he kept Patrick's gaze, just steadily pushed inside him until his balls rested against Patrick's ass.

They both panted, and Kieren lowered to his hands, dropping a kiss on Patrick's mouth. "I don't know how long I can hold back."

"You don't need to hold back. Just fuck me," Patrick said.

Kieren's eyes flared, and he inhaled. "Okay."

He withdrew and thrust forward, setting a punishing pace that sent Patrick higher. Sparks tingled at the base of his spine, and he gripped the sheets, trying to keep his bad hand loose beside him.

Kieren rose to his knees, gripped Patrick's hips and slammed harder. The muscles in Kieren's jaw clenched, his hold bruising, and Patrick loved every moment. He lifted his knees a little, giving Kieren more room, and he took advantage of it, pounding deeper and hitting Patrick right where he needed it.

"Fuck! Right there!" His good hand clenched against Kieren's forearm.

Sweat trickled down Kieren's face, the drips falling to Patrick's skin with Kieren's movements.

"Come for me, Paddy. I'm close," Kieren gritted out.

Patrick wrapped his hand around his cock and stroked to the rhythm of Kieren's movements. It didn't take long. "Now!" he gasped as his orgasm overtook him. Streaks of his release coated his stomach and chest, and for the first time, he felt the warmth of Kieren's release coat his channel. It was a moment he would never forget, despite it being dulled by the sensation of his own climax.

As his body calmed, jerking in times with the aftershocks, he lifted his eyes to Kieren. Something passed between them when their gazes met. *Mine.* Patrick wanted Kieren with every fibre of his being, and he hoped to convince Kieren to take a chance on them. After all, they were already in some type of relationship. He just wasn't sure what.

He reached a hand up to Kieren's cheek, cupping it and encouraging him to lower himself down. Instead of lying on or beside him, Kieren lapped up Patrick's release from his skin, his cock sliding free of Patrick's ass. Patrick closed his eyes and smiled when he felt some of the come escape. It was something he wanted to feel every day.

When Kieren finished, he rose and fetched a flannel, wetting it at the sink before bringing it back and cleaning Patrick's ass.

"I shouldn't feel like this, but seeing your ass leaking my come is hot as fuck," Kieren said.

Patrick grinned. "You should feel it. It's decadent." He wriggled on the bed. "Are you going to join me?"

Kieren hesitated, and Patrick ignored the coaxing words that wanted to fly from his lips. "Sure."

Patrick exhaled silently while Kieren put the flannel in the basket by the door. He lay next to Patrick on his good side, resting his head in his palm, and traced a finger over Patrick's stomach.

"Penny for them?" Patrick asked when the silence lengthened.

Kieren sighed. "I don't know if I can be what you need, Patrick."

"And what do I need?"

Kieren met his gaze. "Someone who can watch you put yourself in front of people who could just as easily shoot you down."

Patrick inhaled. "I could say the same for you. You put yourself in danger every day by being with me, by being willing to jump in front of bullets. You're already doing it. What would making our relationship official change?"

When Kieren said nothing, Patrick sighed. "Think it over some more, Kieren. We have the Halloween charity event tomorrow night. There's no rush to decide what we're doing."

"Isn't there?" Kieren studied him.

"Not at all. Rome wasn't built in a day, as they say. We'll carry on as we are and see where it takes us." It wasn't what he wanted to do, but he didn't want to lose Kieren by pushing him too hard.

He refused to lose the best thing to happen to him, especially through his own impatience.

"Oh, darling! Look at you!" his mother cried, hands covering her mouth as Patrick wandered towards the front door.

He was in his black tuxedo, ready to slay at the auction. He was the auctioneer for the event, though he'd never done it before. He wouldn't do "the chant," as it was called—the speaking fast to get through the bids. It wasn't that type of event. The event was for a charity that helped those who were victims of domestic violence. It was one of the few charities in the country that helped both women *and* men in the situation and was close to his heart.

"Thank you, Mother. You look amazing."

Victoria wore an ankle-length, royal blue gown with white heels and a white bag. She had styled her long hair in an updo and looked fantastic.

"Thank you, dear. Your father and I will arrive slightly later than planned, unfortunately. But we will be there. You go on, and we'll meet you there before it all starts."

He kissed her on both cheeks. "Okay. I'm heading over there now. I don't want to be late."

"Of course."

He waved goodbye and climbed into the car, eyeing Kieren, looking tasty in his black suit, as he settled into the front seat as usual. Wanting nothing more than to order him to sit in the back with him, he distracted himself by checking his phone. His cousins were coming to support him, but he wasn't sure who else would be there.

The journey into the centre of London took the better part of an hour and a half due to the traffic. When they reached their destination, the media were already behind the crowd control barriers, cameras flashing towards the car. Patrick's stomach fluttered as he stared at them, the idea of being in front of them never getting easier, no matter how many times he'd done it.

Kieren climbed out of the car, and the din of the crowds rose as the door opened and lowered as he closed it again. He wandered around the front of the car, eyes on the crowds until he reached Patrick's door. There was a pause before he opened the door, and the noise level rose again. Patrick swallowed and climbed out, smiling as he fastened his jacket button, then waved at the crowds.

"Don't linger too long, please," Kieren muttered.

"Bossy," Patrick replied, keeping the smile on his face.

He took the steps, covered in red fabric, and paused a couple of times for the media to get photographs, then entered the building, sighing as the noise reduced again.

"Your Highness!" He turned, and the organiser, Augustus Milden, held out her hand. "I'm pleased you were available for this event. I'm happy you're here."

"Augustus, thank you for having me. As you know, this is a worthy cause. I'm more than happy to help."

They went through the plans for Patrick's job briefly—they'd already been through it several times, but he understood things could change at short notice—and he joined the guests milling in the ballroom. This was the part he hated the most—mingling.

Kieren was by his side the entire time, which helped, but a deep-seated need to hold his hand as he went through the hell he was in had to be pushed back several times. As if he'd noticed, Kieren kept close, brushing their arms together occasionally, which helped to centre Patrick more than anything else.

They invited the guests to take a seat at their tables, and Patrick moved to the table closest to the stage. Originally, they had been placed in the centre of the room, right at the front, but after some discussions about security, they had been moved to the side of the room instead. It would be easier to get Patrick out of the room if he wasn't surrounded by people. When he got there, Christian and Oscar were already there.

"Hi," he greeted them both.

"How are you holding up?" Christian asked. Patrick smiled

and turned his back on the guests before pulling a face, then smiling again. Christian chuckled. "Like that, huh?"

"I'm excited to be a part of this." Patrick gave his rote answer and sat beside his cousin. "Not as much to be standing up doing an auction," he whispered.

Before he could get another word out, Douglas, Mav, Henry, Robert and Kean arrived, seating themselves at the table. Patrick glanced at Kieren and caught a grimace as he looked at the table. A source of contention for all the security involved. Having that many royals under one roof was not a good thing, according to them. Patrick could understand, but they couldn't stop attending these things just in case something happened. Luckily, they had an amazing security team.

"Thank you for being here tonight," Augustus said. "This charity is something close to my heart, and I'm happy you are here to support such a worthy cause." She continued for a short time, explaining the need for such a charity and what they spend their money on. "As you are aware, tonight is an auction. We have been blessed to have such amazing items for you to bid on. And to help us during the event, please welcome His Royal Highness, Prince Patrick."

She clapped, and everyone joined in as Patrick climbed the steps to the stage, his heart pounding painfully. Kieren joined him but stayed on one side of the stage, his eyes scanning the entire room.

Patrick faced the guests. "Good evening, and welcome to Claridon's Domestic Violence Support Auction." He addressed the guests, thanks to George's speech-writing ability, reiterating parts of what Augustus said to highlight them again, then wound down. "Shall we get the auction underway?"

15

KIEREN

*K*ieren hated every minute of this. The security for the event, though good, was not good enough to stop a bullet if someone wanted to do it. Patrick was spotlighted for everyone to see in the centre of a large stage, with nowhere to hide should something happen. Kieren was ready to fly across the stage at a moment's notice, but he hated it all. Patrick so exposed, so vulnerable. But he was also extremely proud of him for getting up there and speaking in front of probably a hundred people or more. Patrick hated it, and Kieren didn't blame him. He hated standing to the side where everyone could see him, but he'd refused to be hidden behind a curtain as it would impede his view of the room.

As the auction started, the staff brought items onto the stage on the opposite side of Patrick, showing them off as Patrick described what they were before going through the bidding part and confirming the winning bid.

"We have movement at the back right of the room," Brett murmured in his ear.

Kieren didn't reply but swung his gaze to that part of the room. Two security guards stood, stopping another man with a camera from entering. He flicked his gaze back to Patrick, checking he was okay, before focusing on the newcomer again. It hadn't gained any attention from the room except for the nearest table, and the scowls on the occupants' faces were not much to go on.

"Congratulations, Mrs Emery. You have the winning bid," Patrick said.

As Kieren went to look back at Patrick, he caught movement from his side and instinctively put his arm out. Christian pushed past him with a muttered, "Charles," and disappeared behind the curtain. He glanced across the stage and saw Charles standing with his arms crossed and a smug look on his face. Kieren checked in with Patrick again, not seeing any indication that Patrick was uneasy, and continued to check between Patrick and Charles. The man didn't appear to have any weapons on him from what Kieren could see.

Christian appeared beside Charles with Brett by his side, which eased Kieren's mind. There was a heated conversation, though Charles never lost his smug expression. He saw Christian's eyes widen, focus on Patrick, then out into the crowd. Then he glanced across at him and mouthed, "Gun."

Kieren went on alert and stared into the crowd, not seeing anything untoward. "What's going on, Brett?" he murmured into his earpiece.

"Charles has implied there is a shooter in the audience. We need to get everyone out."

Kieren was already on the move when a gun discharged. He slammed into Patrick, taking him to the floor as pain flared through his arm. "Stay down!" He covered Patrick's body with his own, palming his gun and aiming it towards where the noise of the shot had come from. Someone lay face down on the floor with their arms behind their backs and two security guards hovering. He turned the gun towards where Charles and Christian had been, seeing Charles glowering as they clipped him into handcuffs. Christian had a gun in his hand, held in a handkerchief. The noise in the room drowned out what they were saying, but Patrick took his attention.

"Shit! Kieren! Kieren! For fuck's sake, you're bleeding!"

Pain splintered through him as Patrick pressed against his arm, and his head swam. He breathed through his nose, blinking his eyes to keep his focus on the two areas of the room that could provide more issues—the shooter and Charles.

"Kieren! Move, for god's sake. I need to put pressure on this before you lose too much blood."

Kieren tried to lift his hand to press his earpiece, but he couldn't. He glanced at where Brett had been standing and saw people coming towards them. Swinging the gun in that direction, they held up their hands, calling his name. He blinked. Blinked again. He saw Brett beside him and let his guard down, the pain intensifying.

"Take…care…of him."

Darkness found him.

Kieren slowly became aware of several noises at once. A muted beeping to his left and snoring to his right. He reached for his alarm to silence it, but pain streaked through him, making him gasp. The snoring stopped immediately.

"Kieren?"

Kieren repeatedly blinked, trying to clear his vision. "What—"

He stopped when his voice croaked. A straw was pressed to his lips, and he gratefully drank the cool water, letting his eyes drift shut again. After he had his fill, he opened his eyes again, the room blurring for a second when they didn't want to stay open. A hand rested on his head, stroking his forehead.

"It's okay. Rest," the voice said.

The next time he woke, he was more alert. He opened his eyes slowly, blinking several times to clear the grittiness. The moment he was able to focus, he knew he was in the hospital.

"What happened?" he rasped.

Someone popped up from beside him, making him flinch and groan as pain radiated from his side. Glancing down, his body gave no answer because a sheet covered him, but he had an IV going into the back of his hand and a clip on his index finger. He assumed they were what was making the machine beep.

"Kieren?"

He faced the voice, smiling at Patrick. "What are you doing here?"

Patrick lifted a straw to his mouth, and Kieren sucked, briefly closing his eyes at the fresh, cool water. He quenched his thirst, then nodded, and Patrick removed the straw.

"What happened? I remember the auction and the shooter and covering you while they tried to get whoever it was."

Patrick chuckled. "Always full of questions. I'm here because I wanted to be. What happened was that you took me to the floor and protected me while they apprehended the shooter and Charles." He stroked his fingers through Kieren's hair. "You took a bullet for me."

Kieren raised his eyebrows. "I did? Go me."

Patrick snorted. "You're an asshole."

"For taking a bullet meant for you?"

"Yes. And for scaring the shit out of me." He sighed. "The bullet nicked something, which was why you lost consciousness. I was afraid…" He shook his head and stared at their joined hands—when had Patrick taken his hand? "It was touch and go during surgery. I thought I'd lost you." The last sentence was whispered, and Kieren wanted to hold him.

"I'm here." He squeezed Patrick's hand. "I'm here."

Patrick leaned down and pressed a kiss to his lips. "Don't leave me, Kieren."

Kieren expected his chest to tighten at the thought of staying, but for once, it didn't. "I won't."

"Let me get the doctor in to check you out, and we can figure out what the plan is from here. Okay?" Patrick said.

Kieren nodded, already feeling tired again. Patrick did something out of Kieren's eyesight, and within minutes, a doctor bustled in.

"Good morning, Mr Young. Nice to see you awake. I'm Dr Green." He picked up the clipboard at the base of his bed and flicked through it. "Well, your vitals are looking great. With what you've been through, I wasn't sure what to expect, but you're strong, and not just in the muscle department." He chuckled at his joke, and Kieren wanted to roll his eyes. He wasn't a fan of hospitals, but the doctor jokes were the worst. "The bullet went straight through your arm, in and out, but, unfortunately, carried on its journey and found its way through the side of your vest, entering your right side and coming to a stop millimetres from your liver. It hadn't exited when you were brought in, but we retrieved it when we performed surgery on you. I have no idea how you didn't sustain more injuries because the bullet missed just about everything. You are one lucky guy, Mr Young."

"How long before I can get back to work?"

Dr Green raised his eyebrows. "If it was just the arm, I would've said maybe two months to be on the safe side. With your side, I want to extend that to at least three months before you do anything too strenuous. I understand you want to get back to protecting Prince Patrick, but if you push yourself too hard, too fast, you'll actually take longer to heal." The doctor stared at him. "I'm sure you know exactly what I mean."

Kieren understood, but he didn't have to like it. He was no use to Patrick now. He'd be replaced, unable to do the job he'd been brought on to do. What would he do now? Maybe Brett could help him find something after he'd healed because he was sure the royal family wouldn't want someone who hadn't been able to work for several months.

Patrick squeezed his hand, and Kieren faced him, realising with a jolt that the doctor had left. Were his senses dulled by medication? He hoped so because, otherwise, he was losing his touch.

"Brett's outside. He wants to visit?"

Kieren nodded. "Sure."

Patrick moved to the door, opening it and beckoning outside. Brett came through, and Patrick glanced back at Kieren, pointed at himself and pointed out of the door. He exited and closed the door behind him, leaving him with Brett. Having Patrick out of his sight was something he hadn't realised would affect him that strongly, but the moment he was gone, Kieren's heart raced, and the monitors went berserk. He tried to calm down but couldn't.

Brett went to the door. "Patrick! Get in here!"

Kieren was about to scold the man for talking to a prince like that, but Patrick returned, racing to Kieren's side. "What's wrong?"

Kieren panted as if he'd run a marathon at sprinting speed and squeezed Patrick's hand while refusing to look away. What the actual fuck?

"I'm here, sweetheart. I'm here. I'm not going anywhere." Patrick's mumblings helped calm him down, and when the nurse came bustling in, she scolded them for making him agitated. After a few moments of checking his vitals, she gave them another speaking to and left.

Patrick threaded his hand through Kieren's and dropped into the seat he'd been in earlier. Calmer now, Kieren faced Brett.

"Sorry," he said. "I didn't expect...that."

Brett's mouth curled. "It's fine. To be expected, actually. How are you feeling?"

Kieren blew out a long breath. "The ache in my side is hurting more. I'm assuming the medication is wearing off. My head is a bit of a jumble, but I pretty much remember everything, I think." He stared down at his boss. "What happened, and what's going to happen?"

Brett grinned. "Well, Prince Charles is currently being interviewed by the Commissioner himself to get to the bottom of why it happened. The shooter, one Harvey Johnson, has been wanted by the police for a long time. Mainly in connection with a previous royal incident involving Prince Douglas. The police had been unable to locate him for over a year, but he slipped up by agreeing to this stunt. From what Harvey is telling the police, Charles is the one who orchestrated it." Brett held his hands out. "Whether that's true or not is anyone's guess."

"I hope they lock Charles away with no chance of bail, but it's highly unlikely," Patrick said, and Kieren squeezed his hand.

Brett glanced down at their hands, smiled and refocused on Kieren's face. "As for what's going to happen, I'm assuming you mean with you?" Kieren nodded. "You're well aware that you can't work while injured, so you're on leave until you're better. That's not up for debate. I have assigned Jade and Nina to you both. They will be your bodyguards for the time being, and we will reassess when you're better. Agreed?"

There was no way Kieren couldn't agree because Brett's expression brooked no argument. It was that or Kieren would probably be let go, and he refused to leave Patrick.

"On one condition?" Brett raised his eyebrows, but a smirk stayed on his face. "I stay on with Patrick as second...fiddle or whatever."

"I thought that went without saying."

The tension left Kieren's body, and exhaustion waved over him. "Thank you."

"One last thing before you drift back to sleep," Brett said. "I've arranged for you to speak to Timothy tomorrow." Kieren opened his mouth to argue. "It's not optional. It's mandatory." He sighed. "I thought Timothy was the better option than a stranger, but if you'd prefer someone else, let me know."

Kieren swallowed hard. He hated the idea of talking through what happened with someone, but he knew he needed to. Even he could understand something was going on with him if he couldn't stand the idea of Patrick being out of his sight. PTSD was nothing to joke about.

"Timothy's fine."

Brett nodded. "In which case, I will leave you in peace. I'll let you know any updates we have as soon as I know them. Having that information will help, I'm told." He glanced at Kieren again. "Make sure you explain but get some rest."

Kieren inhaled. "I will."

Brett left after saying goodbye, and Patrick brought his hand up to kiss his knuckles. "Get some sleep, sweetheart. We can talk later."

"No, I'm okay for the moment. I don't know how long," he smiled, eyes heavy, "but for now." He glanced at Patrick. "How are you? Did I do any more damage to your wrist?"

Patrick snorted. "No more than had already been done. It got jolted, but only an ache. The doctor checked me over and put a stronger brace on it, but apart from that, I'm good."

Kieren closed his eyes and sighed, glad he'd been able to prevent Patrick from getting hurt. "I have PTSD, I think." He rolled his head to look at Patrick again. "That's why the monitors went a little crazy when you left the room. *I* went a little crazy. Sorry."

Patrick brought their clasped hands up to his face and rested the back of Kieren's hand against his cheek. "Don't be sorry. I don't mind at all. If I have to spend every moment with you to make things easier, I will. It's no hardship."

"You might get fed up with me."

"Possibly, but you might get fed up with me, too." Patrick smiled. "I'm willing to try if you are."

Kieren studied Patrick's face and opened himself completely before sleep overtook him. "I'm willing to try. With everything. I trust you. With my life. With my body." He paused, swallowing again. "With my heart," he whispered.

Tears trickled down Patrick's face, and he pressed his hand harder against his face. "I'll look after it. I promise. And just so you know," he rose and paused with his lips above Kieren's, "you have everything of me. I trust you with it all."

A lone tear slid down Kieren's temple. "I hope I don't make you regret it."

Patrick closed the distance and kissed him, soft and slow. "Let's take it a day at a time. We don't need any more than that."

"Okay."

Patrick settled back into his chair, clearing his throat. "I would like to arrange for you to move into my rooms at home. Are you okay with that? I don't want to crowd you or anything, but I wanted to look after you, and after what you've told me about the possible PTSD, it might work well to help you. What do you think?"

Kieren couldn't explain how happy it made him without sounding like a sap, and he nodded. "That's fine, but only if you're sure." He gasped, then winced when his side protested. "What will your parents say?"

"They'll be fine. I promise. They love you anyway. Even more now that you saved me." He chuckled.

"I don't want to be a burden to you or your family."

Patrick glared at him. "Did we not just go through the *I trust you with my heart* thing? That type of relationship is never a burden. I would love to spoil you—I mean, look after you." Patrick winked, and Kieren chuckled, hissing again.

"Okay, duly noted that laughing and gasping are not good things to do at the moment," Kieren wheezed.

Patrick chuckled. "Good to know. Oh, is there anyone I need to let know about what happened to you? Your phone has buzzed a few times, but I've not looked or answered it."

Kieren tried to get his brain to work for a few more minutes. "Only Zane. He's a friend. Feel free to answer or not if it's him. My passcode is 2486." His blinks lasted longer. "I'm gonna… sleep…now."

"Okay. I'm right here." Patrick squeezed his hand, holding the pressure long enough for Kieren to drift off with it in his mind.

PATRICK

As Kieren's breath evened out, Patrick sat back in his chair and blew out a breath. The future he saw stretched out in front of them, and he was overjoyed. The actions of his cousin dampened it slightly. Would Kieren be in the line of fire now, too? He assumed so, and he didn't like it one bit.

He was glad Charles was being held and questioned. Maybe the Commissioner would get some information out of him. Uncle Andrew was good friends with the Commissioner, and they often worked together on things. Patrick had limited interactions with the man, but he remembered how helpful he'd been when someone had accused Douglas of abusing them—it hadn't been true, just a ruse an ex-member of the club had devised to get him back for rescinding his membership. Hopefully, Charles would squeal about what was happening, but Patrick doubted it.

Kieren's phone rang again, and Patrick carefully pulled his hand free and reached for the phone in the drawer. Zane's name flashed up, and Patrick cleared his throat and answered.

"Hello, Kieren's phone."

There was a pause. "Who are you, and what happened to Kieren?" a rough voice said.

"I'm Patrick. I'm his..." He wasn't sure how Kieren wanted to describe them, and he didn't finish the sentence. "There was an incident. He's in hospital, but he's fine. Nothing that some rest and recuperation won't help."

"Patrick. Ah, his protectee and..." Zane chuckled. "Never mind. Nice to speak to you, Your Highness. Can you tell me what happened?"

"Please, just Patrick. I don't need the titles." He sighed. "We went to an event. It's probably all over the news now, anyway. Someone shot at..." He inhaled. "Someone shot at me, but Kieren got caught instead. The bullet went through his arm and into his chest but hit nothing. He's lucky because it could've been much worse, and it was touch and go during the surgery to remove the bullet, but he's fine. He's just fallen back to sleep, actually."

"I never understood why he felt the need to do this job." Zane paused. "Sorry, that sounded shitty. I'm glad he protected you. It's what he would've wanted, especially with how close you are. I just hate seeing him in harm's way."

"I know, and I'm sorry he was there. If it's any consolation, he won't be doing the job for a while."

"But he'll still be by your side, won't he?" Patrick had nothing to say to that. "He's in love with you, you know?"

"I hope so," Patrick whispered. "I feel the same."

Zane sighed. "I won't say I didn't wish he was with someone less...exposed, but I'm glad you have each other."

"Thank you."

"Does this mean I need to add a plus one to Kieren's invite?"

Patrick frowned. "Invite?"

"I've just returned from a holiday that turned into a honeymoon. We're arranging a reception as soon as we can."

"A holiday turned honeymoon?" Patrick chuckled. "Congratulations?"

Zane laughed. "Thanks. A little impromptu, but we're happy. Should I add a plus one?"

"You better speak to Kieren about that. It might be a security problem, and I don't want to take away from your joyous celebration." Patrick gasped. "Not that I think I will take the limelight or anything." He palmed his face.

Zane chuckled again. "I know what you mean. Okay, I'll speak to Kieren about it. What's the plan for him now?"

"He's staying here for a few days to make sure there are no complications from the surgery. Then I'll take him home and arrange for physical therapy and anything else he needs. It'll be a few months before he can even consider returning to his job."

"That's going to be difficult for him to process," Zane murmured.

"I'll get him whatever help he needs. I promise."

"I know you will. Right. I'll leave you in peace, but could you get him to call me when he's up to it, please?"

"Of course."

They spoke for a few more minutes, and then Patrick ended the call. He checked if Kieren was still breathing—it was stupid because the monitors would go off if he wasn't, but he couldn't help it—and wrote a quick note and left it in Kieren's hand just in case he woke before Patrick came back.

He exited the room. "I'm just fetching some tea. I've left a note for him, but if he calls, can you tell him I'll only be a few minutes?" he asked Nina, the bodyguard they'd put in place for Kieren. She nodded. Patrick thanked her and wandered down the corridor to the cafe, which was on the same floor, his new bodyguard, Jade, following him.

He bought four cups of tea and headed back the way he came.

"Are you okay, Your Highness?" Jade asked.

Patrick gave a small smile. "Yes, thank you. It's been a stressful day. And please, call me Patrick."

"I'll try." She grimaced.

He knew it was ingrained in them to stick to titles, but he hated it. "I need to arrange for some clothes to be brought over. I can't stay in this for much longer." He chuckled, plucking at his tuxedo shirt. He'd taken off the tie and jacket hours ago.

"I believe Prince Frederick is on his way with something for you," Jade said.

Patrick raised his eyebrows. "Oh, okay. Thanks." He paused at the door to Kieren's room and handed Jade and Nina a cup. "I never thought to ask, so it's tea. I apologise if you don't like it. I'll get to know you better as soon as I can."

"This is fine. Thank you for thinking of us," Nina said.

"It's only right. After all, you're putting your lives on the line for us. Tea is the least I can do."

He entered the room to see Kieren staring at him, his hand gripped around the note, sweat beading on his head. Patrick rushed forward, putting the cups on the table.

"I'm sorry. I thought I'd be back quicker than you would wake." Patrick slipped his hand into Kieren's and squeezed.

"It's okay," Kieren rasped.

Patrick's heart broke. He wished he could click his fingers and make Kieren all better, but he knew the road would be bumpy. They'd weather it together.

"I brought tea. I checked with the nurse that you could have it if you want?"

"Tea?" Kieren raised an eyebrow.

Patrick grinned. "Yes, tea. You can't have coffee yet."

Kieren's bottom lip came out. "Meanie."

Patrick's laugh echoed around the room. "Maybe, but it'll help."

"So will a kiss."

Patrick's smile never wavered as he lowered his head and touched their lips together. "Better?"

"I don't know. Maybe another one, to be sure?"

The twinkle in Kieren's eyes helped to reassure Patrick that they would be fine. It might take time, but eventually, they would be good. He kissed Kieren more than once. Little pecks on his mouth, cheeks and forehead before returning to his mouth again.

He took his cup and sat in the chair. "I spoke to Zane. He says to ring him when you're feeling up to it."

Kieren nodded. "Thanks. I will. Was he okay?"

"He was. A little upset about the incident, but he's okay."

Kieren winced. "Yeah, he'll take a strip from my hide for it, but I promise it's just because he cares."

"I know he does. I can hear it in his voice." Patrick sipped his tea and opened his mouth to speak when a knock sounded. He put the tea down and opened the door a crack, then held up a finger. He turned back to Kieren. "It's Freddie. Is it okay if he comes in?"

Kieren nodded and put his cup down, trying to push himself to a seated position, but groaned and grimaced instead.

Patrick rushed over, placing a hand gently on Kieren's chest. "Stop trying to move, you idiot. You'll do more damage and end up staying in here for longer than you want."

"It's not right to be lying down when royalty is in the room," Kieren said.

Patrick chuckled. "You don't have a problem lying down when I'm with you."

Kieren paused, staring at him, mouth gaping. "I can't believe you just went there!"

Patrick laughed. "Just lay down and be a good boy, or..." He lowered his mouth to Kieren's ear, "I'll have to tie you to the bed."

Kieren closed his eyes and pushed his head into the pillow. "Patrick!" he hissed, covering his groin with his hand.

Patrick snorted and pulled the rolling table over Kieren's lap, hiding his erection. "I'm going to let him in now."

"Okay," Kieren croaked.

Patrick went to the door, face flaming when he realised he'd left it ajar instead of closing it like he thought he had. He met Freddie's amused expression with his head held high, ignoring his heated cheeks.

"Come on in."

Freddie entered, leaving his two guards outside with Jade and Nina, but not until one of them had checked the room first.

"How are you feeling, Kieren?" Freddie asked, grabbing a chair and settling next to Patrick.

Kieren blew out a breath and winced. "I've been in better health, but I'm good, thanks."

"Thank you for protecting him. It means the world to us."

"And to me." Kieren glanced at Patrick, and Patrick scooted forward and grabbed his hand, making his eyes widen.

Patrick smiled. "Trust me," he whispered. Kieren nodded, and Patrick faced Freddie. "We're together."

"Glad to hear it. Took you long enough." Freddie grinned.

Patrick backhanded him. "Leave us alone."

Freddie laughed. "It was a long time coming, Paddy. George had even picked out a new name for us, knowing it was inevitable." He tilted his head. "Well, after I'd pointed it out, that is."

Patrick covered his face with his free hand and groaned. "Oh, god! Is it bad?"

"It's been worse. We will be called the 'Thirsty Thirteen.'"

"When will he stop?"

"When no one else joins us?" Freddie raised his eyebrows, then focused on Kieren. "Welcome to the family."

Kieren swallowed hard enough for Patrick to see the bob of his Adam's apple. "Thanks."

"Brett came to see us earlier and told us what was happening with Charles," Patrick said, trying to divert Freddie's attention.

With a knowing glint in his eye, Freddie nodded. "Commissioner Thomas was still interviewing Charles when I last heard, but Aunt Charlotte had been on the phone several times to him and Father."

"She called your father?" Patrick gaped.

"Yes. I can't believe it myself. After everything she's done, and after Father practically disowning her, at least privately, she called him, telling him to get Charles out."

"I'm assuming he declined."

"He just said no and hung up on her." Freddie snorted.

Patrick gasped. "He did what?"

"I bet she's causing havoc at the station. She wouldn't go down there because the media are all over the place with them arresting Charles publicly."

"I can imagine. I've not checked the news or anything," Patrick said.

"It's not pretty. For Charles, anyway."

"Good. It might do him some good to have a stressful time of it," Patrick said. He glanced at Kieren when he yawned. "Are you doing okay?"

"A little tired, but I'm good."

Freddie rose. "I'll leave you to get some rest."

"You don't need to. You can visit while I sleep. I don't mind," Kieren said.

Freddie glanced at Patrick, then back again. "Are you sure?"

Kieren nodded. "I'll still sleep."

Freddie resumed his seat. "If we disturb you, let me know, and I'll come back later."

Patrick stood and leaned over Kieren, whispering, "Sleep, sweetheart. I'll be here when you wake." He pressed their mouths together briefly, then brushed his hand over his head and sat again, retaining Kieren's hand. "How are things with Damon? I've not had the chance to speak to you properly about it."

Freddie sighed. "Well, we spent those few days together, but it was exactly what Damon said it was. We were in meetings for the most part. I don't know, Paddy. Something's not right."

"You need to talk to him. Really talk to him, Freddie. If something's wrong, he might need help."

"He won't talk to me. I've tried."

"Try again. Or do you want me to try?"

Freddie shook his head. "I honestly don't know. I feel...out of sorts."

Patrick knew how he felt. It was easy to see on his face and something Patrick could understand. It was also plain to see how uneasy Freddie was. It made Patrick believe his cousin and best friend were on a journey neither expected nor prepared for. At least on Freddie's side.

They spoke for a while longer until Freddie made his excuses. Patrick hated seeing him like that. He'd arrange for them all to get together again and cheer him up. He needed to speak to Mav or Randall to get a date when all their calendars allowed. It was getting harder and harder as they gained more responsibilities.

Hopefully, Charles would let some information free, and they could take Aunt Charlotte down once and for all. It was all he could wish for.

It had taken some talking from Timothy before Kieren felt comfortable letting Patrick out of his sight the following day. Nina had stayed outside Kieren's room, and Jade had followed him when he wandered down the corridors and to the exit. He'd told Kieren he was going home for a short time to see his parents, but he'd be back in a couple of hours. Timothy had agreed to stay until he returned.

Jade sat in the front seat of the car—Kieren's usual seat—and Patrick felt adrift not having the man with him. It was a strange sensation. He wasn't sure if Kieren had realised that as they were now in a relationship, he would have a guard himself. Or maybe they would just give them one guard between them. Patrick wasn't sure.

The journey wasn't long as his parents were meeting him at Clarence House instead of home because he hadn't wanted to be too far from Kieren. When they stopped outside the large white house, Jade jumped out and opened the door for him. He nodded his thanks and headed straight inside.

Clarence House was home to Uncle William and Aunt Lou and two of Patrick's cousins, Louis and Helena, and their partners. Uncle William was the image of Uncle Andrew, and they were of the same minds when it came to a lot of things, which had helped considerably when things with Aunt Charlotte began getting worse. Uncle William had supported Uncle Andrew in his decision and had helped several of them through tough times.

"Patrick!" His mother came towards him, holding out her arms, and for the first time in a long time, he buried his head in her neck and clung to her. His entire body trembled as he tried to withhold his emotions. "My dear, dear boy." She stroked his head, and Patrick breathed in her perfume as deeply as he could, letting it soothe him.

"I love him, Mother."

"I know you do, sweetheart. I can see it. I've seen it for a long time. Everything will be fine. I've already prepared your father for another addition to the family." She chuckled, making Patrick smile.

He lifted his head, and Victoria wiped her thumbs under his eyes, catching his tears. "Thank you," he whispered.

"You don't have to thank me for anything. I'm glad he was there. I can't even think about what the outcome might have been if he hadn't been close. I owe him an enormous debt of gratitude."

"He won't accept it. He'll say it was all part of his job."

Victoria winked. "You're more than a job to him."

"I know, but he's proud of his job. He needs to protect those he cares about, especially after everything that happened to him."

"We'll all be here to help him. Whatever he needs will be given without question. He's family, and you know what family means." She raised her eyebrows.

"Everything," he murmured.

"Exactly. Unless he proves to be a loose cannon like someone we know, he'll be fine." She slid her arm into his and tugged him towards the living area. "William has been chomping at the bit to talk to you about everything, but tell him to mind his own business if you don't feel like talking. He can take it."

Patrick chuckled, the smile staying on his face as he greeted his family.

"I hear I have a new son to welcome to the family," his father said.

Patrick ducked his head, his cheeks heating. "Yes, Father. He's amazing."

Patrick Senior threw his head back and laughed. "I know he is, son. You wouldn't have chosen him if he wasn't. Plus, I know him, remember?"

"Come sit down, Patrick," Lou said. "You must be tired after such a tedious couple of days."

"Thank you. It has been trying to say the least. Kieren is doing well. The doctors say there haven't been any complications, and they're pleased with his progress. I'm taking that as a huge win. Kieren doesn't want to be in there any longer than he has to, though."

"Understandable. Having someone poke and prod at them throughout the night must be annoying," William said. "Congratulations, Patrick, and send them to Kieren, too."

"Thank you, Uncle."

"Now, tell me everything." William grinned, rubbing his hands together.

Patrick spent a relaxing couple of hours explaining everything he knew and what he'd heard from Brett and Freddie. He'd even learnt some new information that William had heard from Uncle Andrew.

"Charles isn't being let out on bail?" Patrick said, mouth gaping.

William smiled. "No. At least, not yet. Brady is keeping him in for as long as he can to make him sweat." Brady was Commissioner Thomas. "He wants to try to get Charles to talk because, at the moment, he isn't. He's saying a lot, but not saying a lot if you get my meaning."

Patrick nodded and dropped his head into his hand. His wrist ached, but he itched to play. It had been far too long since he'd felt the keys of his piano or the strings of his violin. His flute and clarinet would be gathering dust if he wasn't careful. He wanted to let these emotions free in the only way he knew how, but he couldn't.

"Why don't you have a shower and get changed, then you can take the tank of food we've had made for you and Kieren back to him? I bet he's anticipating your return," his mother said, patting his arm.

"More than you realise," Patrick said. He stood. "Thank you for meeting me here instead of at home."

"Don't be silly. If we could, we'd have been at the hospital already, but security is being overly cautious at the moment." Victoria pouted.

"And they have reason," his father said.

"Doesn't mean I have to like it. I want to be with my son."

"Speaking of son, what are the plans for Henry's birthday?" Patrick asked.

Victoria sighed. "He doesn't want to do anything because of what happened, so we're going to have a small family dinner instead. I'm not happy, but it's his birthday to spend as he wishes."

Patrick kissed her cheek. "It will be great, either way."

By the time he headed back to the hospital, with enough food to last them several days, he was exhausted. Sleeping in the hospital chair hadn't allowed him much sleep over the past two days, but he refused to cause Kieren any more upset than necessary. They'd figure things out once Kieren was back home.

17

———

KIEREN

It took everything in him not to climb out of the hospital bed and go after Patrick when he left. His eyes stayed on the door until Timothy spoke.

"It's not easy to allow him out of your sight, is it?" Kieren didn't answer, but Timothy continued, "I've been similar with Eddie and George occasionally. After everything that happened with me, it's difficult to believe neither of them will come to harm without me being there to protect them. Even though I was no use in the past."

Kieren glanced at him, mouth pinched. "How can I protect him while I'm in here?"

Timothy stared at him, and Kieren knew he was going to say something he didn't like the sound of. "You can't. But you have to trust that he can take care of himself and that the people surrounding him can do their job."

"Everyone makes mistakes." Kieren rested his head back, staring at the ceiling, and clenched his fist in the covers.

"Yes. And they can also do their job amazingly well."

Kieren inhaled. "I feel like I have a weight on my chest whenever he's not here. Like I can't breathe without him."

"That's what love can feel like, even without everything else thrown in. You've found someone who means more to you than anything, and you don't want anything to take that away from you."

Kieren closed his eyes, and an image of a plane falling from the sky played behind his eyelids. "I wasn't there to protect my family, either." He blinked his eyes open, returning his gaze to the ceiling.

"Do you honestly believe you could've done anything to stop their plane going down?"

Kieren sighed. "I might've."

"And you might've also been killed alongside them. But you're alive. You're keeping their memory alive. The man they brought up has made a difference in this world."

"Have I?"

"Should I ask for Patrick's opinion? He's alive because of you. He's been happier since he's met you."

Kieren didn't reply. He wasn't sure if that was true. They had admitted they had feelings for each other the previous day, but what if that was just the adrenaline talking? What if Patrick was just grateful for what he'd done?

"Tell me what went through your mind when you decided to run across the stage to Patrick," Timothy said.

Kieren swallowed. "Christian rushed past me to get to Charles. I almost stopped him because he came from behind me, and I hadn't seen him. Christian *or* Charles. I was too focused on Patrick." He paused. Was that why he hadn't seen the shooter until too late?

"What went through your mind just then?" Timothy asked. Kieren didn't see any reason to deny what he'd just thought. "Is it a problem to be focused on the person you are protecting?"

"It depends. If it was because I was checking on him to make sure he was okay, then it's fine. If it was because I was distracted by him and not aware of our surroundings, then no."

"Do you believe you were unaware of your surroundings?"

Kieren frowned, thinking back to the auction. He hadn't seen Charles waiting in the wings of the stage, but he'd seen the commotion by the door and had been focused on that and Patrick. Was that why he hadn't seen Charles turn up?

"Brett brought my attention to something happening at one of the entrances. I was trying to figure out what was happening. Then, when Christian rushed past, my attention was divided. The entrance, Patrick, Christian and Charles, and the audience. I didn't know which way to look. But when Christian mouthed gun to me, I made a split-second decision."

"One that saved Patrick's life."

"Is that why he's with me?" Kieren whispered.

"No. I can see the way he looks at you. And he did that before you saved him."

Kieren thought so, too, but he couldn't help second-guessing everything. Every move he made, every feeling he had, every thought floating through his mind.

"Everyone around you doesn't die, Kieren."

Kieren snapped his gaze to Timothy's face. How the hell had he understood that?

Timothy smiled. "First, I'm a therapist. I understand the way the mind can work. Second, you've been around the royals enough that if you were cursed, they would drop like flies."

"I lose those I care most about," Kieren argued.

"What about Zane and Viv?" Timothy asked, bringing up the friends he'd mentioned earlier in the session. "They're still here. Does that mean you don't care about them?"

"I do care!"

"They're still here, Kieren. Nothing has happened to them because of their association with you. If you were cursed, I would've thought it would touch *anyone* you cared about. Wouldn't you?"

Kieren's gaze darted around the room, trying to make sense

of Timothy's words. Could he be right? He brushed a hand across his forehead, wiping the beads of sweat from his skin. Was Patrick on his way back now? Had something happened on the way? Kieren reached for his phone, but Patrick hadn't sent a message. Should he message and check in with him?

"He'll be fine, Kieren. Deep breaths for me. Get your heart rate under control before the nurses pull rank on us. That's it."

Kieren shakily inhaled and exhaled, listening to Timothy's words instead of the jumble of thoughts whizzing around his head like they were on a waltzer ride.

"It's Henry's birthday in a couple of days," Timothy said.

Kieren frowned. "Okay…" He wasn't sure how relevant that was.

"He's decided to just have a family dinner instead of a party because he doesn't want to put anyone at risk. No one agreed with him, but he put his foot down. Everyone has the right to worry about the people around them. To change their plans because they want to keep them safe. No one is debating that. I guarantee you, though, that if this differed from being a birthday party and was some larger event, he might've been overruled. The people around us would have to adapt like everyone does with every situation, every day. It can cause confusion, upset, arguments even." Timothy paused. "But what every one of these situations has in common is communication. You don't have to like something, but with good communication, things get easier."

"You're saying I need to talk to Patrick?"

Timothy shook his head. "I'm saying you need to talk to *everyone*. Unless they know your situation, they can't give you what you need, which is reassurance." He crossed his legs. "I'm not saying you need to give them your entire history unless you want to, but give them a reason to make sure your worries are heard and acknowledged. That's the only way they can help you feel better about the plans."

"Some people already know."

"That's good. It makes it easier for you. You don't need to be ashamed of wanting to protect those close to you. Of needing reassurance. It will get easier."

"Is it PTSD?"

"Possibly. It could also just be because this is fresh, and you haven't had the chance to settle down and rest properly."

Kieren held his side as he chuckled. "I've done nothing but rest since I've been here."

"Ah." Timothy held up a finger. "Healing is the least restful thing you can go through, despite lying in bed all day. I believe it's because your brain makes up for the inactivity by going ten times as fast."

Kieren rolled his eyes. "It truly does." He sighed. "Thank you."

Timothy smiled. "You're welcome. Would you like to keep these sessions going?"

Kieren tapped his fingertips against his thumb. Did he want to keep talking about all the things that were running through his head? Not really. But did he think it was a good idea? Yes.

"Yeah."

"You'll hate me some days, and other days, you'll worship me. I promise." Timothy laughed. "And I will promise you one more thing. Nothing you say to me will ever be spoken to anyone else. I might have stepped into an interfering family who only wants the best for everyone, but I take my oath seriously."

"Thank you."

Kieren checked his phone again, realising he wasn't as stressed as he had been, but the message from Patrick relieved his tension further.

PATRICK: *On my way back. x*

Kieren closed his eyes and inhaled deeply. He could do this. They could do this.

"Everything okay?" Timothy asked.

Kieren smiled. "Patrick's on his way back."

He and Timothy talked more until a knock sounded, and Patrick popped his head around the door.

"Is it okay to come in?"

"Of course!" Kieren said. His heart rate increased a little at the sight of the man he'd fallen in love with, but not enough to set the monitors screaming.

Timothy stood and shook hands with Patrick. "I'll leave you to it." He glanced at Kieren. "I'll call you."

Kieren nodded. "Thanks."

Timothy clapped Patrick on the shoulder and left, closing the door behind him. Patrick clasped Kieren's hand, leaning forward to join their mouths. The tension left Kieren the moment they touched, and tears escaped down his temples.

"Shh, shh. I'm sorry. I won't leave you again," Patrick said, brushing his hand through Kieren's hair.

Kieren smiled through his tears. "I'm okay. It's okay. I'm just glad you're fine."

Patrick returned his smile. "I'm glad you are, too."

Kieren carefully manoeuvred himself further to the side and patted the bed. "Climb on."

"I can't. You're injured."

"I need to hold you, Paddy."

The corner of Patrick's mouth curved up, and he scratched his head. But he climbed on. "This isn't a good idea."

He moved around until Kieren had his arm around Patrick's shoulders, and Patrick was curled into his body. He inhaled the scent of his man.

"That's the second time you've called me Paddy," Patrick said, resting his hand over Kieren's chest.

Kieren frowned. "Is it? I hadn't realised. Do you not like it?"

"I don't mind now as much as I did when I was younger. It's only my cousins and brother who call me that."

"Do you want me to stop?"

"No!" Patrick pressed a kiss to his chest. "No. I like it."

They stayed snuggled together on the bed for several hours, talking about anything and everything. They ignored the looks the nurses gave them, and Patrick only moved when the nurse insisted on checking over Kieren fully. Within seconds of her leaving, they were back on the bed again, and Kieren never wanted to move.

"You're invited, too, you know," Patrick said as he helped Kieren into a wheelchair, ready to push him to the exit.

Kieren could finally go home after three days of observation. His arm was in a sling and would remain in it for a few days, making everyday activities that much trickier, but it beat being in the hospital. Patrick had helped him shower and change into some decent clothes, rather than the awful gowns, and he was feeling more human.

"You don't need me there when you're celebrating your brother's birthday," Kieren argued.

"I want you there, and more to the point, Henry would like you there."

"But it's a family celebration."

Patrick crouched in front of him, placing his hands on his knees. "And you're now family."

Looking into Patrick's eyes, there was no way he could decline, but he wasn't looking forward to having his food cut up for him or the pitying looks he would undoubtedly get.

"Fine."

Patrick stood, bracing himself on the arms of the wheelchair. "Thank you." He nipped at Kieren's lips and licked into his mouth, taking the kiss they both wanted. When he pulled back, they were breathing hard.

Kieren swallowed back the words he wanted to say, knowing it was too early in the relationship to say them.

"Ready?" Patrick said with a glow on his face that Kieren wished would stay there forever.

"As I'll ever be."

Patrick pushed him to the door, scooted around him to open it, then returned to the back and pushed him through it. Kieren glanced at the two guards, Jade and Nina, as they slipped into place, one in front of them, one behind them. It was the first time Kieren had seen them in work mode—except for guarding the door. He scrutinised everything he saw Jade do in front of them, and by the time they made it to the entrance, he was impressed. He shouldn't be because he knew the royals would only take on those they knew could do the job, and he also knew Brett would've put them through the wringer before assigning them.

Jade paused before they went any further, turning to them. "Just to warn you, there are journalists outside. We've spoken to them, and they've agreed to stay back, but whether they do..." She shrugged. "We're here, though." She focused on Kieren. "Do you have anything you want us to do?"

Kieren studied her and felt himself relax. She knew the job. She didn't need him telling her what to do, but she offered anyway. "Thank you, but you've got this."

Jade nodded, a small smile on her face. "We have." She nodded behind them, presumably at Nina. "Ready?"

"Let's get this done," he said.

Jade led the way through the entrance, the automatic doors making it easier for them, but as soon as they left the confines of the hospital, the noise started.

"Patrick! Are you glad he saved your life?"

"Patrick! Give him a kiss for us!"

"Kieren! Kieren! How are you feeling?"

And so on. They all ignored the hurled questions, and Patrick helped Kieren out of the wheelchair and into the back seat of the car. Nina slid in and into a seat facing sideways while Patrick rounded the car and got in beside Kieren, with Jade closing the door for him. Once Jade was sitting up front, the driver took off.

Kieren was sweating, and not from the exertion. Not from the media attention either. It took everything for him not to grab hold of Patrick and hide him from the world. To keep him cocooned and safe. He closed his eyes, laying his head back against the seat, and breathed. A hand covered his, and Kieren immediately recognised Patrick. He clung to him, unable to temper how hard he was holding.

There was no way he could protect Patrick like this, and he had to have faith in their guards. And he did. Like he'd told Jade, they had this. It just wasn't easy letting go of what had been his job. He wanted to spend the journey planning their next steps, the next moves, the next wave of the journey, but he forced himself to keep his eyes closed, holding Patrick's hand like his life depended on it.

And maybe it did.

Kieren had a feeling he was going to need Patrick to ground him in the days to come, and he hated being a burden.

"We're here, sweetheart," Patrick murmured.

Kieren blinked several times, groggy from having fallen asleep. He sat up and rubbed his eyes, having to let go of Patrick to do it. The sight of Bagshot Park had never been as welcomed as it was right then. Jade and Nina climbed out of the car, then Patrick did, and Kieren slid over the seat to get out of the same door. Patrick helped him to stand and then threaded their fingers together.

"Okay?" Patrick asked.

"Yep." His legs were a little wobbly, but nothing he couldn't stop with locked knees.

Princess Victoria exited the building and came to them. She kissed Patrick's cheek and turned to Kieren.

"I have many things to thank you for. I would like to welcome you into the family officially and want to let you know that if you need anything, anything at all, just let one of us know. You're one of us now. And we take care of our own."

She carefully wrapped him in her arms, rubbing a hand up and down his back. That was what broke him. He hadn't had this maternal caring in so long that it came as a shock. His body shut down, and it was only Patrick's strength that stopped him from taking Victoria to the ground with him.

"Oh, my sweet boy. I'm here. We're all here."

18

PATRICK

When Kieren broke down in his mother's arms, Patrick felt like crying, too. After a brief stop at Kieren's room to get him freshened up, Patrick guided him down the hallways to the dining room. As they walked, Patrick commented, "I've just realised. We can't hold hands properly."

Kieren glanced down at their bodies, then frowned. "Shit, we've both hurt our left arms. No matter which way we stand, we can't." He shook his head. "We should've planned this better."

Patrick cracked up. "I know a solution, though." He took Kieren's right hand in his own right hand and took it up over his head until Kieren's arm was around his shoulders, and they linked their hands at Patrick's collarbone. "I can snuggle into you at the same time."

He was much happier now Kieren was back home, where he belonged. The hospital was excellent in that they looked after him, but it wasn't as good or as comfortable as being home. And it wasn't even Patrick that had been in there.

Patrick paused them a few steps away from the dining room.

172

"Are you okay with this? I know you had reservations, to begin with."

Kieren quirked his mouth. "It's fine. I suppose it's a bit easier because I have met them all before, just not as your boyf —" He stopped.

"My boyfriend?" Patrick finished. "Because that's what you are. At least, I hope you are."

Kieren lowered his mouth to Patrick's, kissing him soundly. "I want that. I just didn't want to presume."

"Presume away," Patrick said, stealing another kiss.

"Ewww! Don't be doing that here! Gross!"

Patrick glanced over his shoulder. "As if you don't do this, Your Highness."

George grinned. "Wouldn't dream of it." He waved his hand. "Come on. We're waiting."

They followed his cousin into the dining room, which was more crowded than it usually was. The five immediate family members that had adorned the seats during his childhood had morphed into a lot more as they'd grown.

"Happy birthday, Henry," Patrick said, hugging his brother.

"Thanks. I'm glad you're here. I wasn't sure if they would let Kieren out in time." Henry turned to Kieren. "I'm glad you made it." Henry pulled him in for a hug carefully.

Kieren seemed taken aback but returned the hug. "Happy birthday, Your—" He swallowed and pulled back. "Happy birthday, Henry." He winced.

Patrick laughed. "It'll get easier. I promise. Your present is in my room. I'll grab it for you in a bit, if that's okay?"

"Don't worry about it."

He spied his sister. "I'm going to grab Mary while I can."

Henry chuckled. "Yes, do. She's bloody flighty, that one." He clapped Patrick on the back and headed off, leaving Patrick to drag Kieren to meet his other sibling.

"Mary!" Patrick wrapped his arms around his sister, clinging to her. "I haven't seen you in ages. Where have you been hiding?"

Mary laughed and rocked them from side to side. "I've been around. Nate has been busy with work, and I've been busy with the kids."

Mary's husband, Nathaniel, was the CEO of a finance company—no need to guess how they met—and spent a lot of time jetting across the world to meet different people for various reasons. Mary, however, stayed at home with their four kids: Nathan, Amelia, Jordan and Denver.

"Are they around? I feel like I've not seen them since Christmas!"

"They're around. I think Chloe took them to the other room for a movie and popcorn instead of a 'stuffy' dinner with the grown-ups."

"Can't blame them," Patrick said. "Mary, can I introduce Kieren? Kieren, this is my sister, Mary."

"Nice to meet you," Kieren said.

"Likewise." Mary eyed him. "What designs do you have on my brother?" She put her hands on her hips.

Kieren stood taller, then winced. Patrick rested a hand on his back, soothing him. "That's between him and me."

Mary froze, then chuckled, dropping her arms. "Good answer." She glanced at Patrick. "Keep him."

"I plan to."

The bell rang, and everyone took their seats. Patrick surveyed their group. His parents were at their usual seats at the head of the table, then his sister and her husband, then Patrick and Kieren, with Henry and Robert opposite them. And so it went. Freddie, Damon, Douglas, Mav, George, Timothy, Eddie, Christian and Oscar filling the sides, and Uncle Andrew, Uncle William and Aunt Lou taking the final few seats. From what Henry had told him, he'd invited Albert and Evanna, but they'd declined. The couple hadn't been seen at many, if any, public events since the altercation with Aunt Charlotte a few months ago. They'd hidden themselves away, hoping they wouldn't receive any backlash because Albert chose his wife over his parents. From what Patrick had heard, they'd not heard anything from Aunt Charlotte since it happened, which wasn't always good news.

His father stood and dinged a fork on his glass. "Good evening, one and all. I'm glad to receive you all in our home for this wonderful occasion." He smiled at Henry. "Our youngest has arrived at the start of another year of his life, and I hope this year, and all the years to come, are as good as the months have been since he found Robert." Everyone cheered. "I won't drone on too much because I know we want to eat and chat, and all I want to say is happy birthday, Henry. I wish you all the very best. Cheers."

"Cheers!"

Henry stood. "I do have one thing I would like to announce." He held out his hand for Robert's. "We have decided on a date for the wedding. 13 May. And..." He peered down at Robert with a smile. "We've decided we want to adopt as soon as we've gone through the process, which we'll start after the wedding."

"Woohoo!" Patrick cheered alongside the rest of the family. Henry and Robert would be amazing parents.

When they all settled down again, the staff brought the food to the table, and several conversations started up around them.

"How are you doing?" Patrick asked Kieren.

"I'm good. A little tired, but I suppose that's to be expected."

Patrick leaned closer. "Do you want to go to bed?" Kieren raised one eyebrow, and Patrick flushed. "I meant to sleep."

Kieren grinned. "I'm fine for now." He gazed around the table. "I can't remember the last time I was surrounded by so many people who wanted to know me. I know it's Henry's birthday, but they're all interested in me. As a person."

"Did you think they wouldn't be?"

Kieren shook his head. "Some of them, yes. But not all of them."

Patrick rested his head against Kieren's shoulder and murmured, "They're interested in you because you mean a lot to me. They want to know who you are. Just tell them what you want to, and if you don't want them to know something, tell them that, too."

Kieren snorted. "Yeah, as if."

Patrick pressed a kiss to Kieren's jaw. "I'm being serious. Not everyone is entitled to information about you. Besides, they'll have to go through me first."

The dinner lasted another hour before Patrick called it quits and dragged Kieren out of there. The man was practically falling down with exhaustion. He led them towards Kieren's room, which was further away from the rest of the family and would give them some privacy. Unless his family suddenly converged on them to make sure Kieren was okay. But he didn't think they would. At least not tonight.

He forewent the shower and helped Kieren onto the bed, undressing him down to his boxers and tucking him under the covers. He was out before Patrick had even finished picking up the clothes he'd taken off him.

Patrick chose to sit in the armchair he pulled into the room from the living area rather than settle beside him because he was worried about hurting Kieren if Patrick wriggled too much. He slid off his shoes and lifted his feet to the side of the bed, wanting some connection to him, then rested his head back and memorised every hill and valley of his face and neck.

The next thing he knew, the sunlight was streaming through a gap in the curtains. He yawned and rubbed his face, stretching his neck from side to side to ease the kink he'd given it from his awful sleeping position. He peered at Kieren, finding him awake and watching him.

"Good morning," he rasped with a smile. "How long have you been awake?"

"Long enough to guess how much your neck would hurt when you woke." Kieren grinned, giving his face a younger look.

Patrick pulled his feet to the floor and winced. "Yeah, a lot. How are you feeling?" He scooted to the edge of the chair, reaching for Kieren's hand.

"I'm feeling okay. A little sore, possibly from sleeping in the same position all night, but I'm good." Kieren licked his lips slowly. "Good enough for a treat," he murmured.

Patrick raised his eyebrows. "And what treat are you thinking of?"

"The kind where you get undressed and straddle me, so you can ride me to the edge."

Patrick tapped a finger against his chin and pretended to think about it. "I don't know. I think you might move too much and hurt yourself." It was something he was concerned about, but if he was careful, they should be okay.

Kieren pulled on the hand he was holding until Patrick had no choice but to move to the bed—or kneel on the floor. The bed dipped as it took his weight, and he made sure not to let Kieren roll and hurt himself.

"Is there something you want?" Patrick whispered against Kieren's lips.

"I want to feel you. It's been too long."

Patrick kissed him, tasting, licking, nipping at his mouth until they were both panting. He moved back, climbing off the bed, and undressed slowly. He wasn't confident enough to give a show, but he could take his time and tease a bit. When he was down to his briefs, he climbed on the bed from Kieren's feet, skimming his hands up his lover's legs, around his hips, over his abs, bypassing the main area he knew Kieren wanted him to focus on. He braced a hand on either side of Kieren's head, trying not to nudge him, then stared into his eyes.

"This will only work if you do as I say." He brought out his Dom voice, hoping it would make Kieren listen more.

"Okay, Sir."

He wasn't sure he believed the quick acquiescence, but he'd soon find out. "You need to stay still and let me do my job. That means no thrusting, no reaching, no touching. Completely still because I don't want to exacerbate your injury. If you move, I will stop." Even if it killed him.

"Yes, Sir."

Patrick narrowed his eyes. "Remember, you move, I stop."

He nibbled at the slight scruff that was coming through on his jaw, noticing a small scar around the left side of his chin. Mentally noting to ask Kieren about it later, he continued his journey down his neck as far as he could with the sling being in the way, then refocused on his stomach. Not having access to his entire upper body was annoying, but he could manage with what he had to play with.

He dipped his tongue into Kieren's belly button, smoothing his hands around his sides and bringing goosebumps to the surface. A harsh breath fell from Kieren's lips, and Patrick peered up at him. His full lower lip was red and swollen as if he'd been biting it. Hiding his smile by pressing a kiss to Kieren's stomach, Patrick continued his journey. He ran his fingers around Kieren's waistband, dipping his fingertips into the fabric at his side and stretching it out as they joined at Kieren's happy trail.

Patrick would never tire of seeing Kieren in all his naked glory. As his cock stood to attention as he pulled the underwear free, his mouth watered, wanting nothing more than to have it between his lips.

"Oh, god," Kieren said. "The way you look at me is..." He shook his head and exhaled.

It's a look of love, sweetheart. But Patrick didn't say it aloud. Instead, he said it with his actions. He stripped Kieren's boxers and threw them to the floor, then straddled his legs and leaned over his shaft. The deep purple, straining erection twitched as Patrick blew warm air over it. A pearl of precome beaded at the tip, and Patrick stared into Kieren's eyes, stuck his tongue out and lapped it up. Kieren's face tightened, and Patrick closed his eyes as the taste spread over his tongue.

Once the flavour dissipated, he licked over the shaft, getting it nice and wet before wrapping his lips around the head.

"Jesus!" Kieren gritted out, and his hips jerked.

Patrick knew it was involuntary, but he had to make a point. He pulled off and stared at Kieren with his eyebrows raised. Kieren grimaced and whispered, "Fuck."

When he'd settled down, Patrick returned to his prize, sucking his cock deep into his mouth and swallowing around it. He took his time, not pushing for the big finale any time soon. He wanted Kieren on the edge for as long as he could keep him there without sending him over because he was saving that for when the man was inside him.

Every time Kieren came close and his body tensed, Patrick eased off, bringing him back down again—but not too far. Sweat coated both their skins, and Kieren's hair was plastered to his scalp. He pulled off the last time and reached for the lube in the drawer. He didn't know if there was any in there, but most men had it. He came up triumphant and wiggled the tube at Kieren, whose cheeks darkened further.

"This is just what we need," Patrick said, sitting back on his heels. He squirted some onto his fingers and spread it generously. He arched his back and reached behind him, pressing against his hole. His eyelids drifted closed as he slid his finger inside his channel. He knew Kieren couldn't see what he was doing, but he could guess from his actions and the noises he made.

"It feels good, but you're going to feel much better."

He speared two fingers inside him, stretching himself as

quickly as he could. His hips thrust back as his fingers invaded, helping with the imagery for Kieren's sake. Patrick could've let Kieren stretch him, but it was fun to tease him.

Kieren's hand squeezed Patrick's leg, and though it killed him, Patrick stopped, meeting Kieren's gaze. Kieren swore and moved his hand, and Patrick resumed his movement, moaning at the feel of being full. He needed more, though. Kieren was a three-finger preparation job, and even then, the man would stretch him further when he filled him. The thought had him dropping his head back and exposing his throat. His cock was rock hard, but he'd learnt how to withstand the arousal.

When he was adequately prepared, he slicked Kieren's dick, giving him a few extra strokes to bring him higher again. Then he crawled up as far as he could without touching Kieren's side or arm and reached between them. Holding Kieren's cock straight, he lowered himself, biting his lip at the sting of the entry. He repeatedly lifted and lowered, gaining a small amount each time. Not because he needed to go slow but because he wanted to make this a morning to remember.

Once he was sitting with Kieren's cock as far up his ass as it could get, he stopped. Sweat trickled down his back and chest, and he breathed deeply to tame the arousal. He didn't stop the small rocking motions of his body, though. They weren't enough to make either of them come, but it still felt fucking amazing.

"Please, Sir! I need..."

"Shh. I know what you need. I'll give you everything. Just have patience."

Kieren's head thrashed against the pillow, and Patrick gave him the benefit of the doubt. He wasn't moving any part of his body that would help him climax, and he let him off.

"That's it, sweetheart. Just lie there while I do all the work." Patrick rested his hands behind him on Kieren's knees. "This doesn't hurt your side, does it?"

Kieren swallowed audibly. "No, Sir."

At that, Patrick circled his hips slowly, pushing against Kieren's groin at the top of the movement and pulling back slightly at the bottom. It was a little tricky because of the positioning of his hands—he would usually use the chest as a place to brace himself—but he managed.

With every circular movement, he could feel the tingle travel down his spine, along all his nerve endings and into his groin, pooling, waiting.

"Colour?" he asked when Kieren hissed.

"Green, Sir."

He was glad because his circles were becoming erratic. He added a harsher twist with his hips and groaned at the spark of electricity. He studied Kieren, noting the tension in his face and the grip he had on the covers.

"I want you to come for me, Kieren. Come inside me. Make me yours."

Kieren bared his teeth and jerked as he emptied into him. The sight of him doing exactly what Patrick had asked without question sent Patrick over the edge, and his release coated both their stomachs. He kept circling, though, until there was nothing left for either of them to give, and Kieren's release began escaping from Patrick's hole.

"Holy crap," Kieren panted. "I never knew slow could be such a killer."

Patrick chuckled and wiped a hand over his forehead. "Yes. Slow and steady wins the race just as many times as fast and furious."

"I'm sure there are movie references within that, but I can't figure them out right now," Kieren said, his eyes closed. "You've killed me."

Patrick eased off Kieren's cock and snuggled on his good side. "But in such a good way."

"Hell, yes."

19

———

KIEREN

Kieren made his way through the hallways of Windsor Castle towards where the security meeting was taking place. Patrick was visiting with Freddie and Douglas while their guards were in the meeting. Kieren, uncomfortable with sitting around and chatting, had decided to see what his colleagues were discussing. He'd been meeting and talking with Timothy every day for the past few days, and although he hated the idea of Patrick being away from him, it was easier to manage, especially in places he felt were safe, like there.

He opened the door to the room and found himself on the wrong end of several guns.

"Jesus F Christ, Kieren!" Brett said, re-holstering his gun, as did the others. "You know better than that."

He did. "Sorry. I wasn't thinking."

"Damn right you weren't." Brett huffed. "Get your ass in here and shut the door behind you."

He did as he was told, sitting beside Nina with a small nod in her direction.

"As I was saying." Brett glared at Kieren. "They have released

Charles. The police couldn't hold him any longer because they had no evidence that he had anything to do with it other than what Christian said he'd told him. He hasn't been forthcoming about anything, and Commissioner Thomas was unable to get anything else out of him. Not for lack of trying, though."

"Is he a threat?" Locke asked. She was one of Freddie's bodyguards.

"Charles? I'd consider him one. Not only because of who he's associated with but because I'm sure he sees this as a mark against our royals." Kieren smiled at the reference to "our" royals. "Keep a vigilant eye out as always, and make sure you let me know if you see anything at all that might be worth noting. Even the smallest thing."

"What about the ongoing threat from them?" Isaac, George's guard, asked.

Brett sighed. "Still the same. We're going on the assumption that they haven't changed their plans, and their next target is the Christmas event, but there's no guarantee. As with anything. If the auction incident was part of their plan and not something Charles did off his own back, then they could've changed things."

Kieren hated they had no idea what they were heading into. But that was part of their job, wasn't it? Dealing with impromptu events and incidents, thinking on their feet.

"In other words, we have no idea where a threat can come from?" Eric, Douglas's guard, said.

Brett raised his eyebrows. "Do we ever really know?" Good point. "Anyway, let's get through this, and our royals can get on with their day."

He stayed quiet throughout the meeting, not having much to add to the conversation, and when everyone stood to leave, he remained seated. Nina glanced at him and paused.

"I'll wait outside," she said.

"Please."

It was strange having a guard of his own, but he knew he was a target now. There had been a lot about Patrick and him in the news—both in the papers and online—and although their relationship had not been confirmed by internal sources yet, they still needed to be careful, which was why he'd not baulked when Brett and Patrick had insisted he had Nina with him at all times.

When everyone had left, he approached Brett. "What aren't you telling them?"

Brett blew out a breath and dropped into a chair, Kieren sitting beside him. The man appeared worn out, but if he was working half as hard as Kieren expected him to be, he would be tired. How he managed to oversee the entire security team as well as guard Christian was beyond him.

"I've received some information from Neil. He says Gia's found an anomaly in the code."

"An anomaly? In what way?"

"I'm not a computer expert, so I'm paraphrasing, but from what I could gather, at first glance, everything is as they figured it out to be. Gia, however, dug a little deeper—for what reason, I don't know—and she found some of the symbols had extra details that weren't picked up on the initial go rounds."

"Extra details? What does that have to do with anything?"

"She believes it's an encoded message within an encoded message. She's currently working her ass off to figure it out."

"Like an envelope within an envelope?"

Brett nodded. "It could just be an error, but Gia's sure she's on to something. It's just a waiting game." Kieren tapped his fingertips on his thumb. "What's up?" Brett asked.

Kieren glanced at him with a slight shake of his head. "I feel useless. I don't know if I can do this for however many weeks or months it'll take me to get back to normal."

"Do you want to get back to normal?"

Kieren scoffed. "Of course I do."

Brett rested a hand on his shoulder. "Do you really?"

Kieren met his gaze. A multitude of emotions flickered over his boss's face, but the most prevalent was understanding. He averted his gaze, rubbing at a spot on his jeans.

"I'm not being an ass, Kieren. When you came into this job, I was over the moon because you're a damn good guard, and I would hate to see you go." He licked his lips. "But...and don't hit me here...you don't need to do this job as penance for your family. Saving other people won't assuage your guilt of not being there for them. All it does is put you in danger instead."

"I have nothing else to give," he whispered.

"I think there's a certain prince who would object to that." Brett grinned. "Now, get your ass gone, and I can get to Christian. I'm sure he's already waiting."

They exited the room together and found Nina and Felix in conversation. Kieren hid his smile when Felix lit up at the sight of Brett. He'd always known there was a connection between the two men, but they were only professional while at work. How they did that when they worked side by side with Christian and Oscar as their detail, he'd never know. It was bad enough keeping his own feelings out of the picture when Patrick was around him, and that didn't turn out well. The media was having a field day about "the bodyguard and the prince" in their articles. He supposed it did sound like something out of a romance novel.

"Do you mind me guarding you?" Nina asked as they wandered back towards where Patrick was.

"I don't mind, but it's weird. I'm not used to being on this side of it." He glanced at her. "How are you finding it? You've only been with us for a couple of weeks."

"It's been a trial by fire. Put it that way." She rolled her shoulders.

He chuckled. "Yeah, I hadn't planned for this to happen a week after you arrived, but I'm glad you're here."

"It's a bit nerve-wracking protecting a bodyguard with many years more experience than me," she admitted.

"It doesn't matter how many years under your belt you have, as long as you trust your instincts, listen to those around you and do the best job that you can. If you stick with those, no one can complain about what happens, regardless of the outcome."

"Thanks."

"Besides, I'm not as important as the royals, so really, you're being eased into it."

"Kieren Young! Get your backside following me right this minute!"

Kieren flinched at the strict, no-nonsense tone of the king. Even Nina's eyes widened. "Yes, Your Majesty."

He followed in King Andrew's footsteps, Nina a few steps behind, probably trying to stay out of sight. They entered the king's rooms, and Nina stayed outside while Kieren stood as straight as he could without hurting himself.

Andrew whirled around and put his hands on his hips. He opened his mouth, then closed it again. "Have a seat, Kieren."

Kieren did, sighing as it took the pressure off his injury. Andrew paced in front of him, and Kieren could honestly say he'd never seen the king as agitated as he was right then. He wanted to ask if he was okay, but he didn't want to make him angrier. Because that's what was wafting off him. But anger at what? Kieren didn't think he'd done anything wrong. Was it because of the media attention? Maybe he didn't want Patrick and Kieren together.

"I can see the thoughts tumbling through your brain, Kieren. Relax. I have no issue with your relationship with Patrick. In fact, I wholly agree and accept it."

Kieren cleared his throat. "Then, could I ask what the problem is?" he said hesitantly.

Andrew paused in front of him. "My problem is what you told your bodyguard."

Kieren frowned, trying to understand what he'd said to Nina that would cause such upheaval. Andrew huffed and sat down, crossing his legs.

"You told her you weren't as important as the royals."

Kieren still didn't get it. "I'm not."

"My dear boy, you are just as important as us. If not more."

"That's not—"

Andrew interrupted, his voice lower but no less significant. "What do you think happened when Louisa died?" The man didn't meet Kieren's gaze.

Kieren didn't know how to answer that because he wasn't entirely sure what the king was asking.

"My life was destroyed. That's what happened." He stared into the distance. "Louisa was the air I breathed, my reason for waking up every morning, the reason I fought so hard for everything we believed in. She was my life, my soul, my everything. Don't get me wrong. I love my kids with everything I am, but when you meet the other half of you," he faced Kieren again, "they become your world."

The pain in his voice sank deep inside Kieren, and if he had been sure he would welcome it, he would've wrapped his arms around the man.

"When she died, I lost my tether. I lost those reasons to live every day. It was only the thought that she would want me to continue, to be there for our children, to see our plans through that I was able to continue breathing each day." He coughed. "Being royal is a pain in the ass. But having someone beside you, supporting you, makes it bearable, worthwhile." He leaned forward in his chair. "*That* is why you are important."

Kieren didn't know what to say. The lump in his throat stopped him from being able to do anything but breathe through the tears that wanted to fall.

"I had been worried about Patrick. He and Henry are the most emotional of us all, but Henry found his tether in Robert.

Patrick was floundering. I doubt you missed that." Kieren nodded once. "Victoria had come to me with her concerns, but we weren't sure how to help. Until we noticed the change in your relationship. At the time, I don't think even you or he were aware of it, but it gave us hope. And now, you are Patrick's tether. I'm not saying that to make you change your mind if you plan to leave, although I hope you would reconsider, but to make you understand how important you are. We, as royals, need someone—or several someones—to love us for who we are and what we have to do. The weight of royalty is not light, even for those who are further down the line of succession." Andrew sighed. "I feel like I'm pushing you into something you might not want."

"No! I do. Want it, I mean. Patrick is…my everything," Kieren said, echoing Andrew's words about his late wife. "I hadn't expected it to happen, but I'm glad it did. We need each other. He's all I have, and I don't want to let him go unless I have to."

He hadn't realised how true all that was until he'd spoken the words. He'd obviously got over the hurdle of being cursed. If he was, it was too late to turn back because he couldn't live without Patrick now.

Andrew smiled and stood. Kieren copied, and the king embraced him carefully. "Thank you for saving his life."

"I couldn't do anything else," he murmured.

"Please remember what I said, but don't use it as an excuse."

Kieren tilted his head. "What do you mean?"

"The weight the royals have on their shoulders is as heavy as the weight on our tethers' shoulders. It's not easy, but it's worth every pound—or so I was told." Kieren nodded. "Go on. Find your man. I'm sure he's worried about what's taking you this long."

Kieren headed for the door, then turned back, seeing the king staring out of the window. "Your Majesty?" Andrew peered over his shoulder at him. "I know you have plenty of people around you, but if you need to talk…I know what you've been through. My family…" He swallowed.

"Thank you, Kieren. I appreciate it more than you know."

Kieren smiled and exited, closing the door and leaning back against it, breathing deeply for several breaths before aiming for Patrick's location. Nina fell into step beside him. She didn't ask what the king wanted, and Kieren was glad because it wasn't something he was willing to talk about. King Andrew's pain would stay between them.

He knocked on Prince Frederick's door and waited for the call to enter. When he saw Patrick, he couldn't help but smile. The man stood and raced toward him, slowing before sliding his arms carefully around his waist and resting his head on Kieren's good shoulder.

"I missed you," Patrick said.

Kieren pressed a kiss to his head. "Missed you, too."

"You're just in time to settle a debate," Douglas called, and Kieren glanced over at them when Patrick groaned.

"A debate about what?" he said and wandered towards them, his arm around Patrick's shoulder.

"Bondage," Douglas announced.

"Douglas!" Patrick said, dropping onto the sofa opposite Douglas, Freddie and Damon.

"What? I want his opinion. We're tied because there are four of us. We need a deciding vote."

Kieren didn't know if he could help with that because he had limited—for now—but he was willing to try. "What's the question?"

"Is sex better when you're tied up?" Douglas said with a grin.

Kieren pursed his lips and thought about his answer. Patrick hadn't tied him up yet, but he'd not allowed him to move the previous day, which was similar. The sex itself was just as good as it had been when they had been together the previous time.

"That's an impossible question to answer," he replied. "It's like asking a parent who their favourite child is. There's no true winner because each one has different good and bad things about it. In this case, being tied up would be a different experience to not being tied up, but when you're with someone who means something to you, it is amazing no matter what."

"See!" Damon waved his hand. "That's what I said!"

"That's such a cop-out!" Douglas said.

Kieren raised his eyebrows. "Are you telling me you would say your experiences with Mav are better or worse, depending on something you're doing?" Douglas snapped his mouth shut, eyes widening. "That's what I thought."

Patrick laughed, kissing Kieren's jaw. "Well played. What took you, anyway?"

"I was speaking with a couple of people." He focused on Freddie. "Have you heard what Gia's possibly found?"

Freddie nodded. "We haven't really much to go on until she looks into it more, but it sounds promising."

"Is the plan still that there are no more large events until Christmas?" he asked.

"That's the plan. Naturally, we have smaller events, but those should be easier to guard. At least, I hope they are." Freddie sighed.

"Usually, yes."

"Do you think they will strike again?" Patrick asked. "Soon, I mean?"

Kieren met Freddie's gaze and saw his minute nod. He sighed. "I think they will, yes. They'll want to catch us while we're supposedly flailing. My best guess would be at whatever event is next."

"Which is me," Douglas said. "I'm at an opening ceremony for a new youth centre next Friday."

"I'll make sure we look into it," Kieren promised.

"Well, let's not think of my potential demise. Let's gather everyone together and visit the club!" Douglas said, standing and flinging his arms wide.

Patrick tensed at Douglas's words, and Kieren kissed his head. "We'll be there for him. I promise. Nothing will happen to him."

Patrick nodded into his neck, and Kieren hated he couldn't do anything more to comfort him. They would not lose anyone else in this fight. If it was the last thing he did, he would make sure they eradicated the evil in this family. No more living in fear. If he had to take the fight to them, he would, but he didn't think he'd need to. He believed Gia had found something that would help them. They just needed to be patient.

In the meantime, they would carry on as if nothing was amiss. Because he refused to let anyone suffer like the king was. Like Kieren had been before he allowed himself to believe in him and Patrick.

In the meantime, they would live and love.

20

DOUGLAS

Despite Douglas's bravado, the moment Mav closed the door behind them in his suite, he sank onto the sofa and dropped his head into his hands. Mav's arms came around him and held him. His body shuddered and trembled as he tried to regain control over it.

"We'll fight them every step of the way," Mav mumbled.

Douglas lifted his head and heaved a sigh. "We will. It's just…" He snorted, but not in humour. "I feel like a complete shit because although it was happening to the people around me, like Christian being held, Mother being…killed, Henry having all the trouble, it was never *me*. I knew what was going on, but it never happened to me, and until now, when I know there's a chance I won't survive, I didn't fully understand. Not truly. Yes, I was arrested, but that was benign compared to what everyone else has been through."

"I don't think the others would think it was benign. Being arrested for something you didn't do."

"You know what I mean."

Mav nodded. "I do. And yes, I understand where you're coming from. But the fact remains that you're all suffering from their actions. No one is free from the repercussions of this. I think, deep inside, you did understand what it was like, but you didn't want to acknowledge it. By acknowledging it, it's real," he said, and Douglas could tell by the tone of his voice that he was tempering his tone to soften it.

Douglas slumped back and gazed at Mav. "When did you get so wise?"

Mav gave a small smile. "Always have been."

Douglas slid his arm around Mav's shoulders and dragged him down with him as he laid on his back and stretched his legs along the length of the sofa. It wasn't the most comfortable, but it was better than his older brother's. Once they were comfortable, with Mav lying on top of him, their legs entwined, Douglas let his body relax.

He pressed his lips to Mav's head and inhaled as much as he could before letting it flow out again. "I feel like we're stronger than ever, but we're starting to come apart at the seams, too," he whispered.

Mav lifted his head, eyes wide. "What? Us?" He waved his hand between them.

Douglas shook his head. "No! The...what are we on now? Tantalising Twelve?"

Mav blew out his breath and lowered his head to Douglas's chest again. "I was worried there for a moment." He fell silent, then said, "I know what you mean."

"Aunt Charlotte is going to pick up the pace because we're all choosing men as our partners. It's going to piss her off even more. God help us all when Freddie gets his head out of his ass and admits he's in love with Damon."

Mav chuckled, the sound vibrating through their chests. "I don't know if he ever will. He's got a lot more pressure on him being the heir. He might forgo love for what he thinks is the best choice for the crown."

Douglas considered that. "I don't know. He might not *have* a choice."

"What do you mean?" Mav rested his chin on Douglas's chest, staring at him with a slight frown.

"I know Damon almost as well as my brother. If he believes he's in the way of Freddie's happiness, he'll leave. And I don't mean for the weekend. If that happens, Freddie will go after him. I guarantee it."

"Do you think it will come to that?"

Douglas shrugged. "I really don't know, but you can see the tension between them already, especially with everything Damon has been doing. Damon's safety has always been Freddie's concern, even if he didn't show it before."

Mav lay his head down again. "Hopefully, they'll figure it out so they're both happy, however that has to be." He sighed. "As for you, we need a game plan. You can pretend with them, that's fine, but we still need to figure out the best way to approach this event. Increased security is a must, and you *will* listen to them. No being a hero."

"Yes, boss."

Mav slapped his side, and Douglas laughed. Despite the gravity of the situation, they needed to keep themselves upbeat. It was okay to fall apart behind closed doors, but to the general public, they needed to be united and free from tension. Once he'd finished wallowing—this release of anxiety—he would be back to his normal self so he could help everyone else. A united front was a must, and he knew he and his family would do just that.

21

PATRICK

Despite Patrick's wrist not being better, he needed to purge the music from his body. He sat in front of the piano, hoping it would be less strain on his wrist, and held his fingers over the keys. The moment they touched the cold plastic, his entire body loosened. Kind of like when it did when he was with Kieren. But his boyfriend was meeting with Timothy, and Patrick had nothing else to do.

He closed his eyes and ran through some scales, warming his fingers from having not played in so long. His wrist twinged, but not enough to encourage him to stop. The scales turned into a tune, and he closed his eyes and let his fingers do the talking for him. His head and body moved in concert with the music, and Patrick smiled at the light, wistful sound.

When his wrist started aching too much, he wound down and finished, breathing deeply as his shoulders lowered. A clap made him jump, but he grinned at his father and stood to greet him.

"I wasn't sure if I should enter, but the music pulled me in. It was beautiful, Patrick."

"Thanks." He hugged him. "What are you doing here?" he asked when he pulled back.

"A meeting was cancelled, and I took the opportunity to come home early. I have far too much work to do, but today, I can't be bothered."

Patrick laughed. "You're playing hooky, as they say?"

"I am." They exited the music room. "How's your wrist?"

Patrick opened and closed his hand, turning it over and back again. "It aches now that I've been playing, but it's not bad."

"Do you miss the training?" At Patrick's raised eyebrows, his father clarified, "The training with Kieren."

Patrick scrunched his face. "Would it be awful if I said not even a little?"

His father chuckled. "No. Although I don't know if Kieren would think that."

"We're both in the same boat at the minute, although he's eager to get back to it. His physiotherapist has told him he has to be patient. It didn't go down well."

"I can imagine. The man is constantly on the move. Being immobile must be bothersome for him."

"It truly is. What do you have planned for this afternoon now?"

His father sighed. "To be honest, I have no idea. I'm going to ask your mother what she would like to do."

They gazed at each other and, in unison, said, "Sit in the garden." They laughed.

"I think it might be a little cold for that, but maybe the sunroom would be a suitable compromise." His father patted his shoulder. "Have a good afternoon, son."

"You, too, Father. Say hello to Mother for me. I'm not sure if we'll be here for dinner or not."

Patrick wandered towards Kieren's room, pausing to knock on the door. As Timothy was there, he wouldn't just walk in like Kieren had told him he could.

"Come in!"

Patrick entered and smiled at the two men. "Am I too early?"

Timothy waved his hand. "No, not at all. We've finished."

Patrick dropped to the seat beside Kieren, who looked worn out, and clasped his hand. "Are you okay?"

Kieren nodded, and Timothy said, "It's been a heavy session." The man stood. "Remember what I said, Kieren. Day or night."

"Thank you," Kieren murmured.

Timothy let himself out, but Patrick focused on Kieren. "Are you sure you're okay?"

Kieren laid his head on Patrick's shoulder, and Patrick wrapped his arm around him as best he could. Steady breathing puffed against his neck, and he thought Kieren might have fallen asleep as quickly as that, but he spoke softly into the silence.

"We talked about Mum and Dad today." He blew out a long breath. "They were such good people. Your parents remind me a lot of them."

"Is that a good thing?" Patrick worried it was too close to home for him.

"It is. Mum would've loved you and your family. Dad would've pretended indifference, but he would've, too. As for Gabby, she would've probably tried to hit on one of your cousins." He chuckled. "Probably would've managed it, too."

It had been the most he'd spoken about his family, other than to explain what happened to them.

"What did they do? For jobs, I mean?"

"Mum was a nurse. She hated the long hours and the politics of it all, but she loved caring for people. Dad was a pilot for a company in London. He was on twenty-four-seven retainer, unless he was on holiday, and got paid extremely well for it. He'd flown the plane hundreds of times. There was no way he'd made an error like they said he did."

"Was it his plane?"

Kieren shook his head. "The company's plane. They had several, and they'd permitted Dad to use it for their holiday."

Patrick said nothing, but the thoughts of what had happened to Freddie flew through his mind. Could there have been something wrong with the plane, and the company hadn't wanted to admit it? They could've easily paid off people to say it was pilot error to ensure they weren't held accountable for the crash. Unfortunately, there wasn't much he could do to help find out the truth. Although maybe he could speak to Christian. His cousin's connections might help, or even Freddie's connections, because he was sure Freddie had more people up his sleeve than even Uncle Andrew knew about.

"Let's get you to bed. I think we could both do with a nap," Patrick said.

Kieren lifted his head, his mouth curved. "A nap?"

Patrick pursed his lips. "Yes, a nap. No hanky panky."

Kieren burst out laughing. "Hanky panky? Where did you get that from?"

"I can honestly say I have no idea." Patrick frowned. He couldn't remember where he'd heard it. "Probably a film or something."

"If I sleep now, I might not sleep later," Kieren said.

"Then I'll wear you out enough later, and you can." Patrick pecked his lips. "Come on." He stood, helping Kieren to his feet, and they both staggered to the bedroom. Neither got undressed nor under the covers. Kieren lay on his back, and Patrick snuggled into his uninjured side, and they slept.

The days merged, and Patrick grew more concerned about Douglas's appearance as time went on. The security team had been through every contingency, but something still didn't feel right. He tried talking Douglas out of it or postponing it, but his cousin wouldn't hear anything of the sort.

When the day dawned, they made their way to Windsor so Kieren could attend the security briefing. Patrick, however, went to find Freddie and found most of their group waiting for him.

"What took you?" George asked. "I was about to call it and eat your muffin."

"Nice try," Patrick said, grabbing the last chocolate muffin from the table. "I bet you've already had two if not three."

George winked. "How is it my fault if my amazing man works at a cafe that sells such delicious baked goods?"

"It's your fault because you hardly ever share!" Henry said.

"I do!"

"Well, Christian has someone in the same situation, and he gives us more than you do," Henry argued.

Christian held up his hands. "Leave me out of—" His phone rang, and he moved closer to the window to answer it.

"You have kitchen staff to make you stuff!" George said.

"How did this get into an argument about who can get more muffins?" Douglas murmured.

Patrick opened his mouth, but he paused, his eyes on Freddie, who moved over to Christian, who had sat in a chair by the window. One by one, the others went quiet until all they could hear was the occasional murmur from Christian. When he hung up, he scrubbed a hand over his face and through his hair. Freddie crouched in front of him.

"What did he say?"

Christian blew out a breath, then grabbed Freddie's hand and stared at each of them. "We have their contingency plan."

"What?" Douglas said, standing.

"The code Gia was trying to figure out? She did it. Mother had added another code within the code I'd made. It details what they would try if we found out their first plan. She said they would step up their game, and their final 'prize' would be to rid the royal family of its current line, and she could take the throne." Christian stood. "Patrick being shot was on there." He glanced at Patrick, then flicked his gaze to Douglas. "As is an assassination attempt on you. Today."

"Then he has to postpone," Patrick said, stepping forward.

"I'm not," Douglas said.

"Douglas—" Mav started, grabbing onto his arm.

"No. Because if I do, they've won. If we go into hiding, they've won. We need to keep up appearances." He stared at Mav. "You know this. If we disappear from view, they will do everything they can to put themselves in the spotlight. And. They. Win."

Mav sniffed and stared at the floor. Douglas cupped his face. "I'll be fine. The security team will be given the information and will figure it all out. I'll be safe." Mav closed his eyes, and a tear trickled down his cheek. "I won't leave you," Douglas whispered. "I couldn't stand it."

Mav wrapped his arms around him, and Douglas held him. Patrick swallowed hard against the emotion threatening to erupt. What Douglas said was right, but it didn't make it easier to acknowledge.

Patrick noticed Freddie and Damon at the window. Freddie had his arms crossed and stared out of the window, while Damon had his hand on the back of Freddie's neck and was speaking to him, their heads close. Freddie closed his eyes and leaned into Damon, their heads touching, and Patrick looked away, not wanting to intrude. He was more and more convinced that Oscar was correct in his assumption that there was something between them.

"What else was in the message?" George asked.

"There were details of one location for each of us."

"Each of us?" Freddie said, turning to them. "Who? List them."

Christian raised his eyebrow. "Hold on." He dialled his

phone. "Neil, who exactly was on the list of targets?" He paused. "Patrick, Douglas, Henry, George, Mary, Freddie, Victoria, Andrew." He raised his eyes to Freddie. "Thanks." He ended the call.

"Everyone in the line before Charlotte," Freddie stated.

Patrick's heart pounded. "Over how long?"

Christian stared at him, tears in his eyes. "Uncle Andrew on 10 March 2023."

"The anniversary celebration," Damon said.

Silence descended. Everyone was seemingly lost in their thoughts. Patrick's were bouncing around his head, but only one thing was clear.

"We have to take these fuckers down."

His lack of filter, when he usually cursed the least of all of them, startled a chuckle out of Freddie. Then everyone followed suit. It was maniacal laughter, to begin with, then gentled until it dropped off.

Freddie moved to them, almost putting them in a circle. "They're not going to win. We have the upper hand now. Let's take the fight to them."

"How?" Douglas asked.

Freddie grinned. "By diverting the targets to their own flesh and blood, their own assets." He paused. "What better way to get our point across than making their co-conspirators pay for who they get into bed with? As for Charles? I'll make sure there's something to take him down. Whoever else is actively involved gets the same treatment. But we'll do it the proper way. No blood. No death tolls. Just a lengthy stay in prison."

"But we've tried this already, and we couldn't find anything to pin them down," Christian said.

"We were focusing on them. We need to focus on who is *working* for them. There's only so much one person can take before they give away their secrets."

Damon grinned. "We've already started that."

Freddie glanced at him. "What?"

"You know those visits you came on?" Freddie nodded. "Information gathering. Companies who we thought could be in Charlotte's or John's pockets or had some link to them. I've been checking them out under the guise of completing audits."

"Wouldn't that put a red arrow above our plan?" Douglas asked.

Damon shook his head. "I've been doing it for *all* companies, not just theirs. Any that are related to the crown in any way gets audited."

"You told me…" Freddie clenched his jaw and looked away.

Damon winced. "I know."

Douglas filled the silence. "I think we need to speak with Father and the security team. We can't just go in, guns blazing. We need them to help."

"I agree," Freddie said. "No time like the present." He headed for the door, and everyone followed.

The journey to Uncle Andrew's suite was fast-paced, and Patrick's heart hammered as he thought about what could happen. There were too many things that could go wrong with what they had planned—mainly one or more of them being killed in the process.

"Randall, is Father in?"

Randall stood, rounding the table and bowing his head. "Your Highnesses. Yes, he is, but he's on the phone at the moment. Is it urgent?"

"Rather than disturb him, could you ask him to join us with the security team when he's finished, please?"

"Of course. He shouldn't be long."

"Thank you."

They retraced their steps, going past Freddie's suite to the security team's allocated room. Freddie knocked and waited. The door opened partially, then further as a guard saw them.

"Your Highnesses," he said.

Freddie entered and shook hands with Brett, who'd have moved over to greet them.

"Your Highnesses. How can I help?"

"Have you received the information from Neil?" Christian asked.

Brett nodded. "Just have. We're in the process of coming up with strategies to keep you all safe."

"Did you happen to see who was on the list?"

Brett's jaw tightened. "I did."

"We have a plan, but we need some guidance," Freddie said.

No expression passed across Brett's face as Freddie's words sunk in. "Understood. Locke, Sam, Eric, could you get some additional chairs, please? I have a feeling this will be a long meeting today."

"Father will be along shortly, too."

"Should we move this somewhere else?" Brett asked.

"If you're okay with us being here, we're okay being here," Christian said, sitting on a chair someone had provided for him.

Patrick glanced around to locate Kieren and broke away from the group to go to him. "Hey," he said.

Kieren pulled him down on the chair that had appeared next to him and kissed him softly. "Hi. What's all this about?"

"We got fed up with being targets." Patrick shrugged.

Kieren raised his eyebrows but didn't reply. Instead, he wrapped his arm around Patrick's shoulders and pressed his lips to his temple. They went through the plans for the event later that day, and what they said seemed to be well thought out. Patrick's muscles eased for the first time that day, and the stress headache made itself known. He rubbed at his forehead, hoping to dispel the pain, but it didn't help.

"Are you okay?" Kieren whispered.

"Headache." Patrick smiled. "I'll be fine."

Kieren put his hand in the air, and Brett glanced at him. Kieren tapped a finger twice on his head and put his index finger and thumb to his mouth once. Patrick frowned. What was he doing? Without breaking his conversation, Brett picked up something from his desk and threw it to Kieren, who caught it with nothing more than a small wince. The man grinned and held out a packet of paracetamol.

Patrick blinked and shook his head. "I won't even ask."

Kieren chuckled. "We get them a lot with everything we have to go through. Brett got fed up with us complaining, and now he makes sure he has some on hand all the time."

Patrick took some with the water Kieren provided, and then Kieren threw the packet back to Brett with a whistle. It was amazing to see them working together on a regular day rather than when they were working. It was a similar situation to the barbecue they'd had the previous month.

The door opened, and Andrew entered. "I hear I have an impromptu meeting to attend," he said with a smile.

Freddie stood. "Thank you, Father. We have something we want to put to everyone."

Andrew nodded and took the seat Brett provided. "Go ahead."

By the time Freddie had outlined the basic idea, several of the guards were nodding their heads.

"It needs work. No offence," Brett said with a wince. "It's possible to get this working in our favour, though."

They spent the next three hours going through plans, finding holes in them, and working out contingencies until they had to stop because it was time for Douglas to get ready for his opening ceremony. Patrick's throat closed at the thought of him being in danger, but he believed in the security team. He just hoped the bad guys weren't too persistent. The worst thing about it all was that they had no clue how the attack would happen. It could be a shooter, a bomb, poison...anything. And only the people who were necessary for the event were allowed to attend. Andrew had put his foot down about that. As much as he didn't want any of them in danger, he refused to put more than necessary in the line of fire.

While Douglas and Mav went to get ready, the rest of them went their separate ways. Before Freddie left them, Patrick pulled him aside.

"Don't be too hard on him, Freddie."

His cousin sighed. "I feel like he's done nothing but lied to me for months. How did we get to this?"

"Talk to him. Properly. Sit down, leave your anger and frustration at the door, and talk. Really talk. From my perspective, you have a lot to say to each other. Why not sort it out now rather than letting it linger and fester?"

Freddie chuckled. "When did you get pushy? I thought that was my job."

Patrick slid his forefinger beneath Freddie's chin and lifted slightly. "You're taking a holiday." He winked.

"Yes, sir," Freddie said sarcastically.

Patrick sobered. "I'm serious, though. This will only get better if you talk about it. We need everyone at their best if this is going to work."

Freddie closed his eyes. "I know."

"Good luck." He hugged him and strode for Kieren. "Let's go home."

"Yes, sir."

2 2

KIEREN

*W*atching Patrick take control of a situation was hot as fuck. By the time they reached home, Kieren's libido was making itself known, and he all but dragged Patrick to his room. Patrick's room, that was.

When they were behind closed doors, Kieren pushed him against the door, getting right up close. "I want you to tie me up."

He'd had a long discussion with Timothy about it because Kieren hadn't believed he could give this to Patrick because of his inability to let go of his need to protect him, but he wanted to try. Timothy had advised that he try, which he planned to, and explain everything to Patrick, which he had yet to do. With everything going on, they were both full of tension, and he believed they were both in need of a release, but a different release to climaxing. Kieren wanted to feel the strikes on his ass, grounding him in the here and now, and Patrick needed the freedom impact play gave him.

He knew they had to be careful with Kieren's and Patrick's injuries, but they *needed* this.

"How?"

It took a minute for him to understand what Patrick was asking, and he swallowed. "I need a knot that I could undo myself. I can't do this without having an escape available to me in case I need to protect you."

Patrick nodded. "I know knots. I can do that. What about your side and arm?"

"I can stretch enough to put both arms above my head. I just need to keep myself from squirming too much."

Patrick smirked. "Good luck with that." He bit his lip. "What do you want?"

Kieren lowered his head to Patrick's ear. "I want to feel it, and then I want to feel you."

"Get undressed," Patrick ordered, pushing away from the door, meaning Kieren had to step back.

He continued stepping back until he knew he was in the middle of the room, then lifted his hands to his shirt. He didn't make the unveiling last longer than was necessary, stripping it off as quickly as possible. His trousers went the same way, and he shoved his boxers down at the same time. Patrick stalked towards him, and it took everything in Kieren to stand his ground. He wasn't afraid, but the power exuding off Patrick would've been a heady experience if he hadn't already witnessed it.

"On the bed on your stomach," Patrick said, lifting his hands to his own shirt.

Kieren followed the directions, resting his cheek on a pillow and keeping his arms by his side for the moment. If Patrick wanted them somewhere else, he would ask. Watching Patrick undress was almost as good as him being naked in the first place. Each inch of skin that he exposed was a trial of Kieren's patience. Patrick finally dropped his clothes to the floor on top of Kieren's. Then he wandered over to his chest of drawers and pulled out two ties.

"I'm going to tie you tight enough that you can feel it but

with a strip that you can pull on to free yourself. But," he said, "you must only use it in an emergency. Being frustrated or wanting to touch me is not a good enough excuse."

"Yes, Sir," Kieren said.

"Onto your knees and arms above your head," Patrick ordered, and Kieren complied with hardly a thought.

Patrick knelt by his shoulder, wrapping the tie around one wrist before securing it to the headboard. "Can you reach the strip?" he asked. Kieren peered up at his hand and grabbed the strip of tie hanging down. "Good."

He climbed off the bed, walked all the way around to the other side and climbed back on again, repeating the tying action with his other wrist.

"Can you reach this one?" Patrick asked.

"Yes, Sir."

Patrick climbed off the bed again and headed for his cupboard. He disappeared for a few long seconds, reappearing with a flogger.

"This one is slightly firmer than the previous one I used on you. It should still only leave a sting, which is short-lived, but it will last slightly longer than the previous one. I'm going to run it over your back, and you can feel what it's like."

Kieren hadn't expected the material to be cold, but he assumed it would warm up as they progressed. Patrick slid the falls of the flogger down his back, over his ass and down his legs and then back again. He did this several times, but on his next journey down, he paused at his ass cheeks and rubbed it harder against his skin.

"I'll start off soft and slow, but don't forget your colours. I'll be asking because we're still learning what you like."

"Yes, Sir."

"Ready?"

"Yes, Sir."

Kieren, with his head buried in the pillow as it was, had no indication other than that to know it was coming, and he waited and waited until a sharp smack sounded and a slightly delayed lick of pain spread across his backside. He hissed on instinct, but by the time the pain flared, it was already receding again.

"Colour?"

"Green, Sir."

The pain flared again, slightly sharper this time, and heat bloomed outwards. Kieren panted, wishing he had known about this kind of play many years ago. Then he shook his head, dispelling the thought. He couldn't imagine experiencing this with anyone but Patrick.

"Colour?"

"Green, Sir."

The responding smack was quicker this time, the bite sharper still. Patrick rubbed a hand over his skin, and Kieren felt a slight easing in the sting. As Patrick had described to him before, it was very similar to when he'd smacked his hand against something too hard and left behind a tingling sensation. It was something he didn't mind because afterwards it appeared to warm him, almost as if it heated him from the inside out. He couldn't really understand how it worked or even explain it should anyone ever ask him, but that was the nearest he could describe it.

"Again?"

"Yes, please, Sir."

Patrick smacked him twice in rapid succession, and Kieren gripped the ties holding him bound—not the strips that would release him, but the ones keeping him tethered.

"More, please, Sir."

Another sharp sting went through him, and he released a breath. Another smack, and another. Patrick's hand returned, rubbing against the skin, squeezing his ass cheeks and sending tendrils of pain outwards. It was almost as if the area around where was being struck was waiting to receive similar attention. He knew it wouldn't, though, because Patrick had explained there were certain areas of the body where it was not safe for any kind of impact play. He also mentioned that some people didn't care about the dangers involved, but that was their choice. Patrick refused to do anything to harm him, and Kieren was thankful for that.

"I think that's enough for now," Patrick said. "Let's get some cream on you, and then we can relax."

Kieren shook his head against the pillow. "No, Sir. Please."

"What do you need, sweetheart?"

"I need you. Please. Please, I need you."

"Are you sure?"

"Yes, please, Sir. I want to feel you. I want to feel you and feel the result of the flogging. I want to feel both at the same time."

He knew he was asking a lot because Patrick had told him he rarely got aroused by impact play, but he was hoping it was different with it being him. Patrick had become hard last time, and he had to hope he was then. He was sure Patrick would say something if he couldn't do what Kieren had asked. He heard Patrick moving around but didn't have the energy to lift his head. Instead, he basked in the warmth radiating from his buttocks, grateful for his wonderful prince for showing him what was possible.

He felt the bed dip by his feet, and a hand rested against his lower back.

"Colour?"

"Green, Sir."

Kieren heard a click and then a coolness against his pucker. Patrick massaged his hole, rubbing the lube around repeatedly. When he made no attempt to penetrate him, Kieren pushed back, receiving a sharp tap on his ass.

"Sorry, Sir."

Patrick resumed his massage, and Kieren gritted his teeth while he waited for more. His side was aching a little, but that was more than likely due to his squirming than anything else. Patrick pressed a fingertip inside him, breaching his ring of muscles and making Kieren whimper. That was the start of a long, drawn-out stretching that had Kieren biting his lip constantly against the need to impale himself.

By the time Patrick had stretched him with three fingers, Kieren was babbling, and not even he could understand what he was saying.

"Ready?"

"Yes, Sir. Please, Sir."

He felt Patrick's blunt head at his entrance, and he bore down, wanting him inside as quickly as possible. He could barely feel the sting any longer, except when Patrick squeezed or rubbed a hand over his skin.

Unfortunately, Patrick didn't go quickly. He did short, sharp jabs forward and back, taking his time, dragging it out. Kieren bit off a curse but planned to return the favour one day. When Patrick was finally all the way inside, Kieren sighed, wishing they could stay this way forever.

Patrick gripped Kieren's hips, his fingers wrapping around the sides, his thumbs pressing in where the flogger had laid its strikes. The bite of pain returned, and Kieren gasped.

"Please, Sir."

"Anything you ask is yours," Patrick said.

Then he withdrew and slammed forward, the smack of their bodies together giving his cheeks an extra spark of electricity and adding to the sensation.

"Oh, fuck. Yes, Sir. Please, Sir. More, please."

"I'm not going to last long, love," Patrick said. "How close are you?"

Kieren couldn't answer because he was already reaching his

peak, and he distantly heard Patrick's curse as he fell over the edge before his mind was a clutter of sensation. He didn't black-out, but he didn't remember Patrick loosening the ties or laying him on his side.

Patrick was pottering around, and Kieren muttered, "Come to bed."

"I'll be there in a minute."

Kieren roused himself enough to watch what he was doing. Patrick brought a tray with some energy drinks, hot drinks and fruit. He perched on the side of the bed, placing the tray on the bedside table. Grabbing a drink, he uncapped it, slid a straw inside and held it at Kieren's mouth.

Kieren sucked, grateful for the liquid to wet his mouth. When he finished, he raised an eyebrow, and Patrick rolled his eyes like a teenager, but he drank some of the energy drink.

"Thank you for taking care of me," Patrick said, his gaze directed at the fruit bowl rather than Kieren.

"You deserve it."

Patrick smiled and picked up a tube. "Let's put that cream on now, then we can have something to eat."

When they finished the fruit bowl and both energy drinks and were onto the hot drinks, Kieren was feeling his normal self again, but Patrick was agitated. Kieren reached for his phone and called Brett.

"Hey, how're things going?"

Brett blew out a breath. "Well, disaster averted, thank god."

"What happened?" he asked, locking gazes with Patrick.

"Someone from the crowd threw a dirty bomb onto the steps. Fortunately, they had rubbish aim. Unfortunately, they set fire to the flag on the front of the building. No one was harmed, though."

Kieren smiled and relayed the information to Patrick, who dropped his head back against the headboard and closed his eyes.

"Thanks, Brett. I'll catch you later. Let me know if you need me at all."

"Will do."

"It seems too simple," Patrick said.

Kieren shrugged. "Sometimes, simple works best. If the person had better aim, they would've thrown it right onto him, and not much would've stopped the flames before it did a lot of damage."

Patrick nodded. "True." He took another drink. "What's next, then?"

"We'll get together again soon to figure out the plan for Henry's event. I doubt they'd bring something together quickly enough to surprise us before then. Evil plans take work and time."

Patrick chuckled. "Evil plans, huh?"

"Is there a better word for it?"

Patrick stared at the ceiling. "I just don't understand why."

"Why what?"

"Why is she like this? Why is Uncle Andrew or Uncle William or Mother, for that matter, not like her? Where did it all come from?"

Kieren exhaled. "I can't answer that. I have no idea." He put his drink on the bedside table, wincing at the pull on his ass and his side, then scooted closer, wrapping his arm around Patrick's waist and resting his head on his thigh. Patrick's hand threaded into his hair, and he closed his eyes.

He hadn't meant to fall asleep. He'd only meant to give Patrick some reassurance, but he woke, alone, in a dark room.

"Patrick?"

No answer.

Groggily, he climbed from the bed, his ass barely smarting at all, and drew on some joggers and a T-shirt, along with some shoes, without socks. He left Patrick's room and wandered to the music room, thinking he was probably playing, even though he should be resting his wrist, but he wasn't there either. It was late enough that most of the household staff would be in bed, and he didn't see anyone he could ask.

His heart picked up speed. Where was he? Had something happened to him? Had someone taken him from the building? Kieren shook his head. No way. No one could've taken him from the house without someone seeing.

He broke into a jog and checked his own room, the kitchens, the dining room, then exhaled roughly when he arrived at the sunroom. Patrick was curled up on a sofa with a blanket covering him while his mother watched over him. She caught his eye and smiled, beckoning him over.

"I couldn't sleep and found him in here," she whispered. "We talked for a while before I told him to sleep. I knew you'd come and find him. I kept watch until you did."

Kieren dropped to his knees beside her, leaning against her chair but staring at Patrick. "Sometimes my fear of him not being with me is too hard to handle," he admitted.

Continuing in a soft voice, she said, "I can imagine. I don't know what I would do if anything happened to any of you." Kieren glanced at her, but her gaze was on her son. "What she's planning..." She shook her head. "I don't know who that is. She's not the sister I grew up with. I don't know where she got the lofty ideas from because it sure as hell wasn't us. Father brought us up to be compassionate, understanding, patient. I think the only thing she took from that was patience because she seems to have that in spades."

Kieren frowned. "When did she start to change?"

Victoria huffed. "In her late teens, I think. She became more opinionated, more defiant."

"Had any of your circumstances changed at that point?"

"No. Mother was still with us. Father was on the throne. Oh, Andrew had married Louisa. Nothing else that I can think of."

Something was niggling in the back of his head. "When did she meet Ernest?"

"She was twenty-two and was at university in Edinburgh. She had refused to go to any universities that we went to. She said we would 'cramp her style.' Ernest was one of the assistants there."

"Isn't he older than her?"

Victoria nodded. "Yes, nine years older. Too big of a gap if you ask me, but they seemed to get on well. Ernest was always willing to do Charlotte's bidding, and she was never afraid to tell him to do something. A slight off-balance relationship, in my opinion, but each to their own. I don't have to live with either of them."

"Whose idea was it for them to get married, do you know?"

"I don't know. They came to Father just after Charlotte's twenty-third birthday and said they wanted to get married. Father could see no reason to deny it." Victoria narrowed her eyes at him. "Why do you ask?"

Kieren pursed his lips. "I'm not sure, but something isn't adding up. I can't put my finger on it, though. I understand teenagers can change, but usually, they settle down again once their hormones have balanced out again. For her to continue, there must have been a catalyst. And potentially a continuous one at that." He tapped his fingers on his thumb. "Unless she'd met Ernest earlier than you all know, and he's hiding something, there's something else we're missing."

"Hmm. I'll speak to Andrew and see if we can think of anything. My brain is not like it used to be." She chuckled.

"There is nothing wrong with your brain, my dear," Patrick Senior said, entering the room. "I came to see if you wanted to try to get some sleep now."

Victoria uncurled herself from the chair and removed the blanket covering her legs. "I think I will try." She patted Kieren on the cheek. "Will you be okay here?"

Kieren smiled. "All good. Get some rest."

They left, but Kieren noted the way Patrick's father wrapped his arm around his wife and pressed a kiss to her head. They were still in love, even after all these years. It was something he could only wish for. He loved the thought of spending years to come with Patrick. What could they accomplish in a lifetime?

2 3

PATRICK

It was becoming a weekly thing that Patrick visited with Freddie or Douglas while Kieren dropped in on the security meetings every Monday and Friday. But this visit had a purpose. As he settled himself on the sofa opposite Freddie, his cousin narrowed his eyes.

"What's wrong?" Freddie asked.

"Let the poor man sit down before you start the inquisition." Damon laughed.

Patrick smiled, but he knew it lacked his usual humour. "I need a favour."

"Whatever you need," Freddie said, and that made Patrick's smile more genuine.

"What I'm about to say, you might already know, but if you don't, please keep it to yourself." He inhaled. "Kieren's family was killed in a plane crash seventeen years ago. The report recorded it as pilot failure, but Kieren's father had been a pilot for years. There was no way it could've been his fault, especially when he had his wife and daughter on board." He lowered his gaze to his hands. "Can you get someone to look into it and see if they can find out anything else?"

"Of course. I know someone who can check into it and see if there is anything untoward about it." Freddie pulled out his phone and typed on it before setting it aside.

"I'm assuming because you haven't asked for more details that you knew about it." Patrick raised his eyebrows.

"I did. It wasn't anything essential to his job, but the security team let me know about it so we could limit his travelling options."

"Limit his travelling? Why?"

"We didn't want him to have to deal with planes or helicopters, and as you don't use them, you were the perfect choice for his detail."

Patrick shuddered. "No way am I going on those unless I have no choice. Thank you for thinking of that."

"It's only fair. We put them through enough without having to deal with any extraneous shit."

"True." He eyed Damon, who had stood and pulled on his jacket. "Going somewhere?"

"More audits to do, unfortunately." Damon winked.

"Yeah, you really hate giving them hell, I'm sure."

Damon laughed. "Of course not. I never realised how much fun it was to make someone run around in circles. Although I only do it when it's necessary."

"Safe journey," Freddie said, drifting over to the side table where he kept his coffee pot.

Damon stared at his back and sighed. "Freddie—"

"It's fine. Go."

It didn't sound fine to Patrick, and by the expression on Damon's face, he didn't think so either.

"I'm trying to help," Damon said.

"I know, and you are. It's fine. Honestly." Freddie sent a smile over his shoulder.

Damon sighed again. "I'll be home on Wednesday."

"We'll be here."

Damon left, and Patrick waited a minute before standing and saying, "Oh, I forgot to ask Damon something. I'll be back in a minute."

As he headed for the door, Freddie said, "Patrick, don't. It's —" The rest of what he said was cut off by him closing the door. He'd apologise later.

"Damon!"

The man stopped and waited for Patrick to catch up. "What's up?"

"Why did you never tell him what you were doing? I'm not upset, but I'm curious."

Damon slid his hands into his pockets. "Andrew didn't want me to. He thought it would distract him, and he was right. Every time I go away now, he's upset with me. That can't be good for his concentration."

"It's not, but knowing where you are and what you're doing goes a long way to help him cope. I think he's more worried about what could've happened to you while he didn't know. Now, though, he can prepare himself." He paused and stared at Damon. "I don't think he's upset because of what you're doing. Do you?"

Damon exhaled. "No. He's upset because I lied to him. Again."

"Exactly. Why not try to be open about everything from now on? *Everything.*"

Damon's eyes widened. "I will tell him everything he needs to know."

"That's not quite what I said, but I suppose it'll have to do." He clapped him on the shoulder. "Have a safe journey and keep out of trouble."

Damon quirked his lips. "I'll try my best."

Patrick wandered back to Freddie's room and entered without knocking. Freddie glanced up at him.

"You should've left it alone."

"I didn't say anything that didn't need to be said." Patrick retook his seat.

"He has a right to do what he thinks is best," Freddie said.

"He does, but he also has a duty to keep himself safe." What Patrick didn't say was that this duty was also to keep Freddie from losing someone he cared about. He didn't want to think how losing Damon would affect Freddie.

"How is the studying going?" Freddie changed the subject, and Patrick let him. There was no pushing Freddie when he'd made his mind up.

"It's going well. I've only started on the first unit, but it's interesting. After this, I have to get back and do some coursework."

Freddie chuckled. "I bet you didn't expect to be back at school, did you?"

"Not even a little, but I'm enjoying it."

"I'm glad." He set his tea on the table. "Have you decided how or what you're going to do once you're finished?"

"I want to give lessons to those who can't afford them under normal circumstances. Maybe youth centres or schools with low budgets. We could work towards an end-of-year concert or something similar."

"Sounds good. Have you been researching it, or are these just initial ideas?"

"Initial ideas. I want to get some more of the course under my belt before I investigate more."

"You'll be done before you know it." Freddie smiled. "How's Kieren?"

"He's good. Wishing he could be back to normal, but he's getting there. His physiotherapist has said he's doing well."

"Good news, then."

After spending another hour with his cousin, during which Kieren arrived, they bid goodbye and headed back home, followed by their guards. When they settled into the sofa in

Patrick's suite with their arms around one another—something that was easier to do now Kieren's sling was off—Patrick took a breath and told Kieren about his new plans for the future. The idea delighted Kieren, and they brainstormed a few ways to provide for those children wanting music lessons.

When their ideas ran out, Kieren cleared his throat. "In the light of recent…transparency between us, I have something to tell you, too."

Patrick glanced up at him. "What's that?"

"I draw."

Patrick frowned. "Draw what?"

"Anything. People, Places, Items." He fidgeted. "You," he whispered.

"Me?"

Kieren nodded. "I have…too many to count pictures of you, but I could never get it quite right. There was always something missing."

"Can I see?" Patrick sat upright.

Kieren shrugged a shoulder, something he'd learnt to do to stop aggravating his injury. "If you want."

Patrick dropped a kiss on Kieren's lips. "Will you show me, please?"

Kieren stared at him for a moment before nodding. "I'll fetch them. You start studying while I'm gone."

"Yes, sir!"

While Kieren disappeared, Patrick retrieved his books, having decided he preferred working with physical books rather than online or ebooks. He opened his textbooks to the chapter he was working on and began reading, losing himself in the background of conducting.

After a short time, he blinked and checked his watch, seeing he'd been at it for over an hour and Kieren hadn't returned. He glanced towards the door and was surprised to see the man reclined in a chair, facing him with a pad of paper and a pencil.

"When did you get back?"

Kieren smiled. "About fifteen minutes after I left. You were engrossed in your work, and I didn't want to interrupt."

"You should have. I want to see your work." He stood.

Kieren held up his pad. "I worked on a new one while you were busy."

Patrick climbed onto Kieren's lap, resting his head against his shoulder. "Will you show me?"

Kieren turned the pad towards him, and Patrick gasped. "Oh, my god! That's amazing!" He studied the pencil drawing of him with his head bent low over his book, the tip of the pen in his hand resting against his bottom lip. "It looks realistic."

He traced the contours of the image with the shading done with gradients of grey. "Do you have others?"

Kieren pointed towards the table where a folder sat. Patrick scrambled off his lap to Kieren's laughter and knelt in front of the coffee table. Reverently, he opened the folder and found another image of himself, this time while he was playing the piano.

"When did you do this one? It's not often I play in front of people."

Kieren glanced at it. "You were playing for your parents. I passed the door, and it was ajar. I couldn't help myself."

Patrick smirked at him. "Stalker." He turned the page and found another of him at the piano.

"There are a few of them. As I said, something was always missing. I couldn't get it quite right. I kept trying, though."

Patrick couldn't see anything wrong with what he'd drawn, but Kieren was the expert. After several pages, he found a new image of him with his head back as he laughed. There wasn't much of a background, and he had no idea what reference to give it, but the happiness in his expression was easy to see. Another page held an image of a young woman with long, wavy hair, wearing a long dress. He guessed it was Kieren's sister, which he confirmed seconds later.

"Gabby," he murmured.

"She's beautiful."

"She was."

Another page and an image of a man and a woman. "Your parents?" Kieren nodded, staring at the paper. He could see the joy that Kieren captured. "These are magnificent, Kieren."

Patrick climbed back onto his lap, wrapping his arms around his neck. "Would you be willing to draw a couple of pictures for me?"

"Sure. What were you thinking of?"

"I want a picture of our group." He rolled his eyes. "The Thirsty Thirteen. I think Mother and Father and Uncle Andrew would love to have a copy each for Christmas."

"I can do that. They're not professional at any rate, but I'd be happy to have a go."

Patrick tapped his shoulder. "They *are* professional. I bet you'd be able to sell these."

Kieren shook his head. "No way."

"Yes, way." Kieren huffed in response. "You would, but you don't have to if you don't want to. Is this something you enjoy?"

"It's what I went to university for," Kieren admitted.

"What? I didn't know you'd been to university."

"I didn't finish because…" Kieren swallowed. "Afterwards, I chose security and worked my way through the various aspects of the job until I landed here." He pulled Patrick closer to him. "I wouldn't want to be anywhere else."

"Me either." Patrick closed his eyes and snuggled his head beneath Kieren's chin, resting his hand over his heart.

"Knock, knock!"

Patrick chuckled at Henry's announcement. "Come on in!" he called back, not moving from his spot.

The door opened to admit his brother. "Good afternoon, brothers. How fare thee?"

"Good, thanks," Patrick replied. "Has Robert finally kicked you out of the shop?"

Henry frowned and straightened. "No."

"That's a yes, then."

His brother settled on the sofa opposite, his eyes dropping to the drawings. "My word." He reached for one, hesitating and glancing at them. Patrick lifted his head and asked Kieren without asking him. Kieren nodded at Henry, who picked up the drawing of Kieren's parents. "This is magnificent. Who did them? I'd love to get someone to draw one of these of Robert and me while I'm in puppy form." He picked up another picture.

Patrick said nothing, waiting to see if Kieren wanted to acknowledge the truth, but he didn't disappoint, making Patrick proud of him.

"I did them," Kieren said.

Henry's mouth gaped. "Oh, my god! You're amazing!"

"Told you," Patrick said, poking a finger at him and making Kieren jump and wince. "Shit, sorry!"

Kieren laughed. "It's okay. I should've expected payback."

"Payback for what?"

"Letting you work when you wanted to see them." Kieren nodded towards the drawings.

Patrick chuckled. "Idiot." He climbed off his man's lap and settled beside Henry. "I love this one," he said, reaching for the one of him at the piano. "Kieren says it's incomplete, but I don't see it. When I get my business running, I want this as part of my logo or poster or something."

"I agree. It's unique and eye-catching. People would flock to you just from seeing the happiness and excitement on your face in this."

"My thoughts exactly." Henry glanced at Kieren. "Do you just do pencil drawings, or can you add colour as well?"

Kieren's face reddened. "Mainly pencil, but I can do colour if I need to."

"I bet Robert would love a picture of someone holding a bunch of flowers. I can just see it. A person in pencil, then the bouquet blooming with colour."

Patrick laughed. "Do you think maybe you should ask before you start filling his calendar?"

Henry ducked his head but peeked up. "Sorry. I get a little excited."

"That's why you're a puppy, I reckon," Patrick said, hugging an arm around him. "It's adorable."

Henry pushed him away and asked, "Do you think I could commission you to do one for him?"

"You don't need to pay. I'm happy to do one," Kieren said.

"I am paying. No arguments, either." Henry narrowed his gaze at him.

Kieren sighed, and Patrick snorted. "Good luck with that. I've already asked him to do a drawing for Mother and Father and Uncle Andrew. I thought it would make a nice Christmas gift."

"Damn it! I should've thought of that. I have no clue what to get them."

"You snooze, you lose!"

Henry shoved Patrick, and Patrick shoved Henry.

"Now, now, children. What's all this noise about?"

His mother entered without knocking, and Patrick thought he might need to bring a new rule that everyone knocks from this point on. What would've happened if he and Kieren were in a compromising position? The idea made him lightheaded.

Henry held one of the drawings and asked Kieren if he could show her. Kieren's face flooded again, but he nodded. Patrick climbed back into his lap and held him, knowing this was difficult for him.

"They love them, sweetheart. They aren't just saying it.

Didn't you want to become an artist when you went to university?" he murmured in his ear.

"I did, but this is…unexpected."

"I know, but look." He moved his head so he could watch his mother's excited expression as she gushed over the drawings.

"Kieren, these are wonderful! You have such a gift." She held up the one of Patrick studying that Kieren had just drawn. "This is like looking at it in real life, just without colour. I love it."

"You're welcome to have that one if you like," Kieren said.

"Oh, no. I couldn't take your hard work," Victoria said.

"Please. I insist."

Victoria smiled at the picture, then frowned. "You must sign it first, though. *I* insist."

Patrick withheld his smile at the standoff, knowing his mother would win because Kieren wouldn't want to upset her.

Reluctantly, he grabbed his pencil and signed the bottom corner, returning the picture to her hands.

"Thank you, dear." She stood. "I got sidetracked from my reason for being here. I just came to tell you that we have requested an early dinner today because your father and I are going to see Andrew. I wondered if you would all like to join us."

"What time?" Henry asked.

"Five o'clock."

"I'll be there, but Robert might not be back in time."

Patrick glanced at Kieren, who nodded. "We'll be there," Patrick said.

"Wonderful. I'll see you in a short while." She smiled at Kieren and held up the drawing. "Thank you for this."

"You're welcome."

She left the room, closing the door behind her. Patrick waited a few seconds before dropping the bombshell on Kieren.

"You do realise that she will tell and show everyone that picture, and you'll be inundated with requests soon, don't you?"

Kieren's eyes widened. "But you can say no to them all if it's not something you want to do. Don't feel forced into it."

"No, it's…" Kieren blew out a long breath. "I just wasn't expecting to get back into it. I'm used to doing it whenever I had a spare few minutes that I never considered trying to make a career out of it again."

"It doesn't have to be a career if you don't want it to be. It can still be a hobby while you protect if that's your preference." Patrick cupped his face. "You decide."

"I…don't know."

"And that's fine, too." Patrick pecked a kiss on his lips several times before pulling back. "There's no rush to decide at all."

Kieren pressed their mouth together again, but this time, he swiped his tongue over Patrick's lips, and Patrick opened immediately to his questing tongue.

"And that is my cue to leave. See you at dinner, brothers."

Patrick didn't hear him leave, too engrossed in what he was feeling. Unable to hold back any longer, he dragged his mouth away and rested their foreheads together. "I love you, Kieren."

Kieren pulled back a little, and Patrick had a momentary panic before Kieren cupped his face and smiled. "I love you, mi corazón."

Patrick bit his lip. "Where's that from?"

Kieren tried to duck his head, but Patrick wouldn't let him. "It's something my father always called my mother. Mi corazón. My heart."

Patrick kissed him. He couldn't do anything else. How he got lucky to have Kieren come into his life, he didn't know, but he would make sure he made the man as happy as he could for the rest of their time together.

HENRY

Henry's heart was light as he closed the door on Patrick's make out session with Kieren. It was something he didn't want to see, but it lifted his spirits that his brother was finally finding his happy ending. At least, Henry hoped he was. Kieren was a good man, and Henry couldn't have hoped to find anyone better.

Those drawings, though… Henry's brain fired with different opportunities for Kieren to give his gift to people. Or rather sell. Although that didn't sound as good. He couldn't give them away because they were amazing. But he could make a full-time living from selling them if he wanted to.

Now that he was with Patrick, he wouldn't need for a job, but as all their partners had told them before, they didn't want to be kept men. They wanted a life of their own as well as one with them. Henry couldn't begrudge them it. If he had a choice, he wouldn't have wanted to be a part of the royal family because of everything that came with it. Their partners were amazing men to be willing to take them on. To take their family on. Especially with the escalations happening now.

That thought soured his mood, and he wished he was with

Robert, but as Patrick had so evilly acknowledged, his boyfriend had told him to stop hovering and go away, but much more politely. It was only because he loved Robert so much. He didn't mean to be a pain in the ass. He wanted to spend as much time with him as possible, but he could understand why Robert sent him away. Henry could be distracting, and Robert knew that. Robert had experienced that.

Henry rolled his lips inwards to contain his smile as he remembered just how distracting he had been when they'd been closing the flower shop the previous evening. Luckily, they'd remembered to lock the front door so no one came in and found them behind the counter.

His phone rang, and he pulled it from his pocket, smiling when he saw Robert's name.

"I was just thinking about you," Henry said.

Robert chuckled. "I hope it was a good thought."

"Hmm. It might have had something to do with that twine from last night…"

Robert hummed. "Yes, that was rather…unique."

Henry laughed. "What can I do for you. I know you're busy?"

Robert sighed. "I want you to come back."

"Why?" Henry frowned. "Is everything okay?"

"Yes. I miss you. As distracting as you are, it's too quiet when you're not here."

"Even with Naomi and Finn there?" Robert's friends and employees worked alongside him all week, but they never stopped talking.

"Even with."

"I don't want to stop you from working," Henry said, and he frowned when a thought entered his head. "Why do you really want me there, sweetheart?"

Robert sighed. "I've found…I don't like it when I don't know you're safe. It's more distracting having you out in the world doing something else than being here talking to me and being underfoot. I prefer the latter."

"I'm fine, Robert. Nothing's going to happen."

"You don't know that, Henry. You of all people should know that."

The unintended barb hit home. He *did* know how unfair and unstable Aunt Charlotte was. He knew all about her little schemes and tortures and hatred for anyone within the LGBTQ+ community. The memories and nightmares still clung to him after all this time, but he understood Robert hadn't meant any harm with his words.

"God, Henry. I'm sorry. I didn't mean it like that."

"I know. I also know you're right. There is no telling what she's capable of, including striking when we least expect it, which could be at our homes or as we're walking in a garden as much as at an event." He sighed, then chuckled. "I'll bring some work with me. It might be enough to stop me bothering you every five minutes."

"Good idea." Robert cleared his throat. "So, I'll see you in a little while?"

"Yes, sweetheart. I'll be there as soon as I can. I love you."

"I love you."

They ended the call, and Henry smiled. As much uncertainty and fear they held, there was also plenty of love and hope to go around. If they kept supporting each other, they could get through this, and Aunt Charlotte would go down.

It was all they could hope for.

25

KIEREN

"Can I make an…out-there suggestion?" Kieren asked.

Brett snorted. "When don't you?" He waved his hand, encouraging Kieren to speak.

"For the events that are targeted—and possibly others if time allows—can we not replace all the staff apart from those who are necessary to the event?"

"How would that help?" Des, Henry's bodyguard, asked. Kieren could understand his concern as Henry was the next on the targeted list.

"Well, the way I see it, it would potentially limit the number of suspects. It's unlikely to be any of the 'necessary' people, though not impossible, and by replacing the staff, if their plan goes ahead and something happens, we've narrowed the pool of suspects to those who were there from the start. It's not fool-proof, but it might help."

Brett sighed. "It's not ideal because there are a damn high number of people involved in events like these, but we can certainly look into it. I'll speak with the king."

There were few royals like King Andrew. Most would delegate something like this, but whenever it involved his family directly, he was always at the front of the line to make sure they were safe, and the people around them had what they needed to ensure that safety.

He waited for Brett once the meeting had finished, and they strode through the hallways to the king's office.

"Hey, Randall," Brett said. "Is King Andrew in by any chance?"

"He is, but you'll only have a few minutes because he has a phone call shortly."

"Understood."

Randal disappeared into the office after knocking, then reappeared quickly. "Go on in."

"Nice to see you, Brett." He shook his hand and turned to Kieren, pulling him in for a hug. "Kieren. To what do I owe the pleasure?"

"You're undoubtedly soon-to-be nephew has an idea to run past you," Brett said with a grin.

Kieren wanted to kill him, but he settled for smacking his shoulder. Andrew laughed. Whether it was at the "soon-to-be nephew" or because Kieren hit Brett, he wasn't sure, but he ignored it.

"I'm all ears." Andrew wandered over to a table and poured a coffee. "Do you want anything?"

"No, thank you," they both replied, making the king laugh again.

"You two are so in sync." He sipped his coffee and sat on the sofa rather than back behind his desk. "Have a seat."

Kieren and Brett sat, but whereas Brett leaned back, the picture of ease, Kieren couldn't. He detailed what he'd explained in the security meeting.

"I agree. Would you take point on this, Kieren? I know you're not yet back to guarding, but if you wanted to, you could do this part instead?"

Kieren perked up. "Really?"

"Definitely. If you want to, the job's yours for now," Andrew said. "Once it's sorted, we can talk about what your future looks like."

"Thanks."

"Don't thank me yet. You don't understand how much of a job you're taking on. You won't be alone, though. Randall does a lot of the delegating, and he'll help you find your feet."

Something inside Kieren eased at having a job. Something other than wandering around like a lost sheep.

A knock sounded, and Randall poked his head in the door at Andrew's call. "Your Highness, your caller is waiting for you."

"Thank you, Randall. Give me one more minute." Randall nodded and left. "Okay, boys. Kieren, see Randall on your way out. Brett, do you have anything to add?"

"No, sir. I just came along for the ride." He grinned, and the king laughed.

"I will speak to you both shortly, then."

They left the office after Andrew had called Randall back in for a quick update, and Brett said goodbye, leaving Kieren with the king's personal assistant.

"Are you ready for a trial by fire?" Randall asked.

"Is there any other kind?" Kieren joked. "Let me send a quick message to Patrick, and I'm all yours."

KIEREN: I'm hanging out with Randall for a bit. I have a new interim job. I'll tell you about it later. If you decide to go anywhere, let me know. x

They spent the next two hours going through the process of how to vet potential staff members, how to delegate and what was involved in organising events. By the time Randall called it quits, Kieren's head was swimming.

"Wow. I know you worked hard, but it seems you have your work cut out for you with all these things," Kieren said.

Randall chuckled. "I've been doing this for a long time. It's second nature to me now, but I will pity the person who ever has to take over from me. Me, though? I love this. Working is my therapy, my solace."

"I find it's that way for many people. Throwing themselves into work is a boon." Kieren changed the subject, understanding the hesitance in Randall's voice. "I have a list of things I need to do now you've got the ball rolling on finding replacements. I'll get started on those. When do you want to meet next?"

Randall clicked his calendar on the computer. "Tuesday? That gives you a couple of days *after* the weekend to do anything you couldn't do *on* the weekend."

"Sounds good."

Kieren said goodbye and pulled out his phone. Patrick had sent an initial message to him but nothing further, and he wanted to track the man down. He dialled.

"Hey," Patrick said.

"Hey. Where are you?"

"Have a guess?"

Kieren snorted. "You have too many people within this castle for me to guess right on the first go."

"Try."

Kieren had no clue which of the princes was busy or not, and he just said, "Freddie."

"Nope."

Kieren sighed. "Henry."

"Nope."

"I give up."

Patrick laughed. "I'm over at Book Drunk with Christian and Douglas."

"I'm assuming Jade is with you?" He glanced at Nina, who had appeared by his side when he'd exited Randall's office.

"She is. Oscar has made a dedicated corner for the body-guards to sit on stools and still be able to see the entire book shop. He thought it best because of the number of bodyguards that come in occasionally."

Kieren's heart calmed. Brett, Felix and Eric would be there with them.

"That's nice of him. I'm sure you all get inundated with people coming up to you when there's that many of you, though," he said as he wandered towards the front exit.

"They're pretty good, actually. Most people leave us alone. At least the people who live around here. It's nothing unusual for them. Tourists are a little different, but we find that if we acknowledge them, to begin with, they then leave us be." Patrick chuckled. "You know this. Why are you listening to me prattle on?"

Kieren smiled. "I like hearing you talk." He side-eyed Nina, daring her to say anything, but all that happened was a small mouth twitch. "I'm on my way."

It took him barely five minutes to reach the book shop cafe across the road from Windsor Castle. At the rate they were going, Patrick would be moving into Windsor with how often he was there. Kieren didn't care where they lived as long as they were together.

He caught the step as he entered the cafe, the thought momentarily surprising him. They'd been living with each other for months—granted, not in the same room—but at the same house. Would he eventually move into Patrick's room?

"Are you okay?" Nina murmured.

"Uh-huh."

Patrick rose to greet him as Kieren reached the table. He wasn't sure if Patrick wanted a PDA, so Kieren just smiled until Patrick leaned forward and pecked him on the lips.

"Everyone knows, Kieren. Don't worry," Patrick whispered.

Kieren hummed and grabbed a seat beside Patrick. He didn't

mind anyone knowing if he was honest with himself, but having people focused on them was a different matter.

"What's this new job?" Christian asked with a smile, making Kieren think he already knew, which he probably did having Brett as a guard.

"I'm helping re-organise some events." He glanced around. He didn't say too much in public because that was a mistake they couldn't make.

Patrick leaned into him, and Kieren slid an arm around his shoulders, holding him close, and pressed a kiss to his temple.

"How's the physio working out for you?" Douglas asked.

"It's going well. I still have to strengthen the muscles back to what they were before, but they say I should be at full capacity soon. I have permission to start yoga and tai chi again."

"I'm glad. Have you decided what your plans are?" Christian asked.

Kieren met Patrick's gaze. "I don't know. We need to talk about it."

Douglas's phone rang, and he answered it with a smile. "Quinn, how are you?" He paused, his eyes roaming across the table as he listened. "That would be great. Let me check in with everyone, and I'll call you back later. Is that okay? Brilliant. Speak to you later." He ended the call. "Quinn's invited us to Kendal's birthday party. Because of…what happened, they prefer not to interact with too many people at once. Quinn believes that they'll be okay with us."

"I'm there," Patrick said.

"It'll give me the chance to check in on some of the other subs, too," Douglas said. "I've not managed it as often as I used to."

Christian nudged Douglas with his shoulder. "You can't be in two places at once. You're doing your best."

"I know. I was doing it a lot when I first met Mav, but life has got in the way. It shouldn't because they're important."

"Doms are important, too," Patrick said.

Christian held up a hand. "Let's go back home to finish this discussion. I don't think today's the day we open our hearts in public about what we do in private." He winked at Patrick, who chuckled.

They said goodbye to Oscar, and the four of them, plus their bodyguards, headed back to the castle. People took photos of them, though no one approached—probably because of the guards surrounding them.

When they were settled into Christian's suite, Christian asked Patrick to continue what he had been saying about Doms.

"We get so much crap heaped on us about being tough, not showing weakness and dealing with things out of our control. The balance needs to be changed. Subs can be strong, and Doms can be weak. It all depends on the situation."

Douglas tilted his head. "True. I wonder if offering some..." He sighed. "Not therapy, but someone or something where anyone can talk about anything, regardless of who they're deemed in public or private. Do you think it would help?"

Patrick shrugged a shoulder. "It depends on if Doms are willing to take the chance. Some might be open to the idea, and if we could get them on board, maybe others will follow suit."

"My eyes have been opened to the downsides of being a Dom," Kieren added. "Teaching subs about Doms and vice versa might be beneficial."

"What do you mean by 'teaching?'" Douglas asked, leaning forward.

Kieren collected his thoughts and turned to Patrick. "Can I explain some stuff?" he asked, not wanting to put their private life out in front of his cousins without his consent.

"I don't hide much from them." Patrick chuckled at the gasps from Christian and Douglas. "Well, you don't really want to know my bowel movements, do you?"

Kieren laughed at their faces. "Without trying to get too...

personal, I knew next to nothing about BDSM or Dominants or submissives before Patrick took me to the club. I'd heard of them, but it had never been anything that pulled me in and made me want to research more. But Freddie brought my attention to something I had *never* considered. Patrick needs after-care, too. How many other Doms do, and their subs don't know it? How many subs aren't getting what they need because they can't articulate what they need? That's what needs to be taught." He held up his hand when Christian went to talk. "I know every person is individual. I know everyone will have different things that work for them. But by giving everyone a lesson in positive and negative care, if something happens and a sub or Dom can't explain, their partner will have more of an idea of how to help."

"Doms do get training, though," Christian said.

"Yeah, *Doms* do. What about subs? Do they not have to be taught that they can say no, that they can change their mind, that there are good and bad things about being a sub, that it is just as much their responsibility to care for their Dom as it is for the Dom to care for the sub."

"And even if they have training, I think it should be repeated more regularly than it is," Patrick added. "And mandatory for members who have caused issues, even minor ones."

"I agree with the repeated training," Douglas said. "Maybe, though, training is the wrong word. We don't need to 'train' submissives because their Doms will teach them about their needs, but instruction on how to have a positive relationship within a BDSM lifestyle and how to identify a negative relation-ship might be beneficial."

He glanced at Christian. "I'd be happy to do it, and if we decide on sub instruction, too, maybe we could ask a variety of subs to help us provide it, or even provide it themselves."

Christian nodded. "I like it." He studied Kieren. "It's a good job you're already busy; otherwise, you would've made a new job for yourself."

Kieren laughed. "I have to start keeping my mouth shut."

Patrick snuggled up to him. "No, you don't. How can we change for the better unless people speak their minds?"

Douglas cleared his throat. "Ever since Mav joined us, things have slowly changed in areas we never thought about. First Mav, then Robert, Timothy, Eddie, Oscar." He glanced at Christian with a smile. "Now you. Each of you brings different strengths to our table. Without each one speaking up about what they see or don't see, we would stagnate. We wouldn't change for the greater good." He sat back, crossing his ankle over his knee. "Father has always told us we need to change with the people. The people are the ones who dictate how we should lead the country. Yes, the Prime Minister officially leads, but the king has sway. He can overrule them in certain areas. But unless our eyes are opened to what we're missing, we can't help."

"Spoken like a true leader," Patrick said.

Douglas snorted. "No, thanks. I'll leave that to Freddie."

"I'm sure he appreciates that." Patrick laughed.

"He has Damon by his side. He has help," Douglas said.

Kieren bit his lip, wanting to say something about that situation but not believing it was his place, when Christian piped up, "I'm not the only one who sees it, am I?" He looked at them in turn, and Patrick and Douglas shook their heads. "Thank god. I thought I was seeing things, and with what Oscar said, it had made me look for the signs."

"I don't know if Freddie understands it or is just ignoring it, but I know for a fact that Damon is in love with Freddie," Douglas said.

"How so?" Patrick asked.

"I asked him."

Patrick gaped. "You asked him!"

Douglas shrugged. "It was annoying me not to know. Don't

worry, Mav tanned my hide afterwards—and yes, literally. The fucker stung for days."

There was a moment of stunned silence before Patrick and Christian burst out laughing. Douglas frowned and rolled his eyes, showing his inner teenager. Kieren covered his mouth with his hand, trying to hide his amusement. It had been easier when he was a guard because he had hardly ever been on the inside of a joke with them, but now, it felt freeing to be one of them in some ways.

"Are we going to intervene?" Christian asked.

"No," Kieren said, not realising he'd planned to speak up. "No. Leave them be. They've managed this long, and if you can see a difference in Freddie, then he's not as oblivious as he appears. Maybe he's trying to figure himself out. If you push him, he might retreat rather than open himself up to the possibility."

"Good point," Douglas said. "All right. At least *we* know. We can support him however he needs it whenever he needs it. Them. Support them." He paused. "I've just realised. Damon is already part of the group, so the name George coined is our final one—Thirsty Thirteen."

They groaned. "Could've been worse, I suppose," Christian said. "Just don't mention anything to him about it being our final name because he might just come up with something different."

"Why we need a name, I do not know," Douglas said. "But that's my little brother for you."

He didn't sound a bit put out about the name, in Kieren's opinion. In fact, he sounded proud.

By the time Patrick and he decided to go home, it was getting late, and the rest of the group had joined them. When Freddie offered them a room at Windsor, Patrick raised his eyebrows, and Kieren nodded, knowing his boyfriend wanted more time with his family, and it would give Kieren some more time to get to know them outside of guarding them.

After devouring several drinks and a table full of food, Kieren had found something he hadn't realised he'd been missing—close friends. In the physical and emotional sense.

26

PATRICK

"Happy birthday, Kendal," Patrick said. He leaned in slowly for a hug, ready to back away if Kendal wasn't ready for contact, but they smiled and returned the hug.

"Thank you," they said, accepting the gold-wrapped present. "You didn't have to get me anything."

"I wanted to." Patrick glanced across at Kieren. "Kendal, this is Kieren, my boyfriend."

Kendal's smile grew. "Nice to meet you, Kieren." They turned to Patrick. "I'm glad you found someone."

"Thank you. You will, too. When you're ready." Kendal ducked their head, fiddling with the bow on the present. Patrick changed the subject. "How are you enjoying the party?"

Kendal peered at him. "It's good. It's nice to see everyone. I don't socialise as much as I used to."

"Well, you're always welcome at ours. Whenever you want or need some company, just let us know."

"Thank you. I appreciate that."

Patrick saw Douglas enter, and he made his excuses, knowing his cousin wanted to check in with Kendal. He grabbed Kieren's hand and dragged him across the room to where the drinks were, but Patrick rested against the wall, watching Douglas interact with Kendal. Douglas held Kendal's hands, rubbing his thumbs over their knuckles, then cupped their face and pressed a kiss to their forehead. Kendal didn't hesitate and wrapped their arms around Douglas.

"They seem to have a good relationship," Kieren said.

"Douglas was the one to save Kendal from Talon last year. They've always been closer than Kendal has to the rest of us, although Uncle Andrew is still in contact with them, too." At Kieren's questioning look, he added, "Uncle Andrew was also there to help. He took over Kendal's care when Douglas left that night."

Kieren passed him a drink, and he absentmindedly sipped it. Could his music help people like Kendal? He'd researched music therapy when he'd begun thinking about a different career avenue, but he wasn't sure about the complexities of it. Is it for people who want to play, or can people just be interested in listening to it? It might be something he could help provide as well as for the youth centre.

"Penny for them?"

Patrick blinked, focusing on Kieren. "Huh?"

Kieren smiled. "What's got you thinking?"

Patrick surveyed the room, noticing the huddles of subs and furtive looks, some interested in the goings-on around them, some unsure. "I was wondering if music therapy would help anyone."

"It might. Is that something that would interest you?" Kieren asked.

"It would, just like conducting does, but I don't think people would really want me to be their music therapist." Patrick scoffed.

"Why not?"

"Can you imagine anyone wanting to open up to me? The first thing they'll see is someone who has anything they want at the tips of their fingers. They won't see someone who they could speak to unfiltered." Patrick shook his head. "I love the idea of it and would love to do it, but I couldn't be the one who ran the sessions. I could maybe help provide ideas for the music used, but it couldn't be me."

Kieren nodded. "Yeah, I can understand what you're saying."

"Sorry to interrupt," a voice said, "but I'd be interested."

Patrick glanced to the side, seeing Quinn stepping closer. "I'm sorry to eavesdrop, but in my defence, you weren't whispering." Quinn's crooked smile appeared, and Patrick returned it.

"It's fine, Quinn. What would you be interested in?"

"Music therapy. Not for myself, but for others. I'm a therapist. Well, part-time, anyway. I firmly believe that music can heal the soul."

"It truly can."

"You would be right, though. No one would feel comfortable opening up with you. Sorry."

Patrick shook his head. "It's as I thought. I take no offence."

"Therapists struggle with finding things that work for some people. When we've tried all the usual avenues, we need to find other ways to help. Music can be that. Funding, however, is an issue."

Patrick nodded. "Yes. I've heard that from Timothy. Private practices have an easier time obtaining other options, but government-funded practices are not as lucky."

Quinn sipped his drink, a bright red concoction which vied with his hair for being the brightest thing in the room. "Very true. If we had someone to help…" He curved his lips and raised his eyebrows.

Patrick chuckled and glanced at Kieren. "It's a good job I don't mind friends asking for something." Kieren snorted into his drink. "I would love to help such a worthy cause."

Quinn pumped his fist in the air with a whispered, "Yes!"

After they'd spoken some more, Quinn wandered off to get the birthday cake ready, and Patrick and Kieren joined his cousins and brother.

"I thought they would be worried about having us around," Henry said in a hushed voice when there was a lull in the conversation. "Being Monitors and all." He glanced at Kean, who nodded.

Douglas shook his head. "No, they feel comfortable knowing we're here. We're not the only Doms here; other subs have brought their partners with them. And besides, the only one who's single is Freddie." Douglas grinned and waggled his eyebrows at his brother.

"Shut it, Douglas," Freddie griped. "Not everyone has been able to meet their soulmate."

Patrick happened to glance at Damon as Freddie spoke and witnessed the wince he gave. He was more convinced than ever that they were both on the edge of something that neither of them realised. How could they not see it?

Kieren slid his arm around Patrick's shoulders and pulled him closer, pressing a kiss to his temple. "Don't get any ideas, Paddy. Leave them be," he whispered.

Patrick sighed and closed his eyes, resting his head against Kieren's chest. He refused to dignify Kieren's words with an answer because he wasn't the meddling one of the family. That was George. But if Patrick gave George some prodding, who was to know?

"It's cake time!" Quinn shouted, and everyone stood and gathered around the table, leaving space between themselves and Kendal.

Quinn placed a cake in front of them, candles burning brightly and a big three-zero on top.

"Make a wish!" someone called.

Kendal flushed, their cheeks colouring, and they cleared their throat before taking a deep breath, closing their eyes briefly and blowing out the candles. A cheer resounded through the room along with clapping, and they all sang *Happy Birthday*. Quinn picked up the cake again and took it into the kitchen area. Several people wandered towards Kendal and hugged them or shook their hands. They gave no worrying side looks, and it eased Patrick's mind.

"They're fine," Kieren said.

"I know, but I like to make sure."

"You wouldn't be you if you didn't."

Patrick kissed his cheek. "Come on. I thought of a game we could play." He dragged Kieren back to the corner the royals had commandeered. "Hey, let's play likes and dislikes."

Freddie groaned. "How old are you?"

Patrick spread his hands. "Hey! There are a lot of new people in our group now. It would be nice to get to know them a little better, and if that means we have to play a 'silly' game, then we should." He knew he was pouting, but he wanted to get to know his family's partners as well as he could.

"You're right," Freddie said. "I'm sorry. I'm tired, and I shouldn't be taking it out on you."

"It's okay."

"No, it's not." Freddie slapped Damon's shoulder. "You're supposed to tell me when I'm an idiot."

Damon rolled his eyes. "You're an idiot." His reply lacked the humour he was usually known for, and Patrick could tell their relationship was treading a fine line.

"Okay, what we have to do," Patrick said, changing the subject, "is to go around, and each of us says one thing we like and one thing we dislike. If someone agrees with you, they put their hand up but are not allowed to choose the same thing when it's their turn. When everyone has had a turn, we go again." He grinned. "I'll go first. I enjoy playing the piano," He paused, waiting to see if anyone put their hands up, which they didn't, "I hate popcorn." There were several gasps, but no one raised their hands. He glanced at Kieren.

Kieren blew out his breath. "I like yoga," He paused, and Eddie raised his hand, "and I dislike travelling in any way except foot or bike."

Patrick inhaled. "What? I thought you just didn't like planes."

Kieren licked his lips and shook his head. "Not a fan of travelling at all. If I could walk or bike everywhere, I would."

Patrick leaned in and kissed him. "I'm sorry. I didn't know."

"It's fine. It's one of those things I have to get used to, unfortunately."

Patrick decided to try to find other ways for them to do things from then on. If they had to use something else, it would be a last resort.

"I like cake," Oscar said. Everyone's hands went up, and they all laughed. "I dislike cats. Could be just because I'm allergic, though." Damon raised his hand.

"I didn't realise that," Freddie said, looking at Damon.

"I'm not allergic, but I don't like them."

Christian sighed. "I like—"

"Reading!" they all shouted, and George and Oscar raised their hands.

Christian chuckled. "I dislike ereaders." No one lifted their hands.

Freddie was next. "I like classical music." Patrick raised his hand with a smile, though no one else did. "I dislike rock music." Damon and Timothy raised their hands.

"I like Indian food," Damon said. All but Eddie and Mav lifted their hands. "I hate cheesecake." No one raised their hand. Unsurprisingly.

They continued in the same vein until everyone had a turn, and when Patrick started the next round, other party guests joined them. It took longer the second time around because, by the time they reached the last person, the entire party guest list had a go. Patrick had learnt that Robert hated bananas, Timothy detested reality shows, Kean loved porridge, and Kendal wanted to live in a chocolate house. At least that's what it sounded like when they shouted "CHOCOLATE!" as something they liked.

When people started leaving, Patrick and Kieren followed suit, leaving his cousins behind. He sent Kendal another happy birthday and a wave, and Kieren drove them home.

"I wish you'd told me about travelling," Patrick said.

Kieren shrugged. "I can't do much about it, really. It's part of everyday life, and even if I wanted to never get in a car or bus or train again, it wouldn't be feasible. Too many things are too far away to walk or bike. I don't mind. It's just not my favourite activity." Kieren glanced at him and winked.

Patrick laughed. "Yes, I think I know your favourite activity now." Thinking of it had Patrick's cock getting hard. "I can't wait to get home," he murmured.

As they walked through the corridors of Bagshot Park, their shoulders bumped, they caught each other's eyes, and when the door closed behind them, Patrick pushed Kieren back against it. He was still careful of his injury, but he knew Kieren wanted to feel the slight bite of impact play. He'd been mentioning it for the past couple of weeks. That night, Patrick would give him another taste.

"Remove your clothes and kneel on the floor at the bottom of the bed, resting your stomach and chest on the mattress."

Kieren swallowed. "Yes, Sir."

Patrick watched him head for the bedroom, and he followed at a slower pace, fetching two bottles of energy drinks and some fruit from the fridge before joining him. He placed them on the bedside table within reach, and only then did he look at Kieren's sensually posed naked body. Licking his lips, he moved to the built-in wardrobe, where he had a supply of floggers.

"This is the same one we used last time. I know we were

going to try others, but as you're injured, I don't want to push you too hard. We can experiment over time, okay?"

"Yes, Sir."

Patrick could hear the anticipation in Kieren's voice already, and he smiled. He laid the flogger in Kieren's line of sight while he undressed, giving him the chance to study it and think about how it could be used. When Patrick was naked, he stopped behind Kieren and ran his hands over his ass and back, soothing him and reminding him to use his colours should he need to.

"How are your side and arm holding up in that position?" he asked.

"They're fine, Sir. The bed is the right height to rest my chest fully."

"Good. If you get uncomfortable at any time, let me know immediately."

"Yes, Sir."

Patrick reached for the flogger, gaze focused on Kieren, who watched the flogger until he could see it no longer. As usual, he ran the falls of the tool down Kieren's back, getting him used to the texture and making him aware of where it was at all times. While he did that, his other hand squeezed and rubbed his ass cheeks.

"Do you know I love watching you train?" Patrick said absently. "The way your body moves, the strength visible in the actions you perform. It's like watching a story unfold. Your body is a work of art, and if I could, I would've loved you to draw what I see every time I look at you."

Patrick slid the flogger over his ass and thighs, then removed it. He stepped to the side. "Ready?"

"Yes, Sir."

He heard Kieren inhale and exhale, then brought the flogger to his skin, the loud slap and answering groan from Kieren heightening Patrick's awareness. It was difficult for him to explain, but whenever he did this, it was as if he tuned in closer and closer to the person and their reactions. Almost like a zoom feature. He blocked everything else out but the person he was with. He could hear every hitch of breath, see every jerk of movement, and he loved it. Add that to the scent of sweat rising into the air as well as the taste of it on his lips, and he was in heaven.

"Colour?"

"Green, Sir."

He brought his hand back and let it fly again, the smack against Kieren's skin a beautiful sound. "You're already blooming into a nice red colour for me." He slid his hand over the blushing skin.

He flogged Kieren several times more, each time dragging moans from his boyfriend. "Lie still for a moment," he whispered.

Patrick grabbed the lube from the bedside table and squirted some onto his fingers. He had a surprise for Kieren, and he couldn't wait to see how he reacted. Stepping out of sight behind the man again, he settled his slicked fingers against his own pucker, biting his lip to hide his sounds as he prepared himself for Kieren's cock. They had never done it this way before. Usually, when Patrick flogged Kieren, Patrick then fucked him, but he wanted Kieren to see what it would be like if he fucked Patrick after such a scene.

When he was ready, he knelt beside Kieren, resting his upper body on the bed and sliding his fingers through Kieren's hair. "Hey, sweetheart." Kieren blinked open his eyes and smiled. "I have something for you." Kieren frowned. "Take me, Kieren. I want your cock in my ass this time."

Kieren's eyes flared, and he paused as if waiting for Patrick to take the chance away.

"I'm yours," he added.

Kieren lifted off the bed, the slight tensing of his facial

muscles the only evidence he felt the flogging Patrick had given him. He stood, using the bed to support him.

"On the bed," he rasped.

Patrick climbed onto the bed on his hands and knees and glanced over his shoulder. Kieren crawled on behind him and pressed his lips to Patrick's lower back. Patrick felt the head of Kieren's cock against his pucker and instinctively bore down. As Patrick had prepared himself, Kieren slid right in, and Patrick groaned.

The sound must've hit Kieren just right because he gripped Patrick's hips and thrust and withdrew to a punishing rhythm. It was perfect. Patrick lowered to his forearms, using them to stop his forward momentum by clenching the covers. His cock bobbed up and down with the motions, and Patrick closed his eyes, enjoying everything about it.

"Fuck, Kieren. That feels good."

"Paddy! I can't…"

"It's fine. Let go."

Patrick stroked his cock, bringing himself closer as Kieren groaned and emptied inside him. Kieren kept pumping his hips as he lowered himself over Patrick's body and the change in position caused him to hit that spot just right.

"Oh, fuck," Patrick gasped and fell over the edge. As the spasms took over his body, Kieren's arm surrounded him, pushing his cock deeper inside him and setting off another round of contractions. His cock spent the last of his release, and Patrick slumped, panting into the V of his arms.

Kieren's fingers threaded through his, and they remained in that position until Kieren's cock slipped free. Patrick could feel Kieren's come leaking from his ass, and it felt divine. He huffed a laugh.

"What?" Kieren asked.

"I was just thinking about how I loved the feel of your come leaking from me. It makes me feel owned."

Kieren moved off him, much to his pouting, but Patrick jerked when Kieren's tongue lapped at his pucker. He licked from his balls to his hole and pushed his tongue inside. Patrick's entrance spasmed around him. Kieren pressed a kiss to his rim, then moved up beside him.

"There you go. All back in again."

"Oh, fuck." Another round of contractions wracked him as the image of Kieren putting his release back inside Patrick so he could feel it leak again washed over him.

KIEREN

*D*espite not being signed on to work the event as security, Kieren couldn't help scanning the crowds to look for danger. It had been his life for many years, after all. Patrick was by his side, their hands joined, but Kieren couldn't rest.

Nobody appeared to be acting suspicious, but that didn't ease him at all. They had no clue whether changing the staff that worked the event would stop whatever Charlotte had planned. They could have missed somebody during the vetting process, or that person or those people could be very good at hiding.

"Relax. You're far too tense," Patrick said. "These events happen regularly, and although I know you don't like the security risk, you need to get used to attending them." He snorted. "And you need to get used to being the centre of attention."

Kieren refrained from rolling his eyes but only just. "Whenever there's a risk to your life or the lives of those around you, I will worry."

Kieren wasn't wearing an earpiece; therefore, he had no idea if there were any dangers lurking. Brett had refused his request to be kept in the loop during the event, citing Kieren's need to focus on Patrick and meeting the people. He knew his boss was right, but he didn't have to like it.

"Patrick! How lovely to see you. I'm happy you could make it." The older woman, who looked like her clothes, jewellery and beauty regime had cost more than Kieren's annual salary, glanced at him in passing, then refocused on his boyfriend.

"Emma, how nice to see you again. I'd like to introduce my boyfriend, Kieren."

Kieren slid his arm around Patrick's waist, noticing the slight widening of Emma's eyes. He didn't know her and didn't know if her reaction was due to the display of affection or that she had been introduced to someone she deemed unworthy. Either way, he made a note to bring it to Brett's attention.

"Nice to meet you, Kieren," she said.

"Likewise." Kieren smiled, unwilling to acknowledge her uncomfortable demeanour.

Patrick and Emma spoke for a few minutes about Emma's business, which just happened to be in the fashion industry. The more she spoke, the more he thought he understood her reactions. She appeared to be someone who didn't like interlopers in her personal bubble. Kieren didn't care, though. His attention flitted around the room while she spoke.

The evening wore on, and soon it was Henry's turn to make a speech. If anything was going to happen to Henry, Kieren would have thought whoever was behind it would try now. Not only for the shock value but because Henry was an easy target standing alone on the stage. His bodyguard, Des, was waiting in the wings of the stage, similar to what Kieren had done when Harvey had tried to shoot Patrick.

As they listened to Henry talk about the event and what it meant to him and the people the charity supported, Kieren kept watch. He couldn't see anything out of the ordinary, and when Henry finished his speech to a round of applause, the prince descended the steps with Des behind him.

"Does this mean we're free and clear?" Patrick whispered.

Kieren tapped his fingertips on his thumb. "We are only free and clear when we all leave this building intact."

He guided Patrick through the crowds towards Henry, wanting to be closer in case something happened but also fighting against his instinct to get Patrick out of there.

"I'm going to give my apologies to the organiser," Henry said. "I feel too jumpy to stay any longer."

"I agree," Patrick said. "The moment you're done, come back, and we'll leave."

Kieren peered at Des and asked him to let Brett know they should leave one or two guards behind to monitor things and see if they spotted anything suspicious after they left. The guard nodded and followed Henry through the mingling guests.

Patrick faced him, sliding his arms around his waist and staring up at him. "You won't be able to stop guarding, will you?"

Kieren caressed Patrick's cheek with his thumb as he pondered his question. "I will never be able to leave it fully because you mean too much to me, but at smaller events or less stressful ones, I should relax further. It's knowing there's a risk that puts me on high alert, and I can't let it go."

Patrick smiled. "I don't mind. If you want to keep doing it, I'm happy to support you, but I don't want you to feel you have to do it. We have other bodyguards to take the stress off you, but I understand how difficult it is. I would never expect you to stop being you."

Kieren lowered his head and pressed a gentle kiss to Patrick's lips. He would never be comfortable making grand displays of affection in front of a large audience, but small gestures he could live with.

"We have plenty of time to discuss what I want to do, but I will tell you this. Making sure you're safe is my singular focus, and it always will be."

Patrick grinned. "I like being your singular focus," he said.

Kieren laughed. Henry came back shortly after, having given his excuses, and they filed down the hallway to the exit, where the cars waited to take them home. To ensure, at least as much as they could, that no one messed with the cars while they had been in the event, Brett had requested each car return to Windsor immediately after the drop-off and return just before they left. Luckily, the event was only within half an hour's drive. It wouldn't stop the chances completely, but it would significantly reduce the chance of someone planting a tracker or even a bomb on a car that had been parked in the same spot for several hours. Even if that car had the driver still in it.

As they settled into the back of a car, Kieren blew out a breath, the aching in his body making him aware of how much tension he'd held.

"Are you okay?" Patrick asked, taking his hand.

Kieren nodded, rolling his head to the side to stare at Patrick. "Always with you by my side."

"Aww, that's sweet." Kieren snorted. "What does this mean, then?"

"It could be nothing at all, but my best guess would be that one of the people we replaced is the guilty party. But it could also mean Charlotte changed her plans because she knows we know. There's no way of knowing for definite without further investigation."

"What happens from here?"

Kieren sighed. "We will get people looking into the backgrounds of those we replaced."

"How many people is that?"

"Too many. I believe it was over a hundred."

"That's like looking for a needle in a haystack." Patrick groaned.

"It is, but we have good people. If there's anything that looks remotely sketchy, they will delve deeper."

Patrick snuggled into Kieren's side, resting his cheek on Kieren's chest. They rode the rest of the way in silence, and Kieren wondered if Patrick had fallen asleep until his head popped up as they pulled into Bagshot Park.

"I thought we were going back to Windsor?"

"I requested everyone to meet here instead of Windsor," Kieren said. "I thought it would be a better option."

Patrick narrowed his eyes. "What aren't you telling me?"

Kieren shook his head. "Nothing. I promise. Windsor is always the place we seem to congregate after an event. I wanted to switch things up a bit, making us less predictable. I should have mentioned it, sorry."

Patrick's expression eased, and he pressed a kiss to Kieren's fingers. "I understand."

They climbed out of the car and headed for Henry's suite. Kieren answered the unasked question. "I thought Henry might prefer his own rooms as the event was focused on him."

Patrick pulled him to a stop, and Kieren raised his eyebrows. "You are one of the most selfless and caring people I have ever met."

Kieren didn't think so, but he knew better than to disagree. Patrick smiled as if he knew what Kieren had been thinking and pulled him along again. Henry, Robert, Des and Matt were already there.

"We have a lot of people coming, Henry. Are you sure you want everyone in here?" Brett said when he entered a few seconds later.

"It's fine."

Robert wrapped his arms around Henry's shoulder, pulling him close. Patrick squeezed his hand and let go, kneeling at Henry's feet and gripping his hand. Patrick spoke to Henry, though his words were too quiet to be heard. Henry nodded or shook his head in response to whatever Patrick was saying, and

Patrick reached for Henry's chin, lifting it slightly with his forefinger. Then he rose and made his way back to Kieren.

"Everything okay?" Kieren asked.

"Yes. He's fine. I think the adrenaline that had kept him going through the event has finally left him. I'm just going to get him a drink and a snack. Do you want anything?"

"I'm good, thanks," Kieren said.

Patrick kissed him, then headed for what Kieren assumed was a small fridge in the corner of the room.

"Kieren." He glanced at Brett. "Thoughts before everyone gets here?"

Kieren frowned. "Personally, I think they know we're onto them. With how heavily guarded Douglas was, and now Henry, they can see we've changed how we work."

"But would that make them think we know, or just that we were being extra careful?"

"Have we been extra careful at the smaller events?" Brett grimaced. "Exactly. If they're looking for clues, we've given them a big one." He didn't say that he'd told Brett. They'd discussed increasing security for each event, not just the targeted ones, but Brett wouldn't agree on the extra manpower for the smaller ones.

"You were right. I'm sorry."

Kieren held up his hands. "I might not be. They might have no idea, and it was just because they couldn't get a replacement scapegoat at such short notice."

"But you don't believe that." It wasn't a question.

"Nobody understands how she thinks. I doubt even her husband understands why she does certain things, but we have to cover all the bases now. They could be in more danger with how unpredictable she can be."

Brett cursed. "We need to end this."

"We will. It's just taking longer than we thought."

"I should have you as my second in command."

Kieren snorted. "No, thanks. Too much like hard work."

The room filled up as more and more people came. The security team and the princes and their partners took up plenty of room. But when the king, Patrick's parents, and Prince William and his wife joined them, even the large room suddenly felt a lot smaller. Patrick and Kieren found a chair, and Kieren sat at Patrick's feet.

Andrew clapped his hands together. "All right. What do we know?"

Brett talked them through the event, what Kieren had done with replacing the staff, what the event had been like, and his initial feelings. Each member of the security team who had been present at the event gave their thoughts on it, as did the princes.

"Kieren?" Andrew asked.

He glanced at Brett, who gave him a slight nod. "I think, after tonight's event, Charlotte knows that we have something or someone who's been telling us what events she's targeting."

"Why?" Andrew said. "How would she know?"

Kieren peered at Brett again. "It's my fault, Your Majesty," Brett said.

"How so?"

Brett sighed. "Kieren came to me with concerns about me focusing on the events that we knew to be targeted. He explained his thoughts about showing our hands and hiding our knowledge behind all the events, not just the targeted ones. I listened but disagreed, not wanting to stretch the team too thin. I think I made the wrong choice."

Andrew remained quiet for a moment, then spoke to Kieren. "What makes you think she knows?"

"We've been too obvious. We had extra security at Douglas's and Henry's events, but not at the smaller ones, like visiting the schools or hospitals. If we didn't know which event they would strike at, we would've increased security for all visits and events and replaced staff at all events, not just some."

"He's right, sir," Brett said.

"Maybe, but that doesn't mean you're at fault, Brett," Andrew said. "Increase security for all events from now on. If you need extra staff, ask, or if you need us to reduce the number of events, we will. Until we have her, we have to be careful."

Patrick's grip on his shoulder tightened, and Kieren reached up to cover his hand, squeezing.

Eric cleared his throat. "We found a couple of suspicious staff from the group that had been replaced at Henry's event. We have investigated them in more detail, but we can't find anything concrete."

"Where are they now?"

"Still being held. We wanted to know what you wanted to do with them, considering the plan to use Charlotte's potential allies as bait."

"I think we should give them some information. Something only the two of them knows, but with a slight difference in each case," Christian said. "If we focus it on something close to us, maybe like Christmas, then if something happens, we will know if either of them went to her."

"We know she used to use the rooms at Sandringham for her..." Henry blanched as he spoke. "Could we say something about what we found there? She might be willing to risk retrieving it if it would point the finger at her."

"Yes," Freddie said. "Something with her fingerprint on it, maybe? Or Charles's? Would she fight for her son or leave him to the wolves?"

Andrew snorted. "She willingly rang me to get her son out of prison. That was either to reduce the chance of him talking or because she cares for him. Either way, it's something we could lean on." He nodded. "I like the idea. William? Victoria? Thoughts?"

William rubbed a hand over his jaw, the scratchy noise advertising his five o'clock shadow. "I think it would work. If I know her as well as I think I do, she wouldn't have got her hands dirty, but when it comes to her son, she'll want him to keep quiet. Even if he's not privy to all her plans, he'll know enough to put her behind bars. She won't want to chance that."

"I agree," Victoria said. "She would want to pretend she was ahead of everyone, even if she wasn't. She never liked being the last to know something."

"Okay, so focusing on Charles then. If she doesn't bite, we can try again with something else," Freddie said.

"Damon, did you find anything of significance in your work?" Andrew asked.

"I have three companies who, although passed the audit, appear to have dummy businesses on their books. I didn't high-light them at all, but I made a note of who they were." He pulled out his phone. "Jamison Investments, B.G. Construction, and Elemental Financials."

Andrew shook his head. "I don't recognise any of those, but that doesn't mean anything. I don't know the names of all the companies involved with the crown. Why do you say they're dummies?"

"When I looked into them, I was rerouted through several other companies and still didn't find a significant name to pin it on. I need someone with better computer skills."

"I can help with that," Brett said. "I know someone."

"Okay. Are we doing this at Christmas, or can I suggest doing it a few days before, and we can actually have a nice Christmas break?" Victoria said.

"Just before would work better," Brett said. "We have less staff over the three days of Christmas when you stay at Sandringham, remember?"

Andrew nodded. "Good point." He sighed and checked his phone. "Let's leave for Sandringham on the Wednesday. That gives us two days to work on the plan before we quit and celebrate, regardless of the outcome. Can the team manage that?" he asked Brett.

"Yes, sir."

"Set the wheels in motion, Eric. You take point on the two people you found. Give them something about Charles and evidence, and we'll see if it nets us results."

"Yes, Your Majesty," Eric said.

Andrew smiled and shook his head. "One of these days, you'll all call me Andrew."

"Never, Your Majesty," several of the security team said, resulting in laughter from all.

The security team said their goodbyes, as did Andrew, William and Lou. Victoria and Patrick Senior disappeared with Henry and Robert, leaving the rest of them in Henry's sitting room.

"Should we leave them to it?" Kieren asked.

"No," Christian said. "They'll be back out soon. They just want to reassure themselves Henry is fine. Henry will need the distraction. He might even need to be a pup. I'm sure if he does, he'll find someone to play with." Christian grinned at Oscar, whose eyes lit up. "Yeah, I thought so."

"How are you finding all this cloak and dagger stuff?" Christian asked Kieren.

Kieren blew out a breath. "I think I prefer being able to see the threat and get rid of it rather than having it play hide and seek through nefarious means."

"True. We'll get her, eventually. I'm sure of it."

"My concern is how widespread it all is. Who else does she have in her pocket?"

"Well, we can count on my father to be there," Christian said bitterly. "And my siblings. Possibly Uncle Arthur and his family. They were close with my parents when I was growing up."

"In other words, there could be plenty of people we miss when we chop off the head of the snake," Kieren said.

Christian nodded but said no more. Patrick leaned forward and wrapped his arms around Kieren's neck.

"We have each other," he said, pointing at those in the room. "We'll get through this."

Kieren could only hope he was right.

28

CHRISTIAN

Kieren's words hit home. Chopping the head off the snake was only the beginning. There were probably plenty of people involved who could and would take over from Aunt Charlotte. Mainly his father.

He wished they had someone on the inside. Someone who could help them prevent whatever plans they had coming to fruition, but they didn't. Neil, Daniel and Gia were still working tirelessly trying to glean any piece of information from the data they had and ideas they'd come up with for what *could* happen. Commissioner Thomas was also digging as much as he could.

They—the good side—had plenty of people helping them, but with their hands tied to do it *lawfully*, they didn't have as much freedom as Aunt Charlotte and her followers did. Aunt Charlotte, John—he refused to call him "father" any longer and was considering dropping the "aunt," too, but habits died hard—Charles, and whoever else they had on their side would stop at nothing to make their plans succeed. And that was the worrying part. They had no qualms about breaking the law if it fit in with their "beliefs."

While he thought about it, he pulled his phone from his

pocket and noted down all the names he believed could have something to do with John. He'd gone through this with Neil already, but he needed to do it again in case he had forgotten someone.

"Everything okay?"

Christian smiled across at Oscar, stowing his phone again and wrapping his arms around his boyfriend. "I'm good."

"Your brain is going a mile a minute, isn't it?" Oscar whispered.

Christian chuckled. "I can't help it. When this topic comes up, it's hard to switch off, as you know." Oscar rubbed Christian's chest in a soothing gesture. "I still feel like we're missing something."

"Well, I think Charles has gotten too cocky and made a mistake, and he's going to say something he shouldn't and set the ball rolling in our favour. I truly believe that."

"I hope you're right."

They stayed entwined while Christian's thoughts tapered off again. Hopefully, the "incriminating evidence" they gave to the two members of staff would net them some leads, too. Nobody likes to believe they'd left something behind, and if it's something unique enough to be traced back to Charlotte or Charles, then they might be willing to risk taking it back.

When Henry and Robert came back into the room, everyone refocused. Henry and Patrick's father had left a few minutes before, and Henry had changed into his pup gear. Robert hadn't changed his clothes, but he had removed his jacket, and he stroked his hand on Henry—Dusty's head.

Christian tightened his hold on Oscar. "Are you feeling playful, sweetheart?" Oscar nuzzled into his neck and nodded. "Do you want to get changed today?"

"No, Daddy."

Christian smiled. It had always surprised him how quickly

and easily Oscar moved into his little space, but it made him all the more delightful.

"Okay, Ozzie. Why not find a ball for Dusty?"

Ozzie plastered a kiss on Christian's lips and scrambled off the sofa. He raced across the room towards the box he knew held Dusty's toys, and Dusty scampered after him.

"Thank you," Robert said, settling beside Christian.

"You don't need to thank me. Oscar loves this."

Robert clasped his hands in his lap, but his eyes never left Dusty. "Henry needs time to decompress, and this is the best way for him, other than..." Robert chuckled. "That."

Christian laughed. "Yes. It's probably best to keep *that* behind closed doors. This is the next best thing."

Robert smiled, then sighed. "Do you think anyone was there to hurt him and they just didn't do it, or it failed or something?"

Christian inhaled. "I honestly don't know. I have been wondering if they have a plan for every event and then decide on the night whether it's going to go ahead or not, but it seems excessive. But if Charlotte is...beginning to worry, then there's no telling what she might do. What she might get *others* to do."

And wasn't that circling back to the original question. Who else is involved that they didn't know about?

29

PATRICK

*P*atrick's phone rang as he waited for Kieren to finish getting ready for the wedding reception. His best friend, Zane, and his new wife had finally set a date for them to celebrate with everyone—three days before they left for Sandringham. Neither of them minded because it gave them the opportunity to get away together for a few days.

The reception was being held in Gloucester, Zane's hometown, and Patrick and Kieren had chosen to stay for a couple of days. They'd arrived the previous day and would then head over to Sandringham the same day as everyone else planned to, giving them a lovely three-day break. For the first time, Patrick wasn't attending Uncle William's charity event—the annual event they held to ease the financial burden on those families who spent the holiday in the hospital or away from their family.

His mother and father had insisted on paying for the hotel they were currently in. Kieren's eyes had widened comically when he'd seen the place, but Patrick had told him to get used to it. He wouldn't, and Patrick had been joking, but it was something Patrick wished he didn't take for granted some days. He felt awful knowing people couldn't afford the basic amenities when he was staying at extravagant places like that, but he also realised that he was helping those he could whenever he could. It often felt like a huge balancing act.

"Hey. What's up?"

"I have the information you asked for," Freddie said.

Patrick glanced over his shoulder and headed for the balcony. He would tell Kieren whatever he found out, but he wanted to gather all the information together before he did.

"And?"

"It was a mechanical failure, not pilot error."

Patrick's heart missed a beat. "How do you know?"

"I found someone who worked for them. They were willing to tell the truth as long as nothing came from it. They won't go up against them, and if we try, they'll deny everything."

"There's no way to prove it?"

"He said they wrote nothing down regarding the truth of the matter. They paid off everyone who knew about it to lie about the circumstances; otherwise, they and many others would lose their jobs."

Patrick sighed. "I can understand why they did it, in some ways, but why drag a man's name through the mud to do it?"

"According to this guy, they thought it wouldn't matter because he and his family were dead. They didn't know about Kieren."

"I bet it wouldn't have made a difference."

Freddie hummed. "I agree."

"Thank you, Freddie."

"Are you going to tell him?"

Patrick smiled. "Yes. He deserves to know the truth. I don't know if it will help him heal or not."

"He has you. He'll be fine."

"Thanks again. See you in a few days."

He ended the call and stared across the expanse of the horizon he could see from his vantage point in the penthouse. It was cold—he should've pulled on a coat before standing out there—but there was no hint of snow in the air. He wanted a white Christmas like they used to have when they were kids, but in the current weather climate and with all the changes happening, it was unlikely to happen.

"What are you doing out here?" Kieren asked, draping a coat around his shoulders and keeping his arm around him.

"Freddie rang. I forgot to grab a coat." Patrick smiled at him. "I have some news for you. Let's go inside."

They settled on the sofa side by side, and Patrick threaded his hand through Kieren's.

"You're worrying me," Kieren said.

"Sorry. It's nothing to worry about, but I don't know if you'll be happy I did it."

"Tell me."

"I asked Freddie to look into your family's crash."

Kieren stopped breathing and went completely still. "And?" he croaked after a short time.

Patrick sighed and held on tighter. "It was a mechanical failure, not pilot error. Unfortunately, there is no way to prove that. They put nothing in writing. No one is willing to go against that company your father worked for. It's the truth, but there's no way to fight for acceptance of it."

Kieren closed his eyes, his body sinking into the sofa. "I knew it," he whispered.

Patrick swallowed, not knowing what Kieren would want to do with the new information.

Kieren opened his eyes again, staring directly at Patrick, and smiled. "Thank you."

"What are you going to do?"

Kieren smiled. "Nothing."

Patrick jerked. "Nothing?"

"I don't need to do anything. I certainly don't want to jeopardise their jobs. All I wanted to know was the truth, and I have it. Thanks to you."

Patrick scrunched his face. "Freddie, really. I just asked him."

"I wouldn't have thought to ask him, though. Thank you."

Kieren pulled Patrick into his arms and squeezed him, burrowing his face into Patrick's neck. Patrick kept a tight hold, feeling the emotions working their way through Kieren's body. He might be glad of the truth, but he was sure the man would be dealing with the knowledge for many weeks to come. Kieren pulled back.

"I'm going to set a day to speak with Timothy again after Christmas. I want to forgive and not forget but set aside the anger and sadness I feel whenever I think of them. I need to remember the good times, which include taking planes." Kieren stared at him. "Will you help me?"

"With everything you need," Patrick promised.

Patrick held him again, then cupped his face. "Let's go celebrate with your friend. What better way to remember them?"

Kieren blinked, his eyes bright with unshed tears. "Let's go."

When they arrived at the location, with Jade and Nina in tow as well as a couple of extra guards for that day only who were already at the party, pretending to be part of the venue security, Patrick threaded his fingers through Kieren's trying not to let on how nervous he was. He'd only spoken to Zane that one time, and he was worried the man wouldn't like him.

"Kieren!"

Kieren let go of Patrick when a tall, muscular guy threw his arms around him and lifted him clear off the ground.

"Put me down, you jackass. I'm injured," Kieren said.

It took him a minute, but he did. The man gripped Kieren's biceps and held him at arm's length. "Well, you ain't changed a bit, have you?"

"Neither have you, Zane." Kieren shook his head. "Congrats."

"Thank you. I'll take you to meet Viv in a moment." His eyes flicked over Kieren's shoulder to Patrick. "I believe you have someone to introduce first."

Kieren chuckled and reached for Patrick's hand. "Patrick, meet Zane. Zane, be nice. This is Patrick."

"Nice to put a face to a name," Patrick said.

Zane clasped his hand, shaking with no extra strength, even though Patrick had expected it. "Nice to meet the man who has stolen Kieren's heart."

Patrick and Kieren flushed, then laughed. "Shut up," Kieren said. "Take us to Viv. I haven't seen her in far too long."

Zane clapped him on the shoulder, making him wince, and led the way.

"Kieren! I'm glad you could make it!"

A woman with big brown curls that barely came up to Kieren's shoulders hugged his boyfriend, and Patrick admitted he was a little jealous.

"Hey, Viv. Why did you agree to marry this lug?" Kieren thumbed at Zane. "You can do so much better."

"I know, but he can't, and I can't make him unhappy because it makes me unhappy. It's a lose-lose situation." She seemed earnest. Patrick had to take another look at them all, but then they burst out laughing, and Patrick shook his head.

"I can see why you said they were perfect for each other," he said to Kieren.

"Yes. No one else could put up with either of them." Kieren nodded solemnly.

"Aww, babe. He said we were perfect for each other," Viv said.

Zane rolled his eyes. "Anyway, are you ready for your best man's speech?"

"What?" Kieren asked.

"If you had been at the wedding, you would've been my best man." He gestured around them. "Wedding reception, therefore, speech. Good luck." Zane clapped him on the shoulder again and wandered off, dragging Viv behind him.

"Shit."

Patrick pulled out his phone and dialled. "George, we need your help. Quick." He explained the situation and then passed the phone to Kieren, who took it with a frown. He answered the questions George threw at him and then handed it back to Patrick.

"Give me half an hour," George said.

"Thanks." He ended the call. "In half an hour, you should have a speech."

"How?"

"George is an anonymous speechwriter. He has written a hell of a lot of speeches for people, famous and not famous, though no one knows it's him. It's all done anonymously through Randall."

"How the hell did he keep that quiet?"

Patrick smirked. "How can we keep the club quiet?" He stared at Kieren, letting understanding wash over him.

"Understood."

Patrick chuckled. "Shall we get a drink?"

"I think I'm going to need one."

Several of the guests accosted them as they made their way to the bar, asking for photos or signatures, and they gave them, not wanting to put a dampener on Zane's day. They did it quietly, without fuss, then grabbed some drinks and found a corner to sit in, away from the crowds.

"I don't know if I'll ever get used to this," Kieren said, his arm around Patrick's shoulders.

"What? People thinking we owe them a photo and information about our private lives? Yeah, me either." He sighed. "It's too much sometimes."

"I'm assuming it's worse for Freddie?"

Patrick nodded. "He's in the limelight all the time. Every

move is photographed and pulled apart for hidden meanings. It's awful, but he does it all with a smile. He's braver than all of us."

Patrick's phone rang. "Hi."

"Check your emails. I've sent it. Get Kieren to check through it and change things as he sees fit."

"Will do, thanks."

"Welcome."

Patrick pulled up his emails and copied and pasted it into a note app, then passed it to Kieren. "See what you think."

Kieren read through it, his lips moving as he read the words silently. He smiled and nodded. "This is amazing."

"Change anything that needs it because I don't think you have long," Patrick murmured.

He kept quiet while Kieren worked on Patrick's phone, people-watching and drinking his beer. When Kieren sat upright, he peered at him. "All done," Kieren said.

"Glad to hear it. And just in time, too."

"Kieren, are you ready?" Zane asked.

"As I'll ever be." Kieren stood. "You coming?"

"I'll wait here with Jade."

Kieren leaned down and pecked his lips, then followed Zane with Nina on his tail. Jade took Kieren's seat and crossed her legs.

"Does he not like talking to crowds?"

Patrick chuckled. "I don't think it's his favourite activity."

A tap on a microphone made everyone quieten. "Hello and good afternoon to you all. My name is Kieren, and I hold the badge for the most crap I put up with from this guy." He thumbed over his shoulder to laughter. He held up Patrick's phone. "My speech is on here because I had less than an hour's notice that I had to have a speech ready, so..." He turned the screen to face him again. "Zane, you are my one true... Oh, hold on a minute, wrong section. Ah, here we go." Laughter sounded again.

"He's good, even if he doesn't like it," Jade murmured.

Patrick hummed.

"Zane, you are my best friend, and as such, you should be ashamed of yourself. Leaving me in dreary England while you went on holiday to somewhere I'd hate, and then getting married without me being there. What kind of friend are you?"

"One of a kind!" Zane shouted.

Kieren chuckled. "Truly. I have plenty I could say about Zane, but most of you would know it all, anyway. He's a good person. That's all there is to it. No sugar-coating it. He just is. There's nothing about him I could ever imagine being able to put up with longer than a night. Good luck, Viv." He winked. "Although, if you've managed with him this long, maybe I should say, good luck, Zane." He scratched his head.

The guests were howling with laughter, and Patrick was proud of him. He continued in the same vein until he came to the end, highlighting again just how perfect they were for each other. He left the stage to a round of applause and took the seat Jade had vacated. His face was coated with sweat, but Patrick pulled him in close and fitted his head into his neck, anyway.

"Well done, sweetheart. You were perfect."

"God, I hate that," he murmured. "I hate it more that they will plaster it over the newspapers by morning."

"Hopefully, it won't because Zane had everyone put their phones away, saying they weren't allowed to take photos or videos of the speeches. It's not impossible that someone didn't, but hopefully, they'll accept it."

Kieren inhaled and breathed hot air against Patrick's neck. "Thanks." He sat upright, wiping his face. "I need a drink." He put his mouth against Patrick's ear and whispered, "For everything you've done for me, I have something for you when we get back to the room tonight."

Patrick smiled. "Oh, yeah? What's that?"

"Complete restraint," he whispered.

Patrick's eyes widened as understanding settled inside him. Kieren was giving him complete control over his body. He stared at his boyfriend, checking his expression, noting his lack of tension, and smiled. "You're sure?"

Kieren nodded. "Completely."

"When can we leave?" Patrick croaked.

"Not for a few hours yet," Kieren said with a laugh.

"That's mean."

"You had to learn patience for your work. You'll have plenty of strength to draw on."

Kieren stood and left him clenching his jaw. Not in anger, but to stop him from grabbing Kieren and running to the nearest bedroom.

When he came back, he had a smirk on his face. "Everything okay?"

Patrick smiled, intending to pay him back later. "Fine."

"Would you like to dance?" Kieren asked, holding out his hand.

Patrick's smile widened. "I'd love to."

Kieren tugged him along behind him as he wound his way through the tables to the small dance floor on one side of the room. He spun Patrick around and pulled him close, holding his hand to Kieren's chest and an arm around his waist. Patrick, being a couple of inches shorter, rested his head on Kieren's shoulder and closed his eyes, enjoying the sensation of being with his boyfriend in a place that was less stressful than the large events he had to do.

"I haven't been this relaxed in a long time," he murmured.

"Hmm. We definitely need to do this more often."

"What? Attend wedding receptions?" Patrick chuckled.

"No, get away from it all. Take some time for ourselves. I

don't think any of the royal family takes enough time away from the spotlight. It really should be mandatory."

Patrick lifted his head. "We'll have to take it up with Uncle Andrew."

Kieren's eyes widened. "I don't have to call him Uncle Andrew, do I?"

Patrick's laugh started small and grew until he had to muffle it against Kieren's chest. When his eyes had stopped leaking, he wiped them with his hands and smiled up at his man. "I'm sure he would love it if you did, but you don't have to. I'm sure it's weird to even hear me call him 'Uncle.'"

"Just a little."

They finished out the song and headed back to the chairs they'd found earlier. Jade had collected a couple of bottles of water for them, and they drank heartily.

"How long do we have to stay?" Patrick asked.

Kieren squinted at him. "Long enough."

"Long enough for what? Me to go out of my mind?" Patrick huffed and crossed his arms.

Kieren leaned closer. "You're not the only one. Think of it as foreplay."

Patrick could do that. He was good at making foreplay last a long time. His mouth curved. By the end of the night, Kieren was going to wish he hadn't put that thought into Patrick's head.

Between eating the food as if it were an orgasmic experience, dancing close enough to rub against him and teasing him with kisses and nips, it didn't take long for Kieren to lose his patience and give their excuses to Zane and Viv. They promised to visit them again soon, but they drove back to the hotel and spent a very enjoyable night in each other's arms.

And if they went through an entire bottle of lube, who would know?

30

KIEREN

After spending a couple of days in the haze of pleasure, Kieren felt invigorated instead of drained. They had left their suite a few times for food and fresh air, but they spent most of their time behind closed doors, enjoying everything about each other. And he was glad they had because he'd learnt even more about his boyfriend than he could've hoped for over several years.

Now, they were in their suite at Sandringham just before having dinner with the rest of the family. Everyone had arrived earlier that day, including themselves, and Andrew had insisted on dinner together before Charlotte could react to their plan.

"Do you think it will work?" Patrick asked, sliding his jacket on.

The muscles Patrick had slowly gained since they restarted his training distracted Kieren. He hadn't been able to do anything too intense, but he'd asked Jade and Nina to help him. They'd been happy to help, and they had put Patrick through a gruelling training regime while Kieren continued at a slower pace to ensure he didn't exacerbate his injury. It was much better than it had been, only the occasional twinge now and then, and he could do a lot more than he could when it had first happened.

"Kieren?"

Patrick's amused tone pulled Kieren from his musings, and he looked into his eyes. "Yes?"

Patrick chuckled and sauntered over, sliding his arms around Kieren's waist. "See something you like?"

"Always." He kissed him. "And to answer your question, I don't know. I don't know her personally, and I only have my observations and what other people have told me to go on. But based on that, I would say she would react to the perceived threat to her plans. I doubt she would come in person, especially with how she'd left things with Andrew, but she'd send someone."

"Charles, maybe?"

"Possibly, but again, because she knows of his antagonistic nature, he might not be the best choice for trying to get in and out quietly. He seems the type of person who would want to cause trouble just for the sake of it."

"He is." Patrick pulled back. "Who then?"

"Possibly someone you wouldn't expect. Maybe turning up unannounced and waving a white flag. Someone behind the scenes." He shrugged. "I'm just guessing."

Patrick sighed. "It's the not knowing that I hate. When I know who it is, I have someone to focus on, but when we don't know..." He shook his head.

Kieren cupped his jaw and pressed another kiss to his mouth. "I know. We just need to be vigilant, that's all. Besides, we have a lot of guards here. Everyone should be fine."

He made himself sound surer than he felt because he wasn't at all certain they were safe. The predictability of their Christmas routine had never sat well with him, but he refused to make them change something that meant so much to them, especially as this was the first Christmas since Queen Louisa had died. They all needed this time together, even if it was fraught with danger.

What he hadn't told Patrick—but he would if he asked—was that there were several guards hidden in places around the property, posing as household staff. No one knew except the security team, and they wanted to keep it that way. The fewer people who knew, the better the chance they had of keeping it a secret.

"Come on. Let's go see everyone," he said.

They wandered through the hallways with Jade and Nina by their sides. He was slowly getting used to having a guard of his own, but he couldn't ignore his need to check their surroundings as if it was still his job. He would always do everything in his power to keep Patrick safe, but he was glad there were two other people around to help him. This was only while they were walking the corridors, though. When they were having dinner, the guards would have a break while four guards stayed on duty outside the room.

They greeted everyone and sat at the table, laughter and banter being thrown around as usual. Kieren loved this part. It made him feel like one of them because they didn't leave him out. Whether it was George making fun of him or Christian joking with him, everyone made him feel welcome.

"Okay!" Andrew called, standing and holding his glass high. "Let's make a toast. To family, new and old, those who are no longer with us," he swallowed hard, "those who need our support, those who are too far away. We make family from those you wish to bring into the fold, not only blood relatives. As we can see here, our family is unique, and I wouldn't wish for anything different. Cheers."

"Cheers!"

The staff brought out the food and set it in the middle of the table so everyone could reach it. As he met the gaze of a household staff member, a thought niggled at him. When they were alone again, he asked Andrew, "Have all the staff been vetted and checked recently?"

"Yes. The staff here have been with us for a long time, but, earlier this month, I did request that they were all checked again," Andrew said.

"And they all came back okay?"

Andrew frowned. "I've not been told otherwise." He paused, tilting his head as Kieren had seen some other family members do. "Why?"

"If she used this place as Henry described, she would've needed help from people. Are those people still here? Who were they? If they are still here, a phone call could easily persuade them to search for what we mentioned we found. Charlotte wouldn't need to make the journey at all."

"Shit," Freddie said. "How did we not think of this?"

Andrew rubbed a hand over his mouth. "I can give you names of those who I feel were closer to her than others were, but I have no idea if they were part of her scheme or not. I assumed if anyone came back with a mark against them after being vetted, they would no longer be employed, but I've not been told if that was the case."

"Who was in charge of vetting them?"

"I asked Tobias to speak with Brett." Tobias was one of Andrew's guards.

"Excuse me." Kieren stood and pulled out his phone, already dialling when he left the dining hall, noticing how quiet it was. "Brett, where are you?"

"In the security room. Why?"

"Did you recheck everyone who works here?"

"No, why?"

"Fuck! Where's Tobias?"

"He should be with Aaron, Locke and Eric outside the dining room."

"I'm standing outside the dining room, Brett. No one's here."

"Fuck!" A muffled sound came, then shouting. "Everyone, get to the dining hall! Now!"

Kieren ended the call and studied the quiet corridor. There was no sound apart from the muted conversation coming from the room behind him. He hoped the guards were okay—those that weren't in Charlotte's employ, anyway. He stepped back towards the dining room door when he heard footsteps approaching. He had no gun or anything to protect the royal family with.

Slipping back inside the room, he closed the door behind him. "We have a situation, Your Majesty."

Andrew stood. "What's wrong?"

"The guards at the door are gone. I don't know if it was by force or if they're aligning with Charlotte, but you're sitting ducks here."

He grabbed a couple of chairs from next to the door and pushed them under the handles. It wouldn't stop anyone from getting in, but it would slow them down.

"What do you need us to do?" Freddie asked.

Kieren paused. "Who can fight?"

Several people gasped, but Patrick stood, as did William Senior, William Junior, Damon, Douglas, Christian and Freddie.

Kieren glanced at Freddie and shook his head. "Not happening, Your Highness."

"You need people," he gritted out.

"Yes, but you're the heir to the throne. You and Andrew need to be the safest of us all."

Douglas gripped his brother's shoulders. "You know this, Freddie."

"I need—"

"I need you to help keep the rest safe," Kieren interrupted. "I have no idea what we're up against."

The door to the kitchen burst open, and Damon, who was the closest, took the man to the wall with a hand to his throat and another hand to the wrist holding a gun.

Kieren raced over. "Who are you?" he asked, though he knew, having memorised the faces of the hidden guards.

"Landon Kirk, Brett's hidden guard," the man gasped.

"Code?" Kieren asked, knowing they had given every hidden guard a unique sentence.

"The sun shines on the east of Windsor."

Kieren relaxed marginally. "Let him go, Damon." He clapped Freddie's best friend on the shoulder. "Good, fast work. Nicely done." He focused on Landon. "Do you have a spare gun?"

Landon stood tall and reached behind him, holding out another gun, which Kieren took. "Be my guest."

"Thanks." Kieren felt better with a gun in his hand. "Has Brett been in contact?" he asked Landon.

Landon nodded. "He relayed what you told him. The kitchen is secure. There were three of us in there."

A knock sounded, but Kieren ignored it.

"Good. That might be our only way out, depending on what else is happening out there." Kieren faced the royal family, ignoring more shouts and knocking at the door. "Okay, I'm splitting us into two groups. I need William Senior, Damon and Christian to stick with Andrew, Lou, Freddie, Henry, Robert, Kean and Oscar. Landon, you're in charge of getting them to the safe room. Douglas, William Junior and Patrick," He swallowed hard at the thought of the royal family in danger but knew he had no other choice, "you need to stick with me, Mav, George, Timothy, Eddie and Sophia." He focused on Landon again. "Leave one of the other men behind with me. Take the other with you. If you are not sure if they are friend or foe..." He didn't finish the sentence, hoping Landon realised what he meant.

"Understood."

Someone began banging on the door. "Go," he said, gripping the gun tighter as he moved towards the entrance door. "I want everyone to plaster themselves against the walls here." He pointed to the wall where the door was. "Either side, press as close to the walls as you can. Usually, when a guard enters, they'll sweep from one side to the other. If you're hidden behind the decorative beams, they shouldn't see you."

"What about you?" Patrick asked.

Kieren grimaced. "I'll be waiting, front and centre."

"No," Patrick said.

Kieren took a second to cup his chin. "I need their focus on me, not you. They'll see me as a threat, not you. You can surprise them." The banging continued. "Go."

The royals did as he'd asked, and Kieren positioned himself in front of the doors.

"Who is it?" he shouted. When there was no answer, his heart sank. It looked like his group had drawn the short stick. Hopefully, the other group had escaped through the kitchen and met up with Brett. "Get ready," he murmured, lifting his gun to point at the door. He flicked his gaze to Patrick's wide eyes, then refocused on the door. This was one time in his life he couldn't miss.

The door gave just as he thought that, and a man he didn't recognise burst in, sweeping his gun as Kieren had told his group he would. Before the man had the chance to do anything, he was dropping to the floor. Another man entered, aiming straight for Kieren, but Kieren was too quick, and the man went down. Two more filed in, and Kieren aimed for one. From the corner of his eye, Patrick jumped out of his spot and gave a high kick at the second man's wrist, sending his gun flying. Kieren took the third man down while Patrick punched the fourth man, knocking him to the floor. He straddled him and grabbed his arms, holding him down.

Kieren took his eyes off his man and raced to the door,

pointing his gun out and checking the hallway. There didn't seem to be any others he could see, but he didn't know for definite. They had no choice, though. They needed to get out of the dining room. He heard a commotion from the kitchen. Kieren moved to the man Patrick was holding and smacked the handle of the gun into his temple, knocking him out cold.

"Everyone out. Now!" he said. "Grab the four guns. We might need them."

He led the way with Gerald, the other hidden guard, picking up the back. They kept to the walls as they hustled down the corridors, pausing at every corner. Kieren stopped everyone when he heard shots firing in rapid succession. They were close to the secondary safe room but not close enough.

"Gerald?" He moved closer to him. "I need you to take lead and get everyone to the safe room on the west side." He glanced at William. "Are you willing to be my backup?"

"I will," Patrick said.

Kieren shook his head. "I can't focus if you're in danger right next to me. I need you to look after everyone. Please." Patrick clenched his jaw but nodded. "William?"

"I'm with you."

"Be safe," he whispered to Patrick, kissing him.

William hugged his wife, and the two men stood at the end of the corridor, guns pointed towards where the gunfire sounded as Gerald led the group down the other stretch of floor. The gunfire drew closer.

"Are you ready?"

"Six years in the Army? I'm good."

They moved further down the corridor towards the gunfire. "We need to draw them away from where the group is—"

Silence descended suddenly, and Kieren paused, holding his hand to stop William from asking anything. It was too quiet. No gunfire, no footsteps, no talking. He wanted nothing more than to call Brett and find out what the hell was happening, but they had a rule that no one would call if something like this happened, so they didn't inadvertently give away another person's location.

Should he go forward and check the location of the shots or go back and keep his group safe? He blew out a silent breath.

"Let's go."

He stepped backwards, heading to where they'd left the group. His job was to keep the people safe, not try to find trouble.

"What about—" William started.

"We need to keep them safe."

Kieren led the way, taking things slowly, and they eventually made it to the safe room with no further incidents. They saw no one at all, and Kieren couldn't decide if it was a good thing or not. He knocked on the door of the safe room, putting his face to where he knew the camera was.

"It's Kieren and William," he said.

The door unlocked with a clunk, the steel hidden behind a wooden exterior to resemble their surroundings. They slipped in, and Kieren immediately had his arms full of Patrick. The door clunked shut again, and he quickly did a head count.

"Don't ever do that again," Patrick whispered into his neck.

"I can't promise that, sweetheart." He held on, though, knowing exactly how Patrick felt. He glanced at Gerald. "Have you heard anything?"

Gerald shook his head. "There's a computer in here, but I don't have access to it."

Kieren pulled Patrick to his side, reluctant to let him go, and headed for the computer. He input his details, making sure no one but Patrick could see it, and it fired up. A message waited.

Incident over. Them: six dead, seven locked up. Us: four non-fatal casual-ties, one touch and go. Royals: ten accounted for, unharmed. Please report. Brett.

Kieren blew out a breath. "It's done." He quickly typed out a message and sent it. "We need to wait here for further instructions, but we should be good to go."

"I doubt I'll sleep after all this," Sophia said. William wrapped his arms around her, reassuring her.

Kieren opened his mouth to speak when his phone rang. "Hello?"

"It's Brett. How is everyone?"

"Shaken, but we're in one piece, as I said."

"All right, smartass. I've sent Jade, Isaac and Owen to your location. They will help get you to us."

"Is that a good idea?" he asked.

"I want everyone in one safe room where we can protect them better. Once we've spoken with the people we locked up, we can decide from there."

"Was it Tobias?"

Brett sighed. "Yes. And Aaron. I have no idea how they got through, but someone got to them. We need to find out who and how."

"They're still alive?"

"For now," Brett growled. "I don't know for how long once His Majesty gets hold of them."

Kieren snickered, despite the seriousness of the situation. "I wouldn't bet against Andrew at this point." Patrick frowned at him, and Kieren smiled. There was a knock at the door. "Are they here already?"

Brett was quiet for a moment. "Yes. Check the camera, just in case."

"See you shortly, boss."

Kieren let go of Patrick and headed for the door, checking the screen and seeing the three people Brett had sent. He unlocked the door, and the guards piled in. They closed the door again.

"We just want to check you're okay before we make our way back," Isaac said.

Kieren glanced at the group. "Any injuries or anything that we need to know about before we get out of here?"

Everyone shook their heads, and Kieren faced the guards. "We're good to go."

"Let's get to it, then."

This time, Kieren and Jade took the rear, with Gerald in the middle and Isaac and Owen in the lead. They didn't go directly because they wanted to ensure they weren't followed. Even with Brett's assurances they had all the bad guys, Kieren didn't want to take any chances.

By the time they arrived at the primary safe house, he was strung tight. They needed to get to the bottom of this. This was a nightmare of epic proportions. He had never imagined Charlotte would be bold enough to send an assassination squad to Sandringham to take them all out. Yes, it had been a chance to have everyone under one roof, but he never truly believed she would attempt something like that. It blew his mind.

If she was willing to try this, what wouldn't she try?

3 1

FREDERICK

Freddie clenched his fists and paced at the back of the safe room. Not being allowed to help protect the others had set aflame a ball in his stomach, and he hated it. Yes, he was the heir, but he was as strong as the rest of them. He could protect them. He gritted his teeth and moved back and forth across the space.

Someone spun him around and pushed him into the wall beside the filing cabinet, partially hiding him from the rest of the occupants. It was only when his back met the wall that he saw Damon looming in front of him.

"What?" Freddie glared at him and tried to step forward.

Damon pressed a hand to his chest and slammed him back again. "Stay there," he said through gritted teeth.

"What the fuck, Damon?" he whispered. "Let me go."

"No." Damon got in his face, almost nose to nose. "You stay there and calm the fuck down."

"Don't tell me to calm down."

"Someone needs to. You're going to combust in front of all these people, and you don't want that to happen. You'll regret it because you'll say something you don't mean to."

Freddie's chest heaved as he stared down his best friend. "You don't know—"

"Yes, I do." Damon stepped closer if that was possible, plastering their fronts together and gripping his chin. "You feel like you could do the job as well as anyone else. You're right. You feel like you've been punished by not being able to help. You're not. You feel like no one is listening to you. They are. You feel like you're not worthy enough to be saved." Damon swallowed hard. *"You are."*

With every word, Freddie felt his body lose its tension, and if Damon hadn't been standing so close to him, he would've dropped to the floor. Damon slid his hand around to Freddie's nape and rested their foreheads together.

"Don't give up on yourself or on me," Damon whispered.

Freddie slid his forehead from Damon's to his shoulder, giving in to the need to be held closer. Damon's hand released his shirt and wrapped around his back, and Freddie clung to the back of Damon's shirt. They both tightened their grip until Freddie could hardly breathe, but he didn't want to. He didn't want to let go. He needed this tethering because Damon hit the nail on the head. Freddie didn't believe he was worthy of being saved. He didn't think he was the best choice for being the heir, despite what everyone else was saying. He second-guessed himself all the time, and what king did that? His father certainly didn't.

Damon's hand rubbed up and down Freddie's back, and Freddie let the tears flow, knowing no one could see him with Damon hiding them. For the first time in a long time, he let his best friend bear the brunt of everything, and Freddie just floated.

He had no idea how long he'd stayed that way, but when he came back, they were sitting on the floor, in the same place, with Freddie curled in Damon's lap. He should've felt embarrassed about it, but he found he didn't care. He was worn out, and he couldn't have brought himself to move even if he had the energy.

"How are you doing?" Damon whispered. Freddie didn't answer, just squeezed the hand holding his. "That's okay. Stay there as long as you need. I'm here."

Freddie squeezed again, then tucked himself in tighter. Damon's arms tightened briefly, and Freddie allowed himself to let go of everything again. When the time came for them to move, he would, but right now, he needed this.

Right now, his entire world circled around the man holding him.

And for once, Freddie didn't fight himself about the thoughts that ran rampant in his mind. For once, he allowed his mind to imagine what life would be like if he chose what he'd been thinking about more and more lately.

What he'd been wanting more and more.

Damon.

32

PATRICK

If Patrick didn't see a gun again in his lifetime, it would be too soon. He knew the guards needed to carry them, but the incident had tested his limits. How he'd managed to take down that guy, he'd never know, but all he could do was thank Kieren for having trained him as well as he had. He still needed a lot more to make it feel like he could do it, but obviously, something had imprinted on him for him to act without thinking.

They were staying within the safe room for a few more hours until Brett and those he trusted swept the estate. He wasn't sure if the people who'd attacked them were the only ones involved in the attack or if there might be more around the estate hidden somewhere, but either way, they needed to check everything was clear before they resumed their normal Christmas activities. If they felt like they could, anyway.

Henry was shaken, unsurprisingly. The incident had brought back too many memories for him, and they'd taken a corner of the room, and Robert had pulled Henry into him and tucked his face into his neck. Everyone had left them alone. Robert would get Henry back to his usual self as quickly as he could, but Henry needed time to recuperate.

As they all did. No one had expected an attack like what had been orchestrated, and they were all a little shaken.

Freddie had retreated into himself, which was a shock. Seeing him curled in Damon's lap, however much hidden behind the filing cabinet at the back of the room, while Damon looked wrecked had gone a long way to worrying Patrick until Damon had given him a small thumbs up. He'd never seen Freddie like that before.

Kieren had gone out with Brett and the others, and Patrick wanted nothing more than to keep in contact with him, but they'd requested phone silence, understandably. It didn't help Patrick's nerves, though.

What did Charlotte think she'd accomplish? Because it had to be her. No one else would've reacted to the message Andrew had left for her when they first arrived at Sandringham. Not with brutal force, anyway.

"Patrick?"

He turned to Uncle Andrew and tried for a smile. "How are you doing?"

"Well, the ticker's still going. I count that as a win," he said with a soft chuckle. The strain of the event was visible in the depth of the lines on his face and the rounding of his shoulders. The strong king was feeling the pain of betrayal, and Patrick wished there was something he could do to help.

"Definitely a win," he murmured. "Plus, she didn't succeed in whatever she was trying to do." He didn't mention the act of treason and how she had likely signed her death warrant through the assassination attempt. It all came down to whether they could prove it.

"True." Andrew surveyed the room, leaning back against the wall. "She nearly succeeded, though. If Kieren hadn't asked that question at that time..."

Patrick had thought the same thing several times over the last few hours. "But he did. And we can thank him later for it."

"He deserves a medal."

Patrick chuckled. "I doubt he'd accept it. He sees it as his duty, even if he's not doing that specific job right now."

"He still deserves it. He organised everything as if it were second nature, which I suppose it is, but he never flinched once. Even my personal guards flinch in some situations."

"He had a lot of people's lives in his hands. He had to trust himself to get them to safety. That's why he didn't flinch. He just did what he had to do."

Andrew rested a hand on Patrick's shoulder. "You have a good man there, Patrick. Keep hold of him."

"I plan to."

A knock sounded, and everyone tensed. He could see it in the way they all froze. They had been left with two guards, Gerald and Landon, and Landon checked the camera and then opened the door. Patrick tensed, not trusting anyone but Kieren at this point, but when Brett, Felix, Locke and Kieren stepped inside and closed the door, he relaxed. He wanted to throw himself in Kieren's arms but stayed back, knowing Kieren had a job to do.

Kieren obviously had no qualms with it because he strode right over to him and dragged him into his arms. Patrick breathed in his scent and closed his eyes, wanting this to be over.

"The entire estate has been checked and is clear. We have quarantined all household staff for questioning. As much as some of you would like to leave, I would suggest you stay here as this is likely the safest place in the country right now. We won't stop you if you wish to leave, but you will leave with guards whether or not you came with them," Brett stated in no uncertain terms.

Andrew stepped forward. "I would like you all to stay. Not

only because, as Brett says, this is probably the safest place right now, but because I want to celebrate Christmas with you all. This is a difficult time for us, and to allow us some time to decompress, it would be an honour to have you all here."

"We have no place we'd rather be," William Senior said, his arm around his wife, Lou.

"Us either," Willian Junior said. His wife, Sophia, held his arm and rested her cheek on his shoulder.

In the end, they all agreed to stay, which made Andrew's smile wider than it had been since everything had happened.

"We have set the house back to rights, but if you notice anything out of place, please let one of us know," Brett added. "You all have your own guards that you've brought with you, and those who don't, I have allocated a guard to you. If you're unsure about anything, please ask." Brett turned to Andrew. "I've allocated Landon and Selena to be your additional guards for now until you choose two to replace them."

The family began leaving, hugging others as they left, but Patrick and Kieren stayed back until the end, making sure everyone was okay before they went back to their suite. The moment the door closed them inside, Patrick threw himself in Kieren's arms and held on tightly.

"That was awful," he murmured.

"It truly was," Kieren said, rubbing a hand up and down his back.

They stayed that way for a long time until fatigue hit him hard. Kieren must've felt his energy deplete because he picked him up, putting his hands under his ass, and Patrick wrapped his legs around his waist. His boyfriend deposited him on the bed, and Patrick had to let go, much to his disapproval. But when he did, Kieren took his time removing Patrick's clothes and shoes. Once he was naked, Kieren pulled the covers from beneath him and tucked him in.

"I'll be with you in a few minutes. I have to shower first."

Patrick sat upright. "I can come with you."

"No, get some rest. I'll only be a few minutes. I'm not going anywhere."

And wasn't that the issue Patrick had? Although he'd let Kieren do his job earlier, now that he was back in his arms, Patrick didn't want to let him out of his sight.

"I promise. Five minutes maximum, and I'll be back." Kieren kissed him.

Patrick nodded and settled back in. They had all been close to losing those they cared about, and all because someone didn't like how someone else lived their life. It was a crazy thought.

He must've been lost in his thoughts because he didn't hear Kieren finish in the bathroom; he only noticed the dip of the bed when Kieren slid in beside him. Patrick automatically rolled to his opposite side and snuggled into him.

"What's going to happen now?"

Kieren exhaled. "We're going to question Tobias and Aaron tomorrow. Find out as much as they will give us." He sighed again. "I never would've thought Aaron would be involved. He's been close to Andrew throughout all this, from what both Andrew and Brett told me. How they persuaded him otherwise, I don't know."

"Who's going to question them?"

"Brett, and maybe me. Commissioner Thomas is making the journey up here to be witness to anything."

"He doesn't trust us."

"He does," Kieren said. "He just wants to make sure Andrew is covered. No one wants the king accused of anything. How is everyone?"

Patrick gathered his thoughts. "Shaken. Scared. At a loss for what to do now. How are you?" He lifted his chin to stare at him, though Kieren's gaze was on the ceiling.

"Same, really. I was scared we wouldn't get you all to safety," he whispered.

"But you did. You all did."

They lapsed into silence, and as the new day's sunlight began filtering through the curtains, they fell asleep, still wrapped around each other.

Patrick and Kieren made their way through the same corridors that held so much fear the previous day and stopped outside the dining room.

"Are you ready?" Kieren asked.

"To face the place where I took down a man I had no business taking down? Hell, yeah." Patrick smiled, though it was strained.

Kieren grinned. "You did well. I'm an excellent teacher."

Patrick snorted, and Kieren opened the door. Several family members were sitting at the table, eating lunch. Douglas came out of his seat immediately, enfolding Patrick in his arms.

"You kicked ass yesterday! I didn't get the chance to tell you. How the hell did you do that?" He let go again.

Patrick's cheeks heated. "Kieren's been teaching me a few things."

"A few things? Maybe I need to learn."

"I think you can hold your own without any more training," Mav said, sidling up beside him. "I don't need you getting into more trouble." He winked at Patrick.

Douglas slid his arm around Mav. "I don't know what you mean. I'm the perfect royal nowadays."

"Hmm," Mav replied.

Patrick enjoyed the easy banter, and they sat at the table for their lunch. They'd missed breakfast because they'd slept in longer than they'd planned, but they didn't care. Nothing was going to happen until this afternoon, and although Patrick knew they had to talk to the guards, he wasn't sure he wanted to know what Charlotte's plans were.

When the time came for Kieren, Brett and Andrew to question the guards, Patrick stayed with his brother and cousins. They chose the movie theatre to relax in and put on a Christmas film to try to distract them. It didn't work because, within minutes, they were all discussing what had happened and what they thought Charlotte was going to do next. Patrick, however, stayed quiet, not wanting to think about what else she could come up with. He stared at the pictures flowing across the screen, letting the conversation fall to the background.

When would this end? They'd lived in fear for so long now, but he didn't want to become accustomed to it. He wanted to live—for them all to live—without the hatred, the fear, the anger coursing through them all. He wanted to go back to how it was when they didn't know about Charlotte and her schemes. He wanted Henry not to have experienced everything he had. He wanted a normal life. Well, as normal as it could be for a prince.

He had no sense of time passing, and he jumped when someone sat beside him. He glanced to the side and almost threw himself into Kieren's arms, just like he had the previous evening. He had a feeling it would be a while before he could fully relax when Kieren wasn't with him. When anyone wasn't with him. He'd be worrying about his family until all of this was over.

Pulling back, he wiped his eyes. "Everything okay?"

Kieren nodded, though his smile was sad. "Yeah. We got next to nothing from Tobias, which is what we expected. It seems he had nothing against Andrew, he just needed the money, and Charlotte gave him the opportunity."

"He did it for money?" Christian asked.

Kieren nodded, keeping his gaze on Patrick. "As for Aaron, well. He's been very helpful, although he doesn't have a lot to give us. Charlotte has been extremely careful, but Aaron has been pronounced dead." Everyone started talking, but Kieren held up his hand. "Sorry, I should've added, he's not dead, but we're pretending he is."

Douglas cursed. "Can you explain before our heads explode?"

Kieren chuckled. "Okay, basically, Charlotte, or rather one of her people, has been threatening Aaron's son. He's nineteen and is gay. Charlotte told him they would leave his son to live his life if Aaron did what they asked of him."

"He did it to save his son," Patrick said.

"He did. At least, that's what he's saying. Currently, we have no way of confirming that because he has no evidence. He wasn't being paid. Every message he received was from a burner phone, and every interaction he had was planned meticulously to ensure there was no evidence left."

"He could be telling lies," Henry said. Kieren nodded. "Then why is he being pronounced dead?"

"We don't want to take the chance that his son will be harmed. If he's listed as one of the deceased, his son should be free."

"Should be."

"As much as we can guess. We can't guarantee it, but we also can't send someone to check in on him because it will show an interest in him we don't want to highlight."

"What's going to happen with Tobias?"

"He's going to jail, no doubt about it. He has no remorse for it. How his uncaring nature was ever hidden, I don't know." Kieren rested his head back against the seat.

Patrick could see how much of a toll this had taken on him, on all of them. "This has to stop," he said. "She can't keep doing this to us. How much more can we take?"

"We will take as much as she throws," Andrew said as he entered the room with William Senior behind him. "We will never give up because she's wrong, and she knows it. She gets backing from those who feel the same as she does, or she blackmails people into helping her. By resorting to blackmail, she is becoming weaker, and those supporting her can see it. We see it through. Whatever she throws our way, we will weather because we are in the right. We stand by those who deserve to live in a free country, not scared to step outside their doors. We fight for them as much as ourselves."

It was moments like that Patrick remembered why Andrew was king and why he should continue being so as long as he could. Freddie was becoming the image of his father, and Patrick was not at all concerned that something would change when his cousin became king.

"Damn straight," Douglas said.

"Right. This is the end of this. As of now, Christmas has started. We're still on high alert, just in case, but we need to forget about it for the next few days. I refuse to let one spoilt brat ruin Christmas." Patrick muffled a laugh at his uncle's description of Charlotte. "Tonight, we will have dinner and finish it as it should have been finished yesterday. Tomorrow, we can do whatever you want to do, and on Christmas Eve, we can spend it together as usual. There will be a couple of minor events I need to appear at over the next couple of days, but from Christmas Eve onwards, I'm yours." He smiled. "Get some rest. I'll see you at dinner."

Patrick and Kieren said their goodbyes and headed for their suite, and once the door was closed, they sank into bed and talked until they dozed. Kieren, luckily, had set an alarm, and it woke them with enough time to have some time in the shower together. They'd both been too tired the previous night and that morning to do anything more than hold each other and kiss, but

Patrick insisted on dropping to his knees and reminding Kieren of just what he was capable of.

As he worked Kieren's cock with his mouth and played with his balls and hole with his hands, Patrick thought about their relationship in terms of a BDSM lifestyle. When they used bondage and impact play in the bedroom or club, Patrick was the Dom and Kieren the sub, but at home, anything was possible. And Patrick loved every minute of what they shared.

He remembered the first time he'd visited the club, scared it wouldn't be anything that he wanted, and when he finally entered the building with Freddie, he'd been surprised. He'd been lured in by the possibilities of being able to play a body as well as he could his instruments, and at that moment, he believed he could play Kieren's body better than he could his piano. There was art in giving someone an orgasm, music in the sounds they made, and a melody in the undulations of their body. As much as Kieren could capture that feeling on paper with his drawings, Patrick could work a body and capture the same emotion in real life. The pair of them together could be a force to be reckoned with if left to their own devices.

But his mind was running away with him. He needed to bring Kieren to the very edge and let him hover there for a short time before allowing him to fly. He wanted him wiped clean and relaxed, and they could enjoy the evening with their family because Kieren was part of the family now, too. And if everything went to plan, the ring hidden inside his sock drawer—hardly a unique hiding place—would have pride of place on Kieren's hand by the end of their Christmas holiday.

He was scared Kieren wouldn't be ready, but he would never push for him to say yes if he wasn't in the right frame of mind for it. Patrick would wait however long Kieren needed him to. He was worth everything.

As Kieren finally cried out in release, Patrick climaxed at the same time, happy to share all this with him. For the first time in a long time, despite everything going on around them, Patrick was content.

And it showed in his music. When Andrew asked him to play for them, Patrick's heartwarming Christmas melodies helped lift their spirits and remind them what they were working towards.

33

KIEREN

*E*veryone had been doing everything in their power to keep the spirits high in the run-up to Christmas. Patrick played the piano, George created games, Eddie made them Christmas drinks—much to the chagrin of the household staff—and Henry fascinated them with the history of Club Royal he'd found out in his research. Kieren had enjoyed every minute of it, but when Patrick suggested they take some time to themselves on Christmas Eve, he agreed wholeheartedly. According to Patrick, Andrew had cancelled their usual Christmas Eve black-tie dinner with the local residents this year, so they had the entire day free, and tomorrow, they would only need to attend the Church service in the morning.

"Horse riding?" Kieren said, staring at the horses currently eating hay in the stable. "I don't know…"

"Have you ever done it before?" Patrick asked, opening the door that separated them from a large black horse.

"No. It never crossed my mind."

Patrick stroked a hand down the horse's shiny coat. "This is Beauty. She has been a favourite of mine for as long as I can remember. She's gentle and easy to ride. You'll be fine with her.

302

We're not going to go far or fast, and I'll be by your side the entire time."

"Okay," Kieren said hesitantly.

Patrick got Beauty ready, then closed the door and entered the stable of another horse, this time a chestnut-coloured one. "This is Roman. He is Henry's favourite. A little temperamental sometimes, but nothing I can't handle."

Kieren was fascinated with Patrick's sure actions. "How many times have you done this? I would've thought—"

"Someone would do it for us?" Patrick chuckled. "They do sometimes. I enjoy getting them ready myself. It gives them time to get used to who is going to ride them, in my opinion. The only time I don't do it is if I'm in a rush."

Patrick explained what he was doing and why until both horses were ready to go. He led Roman out of the stable, handing the reins to a stable hand, and returned for Beauty. Kieren walked beside the black horse, nervous tension running through him.

Patrick stopped beside him. "Relax. Once you're up there, you don't need to do anything except enjoy the ride." He smirked, and Kieren's thoughts went to places they shouldn't. He cleared his throat.

"How do I get up there?"

Patrick showed him, and Kieren managed it on the first try, although it wasn't as easy as Patrick made it seem, and Patrick leapt up onto Roman's back.

"Thank you, Ren."

"You're welcome, Your Highness. I'll be here when you get back. Just holler."

Patrick smiled and nodded. "Ready?" he asked Kieren.

"As I'll ever be."

Patrick clicked his tongue and did something with his foot, and Roman began moving.

"Patrick, what do I—" He stopped when Beauty started walking without him doing anything.

Patrick smiled over his shoulder. "She'll follow Roman's movements. You don't need to do anything."

Kieren relaxed marginally, knowing he wouldn't have to learn how to steer the horse. Patrick laughed when he voiced that concern.

"You don't need to learn how to 'steer' the horse, Kieren. Leave that to me."

The horses stayed side by side, and Kieren's tension left his body as he got used to the rhythm. He inhaled the cold, fresh air and exhaled, surveying their surroundings, but not in a protective way, although he couldn't leave that completely at the house.

"It's beautiful around here."

"It is. One of my favourite places, other than home," Patrick said. "If we continue on this path, it will take us to the lower lake."

The chill in the air made Kieren glad he'd worn gloves and thick clothing, but the views were fantastic.

"I know you said you preferred walking and cycling, but I thought I could show you another way to travel," Patrick said.

Kieren smiled at him, knowing it had been something that had played on his mind. "You don't need to worry. I'm used to cars. No matter what we travel in, I'll get through it." He inhaled again and let it out. "I've been speaking to Timothy about it. He said some people benefit from... I think he called it 'immersion therapy,' which is kind of like doing what I don't like over and over again until I can get used to it. I've not been on a plane since before my family died, and I don't know how I'll react, but it's something I need to do. Sooner rather than later."

"There's no rush, Kieren. Take your time. And if you're never ready, that's fine."

"I know, but visiting other countries is something I know you want to do, and I want to go with you."

"I would never push for that, especially as planes and helicopters are not my favourite method of travelling. If I ever go to other countries, it will be by car, train or boat."

Kieren smiled at him. "I know you wouldn't. But I want to push myself for that."

They lapsed into comfortable silence until they reached a lake. Patrick stopped Roman, and Beauty followed suit. Patrick jumped down and reached for Beauty's reins to let Kieren slide down, rather ungracefully, especially as his legs were rubbery. Patrick chuckled.

"You'll get your muscle memory back in a minute. I'm just going to tie these up."

Patrick walked the horses to a wooden fence post and wrapped the reins over it, then wandered back towards him, carrying a blanket. Kieren smiled as his boyfriend flicked the blanket out flat and gestured for him to sit.

"It's a little cooler than I expected. I always seem to forget it's colder at the lake," he murmured, wrapping his arms around Kieren.

"It's beautiful, though."

They watched some birds flying, though Patrick told him there was a lot more to see during the summer months.

"I want to ask you something," Patrick said.

Kieren leaned his head back against his shoulder. "You can ask me anything."

"Will you marry me?"

A small black box appeared in front of him, and Patrick opened the lid. Nestled inside was a shiny gold band with two lines of amber and one line of blue between them, encircling the entire ring. Kieren's heart missed a beat.

"You don't have to answer now." Patrick's voice trembled. "I just want you to know how I'm feeling. I love you so much. It would be a great honour to be by your side for the rest of my days, but I know it might be too sudden—"

His words stopped when Kieren slammed their mouths together. He took him hard and deep, then gentled it, finishing with a couple of pecks on his lips. Tears trickled down both their cheeks, and Kieren smiled.

"Yes. I will marry you. I love you."

Patrick kissed him again, and when they pulled back, he lifted the ring from the box. "I have no idea if this will fit."

The ring slid on, maybe a little tighter than Kieren would've liked, but it fit. That was the main thing. It sparkled in the muted sunlight.

"I thought of you when I saw the colour of the blue. It reminds me of your eyes."

"And the amber? Does that have significance?" Kieren asked.

"Nothing official, but it made me think of the royal crown. I thought it was apt to have something related to the royals. As you'll become a prince, after all."

Kieren's mouth opened and closed several times, but he couldn't think of a thing to say to that, apart from, "Holy crap!"

Patrick laughed and held him tighter. "It's funny how none of you—and by you, I mean the partners of my brother and cousins—none of you realise you're going to be princes when you marry. It's as if you all push it aside and see us as actual people. It's wonderful."

"That's because you are a person first, a prince second."

"Not to the rest of the world."

"But to those who matter most."

They drifted into silence again, broken only by their kisses and random musings. When they both became too cold, Patrick helped Kieren to climb back onto Beauty, and they rode to their temporary home. The pressure around his ring finger was strange but not unwelcome. Every time he moved, it rubbed or pressed against his fingers and gloves, and it reminded him of what his future held.

When they arrived back at the stables, he stopped Patrick from heading back into the house with a question that had concerned him. "Do you want people to know straight away, or should I put the ring back in the box for now?"

Patrick wrapped his arms around his waist and smiled. "I want the world to know, but only if you're okay with that."

Kieren kissed him, the cold tip of his nose brushing against his skin. "I'm okay with that."

"Good. Let's go tell Mother and Father."

Kieren couldn't help but react to Patrick's enthusiasm, but the closer they came to Patrick's parents' suite, the more nervous he became. He loosened his coat and scarf, removing his gloves and putting them in his pockets.

"Stop worrying. They love you."

He thought they liked him, but there was always that niggle of doubt in the back of his mind that they were only saying that for Patrick's benefit. When things appear to be more permanent, they might change their minds.

Patrick faced him as they stopped at the door. He grabbed his hands and squeezed. "You have nothing to worry about. I promise you."

Kieren swallowed, inhaled and blew it out. "Okay," he said with more certainty than he felt.

Patrick knocked, keeping hold of Kieren's ring hand. There was a call for them to enter, and Patrick led the way.

"Good afternoon, boys! How was your ride?" Victoria asked, coming forward with her arms open. Patrick hugged her, and so did he. "Come sit."

They removed their coats and put them on the coat stand, and Patrick grabbed his hand again and pulled him to the sofa. Victoria sat in an armchair to their left and asked her assistant for tea for them all.

"Tell me. How was the ride? I bet it was chilly." She rubbed her arms and chuckled.

Patrick laughed with her. "It was colder than I thought it would be, especially at the lake."

"I can imagine. How did you enjoy your first ride, Kieren?"

He cleared his throat. "It was good. A little nerve-wracking, to begin with, but I got the hang of it."

"Good. Patrick loves to ride, don't you? You don't do it as much as you used to, though. Maybe you could get back into it now?"

"I'd like that. I'd have to see how much time I have with the coursework I have, but it would be nice to do it to relax." He glanced at Kieren. "Did you enjoy it enough to do it again?"

Kieren nodded. "Yes. It's another way I could see myself travelling." He laughed. "Although, I don't think the horse would like to ride all the way from Bagshot Park to London every day."

They laughed with him, and Patrick squeezed his hand, telegraphing what he was about to do. "We do have some news," Patrick said, staring at his mother. "Is Father here?"

She raised her eyebrows, her mouth curving slightly, and Kieren knew she had already guessed. "No, he's with Andrew and William. I'm not sure what they're doing, though. Do you want to wait for him?"

Patrick shook his head and glanced at Kieren, smiling. "I asked Kieren to marry me, and he agreed." He turned back to his mother.

Her hands covered most of her smiling mouth, and she looked like someone who'd been given the best gift ever, settling Kieren's concerns.

"Oh, my! I'm so happy for you! We have to celebrate!"

Patrick shook his head. "No. We'll announce it at dinner this evening, but we're not making a huge thing of it. It's a Christmas celebration, after all."

Victoria pushed to her feet, and he and Patrick followed suit. She enfolded her son in her arms again, whispering something in his ear, and moved to Kieren. When her arms tightened around him, he had to swallow hard to stop the emotion from overflowing. More so when she whispered, "You are an amazing man, Kieren. I couldn't wish for anyone better for my son. Welcome to the family, son of mine." She cupped his cheeks when she pulled back, and he smiled, though his chin wobbled.

"Well, regardless. I think we should celebrate. Both my sons are engaged! What more could a mother ask for?"

When everyone was sitting at the dinner table that evening, and before they had served the food, Patrick stood and clinked his glass.

"Happy Christmas Eve, everyone." Murmurs replied to him. "I just want to say a quick word because I have some news. Or *we* have some news." He reached a hand down to clasp Kieren's. "We're getting married."

Everyone spoke at once, and Patrick laughed, the joyous sound barely muted by the almost thunderous noise of conversation. After everyone settled down, and they received the congratulations, the household staff served the food.

Kieren closed his eyes and just listened to the people around him. Never in his wildest dreams as a young man had he ever believed he'd be living a fairy tale. He was marrying a prince, and although the fairy tales of his childhood were completely different to reality, the truth remained the same. He, a commoner with no family to his name, was marrying the love of his life. The man he couldn't live without. The man who came to him with a family whose hearts were large enough to take him in.

"Are you okay?" Patrick whispered in his ear.

Kieren stared at his fiancé, and his heart missed a beat. "I love you so much."

Patrick smiled and pecked a kiss on his lips. "I love you."

"Whoop, whoop!" someone shouted from down the table, and Kieren laughed. If he hadn't been surrounded by the parents of the men and women at the table, he would've put up his middle finger to them all. Instead, he ignored them and focused on his food.

Life would not be easy for them. For any of them. Charlotte, though they knew it was she who was the mastermind behind all the incidents happening, couldn't be touched because there was no physical evidence to prove it. She was smarter than he'd given her credit for, but he was determined that they would find a way for her to pay for what she'd done. She'd got away with it for far too long, but the end was coming. He could feel it.

He peered at the occupants of the table, noticing the smiling, happy faces in all but four people: Freddie, Damon, Kean and Andrew. He understood Andrew's expression; although happy, he was hurting, and when the man caught his gaze, Andrew gave a small smile and nod, answering Kieren's unasked question of whether he was okay. The loss of his wife would be closer to the surface than ever during this time. Not only because it had been her favourite time of year, but because of the incident. It brought home how close he'd come to losing more of them. He only knew that because he'd been to see the man earlier in the day to check on him. They'd had a long discussion about Queen Louisa and what he wanted to do in her memory, and Kieren was all for it.

As for Freddie and Damon, he wished there was something he could do to help. Patrick had told him of his opinion about their relationship, or rather, the relationship he thought they were teetering on the edge of, and Kieren could see it. But they had much they needed to talk over before they could be happy. Not only the issue that everyone presumed Freddie was straight, even Freddie himself. If that wasn't something that needed to be discussed, nothing was.

Kean, on the other hand, had lost his brother, Simon, the previous year, and it was still fresh in his mind from what Patrick had told him. Kean had been close with the family and best friends with Henry for years before a misunderstanding caused them to split. It had taken over a year for them to become friends again, but Kean still had a sadness about him. Maybe he'd mention it to Henry and see if there was anything they could do to help him.

Everyone else was full of the joys of Christmas, despite what had happened earlier that week. They were eager for the next day when they would have a large present opening event after they'd been to the church for morning service. Kieren had bought two presents for Patrick. One he could open in front of everyone else and one he would be opening tonight before they went to bed. Something for the two of them, really.

Now that Kieren was fully into the impact play Patrick had introduced him to, he'd been researching and found a flogger and some restraints he wanted to try. So, although they were a gift for Patrick, it was definitely for them both.

How he ever believed he could live without Patrick in his life, he'd never know. But it goes to show that fate sends what people need when they need it.

He reached for Patrick's hand and kissed his knuckles. "Merry Christmas Eve, sweetheart."

"Merry Christmas Eve, Kieren."

They shared another kiss, and Kieren wished for many years to come with the man beside him and the family surrounding him.

Thank you for reading Patrick and Kieren's story. I hope you enjoyed it. Order Awakened Royal to see whether Freddie can put aside his qualms and start something with his best friend, Damon.

Would you like to know what the princes got up to during the triple birthday bash? Here's the short bonus story, Triple the Trouble.

Sign up to my newsletter to get some free short stories and regular updates and exclusive content.

Would you also consider leaving a review?

ABOUT ELOUISE EAST

Elouise East writes sweet and steamy connections in gay romance. She also touches on taboo stories under the name Elouise R East.

Books that tell the stories where friendship and family are the focal point - be it blood family or chosen - are very important to her. That's why she includes a variety of personalities, talents, ages, situations and abilities as she believes a story or character needs. She wants her characters to be real, to be relatable, to be free to have whatever views they tell her they have. And trust her, most of the time, she does not have *any* say in the matter!

Her characters come to life on the page for her as well as her readers. Their stories unfold in front of her as she writes, and she has very little input into how they want to be shown. Just like real life, the lives of her characters change with every choice, every interaction and every conversation. And she wouldn't have it any other way.

She writes books that are emotionally realistic, even if liberties are taken with other aspects of the stories. She doesn't know any other way to write. It comes from deep inside.

Who is she? A single parent to two children living in the UK. An avid reader who still tries to devour every book she can get her hands on. A student of learning about any subject that takes her fancy. An author of books she would read herself. And a romantic at heart who loves anything cheesy.

Who's joining her on her journey?

Stalk her here… ;-)
<u>Website</u> https://elouiseeast.com
<u>Newsletter</u> https://readerlinks.com/l/2368814
<u>All links</u> https://linktr.ee/elouiseeastauthor

BOOKS BY ELOUISE EAST

<u>CLUB ROYAL</u>

Rogue Royal

Secretive Royal

Grieving Royal

Disowned Royal

Trained Royal

Awakened Royal

Commanding Royal

<u>ILLUMINATE MATCHMAKING</u>

Ignite

<u>BOYS, DADDIES, SNUGGLES & MORE</u>

Need Him

Trust Him

<u>DADDY</u>

Love Me, Daddy

Soothe Me, Daddy

Spoil Me, Daddy

The Complete Daddy Series

<u>LOVE IN FLAMES</u>

Out of the Frying Pan

Smokescreen

Breathing Fire

CRUSH

Love Conquers

Crush Series Page

Crush Box Set

JUST A LITTLE CRUSH

He's Behind You

A Special Love

Three Thirds

STANDALONE

Treehouse Whispers

Star-Crossed

Protecting the Thief

Sizzling Chauffeur

BY ELOUISE R EAST (TABOO)

DARK & DIVERGENT

Forbidden Temptation

Too Many Secrets

COLLIDE

When Fantasies Collide

When Dreams Collide

When Pleasures Collide